CALL OF DEATH

A JASON McCRAE: PSYCHIC FOR HIRE NOVEL

MATTY BAGGINS

PLAYLIST

"What If?" - Goodbye Misery

"Thank You For Hating Me" - Citizen Soldier

"BEG!" - Vana

"Do Your Worst" - Outline In Color feat. Loveless

"Sinematic" - Motionless In White

"Strong For Somebody Else" - Citizen Soldier

"Not Enough" - Outline In Color

"Wasp" - Motionless In White

"Wolf In Sheep's Clothing" - Set It Off

"Animal" - Magnolia Park feat. Ethan Ross & PLVTINUM

"Primitive" - Not Enough Space

"Fuckin' Perfect" - P!nk

"Dance With The Devil" - Breaking Benjamin

"On My Own" - Ryan DeBlanc

CONTENT & TRIGGER WARNINGS

The story of Call of Death is the continued saga of Jason and his partners Adelaide, McKenna, and Haley. This is a tad darker than the first book so I would advise some caution going into this follow up novel. This novels contains:

- Forced Captivity
- Reliving trauma at the hands of an abuser
- Rape/Sexual Assault (not depicted)
- Blasphemy
- Possession
- Grief, loss, and feelings of inadequacy
- Death
- Willing decapitation
- Cannibalism
- Soul Ownership
- Detailed sex scenes between constenting adults featuring: Biting, Marking/Claiming, Voyeurism, Praise kink, DDLG, Headless Shenanigans, & Unconventional Relationships

If you have any questions about specific trigger and content do not hesitate to reach out to me on Facebook, TikTok, Instagram, or Bluesky: @mattybagginsauthor

Have fun and read responsibly.

This one goes out to the fighters, survivors, and outcasts;

Outlive your demons and then fuck on their grave.

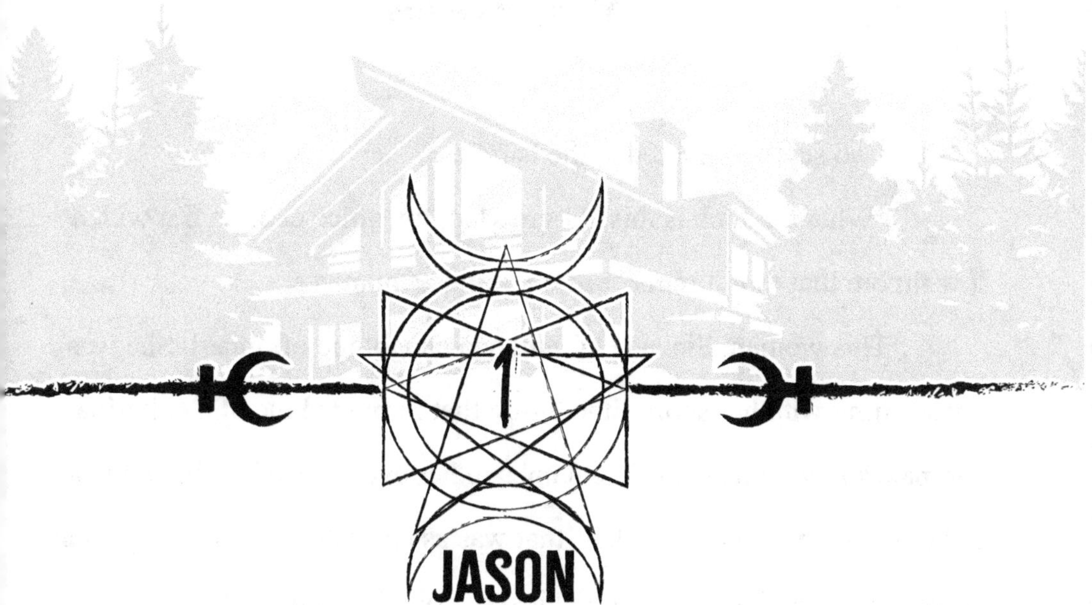

PAIN SHOT THROUGH MY HAND AS BLOOD CASCADED DOWN MY PALM.

However, as much as I wanted to look down to see how badly I was bleeding, I couldn't take my eyes off the woman in front of me. Not due to the threat she posed - the gash on my hand was a testament to it - but because of her eyes. Ones glowing with a brilliant cyan-colored aura as blue flames licked outward from them.

I hissed and gritted my teeth harder, spittle trailing down my lips as the pain intensified with the growing flames in her eyes. She remained unmoving, glaring at me with a coldness born from stoic hatred before I gave in and looked down at my palm. Blood was no longer pouring from the wound. Instead, I found a viscous black liquid oozing from the cut. It stretched and crawled across my skin like a sentient thing before embedding itself into my flesh. It had tattooed a small crude design into my palm.

Two scythes crossed at the handles.

"What the fuck is this?" I growled, my voice coming out with a low timbre that didn't register in my mind as human.

This woman, Sinead O'Hare, had caught me off guard. She was unassuming with her short, lithe figure that reminded me of a ballerina, and pale snow-white skin. The flames in her eyes danced in the reflection of her long white and silver hair that was as smooth as ice. Her expression, despite the blue flames, remained just as cold. I told myself I could have been on guard if I hadn't been in Grandma Ruth's bookstore. I'd seen plenty of women perusing the shelves dressed to the nines in gothic lolita fashion or looking like Wednesday Addams.

However, ones that carried a pair of small, sickle-shaped blades? That was definitely a first.

"That is but a warning, Jason McCrae," she said dryly while she spun the blades in her hands as if she were a desperado in an old western film. "My master sends his regards."

The hushed voices that had been around us turned to shrieks of terror as the few patrons in the store took notice of what was going on. The one closest to me had noticed that I was bleeding and that the petite woman in front of me had weapons in hand. The others took notice when the wisps of black smoke leaking from below Sinead's black lace choker became darker, and thicker, and began crawling along the shelves.

It took all of thirty seconds for the handful of customers to scramble out the door, leaving the two of us alone.

"What does that motherfucker want?" I sneered, my fists clenched tightly despite the pain in my left palm.

"Jason!"

My eyes shot toward the sound of familiar voices at the back of the store as McKenna and Haley burst through the door. Behind me, in my peripherals, I saw a series of dancing, spectral lights and felt the familiar weight of Adelaide pressing into my back. The two shifter women bound toward me, clad in little more than a t-shirt - both of which were mine - that clung tight to their forms.

I found myself grateful that the customers had bailed on the situation. If Sinead's bladed threat hadn't sent them running, then a pair of bright chartreuse and liquid gold irises surrounded by black sclera would. With their combined rage, the two women had gone into the first stages of their shift leaving both of them with tapered ears, lengthened fangs and claws, and, in Mickie's case, a series of ringed spots darkening her bronze skin further.

"Get away from him, you bloody fucking cunt," Mickie screamed, her English accent becoming harsher amid her anger.

"Three days, Jason," Sinead said, unmoved by the two women racing toward her. Her gaze then found its way to Adelaide who stared back at the smaller woman with eyes that were stricken. Haunted. "I suggest this one attends the meeting as well. In fact, her presence is required."

As Sinead spoke, her body caught fire, a wash of blue flame engulfing her. Her body evaporated into dust, ash, and smoke as she disappeared before us. Mickie, claws extended, took a swipe at the flames as she barreled forward and found nothing of purchase. Instead, her body crashed hard into mine, leaving me out on the floor on my back.

"Puta pendejo!" Haley snarled from a few feet away.

From where I lay with Mickie on top of me, my werewolf girlfriend was stalking across the top of one of the shelves. Her nostrils flared wildly while her head snapped back and forth in rapid motions, searching for any trace of Sinead. When she found nothing, she began muttering angrily under her breath entirely in Spanish.

"Fucking hell," Mickie groaned as she lifted herself off of me and began searching for my assailant as well. "What in the bloody hell was that?"

"Better yet, *who* was that?" Haley growled as she jumped down to my side.

Both she and Mickie extended their hands down toward me and I took their helpful gestures. Granted, taking Haley's hand with my left was a far more ginger touch compared to the firm grasp Mickie held me with.

"Sinead," Adi answered softly, her voice quivering from being on the verge of breaking down. As the three of us came to stand by her, she hung her head and hugged her arms close to her chest. Her posture said that the ghost woman was seconds from shutting herself down entirely. "She… she was - *is* - like me."

"Love, what does that mean," Mickie asked, her voice regaining its normal sweet contralto tone while her hands found their way to gently cup Adi's arms. She didn't force movement, however, she made the effort to be reassuring and place herself so that they at least faced each other.

"And why was she here, la novia?" Haley asked, her tone matching the same caring and gentle tone as Mickie's. She took a position behind Adi, gently resting her hands on the woman's shoulders, and stifled a shiver as she began to calmly massage Adi's shoulders.

Adelaide remained unmoved.

My eyes trained on Adelaide, watching the short, curvy woman carefully before I chose to move closer to her. I attempted to reach out for her, my fingers inches from her pale semi-translucent flesh before she stiffened and flinched. Seeing her body language, my arm fell limply to my side.

Sinead had told me she worked for Samael and that was enough to know the reason for Adi's sudden change in behavior. After all, he'd been the demon who'd taken the strong, confident woman who I'd come to love and turned her into his victim. She had spent a century being his treasured toy for his sick gain and pleasure, the one he'd spent a hundred years torturing and tormenting repeatedly day in and day out.

Even after I'd found the amulet that her soul was bound to when I was a teenager, she'd been terrified to sleep. She never rested because his face would be the one she saw. She pushed herself to be an everlasting light in my presence because she tried to hide the pain and trauma he'd caused her.

Samael was her boogeyman.

"Scheiße," Adi finally hissed as she sunk back into Haley's grasp and pulled Mickie forward to comfort her with the taller, stronger woman's embrace. She sandwiched herself between them, hoping to ground her emotions in their combined warmth and strength. Then, with one hand, she gingerly took my left palm and inspected the wound before her hazel eyes met mine. "How many days did she give you?"

"You recognize it then?" I asked, my eyes narrowing onto the two crudely drawn crossed scythes. As Adi inspected it, I saw her eyes darken with a cloud of rage.

"It looks like a- Ow! Fucking bloody hell," Mickie hissed as she retracted her hand quickly from trying to touch my palm out of curiosity.

"It hurt you, babe?" Haley queried, her eyes narrowing as she looked back and forth between the gash on my palm and Mickie's pained expression.

"It's a blood curse," Adelaide answered coldly. "How did you let her get that close to you?"

"I was on the phone with Thomas and taking a job request from him. I had no idea she was behind me until I bumped into her," I answered truthfully, furrowing my brow at her.

Thinking of the phone call with our Odin reminded me that this wasn't the only big fish I needed to fry. The blue flames that had swept through Sinead's eyes and her entire form hadn't been the only time that those blue flames had been mentioned in the last hour.

Thomas, the Odin, or wolf king, of the Granite Pine Clan, had called in a favor for a close friend or lover of his. An explosion of blue-tinted flame had decimated her high-rise office in downtown Salt Lake City, destroyed over a million dollars worth of office equipment, and made it rain across Main Street. It had also injured her in such a way that she was now in a hospital bed with Thomas glued to her side waiting for the woman to wake up.

As his Muunin, someone who had magical capabilities associated with the pack but wasn't a member of the witch's coven they worked with, I was duty-bound to attend to the favor. But as Adi's boyfriend, her long-time best friend, and someone who once swore that I would destroy the demon who'd hurt her for so many years, I was conflicted.

No, fuck that, Adi takes priority.

"And she said… fuck, what did she say," I asked more to myself than anyone as I pushed aside my pain and anxiety to conjure up Sinead's words. "I have three days to grace, or whatever, Samael's presence. If I don't, at midnight on that third night, a pale horse will ride, and… she'll take my head and soul?"

"The bloody cunt is bluffing, right?" Mickie snorted with a humorless laugh as she watched both Adi and me.

"I wish," Adelaide mumbled. She then let out a deep exasperated breath before reaching her hand away from mine to stroke it through her long reddish blonde hair nervously. "If we don't pay him a visit, Jason will die."

"We are not going to see that pendejo, Adi," Haley retorted sternly, a trickle of an animalistic growl reverberating in her throat. "Not after what he did to you."

"Maybe you didn't hear ze part about Jason ficken dying," Adi snapped back, anger making her Germanic accent sharp and her eyes go completely black as a raven's. "We are not trading him for me."

"I-"

"We are not trading anyone," I interjected, stopping Haley and Adi from fighting further. My eyes trained on the crossed blades and then looked at both of them with a finality that left no room for either of the two women to deny my words. "Give me time to figure out how to deal with Samael. Until then, Mickie, Haley, babes, you need to get ready for work."

"JJ! You can't be serious," Mickie scoffed, cocking her hip to one side as her eyes trained on me, having gone back to her bright green human eyes some time ago.

"There ain't no way, I'm going into work after this," Haley snarled, wrapping her arms around Adi's shoulders and neck to hold her possessively and shoot me an angered glare.

"I am serious and yes you are," I said matter of factly.

Using my unmarked hand, I sank my fingers into the black fabric loosely adorning Mickie's form. I jerked her forward, letting a stern growl trickle through my own lips before I crashed them into hers for a rough kiss. It wasn't the hungry and passionate kiss I would have greeted her with when I returned to our shared apartment. However, it held the same feelings for her I always had for the taller, darker-skinned woman before me.

She returned that same fierce snarl and *humphed* when I trapped her lips between my teeth and gave her the usual love bite I always enjoyed delivering. One that held all of my love and adoration I had inside me toward her. I loved her - I truly did - and I appreciated her trying to be the big scary wereleopard she wanted to be. However, at that moment, she didn't need to be my fur-covered guardian angel - or rather leopard - she needed to get ready to be that and more for her students.

They needed their Coach Taylor and I'd be her aloof psychic.

With her still held with one hand I moved to trap Adi between Haley and me as I delivered the same fiercely passionate kiss to my golden-skinned wolf. Instead of holding her with my marked hand, I balled it into a fist and pushed on the small of her back, forcing her into me as I nipped and bit at her bottom lip and chin. Between the growl and the rough kiss, I left Adi and Haley breathing a little quicker and Haley's eyelids fluttering lazily.

"Now. Go get ready and take care of your kids, kitten," I said, directing the last word toward Mickie with a low tone that carried as much of a promise of sex as I could deliver. It wasn't nearly as good as she could deliver, but the way her entire body shivered under my grip said it worked just as well. "Same goes for you, pup. Understood?"

Haley shivered the same as Mickie as soon as my loving pet name for her left my lips. Then, because I wanted more of those reactions, I decided to brutally tease them both. "If you don't, no Adi or me for a week."

"Fuck," Mickie sighed, letting out a shuddering breath, while letting her teeth pinch her bottom lip and a small playful smirk tug at the corner of her lips. "You are such a bloody arsehole, you know that?"

"Ay dios mio," Haley whispered with a shuddering breath. "You are too damn good at turning us into puddles. You been snooping through Adi and I's library?"

"I know. And yes, I have," I snickered, letting my grip on the shirt Mickie was wearing loosen, but not before letting my eyes take a once over on her and the way the fabric tightening had outlined the shape of her toned, voluptuous form. "And that's why you love me."

"I love you too, asshat," Mickie sighed with a wide, fang-baring grin.

"Te amo, cara de idiota," Haley giggled with a pleasant whine and a grin.

They both pressed a chaste kiss to my nose before allowing me to lean back. They could call me names all they wanted, however, I knew it was out of the same love and adoration I held for the two of them. Then I turned a knowing smirk toward Haley, I may not be fluent in Spanish but I knew the gist of what she'd said.

"Hales, I will be fucking that pretty face later, you can count on that," I teased, giving the wolf woman a wink before turning back to Mickie. "And Mickie, when you're off later today, we'll meet you at the gallery so you and Adi can have your dinner date. The four of us can see how we can help Thomas' friend afterward."

"Yes, *sir*," they replied in unison, adding a sizzling tone with the second word. Mickie and Haley giggled as they watched my eyes flutter and my neck kink from the sudden rush of butterflies that soared from my chest and down my spine.

"You're sure you still want to go?" Adi asked with a small blush on her cheeks as she nibbled on the tip of her thumb while her eyes focused on Mickie, Haley, and me with laser precision.

"Yeah. I can't really cancel on Zi. You know how they get with short notices," I shrugged, giving her a soft smile.

"Before we head out," Mickie purred, her smile widening as she swept Adi and Haley into her arms.

The taller wereleopard cradled Adi, our shared Valravn girlfriend, caging her cheek with one of her hands while the other sank behind Haley, our shared werewolf girlfriend. The sudden purring sound leaving Haley's throat gave me a clue that Mickie had just groped the curviest of the three women roughly. Adi was left softly moaning in pure bliss as she was put on the receiving end of a dual attack, Mickie kissing her lips roughly with a possessive snarl. Haley, meanwhile, took advantage of Adi's craned neck and sunk her teeth into the pale glassy flesh offered up to her.

Once the kiss was broken, Mickie leaned in to whisper something against Adi's ear that I couldn't hear but left all three women smiling wide and laughing. It felt normal to watch their affection toward each other and I soaked up the infectious joy present when they were together.

I enjoyed the moment before the two shifter women stepped away and began their trek back up to our apartment. However, they only left after they wound back and gave Adi a dual swat. The sudden impact made Adi squeak with surprise as Mickie and Haley gave Adi's plump, round ass a firm smack and then darted off before she could retaliate.

"Before we go," I began as Adi turned her flushed attention back toward me. "I'm going to go up and figure out what blue fire means, see if we have anything in the office library that mentions it. Can you call Tori for me?"

"Sure?" Adelaide answered with more of a question in her tone and cocking her eyebrow. "Why's that?"

"Because I'm going to do a ritual and put up a protection circle and I need her help. Samael or anyone associated with him will not step foot in the store or find us here at home," I said with finality.

Adi nodded slowly with my declaration but remained motionless, even as I began walking forward, determined to start my research. When I felt a hand wrap around my wrist, I paused from the surprising amount of strength. When I looked back, I found Adi still staring forward with an expression of fiery determination etched across her soft features.

"Look, Jason, I appreciate you wanting to try and play this as easygoing as you can… But I'm worried," Adi said quietly in almost a whisper which had a cold edge that mixed a sense of overwhelming fear and anger into one emotion. "What if-"

"He touches you?" I asked, watching her reaction carefully to read her every movement. I flexed my fists, ignoring the surge of pain that my wounded palm sent crawling through my body, and focused solely on my girlfriend. "If he tries anything, if he tries to take you, touch you, or even look at you in a way that I don't like… Mickie or Haley will be the least of his worries."

"Jason, it's not just S… him. Sinead is dangerous too," Adi reaffirmed carefully.

"I don't care," I shrugged and then used the wrist where Adi clutched me to turn her and pull her forward.

I let her sink into my grip, one hand coming to cup her chin so she looked up at me while the other went south. I smirked softly as I coaxed a gentle squeak and a playful smile out of her as I palmed her ass with my uninjured hand. There was something about the way that these shared women of mine always seemed to help stir a sensation of confidence and determination out of me. Even if part of me still questioned how in God's name I'd ever gotten lucky enough to attain not just one of them but Adi, Haley, and Mickie together. I ignored it.

I would bask in that luck with everything I had.

And part of me, the one that loved the three of them with everything I had to offer, said that I wasn't just lucky. In Mickie and

Haley's cases; it was fate. According to them the gods themselves deemed it was fate and I was meant for them just as they were meant for me and for each other. There was no question that I loved them for their differences, and their commonalities, and my job - more than anything - was to be there for them.

I was meant to protect and love Adelaide. It wasn't just Mickie or Haley's self-proclaimed duty, it was mine too.

"Adi, little bird, if any of them touch you. I swear to fucking god," I said firmly, watching her eyes go cloudy with lust and adoration while her cheeks flushed and her knees wobbled. Then I let her watch as my eyes darkened the way they did whenever I said that she was mine. Because she was. "I. *Will*. Kill them."

PART OF ME WONDERS IF I'M A BIT OF A MASOCHIST.

The pain I receive from getting my tattoos freshened up shouldn't feel as therapeutic as it does. However, it is. The way the steady vibrations and humming seemed to lull me into a sense of calm like it was a form of white noise made for sleeping. The way it revved and the RPM increased with every touch of skin drew me closer to the same calm that sleep - true sleep - provided. The way that the needles drew across my skin, dying my flesh to black, turned me into a living canvas.

The biting pain like that of a cat's claws throughout my back brought me comfort.

Enough that I'd let my mind wander to what I'd been able to research about blue-colored fire which, admittedly, hadn't been much. My research had brought up millions of search results featuring an animated depiction of Hades, none of which did me any good. Unless I were to find magical inspiration somewhere in the voice of James Woods. Which was doubtful at best.

Truthfully, I hadn't been here to get my arms freshened up. Once I saw Adi and Mickie leave - with an exaggerated sway of their hips to tease me of course - I rolled onto my stomach and let Zi get to work on a piece for them. I called it their early Christmas present.

"Aight, just a spot more of shading and then we'll get you outta here, brotha," came a familiar voice as the tattoo gun let off its revved motor.

One eye opened to trail toward its source and found the fabric of a gold-colored bandana hanging loosely in front of me and obscuring my vision of the dark umber skin of its owner. As the machine turned off, the dark outlines of a portrait of Anubis entered my field of view as the artist sat back and let out a deep breath. I took in the sight of the jackal-headed man, his face sternly judging me as always, before following the intricate banding up Zi's arm to their bicep where it spawned into a portrait of Ammit, a shapely and voluptuous crocodile-headed woman.

"Sounds good, Zi," I replied lazily as I watched Zi, my lithe African American non-binary friend, bring the tattoo gun back to life and lean forward with their tongue pinched between their teeth.

As Zi's bright brown eyes narrowed in concentration, I felt their hands, covered in black nitrile rubber gloves, press firmly against my back to halt any movement. The spike of pain increased with the more vigorous motion and I let out a hissed groan as black ink poured into my skin to create shadows and depth on the designs that now adorned my spine.

"So you never said what these were for," Zi said, their tone strained from focus on my back. "And knowing you, all your shit is symbolic."

"These were," I started and then paused mid-sentence, trying to find an excuse for an explanation. "Just… for fun?"

The hum of the tattoo gun stopped instantaneously, as did the pressure on my back before I heard the squeak of Zi's chair. Their golden eyes met mine with the same stern and judgemental expression as the two Egyptian gods inked across their left arm. It was a piss poor excuse and I knew it.

I turned my head enough so that my eyes met Zi's and they returned my pensive expression with one that was ice cold. It made it so that their soft features and high, rounded cheekbones became more pronounced and striking. It was the same look Zi had given me when we met. I'd spent the entire session working on my right wrist band awkwardly apologizing to Zi for misgendering them when we first sat down.

Zi said it was fine of course, however, everyone knew that saying fine didn't mean how it was defined in the dictionary. Fine was the F-word worse than fuck.

Frustrated. Insecure. Neurotic. Emotional.

It had annoyed Zi that I had been persistently apologizing for something they had come to terms with, something they thought wasn't a big deal. It happened a lot, and Zi preferred people to say sorry once and move on, or not at all.

Today Zi wore their usual gold-colored baggy harem pants, black tank top, and gold bandanas on their wrists and neck. A look that put more emphasis on their toned arms and leanly muscled runner's build and more masculine features. The day we'd met, Zi had been in a pair of black leggings that accentuated their hips and waist and a white crop top that looked like they had been wearing a sports bra underneath. Zi also happened to be the only person, who sometimes identified themselves as a man, I knew who frequently wore large hoop earrings in their ears and more mascara than most women I'd ever met.

I'd grown up in a sheltered home and Zi had been the first person I'd met that identified themselves on the LGBTQIA+ spectrum. They were my first and only friend who went by they/them pronouns and identified themselves as non-binary outside of work. They also may or may not have been the first person to make me take a hard look in the mirror and begin questioning my own sexuality. I was - am - at the very least bi-curious thanks to Zi.

"Dawg, please tell me you didn't come to me with some dumb shit," Zi deadpanned.

When I gave Zi a weak smile in lieu of words, they took an annoyed breath, shaking their head while they grabbed the spray bottle from his artist rack. I groaned as the cold liquid soap misted my skin before Zi idly began cleaning the fresh artwork and wiping it down. When I still didn't budge, they rolled their eyes as they placed a thin, clear membrane across the top of the tattooed area of my back.

"Bro, you know that's a bad omen," Zi grumbled as he rubbed the adhesive second skin down flush against my back. "How many times do you think I gotta cover pieces up 'cause some dumbass got they baby daddy's name?"

"A few a day," I chuckled weakly when I felt Zi tap the small of my back before scooting their rolling stool away from the leather recliner.

"Facts," Zi snipped while they began cleaning up and disinfecting their workstation.

"But," I said, sarcastically letting the word hang in the air before giving Zi a cheesy look. "I didn't get names, just an art piece to represent them."

"Uh-huh," Zi deadpanned incredulously. "And what happens if you get a new girl to replace one of 'em or, shit, maybe you lock up one of your homeboys?"

"Please," I scoffed, rolling my eyes at them. "You think with my track record I would've ever landed them three months ago? And while you're thinking about that, think about my track record of being a heartbreaker or player. And… you do realize you'd probably be on that list of homeboys, right?"

Zi paused at that, furrowed their brow, and then shrugged once they'd mentally come to a conclusion.

"Okay, okay, you got me there," Zi chuckled, tossing their nitrile gloves into a garbage can.

"Besides," I said, walking around the chair to look at myself over my shoulder in the full-length mirror in the corner of Zi's booth. My eyes traced over the fresh ink, now slightly hidden under the translucent membrane holding back a mixture of skin moisture, blood, and plasma. "I'm not going anywhere anytime soon if I have anything to say about it."

I smiled wide at the design, knowing exactly what was now branded into my flesh but obscured by the fresh healing process that had already begun. I grabbed my shirt off of the end of the table and turned in time to catch Zi fixing their gaze from where it had been lingering. I shrugged, not minding the extra attention before pulling my shirt on, hissing at the pain of my muscles pulling at the opened skin before the dark red shirt fluttered down my chest in time for the front door to chime and see two women bouncing happily toward the front desk.

Adelaide paid for my new tattoo before I even had a chance to tell her no. It was a kind and loving gesture that I appreciated. However, part of me wanted to pick at it like a scab. I'd already owed her a lot before we became an official couple. Now, at this rate, I would never be able to repay her; especially for being by my side all of these years.

"Shit," Zi snickered, shaking their head as they watched the exchange. "Baby girl's been around for a fat minute, you ain't getting rid of that one for sure. And her? Hell, you'd be adding before I have to schedule you a coverup."

"Dude, I'm already up to three," I laughed, before giving Zi a mock Boy Scout salute instead of the usual fist bump they gave their other clients. "Now who's dreaming?"

I paused then because part of Zi's statement fell into place and clicked long after they'd said it. Zi had been looking at Adi when they called her *baby girl* and mentioned she'd been around for a long time.

"Zi, you-"

"Eyes of gods see all, my brotha," they smirked, tapping their left arm and pointing the gazes of Anubis and Ammit toward me. Zi then waved and began walking into the back of the shop, ignoring my insistence in flagging them down and offering me a call over their shoulder before disappearing. "See you soon, Ghost Whisperer."

ADELAIDE

TODAY WAS SUPPOSED TO HAVE BEEN ANOTHER WONDERFUL DAY.

I had anticipated a day filled with new memories, experiences, and warmth that had been filling the void my afterlife had become. One more day to help continue to scrub away the grime and decay that my soul had been bathed in from the time of my death. Anything to make me forget about the decades of eternal darkness and then being hunted by nameless things I'd wished to never know existed. And to help me forget the 115 years of agonizing despair brought on by the hands of *him*.

I'd spent the last three months trying to relearn how to live to my fullest potential thanks to the benefits the power of the Valravn had given me. I'd tried every food I could taste, touched every book I wanted to its fullest, and filled my ears with new music I'd never cared to try before. I was allowed to drive the Bronco without repercussions and even tried driving Mickie and Haley's motorcycles. And I spent every waking hour being able to touch, hold, and taste Jason, McKenna, and Haley; my most treasured moments.

The morning had started with perfect anticipation. Being the last one to wake meant that, when I did, it was to the feel of Mickie's lips and fingers along the inside of my thighs. The feel of Haley's lips and fingers along my neck and breasts hit me better than a hot cup of coffee. It was their favorite way to start the morning before leaving for work; spoiling me with attention and turning me into their dessert before breakfast.

Then a sense of cold dread and pain filled me through my connection with Jason. In the same instance, the two shifter women froze while their noses flared. They dressed quicker than I'd ever seen them do so but the panic that filled the three of us was clear. I'd felt cold pain and they'd scented blood. Jason's blood.

It had been the first time in nearly a decade since I'd seen Sinead O'Hare, the one who'd come to be an omen to my abuse and torture. Samael's obedient little lap dog and the warden of my confinement for the final decade of my servitude. I'd come to both fear her arrival and hate her presence with the same vitriol I held for the bastard demon himself.

However, part of me knew better. She was his victim just as I had been. The only difference was that I had persevered, I had the strength to not break to his will. I still had fight left in me long after her will had been decimated by his abuse. I couldn't - and shouldn't - blame her for that.

Part of me prided myself in being strong enough to outlast him as long as I did. Part of me hated the others for not being strong enough.

To rid myself of those pressing thoughts I had called Tori while Jason had begun his research. Then I wiped the slate clean and sated my carnal needs, stealing my man away to have him in every way and position I needed before we had to leave. Absorbing Jason's seed made my body glow with spiritual energy and resonance and I was positively doing so by the time we made it to the Elite Gallery for his appointment with Zi.

The short time between the start of Jason's appointment and my date with Mickie had given me something else to think about as well to rid myself of the memory of Sinead and Samael. A fantasy I'd been harboring since my first time meeting Zi. I found myself focusing on the thought of what it would be like to watch the two of them finally fulfilling that unrequited desire, lust, and tension.

And what it would be like to be in between them.

Between those thoughts, filling my belly at the Ethiopian restaurant Mickie introduced to me on our date, and her whispering carnal threats while we kissed I felt like myself again. More so once I got to hold Haley again and she dragged me out of my spiral completely with our shared passion.

"Really? You preferred Kenzo over Diesel?" Haley scoffed sarcastically as she walked backward, arms folded behind her head as she entered the elevator ahead of me, Jason, and Mickie.

"I found him charming and kind of sweet," I chuckled, shrugging my shoulders as I thought about the newest of my fantasy lovers.

And yes, I did eventually pick up her first book recommendation when we had first bonded. And yes, it was for the shallow reason of the main character having a name similar to mine and that haunting was in the title. Sadly, I found no ghosts, however, that didn't stop Zade from haunting my fantasies when I slept.

"Speaking of charming and sweet," Haley grinned as she leaned back against the glass of the elevator wall, giving me a wry grin. "I found a new book, it's about two serial killers-"

"Fuck, here we go again," Mickie drawled with an exasperated sigh.

"Babe, careful," Jason chuckled, hitting the button for the top floor of the older high-rise building.

"I'm just saying, little bird and our pup, have enough books," Mickie said, rolling her eyes as she slumped into the corner of the elevator, pulling me with her. "Too many honestly."

She folded her arms tightly over my shoulders and hummed as her large breasts melded into my back. It would have served as a perfect delightful feeling, however, her comment had been blasphemous. And blasphemy needed to be addressed.

"There is no such thing as too many books," Haley and I said in unison, both of us turning an indignant scowl at the taller woman.

Haley leaned herself back against Jason, pressing him into the opposite corner while his arms encircled her. His arms served to lift her moderately plump breasts into my direct line of sight while she indiscriminately pressed her rear tight against Jason's waist. The sight made my voyeuristic side hum to life, hoping to get the chance to watch them together again. Because I thoroughly enjoyed watching *my* tall, toned, red-headed, blue-eyed man with *my* short, curvy, black-haired, golden-skinned wolfess.

"And you can't tell me either of you wouldn't enjoy watching JJ make some more bookshelves. *Again*," Haley cooed, wiggling her eyebrows suggestively while reaching behind them to run her fingers through his hair.

"No. No, I would not," I sighed dreamily under my breath. However, I knew that in an elevator with a werewolf and wereleopard, I may as well have shouted it thanks to their fine-tuned hearing.

"Fair," Mickie snorted, rolling her eyes.

I vividly remembered the night while Jason was working on a poltergeist case and Haley brought planks of wood and varnish to curb his ADHD. Jason had ended up shirtless and covered in a fine sheen of sweat and wood stain as he completed a hand-made built-in bookshelf in the corner of our bedroom. It was me and Haley's personal library now and had been christened that night - all night - by Jason taking turns on the three of us against it.

That memory, mixed with the lingering desire to see Jason and Zi together made me hum with happiness in Mickie's arms. I'd known before that I was far from straight, however, being labeled as bisexual didn't seem to fit either. My father would be rolling in his grave if he saw me now being a not-so-old-fashioned woman. Instead, I was my happy little Pandemic self - as Mickie called it - someone who had both pansexual and demisexual tendencies.

Especially since I now knew I was far from monogamous as well.

The ding of the elevator brought me out of my thoughts and back into reality, though Haley had tried to make it a hard task. Especially as she ground herself against Jason, whispered sweet nothings in his ear in Spanish, and then sauntered out of the elevator. My eyes drank down the sight of her hips swaying hypnotically, and then I stifled a giggle as Mickie and I watched Jason. He, of course, needed to adjust himself in the corner of the elevator before the three of us followed after our tease of a werewolf toward the double doors of the penthouse office.

What remained of the broken glass was large black ink blot graphics that created some illusion of privacy before they melded into the large, rough-edged block lettering of an R, M, and A stacked together. The logo of our newest client Aniah Lebeaux, CEO of Republik Marketing and Advertising.

Mickie fell into pace behind Haley, the two of them letting out unamused whistles as their eyes set onto the destroyed penthouse office. Both of them had their hair blowing in the wind that had gained entrance through the deluge of windows that were shattered and rendered useless and, set against the sunset, both of them looked captivating.

Turning away from the two women, I found Jason still at my side in the mouth of the hallway being sobered by the sight in front of us. I saw his mind already beginning to work through possibilities of what could have caused the destruction in front of us and I smiled.

"Ready?" I asked, reaching out a hand in an offer for him to take if he decided to do so.

I felt his warm, strong hand encircle mine before my slender fingers intertwined with his thicker digits. He then took in a long, deep breath, readying himself for whatever would be beyond the safety of the hallway and his eyes narrowed in determination. He had a fierceness that made his cerulean eyes become deep boiling oceans before he took one step forward and grit his teeth to let out a trepidatious growl of confidence.

"All right, let's find us a fucking demon."

One step forward.

Then two.

And then, before we could register anything, Jason and I went through the doorway with Mickie and Haley. The only contortion or signs of pain that registered on Jason's expression were confusion and none of his usual ticks that I'd come to determine as pain.

Then confusion spread across me, Haley, and Mickie's faces because, once Jason was through the door, he walked around the ruined office as if nothing had happened. All of us scanned the walls which once had been white, decorated with graphics that imitated large ink blots and paint splatters. The graphics now looked like they had been the original wall color and the white and dark brown charred splotches were the intended negative spaces.

Jason walked around as if the many desks, computer equipment, lounge chairs, and couches had always been thrown across the floor, creating small mountains of twisted wreckage. As if the large, almost star-like pattern in the middle of the black carpet that had been burned away to reveal a layer of concrete underneath had always been the room's focal point.

"Are you getting anything?" I asked, watching him with a mix of caution and anxiety.

"Not a thing," he answered, that same mix of confusion and nervousness coating his voice. It felt like he almost wanted to laugh at the absurdity of it all.

"So, what does that exactly mean?" Haley asked, her light brown eyes tracing back and forth between Jason, then to Mickie, and then to me.

"I'm guessing it means no demon," Mickie said, shrugging as she looked at Jason and me for confirmation.

Jason simply nodded, furrowing his brow as he began pacing in small circles around what looked to be the explosion's origin. He was walking around ground zero like it was nothing other than it was frustratingly curious. Frustrating and curious from the lack of feeling at all from that point.

"No, because if it was… I think all of us would have been able to sense it. Especially the two of you with your heightened senses," he said, tapping his nose as his eyes met theirs.

That made the two shifter women pause and then flare their noses, lifting their heads to scent the air and let their beasts tell them what they needed to know. I watched as their eyes closed to focus on what they could smell and then saw them both furrow their brows and tilt their heads in confusion.

"It doesn't even…"

"Smell like normal fire," Mickie finished Haley's pondering before the two of them watched each other closely as if to make sure they were on the same page.

"No, and that's the thing," Jason said, now standing in the middle of the blast zone, scratching the back of his head with growing confusion. "If it was demonic, all of us would smell sulfur and brimstone. But this…"

I decided that maybe since I was something other than human I could do something similar to Haley and Mickie. I closed my eyes and let my mind drift to that place where my wrath and the spirit of my raven sat together awaiting me to judge and guide a soul. That bestial spirit, one that looked like I had stopped in the middle of a shift from human to bird, stepped forward and I felt a rush of energy and power begin to flood into my body.

When my eyes opened I felt the comforting weight of my mother's Valravn skull now sitting perched into my hair like a crown that had always been meant to be there. I knew that, if I could see my eyes, they'd become pure black resembling that of a raven as well. I called forth that spiritual guide for one reason; its eyes and nose always seemed to triple my normal senses every time I'd called upon it since it manifested after my first time with Jason and during my battle with Moira Westfall.

Now I could scent in vivid detail what the shifter women beside me were. Hints of rose, possibly the flower itself or mixed with sage that was typically burned at a wake, with traces of vanilla and… rain. It was a mix of scents that felt comforting, almost like a peaceful home.

Curiously, it had the same feel as Grandma Ruth's house.

My mind wandered back to the first time Jason and I had visited

Ruth's home together. Sure, I had been nervous about officially meeting the woman for the first time but there was something else. There was something of a familiarity not only with her home and my childhood home because now that I was consciously thinking of it, the scent reminded me of my mother as well. Moreover, it had been something I vaguely correlated with Sinead as well when she was my warden; the scent of rain and sage.

Especially when her eyes…

"Jason," Mickie said cautiously, her voice pulling me from my wandering mind.

When I blinked back to the here and now, I found the two shifter women crowding around Jason who was standing in the middle of the blast zone. His head was hung back, his stance uneasy and shaky, while he stared up at the ceiling with eyes rolled back so that only the white of his sclera was visible. He was inside one of the psychic-induced trances that left him comatose as his mind filled with memories and emotions of land, people, or objects he physically touched. It was the precursor or after-effect of a rush of surging pain being jettisoned into his mind.

"Is he okay?" Haley asked nervously, her eyes darting back and forth between the three of us.

"Yeah," I answered cautiously as I made my way closer to them and then reached out to take Jason's hand. I let my urge to guide him back to reality take over as my weight against his stabilized him and soon he was blinking himself back into the room with the three of us. With me. "He's okay, he must have finally found a trigger."

"You're so calm about it," Haley replied, furrowing her brow and deepening her confusion as she looked down to where I held Jason's hands in mine and then up at the man himself.

"I'm far more used to it than anyone," I shrugged. "This is nothing compared to what I've watched go through in places like Mountain Meadows, Sand Hollow, or even our first visit to Hounds Den."

"You're just lucky you've had some warning," Mickie snorted, shaking her head with a wry grin. "The first time I brought him through the White Door, I thought I killed him."

"Dios bueno," Haley muttered under a shuddering breath.

Jason rolled his head down so that he met my eyes first and then looked toward Mickie and Haley next. A contemplative expression etched its way across his eyes and brow before looking down at his feet. Without saying another word, he reached down to the center of his stance, picked something up, and then brought it back up in his palm with a hiss of pain and uneasy movements. Whatever he'd picked up had been the source of his wave of memories and emotions and then he held it up for the three of us to see with bated breaths.

An... earring?

More specifically, a small pendant earring that had a stone in the middle, one that looked familiar because it was the same kind of malachite that my soul-bound necklace was. The same one that still hung from Jason's neck which now had a small flash of pink coloring toward the bottom.

"Aniah's?" Mickie asked pensively as her eyes darted back and forth between Jason and the jewelry he held.

"No," Haley and Jason answered in unison.

"She usually wears the big hoops and bangles like I do," Haley continued, shaking her head as she furrowed her brow at the piece.

My eyes went wide at that realization. Aniah hadn't been the only person standing here. Someone else had been in this spot where the blast emanated from.

Mickie and Haley both leaned down, getting closer to Jason's palm, and then took in long, deep breaths. When they came back up and let the sense dance throughout their bodies and minds, they quickly shot each other a look of cold determination and fierceness. They watched each other for a moment, a conversation held with their eyes instead of words that said that they were getting the same scent we had but underneath the rose, sage, vanilla, and rain, there was something else. Something that Jason and I had missed.

In a blink of an eye, the two of them were gone. My eyes only found Mickie as I searched for a small sheen of vermillion hair and found her and Haley with their backs to the wall on either side of a closed door. Their eyes had both rolled to their beast's, black sclera surrounding bright stars of golden green and amber, teeth lengthened to a pair of fangs on each of them. Both also had claws fully extended at the ready as well.

"Girls, wait," Jason said, quickly rushing toward the far end of the office, his hand interlaced with mine and forcing me to keep pace with him.

"So, it's not a demon," I asked carefully as we raced toward the other side of the office, the weight of my Valravn skull disappearing as I shelved that power inside of me.

The two shifter women ignored Jason's prompting and mentally shared a countdown before Mickie grabbed for the handle and pulled, ripping the door off of its hinges and tossing it absentmindedly across the room. The two of them rushed toward the room, ready to strike and kill anything on the other side of the missing door, and then froze in place.

Their shoulders slumped from defensive, aggressive poses to something akin to both shock and pity. Jason pushed faster, forcing me to chase his longer strides with everything we had until we finally reached the two of them.

"It's…"

Jason began speaking and then stopped abruptly at the threshold, looking down into what I found to be nothing more than a supply closet. It was pitch black inside or would have been if it wasn't for the faint glow of blue light that flickered and danced dimly inside.

I pressed myself past Mickie, Haley, and Jason to see inside and my eyes grew wide with astonishment. It took a long, timeless moment for me to understand what I was seeing because part of me found itself not wanting to believe. In the end, I had no choice but to come to terms with what was before me.

Huddled in the bottom of the closet was a figure, lithe and petite in stature huddled over in panic and terror. I recognized the same rocking motions that I had during my panic attacks and it made my heart sink from heightened fear and anticipation to sadness and sympathy.

Pale skin was graced by long sweeping designs tattooed into the skin, creating beautiful displays of artwork I'd seen from old horror movies and rock band posters. However, the four of us paused and no one dared to make the first move. It wasn't merely from the sadness we felt watching someone trying and failing to make it through a traumatic emotional and mental breakdown, it was the hair. Hair that was bright blue from its roots where it wandered upward along the short pixie-styled cut before coming to life in short waves of blue flames.

The figure looked up, her eyes alight with smaller singular flames that danced from her cyan-colored irises, making her face glow with the same soft ethereal blue around her. The woman's dark makeup was smeared, plastered down her face from where thousands of tears had dragged down her cheeks and stained her wrists where she'd been curled into herself tightly. The expression in her eyes and marred across her brows was that of pure fear and regret. Fear of what had happened, fear for the lives of the people around her, and fear of herself.

The thoughts that could be seen playing across her eyes in repeat like a melancholy film said it all. She was terrified of everything that had happened and who she'd hurt because the guilt in her eyes said that she was the culprit that we had been searching for.

"What are you?" Mickie asked breathily.

"Everything is okay," I said, taking in a deep breath and calming myself.

The woman's eyes shot up to the wereleopard, still not trusting my words. She shook her head rapidly as fresh tears began to pour. I shifted forward, lowering myself to my knees in front of her, and mentally cringed as she closed off even more, shrinking herself into a tighter ball like she was scared that I would hurt her.

I wouldn't.

The fire in her eyes that danced through her hair was the same kind that I was all too familiar with. Instead of my eyes being the one full of fear when I saw those blue flames, the roles had now been reversed.

I wouldn't make her feel like I was the omen Sinead had been for me. I was looking into fiery eyes that were broken, sure, but this woman's will hadn't died within Samael's grasp.

Looking into her eyes reminded me of a truth I hadn't brought myself to tell Jason either; that I knew the kind of fire he was looking for. My only logical reason was the pain it caused from thinking about Sinead. Or was it because I had more knowledge of it thanks to the raven spirit manifesting and feeding me memories and information each time I summoned it?

I knew one thing, however…

Hellfire is fucking gorgeous.

As I inched closer, I reached out a tentative hand and gave her eyes that said that I understood the pain she was going through. More than anyone. She sucked in a breath, whimpering before she finally spoke in a voice thick with horror and despair. A voice so quiet that I was the only one who would hear her.

"Help me."

It took a long moment to pry myself from staring at the cyan flames licking upward from the woman's hair. Instead, my focus regained itself when I felt Adelaide's elbow connect with my gut to shuffle me out of the way. I took the hint and moved back while the three women to my side crouched down in front of the woman and began talking with her softly. As they did so, Haley stripped off the flannel shirt she was wearing and wrapped it around the terrified woman.

Realizing she was naked made me turn so that I was no longer facing the four of them. After what she'd been through, I wasn't about to leer at her in any way if I could help it.

"Jason, Meine Liebe, can you get her some water?" Adelaide asked, seeing her out of the corner of my eye as she and Mickie helped the other woman to her feet. "Meine Wölfin, can you get her something to sit on?"

"Sure thing," Haley and I responded in unison before giving each other a shared smile.

As the group moved, I caught a glimpse of a bag of disposable cups inside the supply closet. After I fished one out of the bag, I quickly made my way into the hallway outside the office and filled it at the drinking fountain I'd passed on my way in. When I returned, Mickie and Haley were both moving a second torn-up couch to sit across from one Haley had moved. The mystery woman sat in a guarded manner, her eyes flicking to each of us as we moved, watching for a threat.

As I walked, I realized I still had the earring in my hand and offered it to her along with the water as I approached. My mind was still buzzing from what I'd seen in the visions the jewelry had offered up on a headache-inducing platter. *None* of it made sense.

"I'm guessing this is yours?" I said, holding it in my open palm. She rolled her eyes up to look at me but made nothing further.

"Okay… How about we start with introductions? That sound good to you, love?" Mickie said, watching the tense exchange and a long moment of silence. She leaned herself against the back of the couch across from the woman and gave her the best award-winning smile she could offer. "I'm McKenna but my friends call me Mickie. This is Haley,

Adelaide, and Jason. We're here to help."

As she had mentioned each of our names, Haley and Adi both gave her a friendly wave and a smile. When it was my turn I lightly lifted the cup of water, still offering it to her, while giving the woman a patient smile. After another long moment of cautious contemplative silence, the woman gently took the water cup and earring swiftly before looking down at the floor.

"Lex," the woman answered quietly. She then took a deep breath, cleared her throat, and lifted her gaze to meet Mickie's as she tried again. This time with a more confident, brash tone. "Name's Lex."

"Okay," Adelaide nodded, taking in a deep breath before giving Lex a leveled gaze. "Jason and I run a small business together called Dead Residents. He's a psychic and I'm… something else… the point is, people hire us-"

"Tch," Lex tsked, rolling her eyes indignantly. "So what, you're ghost hunters or something?"

"Sort of," I snorted with a shrug of my shoulders. It wasn't the warmest of receptions but at least the woman was on the right track, if at all as sarcastic as she could be. "Ghosts, poltergeists, curses, *demons…* you name it, we try to get rid of it."

I knew the walls she had because I'd used sarcasm, self-deprecation, dark humor, and more for my own mental barriers. I often used them to dance around the issues of my failing mental health and well-being. They could be great, stone wall defenses lined with iron spikes to keep everyone at bay, however, I knew better than anyone those caltrops went both ways. And I knew that they could cause you more harm than allowing someone to get close if you poked at them for too long. With one singular word, I had put a crack in those walls.

"We were hired by Thomas Rassmussen, I'm sure you've heard that name before, as a favor for a friend," I began.

"Oh, they're more than friends," Haley and Mickie answered in unison, with devilish smirks etched across their lips.

"Right, anyway," I chuckled at the two shifter women, confirming a suspicion I'd had. And then, because I needed to get through Lex's barriers further to even begin helping her, I gave her a stern expression. "Now, this can go two ways. We can call Thomas and let him know we found the person - not a ghost or a demon - who hurt Aniah-"

"It wasn't on purpose!" Lex screeched, jolting to her feet and giving me wide eyes with a mix of regret and pain etched into them. Her irises had also reignited with small trickles of blue flame, as did her hair, which roared into a small bonfire of cyan embers. "It..."

"I get it, you're scared okay. I don't blame you for it," I said, holding up my hands in a disarmed gesture. I watched her flinch as her eyes darted toward the mark on my left palm. Using that same hand, I pointed toward the earring in her hand. "Especially not after what I saw from that."

"And how would you know a fucking thing about that?" She sneered at me.

"He's a psychic," Adelaide answered sweetly, giving me a warning smile. "If he touches a person, object, or designated piece of land, he can gather all of its thoughts, memories, and emotions. It's what he does besides seeing and communicating with the dead and other things."

"Pfft, right and I'm supposed to believe what, that ghosts and monsters are real and shit?" Lex scoffed, rolling her eyes and slamming herself backward against the couch to lounge in a relaxed but defiant and guarded way.

"I mean," I chuckled, rubbing the back of my head, and dragging my nails against my scalp. "Technically, I'm the only human in this room right now."

The comment made everyone in the room freeze. After a moment I moved to drop myself into the couch across from Lex and leaned forward to rest my elbows on my knees to give her a level gaze.

"Lex, I know that Salt Lake has never been your true home. One because we don't have the ocean or a giant cave that disappears after you walk through it. Two, because any Greek architecture we have here in the state is fake as fuck and nowhere near old enough or authentic enough to be what I saw. And three," I said as I reached into my pocket and pulled out my phone. I opened the camera app and turned it so Lex could see herself. "Your hair and eyes are still on fire."

Her eyes widened before she slammed them shut to snuff out the flames there, reaching up and frantically patting the top of her head to try and snuff out the flames there. The fire never burned or charred her skin, leaving her untouched and pale.

"Why does it do that anyway? What kind of fire is it?" Haley asked, leaning forward and squinting her eyes to see any traces of ignition as Lex finally snuffed out her hair completely.

"Hellfire," Adelaide answered, drawing my attention completely toward her. "And before today, I'd only seen it once before. Or rather, on *one* person before."

"Before today, I'd never seen it before," I scoffed, shaking my head with a humorless smile, and then held out my left palm face up. "Now you, Lex, are the second person and I'm really hoping you don't attack me either."

"You're right, you know," Lex sighed, reclining so her head rolled against the back of the couch.

Her posture drooped in unease which left the open edges of Haley's flannel shirt and the water cup now in her lap covering anything indecent. It left her petite lithe figure with pale white, creamy skin exposed to draw a long line from the tip of her chin, through the valley of her small breasts, and abdomen before opening wide to bare her thin hips and long legs, all of which was covered in tattoos of varying designs and colors.

"I'm not human… Mostly. And Aniah is… my adoptive mother so we know Tom is the wolf king or whatever. Which means you two are shifters, right?" She said, waving a finger between Haley and Mickie to which they nodded. Then she gave Adi lazy eye contact. "And yeah you're definitely… something else. But I swear to the fucking gods I didn't mean to hurt Mom, just…"

Lex's voice became distant, her words trailing off as if she didn't know what to say or how to explain what happened. Or how to explain who and what she really was. The walls of her self-defense were crumbling, all because she'd seen the brand on my palm and where my pale skin had begun to turn ashen and dark like a mold was festering from the wound I'd received this morning. My heart broke for her.

"If you don't want to say anything, I can see what you need me to see," I said, offering her a sigh of condolence. "One touch and I'll be in your head. I'll see mostly everything. Just focus on what you need me to see or feel and I'll make it quick."

"Fine, it's your funeral if you want inside that fucked up place," Lex said, standing entirely as she tossed the empty water cup behind her into the pile of wreckage and debris.

"So you figured us out, but I wanna know," Haley said, her tone contemplative as the three of us watched Lex take a step toward me. "What are you exactly?"

She gave the four of us a contemplative look then shrugged and let a small smirk tug at the corner of her lips. As she began gliding towards me, the sway of her hips seemed entrancing in an ethereal sort of way, giving off an enhanced air of seduction and sultriness. It was something I'd only ever seen Mickie or Haley do, which always led to a long night of sex. Moreover, she no longer tried to hide any of herself and I forced my eyes to avert my attention from lingering too long on her form.

For the first time, I heard a genuine giggle of delight and playfulness that rang out like small bells. As I felt her long, slender fingers wrap around the sleeve of my leather jacket and lift my right hand upward, she hesitated. I could sense that there was still an air of nervousness and caution. Her eyes darted between the three women around us, seeking their approval before the bare skin of her clavicle pressed against my palm.

"I'm… an underworld nymph," Lex whispered with a nervous, apologetic smile.

Her words registered just as the first rush of pain entered my mind.

The scent of rain and sage flooded my senses as the strobing visions of memories passed through my mind's eye at a blinding pace. A massive, dark watered river snaked from the mouth of a cave across an overcast, mountainous environment. Its banks were lined with blue-flamed torches that dotted the distance like rows of street lamps. The visage of a riverside village filled my view but the vision couldn't decide which memories to show as it flipped back and forth between showing the village on fire, bodies and gore strewn about the sand and grass, and lively times.

The village's residents all had the same kind of hair as Lex, cyan flames dancing across differing lengths and styles of the women inhabiting it. The overlay of images saw Lex at various stages of her early childhood, playing with others like herself before it flashed to her screaming and running for her life. Even in the visions of her village before it was decimated, a tall ram-headed figure stalked forward, his distance from her jumping back and forth between near and far like a disoriented film.

The vision jumped with the sound of a scream as he got within inches of her before a wall of blue fire filled the view entirely. From there I found the same visions I had from the earring, flashes of a cave from where the river originated opening up. A flash of the ocean and what looked to be Athens in the distance. Athens became closer as it jumped between memories of pickpocketing and living on the streets before stowing away onto a boat. Another blur of flashing memories brought the scene to Salt Lake before settling onto countless memories centered on a short, curvy African American woman whose presence and aura exuded a homely, loving, and powerful nature.

"Shit, is he okay? He's not gonna die is he?"

Lex's voice of concern began dragging me from her memories, as did the pleasant feeling of cool, slender fingers brushing through my hair. As the room came into view, I saw Lex's fearful expression flicking back and forth between me and the women at my sides.

"He's okay, just his gift at work," Adelaide said, her voice pulling me like a lifeline back to reality. "Funny enough, you and Mickie had almost the same reaction to the first time seeing him like this."

"Hah hah, very funny," Mickie deadpanned, which made my lips curl into a grin.

"Holy fuck I killed him," I said, imitating Mickie's tone and accent. Quite poorly I might add.

"You know what, babe, no sex with me and the girls for a week," she glared at me with a sadistic grin. "You're sleeping on the floor."

"Ouch, the accent was that bad?" I snickered and rolled my head to look at Lex, who gave me a confused glance. "See, I'm fine. The memory thing is just a bit of a bitch, even if my pain tolerance is abnormally high."

"Anyway," Adelaide giggled softly from beside me where she continued to idly run her fingers through my hair. "You know about the curse mark, hellfire, you're a nymph from the underworld, and Jason mentioned a cave somewhere in Greece a while ago. Can I assume you're a denizen of the world beyond like myself?"

"Y-Yeah… I," Lex paused as she trained her eyes on Adi for a long moment, her brow scrunched with scrutiny.

Her eyes then began to widen, her pupils shrinking to pinholes just as I looked at Adi in time to see the raven skull materialize. It formed and made its presence known like it had been a crown that she had been wearing the entire time while her hazel eyes became pitch black like that of the bird in question.

"You're from Nekduamortum," Lex whispered, almost like it had been a dirty word. Or as if someone wasn't meant to hear what Adi said was the true name of the world beyond.

"I'm not myself. But before my mother spent the majority of her life in Germany, I believe she would have been born there, yes," Adi nodded, happy for any moment to speak about her mother. "She met my father, gave up being a Valravn for a mortal life, and then had me and my siblings here in the States. But that was lifetimes ago."

"Wait, so exactly how old are you?" Lex snorted, shaking her head in disbelief.

"Well… if you count the time since my death… I'm 197 years old," Adi shrugged.

"Yeah, but we decided we wouldn't count that extra time," Mickie said, folding her arms tightly across her chest, and giving Adelaide a stern glare. Haley and I matched Mickie's expression.

"Fine, fine, if you go by what these three say, then next year I will finally see my 23rd birthday," Adi chuckled softly.

"Which leads me to why I'm worried the most," I said, feeling my expression and words going distant. I held out my left palm in Lex's direction and turned my head, not meeting her gaze. "Where did you see this before?"

"I uh… when I was a little girl," Lex answered quietly, turning her head to look down off to the side of her lap. "In my village before…"

"Where you lived with the other nymphs, by the big river. Which, since you're an underworld nymph, I'm guessing - and I can't believe I'm about to say this - is the River Styx," I said, my eyes and mood brightening from that realization. I would have probably broken down into hysterical laughter if the memories hadn't been so… unwelcoming.

"Hold the fuck up, chico amantes," Haley retorted with exasperation, holding her hands to each side of her head like she couldn't believe what she was hearing. "Are you trying to tell me that Zeus, Hercules, Hades, Poseidon… They're real? Like *really* real?"

Lex nodded sheepishly and then shrunk herself down a little, again like she wasn't supposed to be saying these things with the fear of divine retribution. It was doubly confirmed when Adelaide shifted uncomfortably, drawing our eyes toward her and all she could offer in return was a sheepish smile.

"Technically… all of them are," Lex offered in little more than a quiet mouse-like voice. "All of the gods that mortals worship live on Aardeotheous, the celestial plane, or Elysivanatum, the realm of the eternals. Among others."

All of us paused and froze at her words, letting them truly sink in for a long moment.

"So Selene," Haley whispered softly and then looked up toward the ceiling in an instinctive nature. "She's…"

"Real," Mickie said softly, staring down at Adelaide and me with a solemn look in her eyes.

"I… Okay, we'll circle back to that later. Lex," I began cautiously before I felt my expression and mood darken as I sat up straight and leveled my gaze on her. "I need to know how and where you've seen this before."

Lex took in a deep breath and closed her eyes, not meeting any of ours.

"Okay, so like, you got my memories right? Then you know what happened to my village, what happened when *he* came," Lex said like she was spitting poison from her veins. "The big guy with a ram's head."

"Yeah," I answered quietly with a coldness in my voice. It felt as cold and as distant as the blood in my veins began to feel. Beside me, I felt Adelaide's body go rigid, and her left hand, which had been resting on my knee, flexed tightly.

"He came looking for us specifically, treated the ones his people took like trophies," Lex continued with a disgusted tone.

"And he has this tattooed on his chest, just below his clavicle," I nodded, pouring through Lex's memories inside my own head while looking at her for confirmation. She nodded. "So why don't we start with what happened last night?"

"I'm the art director for my mom, Aniah, worked my ass off since she was allowed to hire me at 16. So when she needs me to meet with high-dollar clients, I'm the one who takes care of them. Sometimes, because of their schedule, it means I have meetings at weird fucking times. Which is what happened with this guy," Lex lamented, scoffing at herself like she should have seen the events coming.

"What was his name?" Adelaide asked, her voice going to a cold and dark place. She was visibly tense, shaken to her core as a cold, frosty wind emanated off of her body. "And what did he look like?"

"He… holy shit," Lex froze as she looked up at Adelaide, her eyes going wider than they had been before.

"Santa meirda," Haley whispered quietly before tentatively reaching for Adi's shoulder.

"Babe, try to breathe," Mickie said softly before she cupped Adi's other shoulder.

"What was the Scheißkerl's name?" Adi hissed, her tone reverting to a thick Germanic lilt as rage began to consume her. The cold wind was replaced by heat as her skin became ashen, her limbs extended, and the skull moved down to cover the top portion of her face as if it were a battle helm. "And what did *he* look like?"

"Tall... uh… six foot something, dark hair, handsome-ish, I dunno… He dressed and looked like one of those rich pompous douchebags. But the cheap cologne couldn't hide the same thing I smelled when all of my birth mothers were taken," Lex continued, becoming frantic like she was staring into the face of a monster trying to devour her. And right then, she probably was. "He… he looked like he was going to hurt Aniah and I… I snapped. I'd never used my fire before but I couldn't let this… Victor Leamas guy take-Ah!"

Adi stood abruptly, raven wings unfurling from her back and ripping through her clothing as she stood to tower over all of us. She had become the creature Mickie, Haley, and I had seen that night in the forest three months ago. The same creature that had torn Moira Westfall into pieces, decapitated her, and then ate her wretched soul. She was, entirely, a true Valravn.

"Ich werde seine verdammte Seele in Stücke reißen" Adi snarled under her breath, her voice now completely in her native language and coming out doubled like some ethereal echo.

"Adi, calm down," I said, reaching out to take her hand and urge the tall, ashen-skinned, and raven-headed creature to sit back down. My grip urged her to calm down and return to the woman I knew and loved who had been beside me through all of the worst parts of my life. "You're not his victim anymore, remember?"

Adi looked down at me with her raven eyes, taking my words in with long consideration. After what seemed like a long eternal moment, her form relented and she sat back down, her body shifting back to her true self. Mostly. Her skin had returned to its normal creamy tan, and her strawberry blonde hair shined once more, however, the raven skull still covered half of her face and her eyes were pitch black.

"Is he… did he come to take me?" Lex said, swallowing a lump in her throat.

"Yes," Adelaide said coldly. "If he's back, he came to get you and do what he did to me. To Sinead, and all of his other slaves. The greedy fucker is after us because we are all children of the world beyond. Creatures who have dominion over death. But it won't happen, not any longer. Not if *I* can help it."

"H-How can you be so sure?"

"Because the next time I see that demon bastard… Whether he's going by Samael or Luciano or Victor," Adi began, a wicked grin stretching across her lips that showed off rows of sharpened teeth. It was a look that made all of us shiver in a mix of fear and anticipation. "I'm going to mount that fucker's head to our wall."

56

ADELAIDE

I TERRIFIED EVERYONE TONIGHT. INCLUDING MYSELF.

Tonight hadn't supposed to have been easy, especially with the worry that we were going to run into a demon. Or something that had the power to hurt mortals and cause the damage we'd walked into. Instead, my past and my nightmares were coming back to haunt all of us.

What had started with the reappearance of Sinead had now come full circle to know that aside from still hunting me, Samael was still hunting others. During our sessions, I always blacked out. Became distant. Trying my best to protect myself from him and his incessant desire to break me and take control over my body, mind, and powers I didn't know I'd had before. All so he could hold dominion over death and not have to answer to the gods who had power over it.

Now that I knew what I was, I understood why he hunted things like me, dullahans, banshees, reapers, nymphs, and the like. Why we became his trophies. His collection.

Greedy fucking bastard.

I ran my finger through the groove through the left eye socket of the raven skull, drawing the comforting feeling it brought me to the forefront. Once I took in a long, deep breath to calm myself entirely, I looked up at the hook Jason had placed above the front door to the apartment. Forcing myself to smile softly, I reached up, placing the raven skull on its perch.

It was similar to what had been its resting place in my childhood home. It's what completed the home for me. Made it *our* home.

After my declaration to Lex, Jason made a phone call to Thomas to let him know of our findings. Haley volunteered to stay with her until he and the Council arrived and made a decision on where to take her. She would be placed under the protective custody of the clan, hoping that having werewolves guarding her would be a deterrent to the demon.

I hoped as much as well.

"You coming to bed, love?" Mickie asked, drawing my attention from the front door to the threshold of our bedroom.

My cheeks warmed and my heart skipped a beat as my eyes drank in her form. Leaning against the doorway, she was completely nude, leaving her dark-bronze skinned perfection in perfect view. It made me instantly want to be in front of her and, with a trail of dancing lights, I was. In an instant, I was across the room and wrapping my arms around her neck as she leaned down to press her plump, pouty lips against mine.

I let out a soft moan as I breathed in the scent of cinnamon and sugar and felt one of her strong hands cup my ass tightly through the jeans I was still wearing. She craned my neck and body as I felt myself go onto my tiptoes to reach her properly while her strong figure held me tight against hers. She was everything I needed in that moment as the touch of her lips and hand on me chased away the remaining anger and fear, replacing it with electric bursts that filled my core with heat and pressure.

"I will be soon," I whispered against her lips. She nodded to my answer, knowing I was waiting for Jason to come back before we joined her in bed. However, with her needing to work in the morning and late tomorrow night, she'd be drifting off to sleep soon. Possibly before either of us made it to her side. "Wake me up in the morning?"

She purred warmly and her hand on my ass gripped me tighter.

"Yes, please," she cooed seductively, then moved to let her purred voice resonate in my ear and fill my core with even more heat and need. "I wanna go to work with you on my tongue and Jason dripping from my cunt."

"That, Miene Liebe, can most - ah - definitely be arranged," I hummed with delight before letting out a throaty moan as her teeth sank into the translucent flesh of my neck.

"Cuddle up tight when you come to bed, little bird," Mickie hummed with delight.

"Yes, my goddess," I sighed with a dreamy tone before her lips crashed against mine once more.

"Love you," she said with a grin, as she backed away slowly and left herself fully on display.

"I love you too," I answered, nibbling my lip as my eyes watched her dark, taught nipples sway hypnotically before she crawled into bed like the giant, lazy cat she was.

I watched her settle in from the doorway, smiling in delight before I giggled and let out a dreamy sigh as I heard her breathing even out, and soft, cute snoring followed soon after. I watched her sleep for what seemed like decades before I heard the front door open and watched as Jason entered our home.

"She asleep already?" Jason asked, lifting a brow as he watched me from across the room.

"Yup," I answered with a curt nod before appearing in front of him in an instant. "She'll wake us in the morning though."

"I can get behind that plan," he grinned and opened his arms to welcome me into them.

Our lips met and I whimpered into his touch as our mouths and tongues began a long, slow dance. He groaned softly into the kiss while his hands found the spot Mickie had vacated before, his strong hands cupping and groping my plump rear firmly.

"I think that's the idea, my love," I sighed as his teeth grazed over my lips and down my jawline.

He nibbled down my jaw and across my neck before laying a firm kiss there. With that kiss he held me close, laying my head into the crook of his neck while his lips planted a soft kiss on the top of my head. His embrace, his presence, was the warmth and safety I needed to let out a shaky breath of relaxation.

"You okay?" He asked while my eyes drifted closed.

Not entirely.

"I will be," I answered with a half-truth, my arms clutching the back of his neck and the small of his back tightly.

"Anything I can do to help you feel or sleep better?" He queried, the sincerity in his voice making me shiver with a mix of happiness and the feeling of his love. It was a feeling that made the heat and pressure in my core rise with anticipation.

"Remind me who I truly belong to," I whispered breathily against Jason's neck and felt him shudder in my grasp. Then came the growl trickling from his throat that always made my knees wobble and my pussy clench.

"Couch. Clothes off and face our bedroom. I wanna see that pretty ass of yours before I get there, little bird," Jason ordered, his voice low and husky with the right amount of grit that only added to my need to have him.

"Yes, *sir*," I cooed softly before disappearing from in front of him and settling onto the couch.

The apartment had come a long way over the last three months. With the help of Mickie and Haley, Jason had framed, sheet rocked, and finished the entire thing, turning the former industrial attic space into a three-bedroom, one-bathroom apartment. Then, once the lease on both Mickie and Haley's apartments had dried up, the two of them filled the space with furniture, giving us a proper guest room, office, and living room.

The couch, a silver-colored L-shaped sectional, had become something of our favorite piece in the entire apartment. And for more than just cuddling up in a pile to watch movies together.

The cool air of the room brushed over my skin as the comforting pressure of the cushions pushed against my knees and bare breasts. I sighed happily and giggled to myself as my eyes locked on Mickie's sleeping form a mere thirty feet away, while Jason's bare feet slapped across the living room floor.

Smack!

Electricity shot through my entire body, making me shudder and let out a whimpering moan as Jason's hand came down on me. His right hand met my left ass cheek first, then the right, delivering that pleasant spike of pain that melted into pleasure as his fingers began kneading the stinging sensation into my supple flesh.

"God, you're perfect, little bird," Jason groaned as his fingers worked me over, his words and touch making me grin wide. My eyes fluttered closed while a whining moan filled the room as the touch of his tongue pressed against my folds. "And you taste- fuck~"

Jason's words, the tickle of his breath against my cunt, and the dragging of his thick, warm tongue pushing me open around him made my body shake and my head float. The heady buzz made me feel drunk as Jason began hungrily lapping at me, the room being drowned in the wet slurping sounds as he tongued my slit and suckled my drooling folds between his lips.

His hand gripped tighter as he pushed forward, suckling on my lips harder while his tongue plunged at my entrance. His nails pressed against my flesh, sending pinching sensations across my backside, melding with the feverous working of his tongue and lips. I felt as if I was floating in the heavens. That buzzing grew, putting more pressure on my core while my skin felt as if it were burning with need.

"J-Jason!" I cried out as his mouth trapped my throbbing clit between his teeth and pinched down. It was all I needed to be sent over the edge for the first time.

He suckled hard on my pearl as my body convulsed, my inner walls fluttering as I hit that peak of pleasure and was forced to ride an overstimulated wave. As I shook and felt that dizzying high begin to wane, my eyes went wide and my breath hitched in my throat.

I hadn't felt Jason move and position himself behind me until the sudden feeling of fullness hit me like a brick wall. I gasped, trying to chase my breath as Jason filled me, stretching my walls around his thick length that was buried to the hilt inside me. The heady feeling came back in full force as his head ground itself against the wall of my cervix and his hips pressed against my plump, round ass firmly.

Without a word, he pulled back until only his head teased my entrance wide around him before he plunged back inside, smacking my ass with his hips and his full, heavy balls slapped my clit. Electricity shot up my spine with the droning mix of pain and pleasure with his cock against my deepest wall, making my body and mind buzz with delight. A feeling that spiked to new heights as his left hand fisted my hair near the roots and his hips began snapping repeatedly. I loved the way he took control of me, put me in a safe place where I could float on every pleasant sensation his body delivered.

"Fuck, Jason! Yes," I squealed as he drove into me repeatedly, and felt his grunting breaths against the crown of my ear. I fucking loved the primal side Mickie and Haley had drawn out of him over the last month, my pussy squeezing hard around him as he pumped harder, making my body jump under his ministrations. "Fick die Muschi deines versauten Vogels."

A low, rumbling growl reverberated against my ear while he pulled tighter. The force bowed my back, making the delicious curve of his shaft ground tighter against the swollen sweet spot inside me. As he attacked that point, my walls rippled wildly, my nectar flowing faster and coating him in my essence. The smacking of his hips against my ass grew wetter with each pass before I screamed in delight as his right arm curled beneath me, cupping my breast in his hand and squeezing in a tight, possessive grip.

"Never forget, little bird," Jason snarled against my ear, my name on his lips filling my mind like a drug. "You're *mine*. I will never let you go. Understood?"

"Gods, yes," I whined, my voice raising an octave as the coil within my core wound tighter. I was on the verge of breaking, as his voice, the sound of his moans and grunts, and his cock filled my entire being. "Please, Jason~"

"You're mine. You're Mickie's and - fuck - Haley's. *Our* baby bird," Jason grunted and moaned, his voice rich with strain to make himself last. Each word was accompanied by a throbbing pulse of his cock that threatened to spread my walls to their limit. I couldn't stifle the screaming moan that escaped me as Jason plowed my tight, dripping pussy again and again. "Mark my cock, baby. Remind yourself who I belong to."

I hit that cliff of pleasure at full speed, soaring off the edge. The overwhelming combination of Jason's cock driving into me, my hair in his fist, and my sensitive nipple being pinched lit my senses on fire. His words triggered the coil inside my core to snap and I called out for him as I came hard, liquid heat flooding around his length, as my body began to convulse uncontrollably underneath him.

"Meine~"

The overwhelming heat and vice-like grip of my dripping cunt made Jason call out as he slammed into me once more and the heat inside my body rose to that of a furnace. Bliss clouded my eyes as Jason - my Jason - swelled and exploded within me. My walls were painted with thick jets of his seed and a hunger inside me was quenched with the warm, pleasurable feeling of his release flooding my greedy pussy.

We collapsed forward as his grip on my hair and breast went limp and I found myself mashed against the soft cushion of the sofa. Jason panted, his heart pounding hard against his chest as the firm flesh of him pressed against my back. With Jason's warmth pressed against me and deep within me, I felt my eyes begin to grow heavy as I settled into that happy place I found myself in every time one of my loves brought me to the peak. I never wanted this feeling to end.

"Better?" Jason asked softly, his voice and breath still strained from our love-making.

"Much," I squeaked happily, grinding my ass playfully against his hips and making him hiss. As I settled, I felt him hug me tightly and I shivered with the sensation of his love for me. "Thank you, Meine Liebe."

"Anytime, little bird," he sighed softly with a tone of his own high. There was a long enjoyable lull of silence as he held me close before he let out a long breath. "He won't touch you ever again. He'll have to kill me to get to you, Adi."

It was a promise he didn't have to make, however, I believed him. And I trusted he'd keep his word with every ounce of his being.

"You know you're more than I deserve, right?" I sighed happily as my hands moved to snake around his arms and grip his.

"Hah, are you kidding," he chuckled, kissing the back of my neck lightly. "You're more than I could *dream* for. Let alone the three of you together."

"In that case, take me to bed so you can get to that dream and we'll figure out where to go with Sinead and Samael tomorrow morning," I giggled softly at his retort.

A soft squeak left my lips as Jason moved, pulling himself from my dripping sex before his hands found me once more and I was swept upward. I kicked my feet and laughed as he carried me from the couch to our bedroom, the small light dancing around my belly lighting our way into the darkened room. Once there, he let me down and allowed me to curl myself into Mickie's arms while he moved to lay me between them.

I was home. Right where I belonged and needed to be and let that comfort begin to drag me fast into the depths of sleep.

"I love you, Adi," Jason said, his voice trailing off as he began to physically crash.

"I love you too, Jason."

AFTER LAST NIGHT, I NEEDED SOME LEVITY.

On the bright side, despite it being a favor, I had a paycheck from Thomas on the way. I could breathe easier knowing I had my own money and didn't feel like I was taking advantage of McKenna and Haley's generosity. I still owed them for all of the materials they bought to finish the apartment over the last two months.

Haley had come home late after performing what she referred to as her duties as the Clan's Skoll, one of two sacred enforcers. She and Lex were able to get the nymph squared away with Thomas who gave Lex an update on Aniah's condition. Gratefully, for everyone involved, she was stable but still unconscious. That was followed by the two of them stopping by the high-dollar condo that Lex and Aniah shared to get her fresh clothes and some of her belongings.

When presented with the knowledge that Lex was being pursued by Samael, Thomas ordered extra wolven guardians for Aniah and placed Lex under the protective watch of several Lupas. She was set up inside a sorority house whose members included a combination of werewolves, a weretiger, and a pair of vampires.

To add to our good fortune, Tori had stopped by earlier today. The witch was a welcome source of knowledge that I'd come to rely on over the past few months. With her help, I was able to figure out more incantations and rituals I could use during my daily work with the dead to help them pass on outside of relying solely on my old tricks and Adelaide's powers.

Again, anything to avoid making me feel like I was taking advantage of the girls.

With Tori's help, I was making headway on figuring out how to find a small buzzing force within my chest. It was where she said my abilities - my magic - came from. Protection wards, once I'd figured out the correct wording and where to draw that energy from had become easier, giving the apartment and bookstore minimal protection for up to 24 hours. After Sinead, I insisted on learning more intricate and difficult wards that would increase protection.

I was still unsure if what I'd done today had actually worked to the level of what we needed to keep Samael, Sinead, and others out. And, before Tori had left when Mickie did, she left me with more questions than answers.

"At this rate, with more practice, you should be able to start developing your own spells without help," she'd said, with a shrug. "Honestly, you might be able to master summoning circles."

That… terrified me.

However, I needed to stop thinking about that and focus on supporting my leopardess.

Mickie had left the apartment three hours ago to get her, the assistant coaches, and her girls ready for the game tonight. Leaving now, Adi and I would meet Haley at the school in time to make shootarounds. Tonight was about supporting Mickie and her team as they took on one of their biggest rivals. The first of two games over the next three weeks which, according to Mickie, could turn into a brawl like they had last year.

We'd seen how high tensions could get over a middle school game, however, that seemed completely insane. Which was why Adi, Haley, Jen, Mark, and I would be there to support her and help keep tensions cooled. At least among the parents. I was still mentally preparing for another game of 21 questions coming from Mickie's girls.

What more could they possibly want to know about me?

I shrugged off the thought as I watched Adelaide happily usher the last of the bookstore's patrons out the door so that she could lock up and we could be on our way. But, of course, sometimes just when things are looking up, reality comes calling to drag you back to the ground.

"It'd be nice if you'd answer your phone for once, buddy."

I recognized the voice all too well and the joyous, admirative smile I had been aiming in Adi's direction fell. It was replaced by one that was forced and didn't meet my eyes. Because the petite brunette, silver-eyed woman storming through the front door was not the person I had been expecting to see today.

"Hey, sis," I replied casually, stuffing my hands into my pockets and watching her as she stood in the doorway with her hip cocked and sizing Adi up. "Sorry, Adelaide and I have been busy with a few cases and I forgot to text you that the four of us would be a little late for Thanksgiving."

"Well, is your phone dead or what? I've been trying to get a hold of you since last night," my sister scoffed, rolling her eyes at my answer.

"No," I answered indignantly and pulled out my phone, bringing the screen to life. "I have maybe one… Okay, 24 missed calls and 39 texts…"

I shook my head at my phone and began swiping up to see her first text message. Bekka, my older sister, was the golden child and received the majority of my parent's affection growing up. It hadn't mattered when it came to her grades being just barely passing or running around with her friends until four in the morning. Me however? If I got anything lower than a B+, I was admonished. Wanted to spend my time playing video games or trying to make friends? That was considered a waste of time and energy. The last nail in my coffin had been stating that I had zero interest in becoming a prophetic mouthpiece and wanted to use my gifts to help people. Especially when my first clients were either non-religious or of a different religion than what I'd grown up in. Or if-

My train of thought froze as I reached the first text she'd sent last night and I read the words.

BEKKA

Mom and Dad got really sick tonight. We had to rush them to the hospital.

Meet us there please!

"They're in the hospital?" I asked quietly, making my way across the bookstore to Adi's side. "Why? What happened?"

"You know, you'd know if you weren't so busy being a homewrecker," Bekka bit back, giving a sympathetic look at Adi, and then turned and shot me a seething glare. "Where are the other ones anyway?"

"Their names are McKenna and Haley," Adelaide answered, careful not to let her voice sound angry. Her eyes, however, narrowed into her own biting glare that she pointed directly toward my sister. "And we were just on our way to see them."

"Oh sure, you can go see the tram-"

"Girlfriends," Adelaide snarled. As I looked down, I watched her ball her fists with so much pressure, that her fingers were bleaching.

"So you can go see your… *girlfriends*," Bekka sighed and rolled her eyes. "But won't even bother with Mom and Dad."

"No, I just didn't know. Like I said we've… been busy," I answered with a level tone while reaching out to take one of Adi's fists into my hand and force her to relax to take it. "Besides, you, Savannah, and Mom made it pretty clear we were barely allowed to come for Thanksgiving anyway."

I scoffed then, remembering the firestorm a month and a half ago that had been created when we decided to do the whole '*social media official*' thing and went public with our relationship. Despite Adi still being technically dead, when she had an overload of spiritual energy in her reserves she appeared completely alive to those around us. It made her want to create an online profile and, when she did so, she joined Mickie, Haley, and me in adding a relationship status.

Given social media didn't necessarily reflect options for those in polyamorous relationships, we'd settled on putting our status to being '*In An Open Relationship*.' We then proceeded to post and tag each other in a slew of photos the girls had snapped; most of which had been without my knowledge. However, it was put out into the world in photos of the four of us cuddling or sleeping together, along with pictures of me kissing the three of them. The message was clear; we were a package deal.

The images of the three women kissing or me kissing Mickie and Haley, unsurprisingly, had the most negative interactions. All of which came from my sisters and mom. Thankfully, Grandma Ruth, a couple of my nieces and nephews, and friends had commented on how adorable we all were. And how happy they were for us.

Especially to Mickie and Haley, Ruth had gone extra grandma on them. She started pinching their cheeks, saying how gorgeous they looked, and hugging her grandbabies as much as she possibly could every time the three were in the same room.

"Do you know how hard it is to explain to my kids?"

Ignoring the fact that her youngest son had been supportive of the four of us.

"Or all of your nieces and nephews of how sinful this all is?"

Again, ignoring that some of them had been supportive like my niece, Alex, who Snapchatted Adi, Haley, and Mickie daily. It wasn't like she'd made the girls feel like the four of them had been besties forever. Not at all.

Bekka groaned, shaking her hands furiously in my direction. After that gesture, she folded her arms over her chest tightly and scowled at me.

"You were happy before. Now you're going down the wrong path. If you don't clean up your act and start going back to church you're going to get hurt and I'll lose my brother."

"Happy?" I snorted with a humorless laugh. "Bekka, you've nearly lost me countless times. Do you not remember that I've wanted to off myself since I was ten? Hell, my last attempt was *literally* eight months ago."

That made her freeze, unsure of what to really say. But only for a second. Adelaide, on the other hand, tensed in anger because she had been the one to nurse me back to health. I may or may not have done the dumbass thing of trying to mix sleeping pills with an entire bottle of whiskey. I was sick for almost a month after that incident.

"Well, I swear you have demons or something inside you," she determined half-heartedly.

"Uh-huh. And I'm guessing one of those so-called demons is yay tall," I said, holding my free hand to be about Mickie's height. "Gorgeous as hell. Just so happens to be black?"

"And I'm assuming the other is this tall," Adi said, holding her hand at Haley's height. "Is a stunning Latina woman and, like me, you knew nothing about until around two months ago?"

"That's not what I meant," Bekka rolled her eyes. "Just… How can we be okay, or moral, if we allow you to date *three* women? Or parade them around and can't keep their mouths or hands to themselves. It's sick. It's wrong."

I couldn't take her seriously.

This was the woman who dated her two best friends in high school at the same time, even going to prom with both guys. She'd also frequently gone skinny dipping and streaking with her girl best friends in high school. To top it all off, she had been the first of my siblings to stop going to church and had only recently started going back. I, on the other hand, had been the last of my siblings to stop attending Sunday services, hadn't even gone to prom, and had never gone streaking before.

"Okay okay, I'll go see Mom and Dad alone first thing tomorrow morning," I groaned, holding my hand up to Adi before she could add more to the argument. "Just… tell me what happened."

Bekka glared at me for a long moment before her expression finally began to soften. She let out a long defeated breath and looked up at me with worry etched across her expression. Her eyes said everything they needed to; she was utterly terrified of the situation.

"Yesterday afternoon, they both got really sick. Savannah and I drove them to the hospital when both of them had a fever of 106. They were in bad shape, Jason," she explained before her voice grew distant. "The doctors have no idea what it is. Or how it happened."

"Yesterday afternoon?" I asked, turning to look at Adelaide. She seemed to have made the same connection as me to the timing. It hadn't been long after Sinead had marked me. "What did the doctor's find?"

"They were in perfect health before… other than Mom's

cholesterol. But they'd never seen the black bruises on their chests before," Bekka replied, making both Adi and I give each other a fearful glance. "They said that bruises don't typically have a defined shape."

"Fuck," I snarled under my breath and then gave Bekka a stern glance as I raised my left palm. "Please, for the love of God, tell me they don't look like this."

Bekka's eyes went wide as she stared at the two scythes crossed on my palm. That was all the confirmation I needed. My sister's eyes shot back and forth between my eyes and the mark on my open palm before her expression became accusatory and offensive. Her gaze deepened with anger the longer she stared at the mark.

"You? This is your fault?" Bekka scoffed incredulously. "What the hell did you do, Jason?"

"I'm going to make a phone call," Adelaide said, turning on her heel and pulling her phone - a recent gift from Haley - from where it was held between her breast and bra strap. "JJ, I'll meet you in the truck."

"Yeah," I sighed, watching her walk away. Part of me felt like I needed to say three words but it didn't feel like the right timing. Instead, I turned back to see my sister glaring daggers at me. "Go see Mom and Dad, I'll take care of this."

"Jason. What. The fuck. Did you do?" Bekka snapped, her fists balling tightly as she got into my face angrily.

"I told a demon to go fuck himself," I said drearily and began pushing forward so Bekka was forced backward out the store's front door.

"Dad told you not to mess with this demon stuff! You know why," Bekka continued, still trying to get in my face just as her feet hit the sidewalk in front of the store.

"Yup. Now, go see them and I'll fix this," I sighed, swinging the door shut in her face and locking up the shop.

"Jason!"

I ignored my sister's pleas and screaming as she began banging on the front door. Instead, I shut off the lights and headed into the back toward our garage. Before, I would find Adi excitedly looking over a new book she'd gotten from Ruth. Now, I found her scowling with her palm clasped against her forehead as she argued with whoever was on the other line. I wasn't sure who she'd called. Part of me didn't care. Rather, I needed to figure out how to get in contact with a demon and somehow kill the bastard in less than 24 hours, or else my parents would be dead.

Sinead threatened me. I had never considered she'd go after my family to force my compliance. I should have known better. Samael was trying to be as cliché of a James Bond villain as possible. I was almost sure he'd even begin monologuing if we saw him and I hoped, if he did, it would buy me time to get in close enough to kill him.

"I know Lex, and I don't care anymore. Just give me the ficken phone number," Adelaide snarled, gripping the phone tightly to the point I feared it was about to break. I felt my blood go cold as I listened to the last of Adelaide's conversation. She said the words that I hoped I would never hear come from her mouth. Words that should have never seen the light of day. Ever. "Because I'm going to arrange a meeting with Samael."

7

ADELAIDE

I WAS A LOT CALMER THAN I SHOULD'VE BEEN.

My former abuser had said to meet at a designated location in one hour. One hour to make sure all of our demands were in order and get ourselves back up. It left little time to do either. Anyone who could help with the fight was an hour away, without the worry of traffic. We also hadn't had the time to make it to Jason's family home where he proposed grabbing one of his dad's guns.

Our last resort had been attempting to call Jen and Tori for help, neither of which were available. Jen and Mark left for their Thanksgiving vacation in Vegas this morning and had just arrived. They were eight hours away - six if Mark drove. And despite being just over a half hour away, thanks to holiday traffic, Tori's ETA had jumped to two hours.

Instead, the witch told Jason to believe in himself, get ready, and know in his mind that he could overcome whatever was blocking him mentally. Something was there, denying him from accessing more gifts, which could be used with the proper encouragement. Tori had not been shy about boasting about the potential she saw in Jason.

I saw it. Mickie and Haley saw it. The Council, Mark and Jen, everyone around him saw it.

Jason, on the other hand, didn't.

He had taken his self-aware criticizations to an entirely new level and I'd watched him admonish himself more than I ever had. He said he feared death, and what it would mean for him, however, I knew that wasn't the entire truth. He feared death because of what that would mean for him, and for us. More than anything, he feared that his afterlife would be just as cumbersome as his mortal life. That he would be just as worthless in the afterlife as he felt in his mortal life.

He tried to hide that fear so I didn't have to see it. He didn't want to seem weak so he refused to show himself as anything less. It's why he refused to let me see him cry. That said, I wouldn't admit to him that I had on more than one occasion. A part of me, however, felt like that knowledge wouldn't bring us closer, he would push himself away.

Instead of admitting that or sharing my own feelings, Jason, Mickie, Haley, and I piled into the Bronco and left for the meeting place. When we arrived in what had once been a cornfield next to the lake, Jason started his frustrated grunting as he tried to figure out something new. He wanted so desperately to set up wards or a barrier for protection around us. He wanted to attempt something different that Tori had shared was a possibility with his power. The problem was that it took more time and energy than we had to spare.

"Jason, Miene Liebe, everything will be okay," I said, trying to reassure him as I placed my hand on his shoulder and forced him to stop pacing.

"I feel like we need more, okay? I'm *not* going to be fucking useless. Not against *him*," Jason snarled, jerking his shoulder away from my touch. He poured harder through the digital tablet he'd brought with us, one that held copies of different spells, rituals, and incantations from the Westfall Coven as well as his own personal Book of Shadows he'd been cureating.

"Breathe, babe," Mickie urged, giving me a pained expression. She didn't like seeing him like this either. "If shit goes sideways, you'll have me, Adi, and Haley to beat the fuck out of the bloody cunt."

"She's right, mi amor. You can lean on us," Haley urged, placing a comforting hand on my shoulder and giving it a reassuring squeeze.

"That's… fuck!" Jason seethed and then screamed at no one in particular, reaching into his hair to pull at it. After a few moments to calm himself down, he leveled his expression into an apologetic gaze that went back and forth between the three of us. "Adi, you shouldn't be here. None of you should be. I… I *should've* been strong enough to cut him off from us. I *should* be strong enough to protect you. But I'm not…"

But you are, Meine Liebe.

I knew that was gospel in my heart. All he had to do was see what Mickie, Haley, and I saw. Had he not noticed that he hadn't needed to exert himself as much anymore? Had he not noticed that the episode he had when he touched Lex the other night hadn't put him out or caused him as much pain as before? Surely he'd noticed that his stamina with the three of us in our bed had grown exponentially, right? Or had he just been that deep into his own mind and self-doubts?

"JJ, you don't have to be strong all by yourself," Haley said, giving him a soft smile. "We're here for you. It's not a bad thing to have a few badass babes that have your back."

"And what kind of man can I call myself if I do that?" He queried, giving Haley a pained expression. "Hales, I'm the man of the house. I'm your boyfriend, your mate, it's my responsibility to make sure the three of you are happy, safe, and secure. What good am I if I can't do that?"

Before he could be questioned, or I could acknowledge a flare of hot wind and energy thrumming from Jason, our sights were drawn to the other side of the field. A black Escalade drove across the grounds toward us, which should have been impossible. Instead of a road where it had appeared, it had come from the end of the field where the shore of the lake was.

I didn't have to question its appearance or who would be inside. I could smell the pungent sulfur and brimstone rolling off of it in massive waves long before it parked. Now, there was no going back because he was here.

The rear passenger door opened and the lithe, petite figure of Sinead stepped out, dressed in her ever-present gothic lolita attire. Her eyes locked on the four of us, her expression stoic as ever as she barely acknowledged our presence before walking around to the rear driver's side door. She opened it like the obedient attendant she was and an overwhelming air of power rolled outward.

A low-hanging, thick, inky fog spread across the field, bathing it in its aura that stunk of death which was rich with the promise of torture and agony long before the end would come. It made my entire body twitch and shudder with the all too familiar feeling of wanting to run for safety but knowing that it was something I would never escape. Then I caught the first glimpse of a pair of ram-like horns that made every part of me want to scream at the top of my lungs.

Stepping out of the vehicle was a figure that was part man, part ram, standing nearly seven feet tall with a pelt of smoothly trimmed white and gray fur. His wide shoulders and barrelled chest created the mass of an imposing form that stretched his tailored black and teal pea coat and vest across him.

He was someone who looked as if he'd walked straight out of high-society Victorian Manhattan. His figure, clothing, and his aura gave him the appearance of someone who had money, power, and influence in spades. He was a man who would be seen as someone with plentiful resources on a vastly attractive masculine frame and would promise you wealth, power, influence, and pleasure beyond your wildest dreams.

If only you gave in.

He still had some of his human features in his face interwoven with being part animal. The same strong, squared jawline, thin blackened lips, a relatively human brow, and lush dark hair that was slicked back with fine grease. His wide nose was contorted, stopping in between taking the shape of the ram's snout and still being human, the rubbery skin black and glinting in whatever light caught it.

His pure black eyes gave no emotion and no direction to which of us he was looking at or sizing up. Instead, the up curl of one of his brows and the corner of his thin lips said he was amused. Despite the four of us standing there, two of which were powerful shifters in their own right, he didn't feel threatened in the least. He was entertained and his glee made the thin smile widen until he bore sharp white fangs.

Looking at him, it was as if he had been the original model for Beauty and the Beast, the monstrous prince that had Belle swooning.

However, this man had no potential to be made kind with affection and patience. This was a beast that had never had humanity to begin with.

This was Samael.

"Oh, what a pleasure it is to see you again," he spoke, his voice dancing across my skin with a sweet honey and whiskey tone that prodded at every nerve in my system. His voice, like his aura and stature, came with the whispering promises of power and pleasure like an aristocratic sex god. "And I see you've finally decided to allow me to meet your friends, little bird"

"You don't get to call her that," Mickie growled, stepping around me to shield my body with hers.

The sensation of something gentle wrapping around my leg with a comforting embrace caused me to look down and find a prehensile leopard tail there. Mickie had already shifted, going to the form that was just between human and becoming her big cat.

"You're going to treat our mate with respect. Got it?" Haley snarled, stepping forward to Mickie's side where I found her thick black and golden-furred wolf tail stiff with anticipation of a fight. She'd taken her beastwoman form just as my leopardess had.

"Ho ho oh!" Samael laughed, bellowing with a full belly of amusement. "Well, I never thought I'd see the day. Seems, the little bird has finally spread her wings and found a momentary perch."

"Not momentary," Jason seethed, stepping around my other side to stand beside Mickie and block the demon's view of me completely.

From the sliver of a view that I could see between Jason and Mickie's arms, Sam nearly began to let out a half-hearted chuckle.

"Mr. Jason McCrae, it is a pleasure to *finally* make your acquaintance, I see you've done well in taking care of my fledgling Valravn," Samael mused in delight. "You did the one thing I was never able to do and brought her into her power, made her realize her true potential. A potential I've come to collect post haste."

"Unwise," Haley retorted, folding her arms across her breasts tightly. "As representative of our Odin, you are formally advised to cease and desist. Adelaide is a member of our clan, our Huugin, and any attempt on her will be seen as a declaration of war against the Rocky Mountain Coalition."

"Ah yes, I was hoping for the pleasure to meet his highness," Samael chuckled humorlessly. It seemed that his amusement was beginning to fade with how many people had blocked his view of me. "The ninth king of the Granite Pine Clan, Thomas Rassmussen. How is Moira these days?"

He spoke Moira's name with delight and familiarity as a shiver of lust ran up his spine. Knowing the two of them were connected made that numbing feeling of wrath begin to swell and take over. He'd hurt me for over a century, hurt and broke the people he'd captured and turned into his minions like Sinead. But he'd also indirectly hurt Mickie, Haley, and Jason. The people I loved.

"Then you know the laws of the fae," Mickie growled, her voice growing angered and vicious. "If you think of yourself as highly as you do, then you know that before entering claimed territory you are to make contact with the territory leaders."

"I'm not really one for law, you know," Samael chuckled. "I live more for chaos and the thrill it brings me to my very soul."

"Regardless," Haley spat back. "Not only did you fail to notify our Odin, but you also failed to notify the other fae kings of this region-"

"Yes, yes, the other kings," Samael sighed with exasperation as if he was bored of the conversation as a whole. "Sebastian and his blood suckers are… too trivial for my time. And don't get me started on that pompous high elf bastard, Cazadelle."

"Trivial or not, law is law," Haley seethed, her voice growing more angered by the second. "And not only did you fail to adhere to those laws, you threatened our Odin's mate and her daughter."

"Oh, the nymph," Samael bellowed with a hearty chuckle. "I simply wanted to see how far she'd come before I collected her as well. I could use fire like that, especially after the others are… how should I say… burnt out."

The second Samael began laughing again at his cruel words, I felt all of my built-up wrath take over. In less than a second, I was no longer myself. Gone was the mild woman known as Adelaide because I was now the bestial raven. My wings unfurled and my body shifted to accommodate a monstrous raven skulled head, strong avian legs, and razor-sharp talons.

Then I was inches from Samael.

He hadn't expected my speed and took a reactionary step back, however, not before my arm had come down in a long swing. I raked my bladed fingernails down his chest, instead of his neck for which I had been aiming. His vest and shirt were torn to ribbons, his exposed flesh opening up in a spray of black viscous liquid as four deep lacerations formed across his chest.

I thrust my other arm forward and drove my talons into him like five long blades cutting through the hunk of meat and flesh that he was. He growled in pain before beginning to laugh, even as those blades tore pieces of flesh, muscle, and gore from him. His laughter was cut short as a pair of long, muscular, leopard-spotted arms wrapped around him and Mickie sunk her teeth into his neck.

She let out a ferocious growl as more of his blood sprayed from the fresh wound and the weight of her on his back pushed him forward back into me. My claws were waiting for him as I let my rage and wrath take over. I slashed at him in the same manner he'd done to me countless times, leaving gashes and deep lacerations across his chest and stomach. In the midst of my fury, I turned the front of him into something that resembled a topographical street map.

Samael ignored my slashing, despite me taking chunks out of him at a time, and reached back to grab Mickie. With brute force he tugged her off of him over his head, her teeth pulling at flesh and muscle in the process. She left thin lines of tendons and muscle connecting his neck and shoulder to her mouth in her wake. Despite the two of us doing significant bodily harm, he grinned and threw Mickie like she was nothing in my direction.

The ragdoll form of Mickie forced me to catch her. The strength at which the wereleopard crashed into me sent me flying, taking my feet off the ground as the two of us were tossed backward nearly fifty yards.

Before the demon could relish in his fortune, however, a monstrous wolven figure just shorter than Samael covered in gold and black fur attacked. The demon took two hard slashing blows that split him open deeper than my talons. Instead of precision cuts like I had delivered, Samael was opened up like he was being cut with a volley of serrated blades.

Haley was tearing into Samael, cutting, slashing, and brutalizing the big half-goat man, forcing him backward. Before long, his chest, neck, and arms looked like they had been pulverized by a meat grinder.

Thick rivulets of blackened blood poured from his wounds in droves and splashed across pristine golden fur. Then he caught Haley.

The two roared in defiance of each other as Samael held the wolven woman's monstrous form inches from him at her wrists, locking them in a temporary stalemate. Still, she persisted against him.

"Sinead, thin the herd starting with the weakest of them," Samael roared with rage.

"Yes, Master," she said dryly before turning her sights toward Mickie and me.

Or rather behind us.

Sinead's brows scrunched as her mouth opened wide and a wailing banshee-like scream erupted from her. A plume of blue hellfire roared upward from her neck, engulfing her head where only a brief glimpse of a white skull was visible through the flames. Her scream was replaced by the crackling of the inferno mixed with a haunting ethereal chorus of dissonant whispers surrounding her.

She began forward, walking with purpose as she reached up and gripped the flaming skull that had replaced her head. Then she plucked it from her form, holding it in her hands and leaving a smooth stump where it once sat. Her neck glowed with embers of hellfire and wisps of thick black smoke that whipped outward around her as if it were searching for her head. Then, with an inhuman amount of speed, she whipped around in a spinning baseball pitch. Like a fireball, the blue flame-engulfed skull was sent hurtling toward us, forcing Mickie to roll us out of the way.

The Escalade's wreckage exploded with dazzling cyan flames as Mickie rolled me out of harm's way and we found Jason rolling not far from us. He looked up once his roll had stopped to check on us before his sights snapped back to the explosion. The flaming skull had begun to hover on its own and shook with rage as it stared him down.

It surged forward and I appeared next to him, tackling Jason out of the way as it hurtled harmlessly over us.

"Looks like I'm the weakest," Jason scoffed as his eyes followed the skull as it rounded for another pass.

"You just haven't had the chance to banish him, Meine Liebe. Then he'll learn not to underestimate you," I offered, making sure he saw the sincerity in my eyes - even in my inhuman form.

Roars drew our attention back to the other side of the field where Samael was being assaulted by a hail of claws and teeth. Mickie, after rolling us out of the way, had returned her attention to Samael. This time, however, she'd taken Haley's lead and now stood as a tall, muscular leopard woman. Her beast form was leaner than that of the werewolves in a more compact frame that was built for blinding speed and agile strikes.

Between the two hulking forms of my mates, they'd done a number on Samael, his strength and speed waning from blood loss. Deep gashes and chunks of flesh had been torn from him in the assault, leaving him badly injured but not yet dead. In a last bit of strength, he swung around and caught both shifters with one leg, kicking them toward the wreckage of the Escalade once more.

The two quickly righted themselves, landing and dragging claws through the dirt to stop themselves before they entered the flames. Mickie and Haley's eyes were glowing with their power as they took a moment to catch their breaths. The glow from them as they glared Samael down was filled to the brim with rage and vitriol as they scratched the ground, readying to pounce on their prey.

The demon chuckled, his fang-filled grin growing wide with sick satisfaction as he reached down to adjust a ring I hadn't noticed before on his right hand. The moment he touched it, his wounds became engulfed in hellfire, peppering his entire body with cyan flames. He hissed loudly in discomfort, the smell of burnt flesh and fur perforating the air around us before the fires died a few seconds later. When the flames dissipated, they revealed his wounds closed up and mostly healed, leaving only small raised tracks of scar tissue and skin.

That hadn't been all, his sounds of pain and discomfort had been nothing compared to the scream Sinead had let out.

When the hellfire washed away from Samael's body, so did the flames around Sinead's floating skull. Her severed head had let out an agonizing scream of unbelievable pain before it had fallen to the ground motionless. Her scream had sounded as if…

He fucking gave her all of his pain.

Despite her head lying on the ground, Sinead's body continued to move on its own. However, she was no longer as fast or agile as she once had been. It looked as if her movements and strikes toward Jason were in slow motion, pained, and sluggish. Which allowed him to easily dodge a swing of the giant grim reaper-styled scythe she wielded and roll around to kick the back of her knees.

Seeing her, I understood that it wasn't just him forcing the pain he felt onto Sinead instead. The hellfire that appeared on him had healed his injuries and as a result, Sinead was moving in tired motions. As if her very life essence was…

"The ring," I said, jerking my head to face Jason. "Sinead is tied to it just like I am to the necklace."

"If I can exorcize the demonic presence on the ring," Jason prodded out loud.

"Then, the bloody cunt can't heal up no more," Mickie finished, grinning wide before disappearing in a flash of speed and glowing golden-green stars.

Mickie soon reappeared solid on top of Samael, having jumped into the air and then rocketed herself back down into him with a double-heeled stomp to the back of his neck. The demon went to the ground before he was attacked and mauled by the wereleopard on his back. His shoulder blades and spine became riddled with claw marks that raked and tore at his flesh. Then, just as Samael had the sense to buck Mickie off of him and get to his feet, Haley was there, delivering crushing blows that drove the demon to step back with each hard thrust and clawed strike.

This was my opening.

I flew forward with a quick burst of my wings, hovering low like a ground-skimming bullet before I tore my claws through Samael's right arm. He recoiled in pain, however, his attention was forced to be on the more powerful werewolf in front of him. I struck and tore at him relentlessly while Haley kept his attention.

Moira had been easier to decimate. I needed more time to get through his flesh, muscle, and bone than I had with her. Mickie was there to give me that time, her jaw clamping around his forearm to tear into the softer and more tender flesh. The attack rewarded her with a spray of thick, black blood to her face as she worried at him ravenously.

Samael screamed and grunted with exertion. He couldn't do anything to get Mickie and me off his arm without risking taking more force from Haley in front of him. With him pouring his efforts and attention into our barbarian wolfess, Mickie and I struck harder and more viciously. Each bite and clawed strike sent more splatters of the demon's blood across our forms for what seemed like an eternity.

Finally, we poured all of our strength into our legs, planting claws into the ground before jerking backward with malicious force. Our efforts rewarded us with a loud, wet squelching sound mixed with thick snapping noises.

With another scream of rage and pain, Samael persevered, lowering his head and resorting to lunging at Haley with the sharp tips of his curled horns. The attack worked to keep her at bay while Mickie and I fell backward with the large muscular arm gripped in our maws. Mickie grabbed his hand, pulled the obsidian ring with a teal inlay off of his finger, and threw it.

Before the two of us could rush to Jason's side to make sure he got the ring, Samael struck me. The force of it sent me into the pile of rubble that had once been his SUV. The twisted metal cut and tore at my skin, making me scream in pain. Then I felt the concussive force of Haley's body hitting mine. The impact forced both of us deeper into the wreckage, making us both cry out in agony as the serrated edges of ruined metal and wreckage tore through us.

Through squinted eyes, I watched as Mickie and Samael, even with one arm, were locked in a stalemate of force and power as they pummeled each other. Even through the pain and the leopard's brute force and twisting motions to disarm him, Samael held strong. The demon managed to dodge several attacks before goring Mickie's chest. As she screamed in pain, Mickie lashed out wildly. However, his horns and angled body kept him just out of range.

Looking over, I found Jason with the discarded ring in one hand and the tablet in another. He was pouring through the grimoires as fast as he could while dodging lazy swings of Sinead's scythe. I growled as I saw her getting closer and felt Haley move to jump back into the fight. As she rushed to Mickie's aide, I went to Jason's.

I tackled the petite woman's headless body to the ground and delivered a hard blow to her ribs. She convulsed from the strike before I forced her movements to still as I kneeled on her chest. I scowled harshly down at the woman, the one who had been complicit in my abuse and torture. If she hadn't had her mind broken she…

I would have been like her.

This woman, she was like me. We were both victims of the same man but part of me had never lost hope for someone to save me. Had she once had that same hope?

"I should have saved you back then," I growled, self-inflicted anger melting over me. "I should have tried to save more than myself. Jason, save her like you saved me."

"Can she be saved, Adi?" Jason asked, pausing his rapid-paced reading to give me wide eyes.

"Do it," I answered, the tension in my body settling as I felt Sinead seem to calm underneath me.

Jason nodded curtly and began reading. Broken Latin flowed as he began chanting loudly, putting his will of intent out for any of the divine who would listen. As the words danced in the air, energy began to swirl around him like a sudden breeze. His voice grew louder with a semblance of an echo while small embers and spittles of green flames began to appear.

"Jason… w-what is-"

As words flowed, the embers grew brighter, and the warm wind grew stronger surrounding Jason. Then it was stifled in an instant. Samael's hand was around Jason's neck, raising him into the air and looking up at him with pleasant disdain. Even still, as his air supply became more finite and his consciousness wavered, Jason continued his incantation.

"I… must admit… you surprised me, Jason," Samael coughed, blood running down his lips as he struggled to speak from a neck wound. However, he hadn't lost his arrogant demeanor. "You-"

Samael yelped in pain and grunted in anger as a line of green fire erupted from where he held around Jason's neck. The sudden rush of pain forced the demon to drop him while a sudden wave of heat pushed back against me.

I was left stunned while Jason looked up at Samael from the ground with pure onyx eyes. My heart began to thrum with panic while Jason spoke the final words of the incantation with spite for Samael in his expression.

Dimittis ligare.

A pulse of frigid cold rushed through my entire body as if a nameless void appeared and swallowed all of the light and warmth around me. I felt cold, and distant, and then felt my body shrink back into my human side, seeping all of my strength. My eyes widened and I was flooded with an overwhelming sense of fear and pain.

I saw the same look in Jason's eyes as his pupils shrunk to pinholes of terror and realization. A hand was around my throat and a hardness pressed against my back. The all too familiar sensation I wished I would never feel again. Samael was no longer standing over Jason. He was holding me.

I saw a flurry of emotions in Mickie's eyes as she ran for me, with Haley just a step behind her. Time slowed down to almost a freezing point. The vision in front of me was a torrential storm of emotions as everyone's worst fears were realized. Mickie and Haley were rushing as fast as they could, my leopardess and wolfess just out of reach.

Strong tendrils of darkness grabbed me and jerked backward as a wall of hellfire and arcane energy surrounded Samael and me. Another sight I hoped to never see; his gates that allowed him to travel wherever he wanted. The familiar sickening pull from jumping through the veil, the feeling I had when being forced into my mother's pendant, hit my gut. Nausea and despair took over.

This was it. I was going back to where I began. To the bitter hell that had been half of my entire being as if I had never been saved. But now I know better. I may be dragged back to a fucking nightmare, however, I was from the helpless woman I had been before.

With that thought in mind, my eyes met those of Mickie, Jason, and Haley. This wasn't their fault. It wasn't that Mickie or Haley weren't fast enough to reach me. It wasn't that Jason had confused the last two words and spoke them in reverse. It was because I had let my guard down, chasing that glimmer of hope that this would have been the end of Samael.

No, I didn't blame them, I didn't want them to ever think that about themselves. So as that wall closed around me and my tormentor, I gave them one last warm smile. And the only words that they needed to hear. Even as the darkness of hell took hold of me, I hoped it wouldn't be forever.

"My darlings. I love you."

McKENNA

I WASN'T SURE HOW LONG I HAD BEEN SCREAMING.

But, bloody fucking hell, did I scream loud and hard enough that my voice went hoarse. My throat was dry and my cheeks were stained with hot tracks of tears. I had cried until I had nothing else to give. Then I screamed some more.

Dirt crusted under my nails and I realized that I had been digging at the earth. As if I could have dug a hole into hell itself to find Adi. Anything to bring her back to me. In the end, it was useless.

I had been useless.

I hadn't been fast enough to make it to her. I hadn't been there when she needed me most. And I fucking hated myself for it.

My attention turned elsewhere when I heard Jason screaming, and cursing into the night amidst the sounds of cracking and smashing. I turned in time to see him throw the tablet and shatter it against the front wheel well of the Bronco. The ensuing impact sent pieces of the device flying everywhere.

"Me and my stupid fucking mouth," he seetheed, kicking at the pieces until one of them shot a dozen yards away, He fell to his knees, sobbing as he pulled at his hair violently. "If I hadn't said those goddamn words. It's my fault! It's… it's all my fault…"

"Correction. The words stated were the intended ones, however, they were not in the necessary order for your true desires," Sinead spoke. It made me realize that she hadn't disappeared when Samael took Adi.

He left the bitch behind.

"You," Haley snarled, stomping toward the petite, pale woman before grabbing her by the neck and slamming her back against the side of the red SUV. Sinead showed no reaction or emotion to the brute force and anger. "What the fuck is that supposed to mean?"

"Where did the arsehole take her," I snarled hoarsely. It was taking everything I had not to tear into her.

Sinead blinked at the two of us lazily, still unmoved by any of our emotions. Instead, she tilted her head as if she found us to be curious.

"Habla o te destriparé como a un maldito cerdo," Haley growled, her claws sinking into the porcelain flesh of Sinead's neck.

Her eyes considered Haley for a moment before shifting to the side and looking over to where Jason knelt. She tilted her head curiously at him before blinking once more. It was like she was waiting patiently for him to do or say something.

"Master, am I to answer this one's queries?" She asked in a soft, yet dry voice.

"Master?" the three of us asked in unison.

"The fuck's that supposed to mean?" Jason continued, his voice hoarse from his screams. "And what did you mean from before?"

"The words you recited were the ones meant for the incantation you were performing," Sinead answered matter of factly. "However, due to what I perceive as elevated stress levels - and your eyes taken away from the device which contained your spells - you reversed the order of the key trigger phrase."

"Yeah, no shit," Jason scoffed, scowling at her.

"You were also in contact with two anam ceangailte artifacts at the time," Sinead continued with a small shrug. "Thus, you released both pacts simultaneously, freeing the valravn Adelaide Winters from the Corvi Catena. As well as breaking the Cumhnant Banntriach, the contract binding myself to the demon lord Samael Luciano III."

"English, bitch," I growled, while Haley squeezed harder around her neck. Crimson rivulets were beginning to bead down her neck from where her claws pierced Sinead's skin.

She stared at me and then Haley again for a long moment before moving to look at Jason. Again, as if she was waiting for him to say something. Like she awaited his approval.

"What she said," Jason muttered under his breath.

"Yes, Master," she nodded with a curt motion before her eyes rolled to look down at me. "In the terms of lamen, both contracts were voided."

"And because neither you nor Adelaide were bound to your pacts, you were both offered up as free real estate," Haley concluded, another growl rumbling up from her chest.

She looked cautiously between the three of us and waited. This constant need for approval was irritating beyond belief. However, it and the lack of reaction to the pain I knew Haley was causing her made my gut flip uncomfortably.

"This is mostly correct. Due to the pigmentation of the malachite crystal that remains of the Corvi Catena, I conclude that only part of Adelaide Winter's soul is contained within. Because her vessel contains a fragment of her soul released from the binding crystal. It allows her to be bound by a new willing patron," she explained, allowing herself to continue to be held up against the Bronco. "I assume since the pigmentation's appearance she has been able to be outside of the predetermined boundary, correct?"

"That's… yeah, she has," Jason answered.

That made me pause. When we first met, Adi had been insistent on staying close to Jason and her necklace. For her to go to the library or the other side of the block from the apartment, the necklace had to be hung up in the corner of their home. It was why she insisted on having Haley and I borrow the necklace for our first few dates and girl's nights. Why she had been terrified the first time we'd gone without it.

"And what would happen if you stepped outside that boundary if your soul was still completely attached?" Haley asked before we waited for another long moment of her seeking quiet permission to answer.

Jason gave her another curt nod.

"Excruciating pain for the first few minutes. Eventually, the rift distortion between an artifact and a bound soul would begin to tear the soul asunder. If left too long, it would begin erasing what reality would perceive as a flaw in its design."

"So what makes *you* so special?" I scoffed, glaring at her.

"Just answer everyone's questions. Stop looking at me every time," Jason said, annoyance and frustration brimming in his voice.

"Yes, Master," Sinead answered.

"And *stop*. Calling me. *That!*" Jason snarled.

Sinead paused for a long moment, a hint of confusion etching into her eyes while her brow lifted ever so slightly.

"What am I to call you?" She asked, the microexpression on her face deepening in her confusion.

"Jason, just… What did you mean by what you said?" Jason asked, coming to stand beside me as Haley held the small woman up off of the ground.

"Very well. Jason," she nodded with confirmation, the movement driving Haley's claws into her throat more. She still showed no level of pain or discomfort at all. It was… unsettling. "This vessel of mine has no soul contained within it. As such, the soul of one Sinead O'Hare resides inside the ring that you now have in your possession. As the owner of this and having broken my contract, I am bound to you unless it comes into possession of another. As such, my soul is free to bind to you in contract if you so wish."

"So what, Jason can just turn you into our fucking slave or something?" Haley snorted, rolling my eyes at her overuse of words and convoluted explanations.

"I assume you meant that I would be your servant as I was to Samael. You're use of the word '*fucking*' is correct to a degree, however," Sinead said with some confusion. "As Jason has possession of an Ananke Ring. If he - like Samael - chooses then, yes, my body, mind, and soul are yours to sate any desire you wish. Including lust and release."

My blood had been boiling with my rage, however, waves of cold began flowing through it as the emotions inside me swirled. There was the anger I felt for Adi being stolen. Then there was the disgust and horror I felt from Sinead's words. They were mixing in a revolting way that didn't just affect me either because Haley quickly dropped Sinead and backed away. We both wore expressions of terror caused by the cold callousness of her words.

"So the glow of the ring," Jason asked as we watched Sinead slowly drag herself back onto her feet in a lifeless, almost mannequin-like stature. "What does that mean?"

"It is an indicator. Not only the strength of the soul and vessel but, ultimately, my life force. As the possessor of the ring, you may use it to absorb my life's essence from me to regain vitality yourself. Much as you witnessed earlier."

"What happens if it stops glowing?" Jason asked and I feared what the answer would be.

"My life force and soul would be forfeit. They would be yours to replenish anything of your health and vitality you have lost. It would effectively act as if I stepped beyond the designated boundary with more expeditious results. Jason needs only will it of me."

"And what if I say fuck that and you live your life as you choose?" Jason growled, his eyes darkening as he understood the same implications of Sinead's words as I did.

"I… I'm afraid I do not understand. Do you not wish to use me as your tool for vengeance, greed, or carnal needs?" Sinead said, her monotone voice showing fractures of something resembling a hint of true emotion.

"You want me to use my will on you? Fine. First thing you're going to do is fix this," Jason said, holding his left palm upward to display the curse mark that Sinead had placed on him.

"Yes, Ma- Jason," she nodded and then produced a small sickle-shaped blade that seemed to form from a wisp of black smoke from underneath one of the long sleeves of her dress.

Haley and I growled when we saw the blade, instinctively flexing our claws to strike. She paused in her motions as my gaze met hers. Her expression was impossible to read. I flashed her a look that said if she hurt Jason, I would tear her limb from limb.

After a moment, she tilted her head with something resembling curiosity in her eyes. The motion made her long white hair curtain farther down one side, framing her doll-like face with a shimmering veil.

"I have been asked to release my plague seal. You may kill me but be warned that, if it is not released, another of my kind will ride at the stroke of midnight. If the mark stands and his head is not collected, the branch from which our Mas- Jason blooms will be cleaved from the tree of life."

I *really* hated the way she spoke.

I hated the way her voice didn't bounce or sway like someone with a heartbeat. It made me wonder what she would sound like if she knew what life actually was. Or if I would always hate her. Because having her here and not Adi had part of me spiraling into madness.

Most of all, I hated the way she called Jason *ours*.

He wasn't hers, and she wasn't his. He was mine. He was Adi's. He was Haley's. Only with the three of us was he ours and for her to use that word…

"Fine," I sneered. "Just make it quick. Bloody fucking cunt."

"As you wish, Mistress," Sinead said, nearly making me choke at the casual use of the word.

Then she raised the blade to the mark and said something in a language I didn't understand. I did, however, catch an Irish or Scottish accent to its inflection. Once the words had been spoken, black ink-like tendrils were pulled from Jason's palm, the blade igniting into a wash of hellfire.

Moreover, the same sparks and embers of hellfire glinted in her eyes, making them glow with an ominous shade of blue while puffs of black smoke emanated from the point of her neck hidden by her choker. The same spot where her head had detached before.

When the fire that engulfed the blade dissipated, leaving only the glow of her eyes, I noticed that the steel of the blade had changed. Where it had been a bright polished aluminum before, it was now a matte black metal finish.

"There's no pain," Jason marveled under his breath, forcing my attention back to him as he flexed his hand and looked at his pale, flawless skin. "So it's done? You don't have to take my head and my parents are cured?"

"Yes," Sinead nodded curtly. "The seal has been voided."

"Good," Jason breathed out, an uneasy relief washing across his face.

"So now what do we do?" Haley asked, scowling harshly at the petite pale woman in front of Jason.

"We find Adelaide," I said as I narrowed my eyes sharply and let her see how close I'd been to tearing into her. And how easy I could've done it at any time.

"That will be a difficult task," Sinead said, her brow furrowing in a way that gave her a nearly human look.

"Do it," Jason commanded, folding his arms tightly over his chest as he stared Sinead down with an equally fierce glare.

Sinead reached out and took Jason's right fist into hers and then deftly spread his palm. In the center, the obsidian ring with a pale blue inlay lay on its side. Part of me swore it had been far brighter when Adi and I had attempted to take it off of Samael. Then I remembered what she'd said and how the ring contained her soul. And how it could be used to heal its owner.

What had once been a bright, glowing cyan color was now a pale blue-gray that faded into the same obsidian color as the ring itself.

"I, like the valravn Adelaide, are all children of the Nekduamortum. It bonds us to one another. Which is why the plague mark would have called to another of my kind. Sometimes we are drawn to one another, which is how I found you the first time," Sinead answered, tentatively touching the ring that held her soul. "However, back then I had the energy and life force to do so."

"So get the energy," I snapped, stepping closer to her with wrath burning in my eyes. "Hurry and find her."

"I am afraid I cannot at this time, Mistress," Sinead answered dryly.

"Then tell me when you can," Haley growled, pushing her face against Sinead's to the point I could see her wolven eyes reflecting in the whites of hers. Part of me hated this woman and was screaming for me to tear into her, telling me I'd delight in bathing in her blood. The rational side of me said that we'd keep her alive, but only until we found Adelaide. "And for Christ's sake, stop fucking calling us that."

"Yes, Mis- I understand," she said, pausing when she didn't know what to call me anymore. Instead, she focused on Jason in front of her.

"The Ananke Rings function similarly to the Corvi Catena, acting as a conduit for energies and magic. The artifact will replenish its energy over time, however, I believe you have broken its regeneration cycle."

"What do you mean by that? English, lady," Haley hissed at her, butting her forehead against Sinead's aggressively.

Sinead sighed, blinking slowly. It was the first real human motion she'd done this entire time. Like there was an honest-to-gods person somewhere inside there. She just hadn't been able to be at her mind's surface. It was… Haunting.

"Adi and I exchanged energy through her necklace. She never went too deep into her spiritual energy for most of the time I've known her except for - maybe - two occasions," Jason said.

It forced me to break eye contact with Sinead and turn to him where I found him gently holding Adi's necklace in his left hand. He furrowed his brow as he looked from the necklace to the ring in his other hand. I watched his shoulders slump with the realization of Sinead's words then he shrugged. He moved to begin putting on the ring.

"Be warned," Sinead said, making him pause. "By wearing it, you will bind my soul into a contract with you. I will be your abettor and herald from this moment forth, Jason McCrae. A servant of your will."

"My will is to find Adi and bring her home where she belongs," Jason spoke confidently, then looked up at Sinead as he pushed the ring onto his finger. His eye twitched in pain from a sudden rush of emotions and memories as he gave into contact with the item. Singular tears formed in the corner of his eyes as they widened while he stared at her. "And you're not my servant or whatever. You're your own person now, not a slave to anyone or anything. Got it?"

"Y-Yes, Ma- Jason. I… am simply Sinead henceforth," she said, confusion and awe thickening her tone.

"Okay. Once you get the strength or energy you need, you are to find Adelaide Winters. That is the only command I will *ever* give you," Jason said with finality. Then his knees buckled, and one of his eyes closed like his body had grown weak, and couldn't remember how to stand. "Fucking shit."

"What the fuck did you do-"

Before Haley and I could turn on Sinead, I felt a familiar touch pressing against my stomach. When I looked down, I found Jason reaching upward to hold both Haley and me back away from Sinead. He gave us a soft smile before holding his right hand up. The inlaid band was now glowing with a shade of cerulean instead of the pale grayish blue it was before.

"I may have been a dumbass and tried to jumpstart the process," Jason chuckled under his breath.

Haley and I shared a look before we both reached down to lift him onto his feet before his weight collapsed into our arms. I was stronger than human but being dead-weighted on annoyed the fuck out of me, even if the person was my hot as fuck, red-haired, psychic boyfriend.

"That was foolish of you," Sinead said, tilting her head as she watched Jason struggling to stand with mine and Haley's help.

"Doesn't matter. You're going to learn real quick that I will do whatever it takes to save someone I love," Jason chuckled, a sly smirk tugging at the corner of his lips.

"You're lucky I love you, you hot, shit for brains, arse," I snorted, no longer able to deny the joy and delight that Jason brought to me. It made me take a deep breath and let it out with a sigh. "Okay, we're getting you home, getting that fucking ring recharged, and then we're getting Adi. Understood?"

"Yes, Mistress," Jason chuckled, my brow twitching with annoyance.

"He is allowed to call you Mistress?" Sinead questioned, confusion deepening in her eyes more as time passed.

"Only because me and him are fucking," I said dryly, narrowing my eyes at her.

"Very well," she said with a shrug.

"Haley," Jason said, turning his attention to our wolfess. "Can you make a call to Thomas and have him triple security? If beings from Nekwhatever are drawn to each other, Lex might still be in danger.

"Good thinking, mi amor," Haley nodded before turning to Sinead. "I'll make the call on the way home."

"Anyway, let's get this arsehat home to get some sleep. I'll figure out what to do with her." I said, glaring at Sinead to make sure she understood that she and I weren't finished yet.

Haley and I lugged Jason around the side of his Bronco before Haley moved to open the passenger door. I laughed when he joked about being the *Passenger Princess* for once before buckling him in and making my way to the driver's side. Haley climbed into the backseat and moved to sit behind Jason while I glared at Sinead. The two of us waited for a long moment, giving her an expectant look as her eyes went back and forth between us.

She blinked for a moment, looking at the back seat, Haley, and then at me. Sinead tilted her head as she read my expression.

I bloody fucking dare you to stab me in the back.

"Your mistrust is unnecessary," Sinead said blankly.

"Get. *In*," I growled.

"I do not need assistance with transportation and I deem it safer outside of the metal box than inside it with your presence," she retorted, still monotone as ever.

"Uh-huh. How exactly am I supposed to get Jason home and watch you if you're not in here with us?" I said, jerking my thumb at the back seat.

"If I may be so bold to make a request, I have means of transportation for myself," she said, making it more of a question than a statement. "If that is permissed, of course."

"Okay?" Jason said wearily, giving her and me both a confused glance. "Asking for favors already?"

"Just this once," she assured.

"Fine," Haley groaned, rolling her eyes at Sinead. "What, can you fly or some shit?"

Sinead turned her head toward the entrance to the field where we had entered, raised a hand, and snapped her fingers. The motion was like any normal person's, however, the sound that came from it was that of a grandfather clock's chime. It bellowed into the night sky with a haunting ring before the distant sounds of rolling thunder began to draw toward us.

I watched as three spots of hellfire appeared out of the darkness. My jaw dropped as a large creature galloped up to the truck and stopped in front of Sinead, puffs of smoke billowing from its nostrils. The creature rumbled and neighed with excitement as it butted its snout against Sinead lovingly then leaned over and sniffed me curiously.

I didn't move. My eyes and brain tried and promptly failed to make sense of what I was seeing. I was left in a daze as I stared up at a light bluish-gray stallion with hellfire for eyes and a mane. While I gawked it shook its head with eager anticipation and excitement.

"As I said, transportation for myself is not an issue," Sinead said calmly. Then, with graceful ballerina-like agility, she jumped, swinging her leg over the horse's back where a saddle sat at the ready. With equal graceful movements, she calmly took the reins of the horse and drew them through her hands. "Do you prefer if I follow or keep pace?"

"Keep pace," Jason said breathlessly.

"What in the bloody fucking hell are you?" I whispered under my breath before I climbed into the Bronco, closed my door, and stared blankly out of the window.

As we drove home, I thought about everything. I caught myself staring at the pale, petite woman as she rode the hellfire-clad horse beside us, racing down back streets toward home. Then several things clicked into place. Sinead's head was removable. And it lit on fire as she threw it. The horse that she was riding was pale just as she mentioned the other morning. Then there was the fact she used scythes and sickles as her weapons of choice.

"Sinead is a fucking dullahan," Jason said with awe-inspired realization as he stared out the front window, his jaw hanging open.

I looked at him as he spoke and all of my elementary school memories came back to me. Back when I'd read a certain book about a headless rider that haunted a sleepy town somewhere in upstate New York. Then I looked toward Sinead riding beside the Bronco with that same dawning expression.

And, at that moment, part of me could have sworn that those matte black lips of hers curled into a genuine playful smirk.

9

HALEY

BLACK FRIDAY SEEMED A FITTING TITLE FOR TODAY.

Without Adi's presence, the apartment felt darker than before. A dark, void-like feeling that I had been all too familiar with after Mickie had rejected me six years ago. A void that had all but been filled up but now threatened to reemerge. The one difference was that I now had Mickie and Jason to surround myself with to stave off the effects of a missing bond.

I knew the signs of withdrawal to watch for.

Signs that had started nearly immediately when we'd gotten home last night. They'd started as soon as we walked into the apartment and Mickie's anger took over while Jason began spiraling into depression. It left me to take charge, first sending the two of them to bed while I took care of Sinead. Adi may have been gone but I knew she'd want me to make sure the two of them were taken care of.

Adi made this house into a home and, until she gets back, it's my job now.

I woke early to take care of breakfast, something I'd spent the last month or so doing with Adi. She had made sure we had always been fed; that was on me now. She'd made sure that Jason and Mickie got out of bed at a reasonable time; that too was on me. I did my best, however, it didn't feel as right as when it was Adi's self-proclaimed responsibility.

After I had gotten them up and made sure we were fed, I had no idea what to do with the rest of the day. I was still getting used to not being alone. It had become so commonplace after my parents walked out when I was a child and Thomas had taken over the responsibility of my livelihood. A commonplace I struggled to replace after Mickie had finally accepted me as her mate, and I was welcomed with open arms into Jason and Adi's home.

Mickie, in her struggles, decided the best thing to do to take her mind off of last night's events was to brave the crowds and traffic. She, like me, was convinced that Adi would return home and that warranted that Christmas shopping needed to be done. She would need to be spoiled. While I agreed, she and I had gotten into a fight about her insisting on going into the droves of people, heightened tensions, and drama that surrounded the unofficial holiday.

"Fine, la novia," I relented and held her tight at the front door.

"Just promise me you'll spoil them as much as they spoil us."

After our leopardess had left, I turned my attention to Jason. He'd locked himself into his office, hiding himself away from interacting with anyone. Despite forcing himself to be away from Sinead and me, I got him a drink and then swiftly pulled the keys he'd gifted me when I moved in from my pocket.

When I entered the office, he was in little more than athletic shorts and a tank top and, despite it being colder than usual, he was sweating buckets. I ventured to guess he was also suffering from nausea and fatigue. Then he was slapping at his keyboard, threatening to break it.

Act fast, Haley. He's got all of the usual signs already.

I padded across the floor of the office to him, grabbed the back of his chair, and pulled him away from his desk.

"The fuck, Haley. What are-"

"Breathe, mi amor," I said, furrowing my brow at him and holding my wrist against his nose.

"What-"

"Breathe, pendejo," I snarled, glaring at his angered expression. He gave me a snarl of his own before he took in a small breath, filling his senses with my scent. A trick I'd learned to help stave off the mate withdrawal years ago. "Now drink this. You're dehydrated."

"I don't-"

"Drink, Jason," I seethed, nearly forcing the glass of water down his throat.

Jason scowled at me while he chugged most, if not all of the glass of water I'd gotten for him. Even in his anger, his cerulean eyes looking up at me made me shiver with need. Once I was satisfied he'd had enough, I bent at my hips lowering myself to place my forehead against his, and shivered at the discovery of how much he was burning up.

"Deep breath again," I ordered as I moved to cradle him into the crook of my neck. He did so, taking in a long, shuddering breath that seemed to calm him even just a little. "You're going through rejection withdrawals, mi amor."

"What does that even mean," he groaned as he took in another heavy hit of my scent.

"It means that without one of your mates around, you're having the same effects you would if you were quitting smoking or hard substances cold turkey. Trust me, it only gets worse," I said, nuzzling my cheek against the side of his head while breathing in his pine and rich earth scent myself. It helped to dull the nausea I was beginning to feel inside my own head. "But I'll help in any way I can. That's what Adi would want right?"

"Yeah," he said, his weight collapsing against me. "H-How.... How do I do this without her?"

"Day by day," I replied, reaching around Jason to hug him tight. It felt comforting to have his hard form pressed against my flesh and I only hoped he felt the same. "Normally, the effects start off mild and grow stronger. However, this isn't a normal situation, is it?"

"He fucking took her. And there was nothing we could do to stop it," Jason admitted with a sob as his arms encircled me and gripped my shirt desperately.

"He planned it that way," I reassured him, pulling him to his feet before taking his hand and forcefully leading him away from his computer. I shot Sinead a warning glare as we entered the dining area, eyeing her with an accusatory glare as she stood at the ready in the living room. "We didn't know he could sacrifice her to heal himself."

"We should have planned better," he growled, his head hung low to avoid catching Sinead in his sights. "We should have-"

"We didn't have time, Jason. That is the fact of the matter," I growled back at him before entering our room and locking the door behind us. Sinead wouldn't be seen by us, and she wouldn't be allowed to see how I planned to comfort my mate. My prime. "That doesn't deny the fact that between you and the girls. We had him on the ropes and he had to cheat to win."

Jason relented to my urgings and plopped himself onto the bed while I moved around it to pull open a drawer of one of the nightstands. When I returned to him, I handed Jason what I'd pulled out of the drawer, all but forcing it into his hand. He took the thick black leather collar and narrowed his eyes at it before looking up at me with confusion.

His eyes followed me as I dropped to my knees at the foot of the bed, turned my back to him, and lifted my long, dark hair. Out of the corner of my eye, I watched him look back and forth between me and the gift he'd gotten me during our second date. We'd gone to dinner and then to a bookstore where we walked and talked hand in hand so we could get to know each other better.

It was where we learned we shared a rough childhood and upbringing. Where he learned that I had to figure out how to control my wolf alone just as he'd figured out how to control his psychic abilities in forced solitude. Then we'd spurred levity between us when he walked me into a sex toy store and we shared a deep discussion about our sexuality, repressed urges, and kinks.

The night he'd gifted me a gorgeous leather collar with a silver metal tag hanging from it. A tag with the words *'pequeño lobo'* etched into it using my claws to do so. One that was identical to Adelaide's collar which sat next to it in the drawer, its tag etched with the words *'little bird'* to match mine.

My eyes fluttered as the comforting weight of the leather wrapped around my throat and squeezed me in the way I liked it. As the clasp clicked shut, heat rushed to my core and a heady feeling blurred the edges of my mind while I pinched my lip under my fangs with anticipation.

"You sure about this?" Jason asked as his hands fell away from me and I turned to see his body slumped with his eyes watching me with remorse.

"The only way to beat the rejection effects is to have a sense of normalcy. Would our baby bird want you locking yourself away?" I asked as I ran my fingers up his exposed calves and under the hem of the shorts to his inner thighs. "Do you think that's what your littles want from you, *Papi*?"

The reaction was almost instantaneous. With a keyword, laced with as much sex appeal as I could muster, it snapped something inside of Jason that had me squealing with delight. His hand found my collar, looping underneath the leather band to pull me toward him before our lips crashed together. The kiss was bruising as I whined and squealed into his lips, his free hand finding the back of my head where he fisted my hair.

The pressure around my neck and at the roots of my hair, combined with Jason's intoxicating scent and taste had me soaring. His lips and tongue went on a feverish attack desperately feasting on me like the supple flesh was a lifeline in the desert. The biting, licking, and suckling left my lips swollen, begging for more as my tastebuds danced with the taste of fall-seasoned spices and the scent of roasting pine.

"Rules?" Jason growled underneath his breath, breaking the kiss so

I was just out of reach.

"Green means go. Yellow means slow down. Oklahoma means stop," I whimpered in response, needing his taste and touch on me.

And yes, Oklahoma was our safe word because there was never going to be an instance that we'd say that. Red hadn't worked because I loved wearing a skimpy red lace combo that had a sheer thong and a translucent babydoll top. Jason loved the way the red, or the gold corset I wore - to match Mickie's pink and Adi's teal identical sets - complimented my skin tone and savored it every chance he got.

"Goal for today?" He breathed out, making me have to come down from my high just to think clearly.

That was another thing me, him and Adi had set up together. If Adi and I wanted to float in subspace, he'd put us there and just let us have the time to enjoy that feeling of care-free submissiveness. We'd get put into that state of mind and then enjoy upwards of two hours just cuddling. If we wanted to ride that high, he'd add teasing foreplay or slow sex that let us prolong that feeling until we came crashing down. And then third…

"Use me. Work out the frustration and remind me who I belong to, Papi," I said with a whimpering sigh and a playful smile.

With a hard tug on my collar, pressing the leather tighter against my skin and making my cheeks and chest flush into a pinkish-caramel tone, I was forced to my feet. With one hand still fisting my collar, Jason's other hand wrapped around my waist, taking my plump ass into his palm and squeezing. The tightness of his grip, his nails pinching through my jeans, sent warm heat throughout my core. Hot enough that his kisses along my belly felt like touches of liquid magma against me.

Adi was self-conscious about her curves and, truthfully, I felt the same about mine. However, Jason kissed and melted those worries away with how he worshiped our bodies. It made me feel like a goddess before him. Every flex of his hand on my ass and collar, the way he trailed his tongue from my delta up, passed my navel ring, to my sternum. I was bathing in his ministrations that had my entire body and soul buzzing with heady desire.

Heady enough that I hadn't even noticed that his hand on my ass had already stripped me of the jean capris and black lace panties I'd been wearing. It wasn't until I felt my breasts fall free with their heft that I realized my surroundings. Jason was standing before me, his hands swiftly pulling my bra away to toss it to the floor to join the discarded jeans, underwear, and crop top I'd been wearing.

"You're fucking divine, pup," Jason said breathily.

Before my eyes and mind could fully become aware, Jason was on me again, tugging at the D-ring of my collar. My body melded against his firm chest and abs, my back arching to reach his lips as our mouths crashed together in a hungry kiss. I whimpered loudly as his teeth pinched and nipped at my lips and tongue, addicted to the way he could feed on me so hungrily.

While his mouth feasted on mine, one strong hand slapped my ass and grabbed tightly, grinding my pussy against the thick bulge straining against his shorts. His other hand, meanwhile, swept one of my breasts into his palm, lifting the plentiful orb for his fingers to find their target. Soon an electric buzzing shot from my taught nipple to my already dripping cunt as his deft touch twisted my barbell piercing.

With his hands on me, I felt myself being lifted onto the tips of my toes as he coaxed me around before I was left to fall backward. I came down on the bed with a splash and a fit of eager laughter and joy. The light buzz of pleasure still coursed through me before it heightened as my eyes fluttered open in time to see Jason stripping in front of me. A sight I loved getting drunk off of with his pale tan flesh, toned chest, and abs, and his length bobbing heavily.

The sight was a dangerous temptation for my hunger. He looked, smelled, and tasted wonderful no matter where my mouth had landed on him, however, that gorgeous cock of his was something else. The perfect length, a wonderfully delicious girth, and just the right upward curve; I fucking needed him. The sight was like dangling a prime cut of steak in front of a rapid wolf which, of course, I was.

"Fuck yes, Papi," I whined hungrily, my eyes following the sway of his length like it was prey. "Is that all for me?"

"You've been a good pup, right?" Jason hummed, his eyes drinking the sight of my body down with feverish hunger as he knelt on the bed with one knee.

His hands dragged his fingers up my thighs, over my hips, and then up my sides, sending rolling jolts of fire and electricity across my skin. That fire became molten as his lips kissed at my knee, my inner thigh, just above my clitoris, and then finally my navel. I was shivering and sinking into a blissful giggling mess as his tongue flicked over one of my swollen nipples and his thick head brushed across my dripping slit.

"Yes," I whispered, my back bowing with anticipation as Jason's rigid length ground against me, my puffy lips parting around him and coating him in my slick, warm essence. The sound of him chuckling against my skin, made a wave of goosebumps rise across my flesh, tensing my skin and making each touch hotter than the last. His lips against my neck and the feel of the base of him pressed against my snatch had me melting with heady bliss. "Please, Jason. Don't tease me, just take what you need."

"Let's get you warmed up, pup," he countered, kissing my neck as one of his hands dropped between my legs. Jason's fingers trailed down the length of my sex, coating him in liquid heat as he parted my folds around his digits. Once he reached the peak, he quickly began circling my thick swollen pearl with firm pressure. "Hearing your pretty voice is what I need, mi pequeño lobo bueno."

"Fuck~"

I let out a panting whine as Jason circled my clit vigorously, sending throbbing vibrations through my core that turned the rumbling heat there into a smoldering furnace. His fingers were like a constant electrical current that made my pussy sing and my body writhe and shake underneath him. That steady buzzing of pleasure tripled as he leaned down, sinking his teeth into my collarbone with enough force to leave a possessive mark. Between the sting of pain that screwed my eyes shut, he rubbed faster on my clit, punishing my pussy with a high stream jet of stimulation.

"Color?" He whispered against my neck as he rolled my clit as fast as he could.

"G-Green. Green. Green. Gree- Ah!"

The overstimulation was too much to take and I was sent flying into sweet agony as my core burst. My pussy pulsed and fluttered, clenching tightly as a heavy wave of heaven took me hostage and I came with a scream. My hips rose to Jason with desperation as his movements paused enough for me to go for my ride and soak his palm in a quick flood of my warm honey. My claws dug into the comforter beneath me as my legs locked up and held my ass high off the bed. I was stuck there as I rode quick wave after wave of pleasure until I remembered I had to breathe.

I collapsed back onto the bed, my chest rising and falling rapidly as I relearned the basic function of my existence. A wide smile stretched across my lips as my eyes opened to little white spots floating above me. There was something about Jason's touch that made me hit that peak so much faster than I had ever been able to do by myself.

Gods, I fucking loved this man's fingers.

Then came the soft kisses, planting their way across my thighs up to my knees before I felt Jason nuzzle his cheek against the crook of my legs. The gentle, loving touches and affection after I'd become a puddle in front of him made my heart flutter for Jason, having to stifle giddy laughter and squealing. I failed miserably as our eyes met and I found Jason's warm, caring smile showering down on me.

"The code is still green, mi amor," I hummed, giving him a teasing 'come and get me' look.

"In that case," Jason chuckled, leaning down to give my belly ring a kiss before he rose and let his eyes darken with a wicked grin. "Come to Papi."

I giggled at Jason's quip - loving that he'd tried his best to learn little Spanish phrases and words for me. However, that giggle turned into a hysterical fit of eager laughter as Jason's hands found me, gripping my thighs and spreading me wide to expose my puffy, glistening pussy entirely for his viewing pleasure. I watched his eyes hungrily admire me in quick glimpses while his body moved me and forced a gasp of surprise from my lips.

Strong forearms hooked under my thighs, spreading me as wide as I could go while my body was pulled toward the corner of the bed and then raised upward. My eyes went wide as Jason towered over me, leaving only my shoulders still firmly on the bed while my legs hovered above me, my knees nearly kissing my breasts in this position. Then his weight came over me, putting pressure on my entire body that shocked me at first before I soon fell into that wonderful blissful headspace.

Jason was completely dominant like this, I was his completely and entirely.

My prime.

"Ready?" Jason said with a dark chuckle as he positioned himself using his hold on my entire body to his advantage. His movements ensured that his rigid member dragged his thick tip down my spine and then upward across my puckered ass to the base of my pussy. "Hold tight, babe."

I nodded eagerly, my eyes screwing shut as they crossed when Jason pressed forward, finding the right angle to spread my wet folds around him and welcome his delicious cock inside me. Jason groaned with a strained breath as he pushed forward, his dick pulsing with every inch that he sunk into me until he was sheathed entirely. The angle at which he entered had me shuddering. This position made me tighter and more compact, however, it also ensured the curve of his length would punish that swollen sweet spot every time.

Nothing could have prepared me for it. Jason began thrusting in slow downward motions that compacted my body, making my pussy squeeze him with a death grip. The tightening meant his cock hugged against my g-spot and put pressure just behind my clitoris with every movement. I was already heading toward an overstimulated buzz and the pressure in my core had risen to hotter, tighter levels than before.

Despite how tightly wound around him I was, the fact that I was soaked to the bone made it so that Jason didn't have to fight friction. Instead, after the few first thrusts used to find a steady, mind-numbing rhythm, something inside him snapped. I subsequently forgot to breathe as his hips began slapping hard against mine, loud wet smacks reverberating as he drove into me with everything he had.

The corner of the bed compressed and sagged out our combined weight as the anchor of his forearms against the backs of my thighs and his grip on top tightened. I felt everything. The calloused pads of his fingers against my smooth flesh, every ridge of his throbbing dick, and a continuous smack against my rear entrance. A sudden forceful thrust made me gasp sharply, forcing me to remember to breathe which coalesced into panting, shuddering screams of pleasure.

"J-Jason! Ah! Querido dios de mierda!"

The whining tone in my Spanish, made him grunt harder, a primal growl trickling through his throat as he gripped harder, steadied his footholds, and began to utterly fuck me. His thrusts were hard, deep, and savage as he filled me, stretching my constrictive walls with every inch of him. He let out long growling moans, my name dancing off his tongue as he took me.

I, unlike Adi and Mickie, didn't typically enjoy having my cervix smashed. The pain of it usually canceled out the pleasure. As opposed to what I loved such as spanking, biting, pinching, or being choked. This, however, the fire in his thrusts, the hungered growls and moans, and the feral need inside the storms of his cerulean eyes flipped a switch inside me.

I was a puddle; soft clay for him to knead and craft like a master. His touch and rhythm pushed me deeper past that floating heady feeling of subspace and into something primal. A place that had me screaming, howling for him like a wolf bitch in heat.

I was fucking *his*.

The harder thrusts made my body shake, my breasts bouncing and heaving wildly as Jason took me. The tag on my collar jangled, with metallic clinging that was drowned out by my cries of need and desire.

The feel of his cock barrelling into me, the constant grinding against that sweet spot, the drone of pleasure mixed with pain had my entire soul buzzing like my skin was a livewire barely grounded by where I connected with him. Then that pressure was just too much to take.

"Pon un bebé en mí, Papi~"

I screamed as my pussy convulsed around him, my body going rigid as I tightened and hung on for dear life while my climax hit me off of that cliff of pleasure. I soaked Jason to the bone as I came, my heated essence coating my inner thighs and his, pooling down the corner of the bed while his pulsing dick throbbed faster and harder like a second heartbeat deep inside me.

"Haley!" Jason called out with a feral roar as his back went rigid, plunging himself as deep as my body would take him as he dove over that same cliff after me.

With Jason balls deep inside of me, my eyes rolled back and I took in a strained breath as he released. His heavy balls, pressed against my ass, tightened as thick ropes of liquid heat poured into me. Jason coated my inner walls with enough of his warm, delicious seed that he began leaking out almost immediately. The warmth of him filling me triggered several more small waves of orgasms that rolled through my body and core. A spreading wildfire danced through my entire being like millions of pleasurable pinpricks which had me writhing and choking on air.

I finally caught my breath as his weight fell onto me, forcing me to breathe and stare up at the ceiling while white danced across my vision in a blissful haze. My legs fell around him and I held him to me as he struggled to move before falling to his knees on the floor. Sweat glistened on my entire body and where I could see his forehead between my legs when I mustered the strength to look up and check on Jason.

"Holy fucking shit," Jason panted before falling back from his knees onto his ass.

"That's… my line," I giggled and then hissed as another wave of pleasure and aftershocks roamed through me.

The two of us laughed as we caught our breath before I managed to scoot my elbows underneath me enough to prop my upper body. Jason blinked rapidly, no doubt chasing away the same stars that refused to leave my own vision. With him down there, I could've so easily teased him and part of me wanted to. Yet, I didn't have the strength to do so.

"You feeling more like yourself, mi amor?" I asked, beaming down at him. Openly showing off the mess he'd made of me to his delight.

"Yeah, I think so," Jason nodded, taking in a deep breath as he got to his feet and wobbled. I sighed in delight as his motions brought him closer and he laid a soft kiss on my lips. "It… was a lot different without Adi here though."

"I know," I responded, forcing a soft smile onto my lips. Instead, I carefully reached up to run my fingers through his hair. "You'll just need to make that same kind of mess with Adi when we get her back."

"That, I can do," he nodded softly and nuzzled his cheek against my breasts.

It was a calming and comforting feeling to have Jason there. A small part of me said that I needed to get us cleaned up and check on Sinead. The part that won out, however, was satisfied with holding Jason close, stroking his hair, and happily enjoying the sensation of his seed leaking down my ass cheeks. It was a part of me that was more than happy to relive the experience of the position that caused it and how he rolled me up like a pretzel. The position that made me scream…

Wait, did I seriously tell Jason to put a baby in me?

IT'D BEEN FOUR DAYS.

Four days since I was forced to watch that fucking ram-headed bastard and his shit-eating grin as his hands wrapped around Adelaide and pulled her into a void. The same void I felt inside me where Adi's presence had once filled. Haley and Mickie had let me vent, the former going out of her way to put me into a headspace where I could take out my frustrations on her.

It had helped. To an extent.

However, one thing remained inside my mind; Adelaide didn't deserve what I had caused her. I had fucked up and now she was trapped in the same place that I had saved her from. That thought was what made me sleep restlessly as recurring nightmares of the event looped countless times while I tried to sleep. The dreams - if you could call them that - were beating my mistake into my skull.

Between the three of us, Haley was trying to keep a semblance of a routine, however, Mickie and I were spiraling. Sunday morning came and we woke up later than usual. Instead of Adi's cooking, the three of us woke up to silence and light pouring through the windows to bring a facade of warmth with it.

We also woke up to the sight of Sinead standing dutifully at the foot of our bed.

"Master Jason, you and the Mistresses have a guest," Sinead said, her tone calm and content with a hint of Scottish accent.

She stood calmly, in a manner that resembled a mix between a butler and a living doll, in an outfit that Mickie and Haley had convinced her to wear. Truthfully, it was intended for the purpose of pajamas, however, she refused to sleep. Instead, she had been swapping this out for her previous gothic lolita attire.

Instead of the frilly Wednesday Addams meets French maid aesthetic, she was clad in nothing but a silk, black spaghetti strap dress that showed off ample amounts of pale, porcelain skin. It had been Mickie's that she wore as a top, however, the size difference between the two fit Sinead like a cropped dress, coming down to her upper thighs. To complete her look she insisted on wearing her black wool knee-high socks.

Part of me wanted to say she looked gorgeous and more human in the outfit. The other part cringed at seeing her in it because the silk top was, of course, partially sheer.

What was worse, standing not too far behind her was a familiar swoop of bright blue hair and pale skin that was covered almost entirely by tattoos. Moreover, the figure's eyes were wide and a light shade of pink flushed her cheeks as she stared over Sinead into our bed.

"Not so bloody fucking loud," Mickie groaned as she rolled away to pull herself from my side and sit up, holding a hand up to shield her eyes.

Mickie was nursing, yet another hangover, from hell. In the last four days, she'd gone through almost the entirety of our liquor cabinets. Adi's disappearance had hit her hard, driving her to find some kind of solace in the bottom of a slew of glass bottles. Ones that I would sure need to make a trip to the liquor store to replace.

"Me duele la cabeza," Haley groaned as she sat up on my other side, the black comforter pooling in her waist and exposing her round, golden-skinned breasts entirely. She squinted harshly through one eye while holding up another to block the sun.

"Wow, okay, you know what? Maybe I should come back," Lex said, clearing her throat and hesitating in her steps to turn around.

"Seriously, what's going on?" I asked, sitting up and letting what little of the comforter had been covering my nude form pool in my lap. "Lex?"

"Yup, that's me," she said nervously, faking a tone of joy and amusement.

Lex muttered something under her breath and then finally turned on her heel to head back into the kitchen. The shadows and light dancing off of her form made it known that she had begun pacing circles nervously around the dinner table. Her hands sank into her hair with frustration and I could hear her muttering under her breath, most of which was some variation of '*fuck.*'

"Everything okay, love?" Mickie groaned, moving to stand up and letting the comforter fall off her completely. She strode to the door of our bedroom, the lighting making her naked skin glow with warmth as she leaned against the door frame and watched the other woman pacing. "Thought you'd be up at the U with the girls?"

"I was! I," Lex froze mid-sentence and mid-step as she stared at the taller woman. Her mouth hung agape as her eyes traced Mickie's form slowly before mouthing a silent '*wow.*' Remembering her purpose, she shook her head and blinked quickly. "Have you guys not seen the group chat?"

"I didn't realize you got added to the server," Haley groaned as she rolled out of bed and strode toward the door to join Mickie. Lex became more visibly flustered with both women standing there completely unabashed by their nudity. "Babe, you wanna check the messages?"

"Yeah, yeah, I got it," I sighed rolling toward the nightstand on Mickie's side of the bed to grab my phone. Picking it up, I found that I had a dozen missed calls from Xan and another unknown number. I also had a new text from Bekka informing me that my parents were released from the hospital. Then I opened the chat server. "Well fuck…"

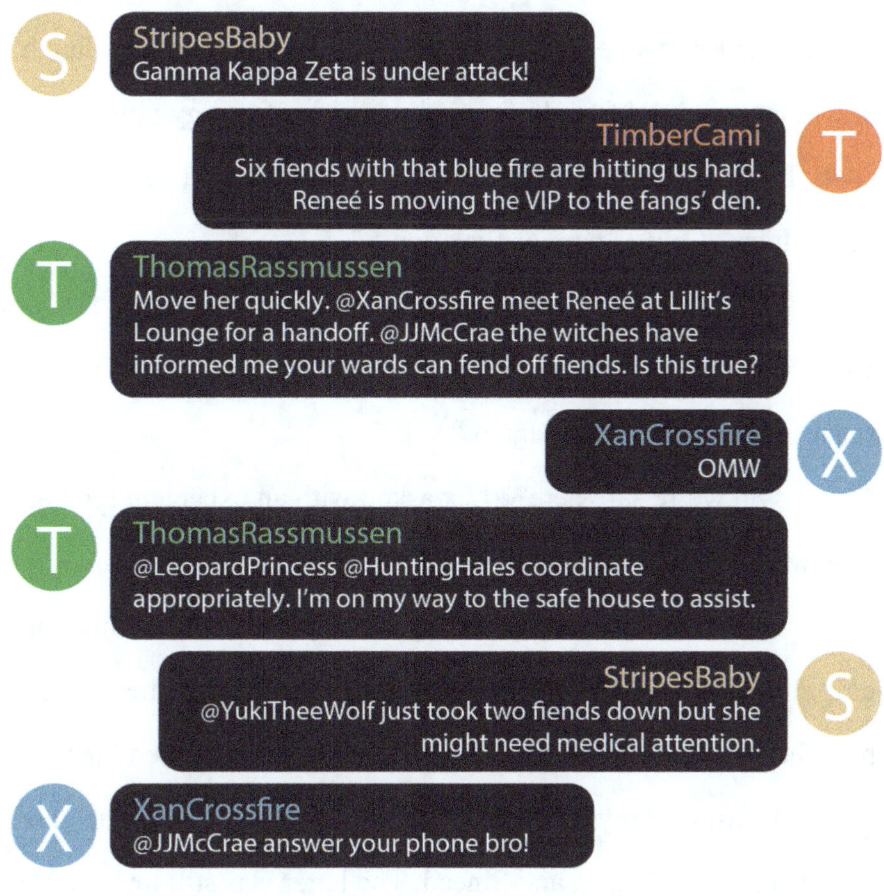

I figured, now was better late than never to answer.

"Well, our Odin definitely has more faith in whatever wards and protections I was able to put up," I snorted with a humorless laugh while I closed my eyes and found that small buzzing of energy pulsing within my chest. I still had no idea what to make of my so-called personal magic or its abilities. "Cause I sure as fuck don't."

"The wards have made our location harder to search for," Sinead confirmed with a curt nod. "I would not be able to find you if I were to be sent out to search for you again."

"So we're safe here?" Lex asked with an expectant look as her eyes went back and forth between Sinead and me.

Her expression was pleading for help and I was folding under her gaze. It reminded me of the first time I'd met Adi. And the last time I saw her when I fucked up the incantation and made her vulnerable to Samael.

I scrubbed my face with my hand and then looked back and forth between Mickie, Haley, and Sinead. The latter was still unreadable. My girlfriends, however, gave me a look that clearly said that if we didn't help Lex, they'd kick my ass.

Fuck it, what do we have to lose? Besides everything.

"Sin?" I said after a long sigh of exasperation. She gave an expectant look, addressing me without words. "I'm guessing you're not going to sleep despite us telling you to?"

"Your presumption is correct," Sinead answered, her shoulders shrugging slightly. "I do not require sleep despite your protests. Rather, I believe it would be valuable of my services to remain on guard. Much like this case presented before you."

"Yeah, thanks," I grumbled and rolled my eyes. "In that case, we have a guest room you can crash in when you're here. It ain't much. And we only have one bathroom in the apartment, but if everyone thinks it's the right call? I can't really put you out."

"Here, I'll show you where it is, love," Mickie said, nodding a thank you over her shoulder before she and Haley pushed off the wall and moved down the newly constructed hallway.

The spare bedroom was in the far corner of the apartment. It had once been the area where I would hang Adi's amulet to allow her to make it to the library across the street; now it shared walls with our bedroom and my office. The bed that was set up had once been Haley's from her old apartment, however, it hadn't been used since she moved in a month ago.

I waited patiently for Sinead to do anything other than stare at me, awaiting another order. One that would not be coming any time soon. She seemed to read my mind and shrugged before cupping her hands in front of her, still not moving from her spot.

"You know, a lot of women would have looked away from me by now. Honestly, it feels a little weird to just have you staring at me while I'm naked," I said nonchalantly.

"Nudity does not bother or concern me if that is your worry. Sa- My former master would frequent his domain in such a manner," Sinead retorted. I watched her eyes briefly scan over me and I couldn't tell if she was enjoying the view or not. Then she looked down at the dress and tugged it away from where it hugged her petite figure. "Truthfully, in his domain, I was required to wear much less than this. He wished that I be ready for him at all times."

"Yeah, well, I'm not that sadistic fuck," I scoffed at her, my eyes narrowing in disgust.

When she remained in place, her body and expression unmoved by my declaration, I rolled my eyes. With nothing else to do, I rolled off the bed and stood, padding across the wooden floor around her toward my wardrobe. I pulled out clothes and dressed, even as she watched the entire display with a melancholic gaze. Part of me registered that her expression had shifted as I walked past her.

Was she... blushing?

Once dressed, I held up my right hand and inspected the ring for the millionth time. The inlay was still a cerulean blue, however, I noticed it was lighter than it had been yesterday. Even more so than it had been the morning after we'd brought Sinead home. The ring was working; recharging her soul and giving her energy, however, at a far slower pace than I would have preferred.

"Is that… a *soul* ring?"

Lex's voice made me pause and I looked up to find her in the doorway, her eyes narrowed into something fierce as she stormed forward. Her bare feet slapped against the hardwood before she was in front of me and looking over the ring. Anger ignited her cyan eyes and they sparked with small licks of hellfire.

She apparently knew what the ring was and its purpose. Neither of which she was happy about.

"The *fuck*, dude? I thought you were better than that?" Lex sneered, glaring at me hatefully.

"Yes, it is an Ananke Ring, I am pleasantly surprised you know of this. However, if it is of any consolation," Sinead nodded with confirmation. Her answer turned Lex's attention toward her with a hesitant yet expectant glare. "Master Jason and the Mistresses-"

"Please stop with the master and mistress stuff," I pleaded, raking my hand across my face.

"Jason, McKenna, and Haley," Sinead corrected herself, her

eyes shifting to watch me. "Have yet to require my presence unclothed. Also, they have yet to require my services to attend to their carnal needs. Furthermore…"

Sinead turned to look up at Mickie standing in the doorway. After a short moment of hesitation, the smaller woman reached out and laid a dainty hand on the taller woman's bare shoulder. She then waited for something, *anything*, to happen. Mickie simply looked at the offending hand on her shoulder and scowled at Sinead with confusion.

"They have yet to punish me for being as bold as this on my own accord. Lord Samael's retaliation to such a thing was often swift," Sinead shrugged and then removed her hand from Mickie. "However, I do not believe it to be amusing to have me resort to using my teeth or feet to perform daily chores."

"The hell's that supposed to mean?" Haley asked, her brow scrunching with equal confusion.

"In my two decades of service, I sought to touch Lord Samael on my own volition thrice. Each time I was punished severely. The first time I was scolded as he beat me. The second time, I spent nearly a year waiting for my arms to grow back," Sinead explained, her eyes floating between the four of us. "On the third occasion, he removed my head and placed it in a box for another year. Afterward, my body was chained to his bed and rendered into what he called his *'personal cock sleeve'* for the duration of my punishment."

The four of us froze completely.

A small look of confusion passed over Sinead's expression before she cupped her hands together in front of her again. It made me realize she was desperately waiting for instruction. Expecting it from me. She'd gotten so used to constantly being given orders and directions she didn't understand what to do with herself.

She'd had no free will with Samael and had completely forgotten what personal bodily and mental autonomy looked like. She had been broken beyond belief and no longer knew what it was to be anything remotely human.

I realized that Sinead had suffered just as much as Adi had at the hands of Samael. The only difference between the two of them was that Adelaide hadn't been broken so wholly. The dullahan had. Sinead's resilience and will to fight had been stolen from her. Adi's resolve hadn't been broken even after all of her trials.

Now he wanted to do that same thing to Lex.

I wouldn't lie, I might have had some delusions which included a sort of savior or white knight complex. I was self-aware enough for that. Aware it all came from a place that hated people who bullied and belittled others. I hated people who broke others down for their own gain and amusement. I was - *am* - a broken man, however, I didn't spend all of my time shielding myself until nothing was left of me. I had turned that into a drive to help people.

Lex needed our help. Our protection.

Adi needed to be saved.

And Sinead needed help just like Adi thirteen years ago.

"That settles it. Lex, come and go as you please. You're safe with us. Sinead, this is your home now, do you understand?" I said with finality, turning their attention toward me. "When you get the energy to search for Adi, bring her home. As for Samael, he's a dead man when I get my hands on him. No one is going to suffer again like you and Adi have. *Ever*."

ADELAIDE

BLOOD POURED DOWN MY BODY. HOWEVER, IT WASN'T ENTIRELY MINE.

In front of me, two figures were sprawled out, sans various limbs from having touched me with their disgusting claws. This was my third escape attempt over the last week and a half and, if I kept going like this, maybe I'd cull Samael's herd myself. Or at least put a dent in his numbers until Jason, Mickey, and Haley came for me.

"Kneel!"

I hissed in pain as Samael's voice boomed throughout the cells and his voice rang painfully through my nerves. The compulsion in his voice made my body betray me, my knees smacking against the hard concrete that made up the dungeon floor. I'd have another pair of bruises to match the rest strewn across my body. His voice pulled on my neck and chest as if a set of heavy iron chains weighed me down, holding me in a position that debased me before him.

His hooves clicked across the concrete toward me, the view of the lesser demons that I'd disemboweled obscuring my view of him. The smell of death mixed with sulfur and brimstone attacked my senses, my gut churning uncomfortably from the pungent odors.

"Looks like you still haven't learned your lesson, little bird," Samael scoffed as he stepped over the bodies in front of me before grabbing my chin roughly. He forced my neck to strain to look up at him. "What am I to do with you?"

"Learn your own lesson," I seethed before spitting a thick glob of blood and thicker things, watching the crimson splash indignantly across his tailored vest. "You could release me and maybe you won't lose a couple more henchmen."

I grinned wide up at him, one eye swollen shut from being bludgeoned in the face several times. He snarled at my act of defiance before I felt a hard crack blossom with heat and pain as my neck was snapped to the side. My jaw tightened from being slugged across the face, forcing me to spit once more to the side and refuse to meet the demon's gaze.

"I would have killed you long ago if you weren't so valuable to my collection," Samael said with disgust as I caught the brief sight of him cleaning his knuckles of blood with a handkerchief. "Nevertheless, I will break you soon, Adelaide. You will be mine to use as I see fit."

"Sorry, my dance card's looking full these days," I snorted, my busted lip curling into a smirk as I forced myself to look up into my nightmare's face. "I'm a claimed woman now, Sammy."

"Ah, yes, the pitiful so-called psychic, the tomcat, and the mutt," Samael chuckled under his breath. His eyes trailed over his fallen minions, his lips curling into a wicked grin as he surveyed the carnage. He looked pleased that the lesser demons had managed to allow me to take my raven's form and decimate them before nine lesser demons managed to reign me in. "The same ones who have left you here? The same ones seducing that useless herald of mine and the tricky minx that decided to try and immolate her adoptive mother?"

"They're coming for me," I snarled back at him. "And I promise you they'll be more than happy to chase you through the Nines to take your head."

"They can certainly try," he snickered as he stood and looked around the room. He then pulled out a gold coin, holding it in one hand while his other snapped his fingers. The sound of it echoed through the empty, spacious room while a wave of arcane energy wafted along the walls, stinging my senses and mind with a sickening feeling. "And if they do come? Are you willing to leave all of them?"

When the sickening buzz mellowed enough that my already struggling eyesight could focus, a cold sickening feeling ran through my entire form. My stomach dropped, leaving me precariously close to throwing up as a horde of lesser demons stepped out of a series of glowing portals around the room. With them came a series of cages that they moved into rows of cells, each holding its own singular inhabitant.

All of them held a similar scent to them that called to my valravn side much like Lex had. All of them had something that was a mix of sage, incense, and rain, filling the dungeon with the scent of a wake. My good eye widened as I surveyed each cage and found a creature that I'd seen or heard of through the many books about cryptids and folklore within Jason and I's library. Spectral figures in long white dresses, hooded skeletal figures, hounds with green and blue fire rolling off of them, and two women no older than Lex with the same blue hair made of hellfire.

All of them were descendants of Nekduamortum.

"So when your saviors do come, will you sacrifice them to save yourself?" Samael laughed as he held his hands out wide and spun with glee in a grandiose gesture.

"Du verdammter Hurensohn!" I snarled, lunging toward him and straining the unseen binding he had on my soul. "Why do you need us? Answer me that."

"Simple really," he smirked as his hooves clicked toward me before my entire vision filled with the ram-headed demon before me. His hand gripped at my hair, pulling hard to force my attention and a scream of pure pain as he threatened to scalp me from the force. "I am the lord of death, remember? The one who controls the fate of everyone in existence. The one who you will serve and render the death gods meaningless before me."

"You… are so… fucking delusional," I grunted as his hands jerked me around with each of his words. My entire body radiated with a mix of the brute forceful pain and the nauseating smell of him being so close.

"You will bend Adelaide Winters," he grinned, his nostrils flaring as he pushed his forehead against mine. "You are the key to my success."

Before I could give him a venom-induced response he pushed forward, his thick, malformed lips locking onto mine. I screamed and tried to move away, however he only deepened the kiss, pushing his tongue forward to invade my mouth and slap mine back. Tears welled in my eyes as I was forced to feel him, forced to taste his filth without a way to use my body to push him off of me.

He tried deepening the kiss, lengthening it until I couldn't breathe, my chest burning from suffocation. I was forced to take him as he wished. That was until I realized I could move just enough to get him off of me. I bit down on his tongue as hard as I could, my mouth filling with the sting of his acrid blood.

He roared and pushed back, throwing me to the ground on my back while I spit to the side of the floor, trying to rid the taste of him from my mouth. His muscles coiled in his arms as he wiped his lips and glared down at me. All the while he tentatively touched his tongue feeling the incisions my teeth had made in an attempt to sever his tongue from his mouth.

"Foul little slut," he rumbled before kicking outward, stabbing at my shin with one of his hooves.

I screamed in pain, however, when I bit back the sound of it I did so with a wide grin that gritted my teeth in pain and satisfaction. I'd caused him pain. Not nearly as much as he had for over a hundred years but it was a fucking start.

Seeing my smile, his brow furrowed and his movements slowed. I saw him concocting something behind his vacant eyes and I felt a cold shuddering feeling race down my spine as I looked up at him defiantly.

"You," he called out, drawing the attention of one of the crimson-skinned, lyre-horned lesser demon minions. "Find me every demon among my army that is endowed as I or larger. Once we have moved all of my operations to the chalet, they will be rewarded. The raven tart will be free use for 96 days."

Hearing his words, I rolled to the side and gave in to the sick feeling. I wretched and heaved a mix of blood and bile onto the ground beside me while Samael laughed hysterically. I might be able to fight off some of them but I couldn't fight that many days nonstop. The overwhelming fear and panic took hold and refused to let go.

"We'll see how full your dance card is then, won't we, little bird," Samael teased in a sadistic, melodic tone.

I looked up in time to see him towering over me, his slacks straining with the monstrous bulge threatening to get out. He didn't shy from adjusting himself, having gotten hard from my pain and panic.

"Retrieve the banshee whore for me and deliver her to my room. I'll break her tonight," the ram-headed demon laughed darkly before his gaze fell down on me. "Take the raven slut to my waiting pen with the bastard."

Samael stalked off, watching one of his minions open a cage to retrieve a pale, nearly translucent spectral woman in a tattered white dress. She floated hesitantly toward him and the unseen weight holding me down released in time for me to be grabbed by a swarm of demonic men.

As I struggled against them, my eyes clenched shut while I began kicking and flailing wildly. I felt my legs connect several times, followed by pained grunts before I was caught again and again. Try as I might, however, their holds remained strong on me as I was hauled up several flights of stairs.

Soon the world went weightless and the restraining holds vanished. I went flying for several seconds as I was thrown before my body hit the floor and I rolled several times. My motion was halted by the hard smacks of several iron bars bruising my skin and I was left to wait for something - *anything* - to happen.

Instead, I sat up slowly with pained groans and grunts straining my vocal chords as I righted myself. When my singular eye opened, I found myself in a large bedroom that I would have called nice, if it wasn't for the iron bars lining the wall and ceiling. It was plain, with no furnishings save for a single queen-sized bed in its center whose sheets were littered with smears of dried blood stains.

My sight fell onto something that caught my attention, my senses picking up a strange scent and the sounds of labored breathing. I strained to stand, my cut leg and bruised knees making the action difficult before I began limping heavily across the room. As I came closer, I found a mess of hair and horns struggling to move away from me.

"Hey, I'm not here to hurt you," I said with a groan, my hand clutching my side where a minion had kicked me in the ribs. "I'm A-Adelaide…"

"The prized pet," she coughed with a mix of pain and irritation before leaning to the side and spitting blood. She leaned back, resting her head against the wall as the rest of her body uncoiled and she focused an intense glare up at me. "Trust me, we all know who you are, *Princess*."

I froze in place as I rounded the bed and caught a clear view of the figure that shared the room with me. A mess of medium-length, feathery, black and dark teal hair draped around a pair of ivory sheep horns that protruded from her temples and curled backward to her sides. The ivory of her horns and mauve skin tone made the black sclera surrounding deep fiery lavender eyes with slitted pupils more striking. As did the strong lines of her cheekbones and pointed jaw that extended to give her facial feature more of an animalistic definition.

Her wide nose ended with a rounded, rubbery pad that tilted her dark lips upward into a never-changing scowl. That, however, didn't take away from the pouty, supple shape her black lips had, nor did the flood of faun spots dotting her cheeks and the thick bridge of her nose. I would have immediately thought of her as cute, in a mythical fae-being sort of way.

Except, her tone and the constant threatening aura surrounding her pushed that thought toward the back of my mind. As did her scent which registered as to what kind of being I was looking at. Rain, sage, and the smoky spice and sweetness of… Paprika? It helped to mostly mask the subtle, underlying scent of sulfur and brimstone; this woman was a half-demon.

I shook my head at her while my gaze trailed over her figure, taking her in completely. She was of average height and had a strong triangular physique, wide hips, and powerful thighs. Thick black and mauve, woolish fur covered her from the lower swell of her hips downward. At her knees, her calves became coated in short, wiry black fur, and became double-jointed.

She wobbled as she stood onto her furred faun legs and took a deep preemptive breath. She gave me a brief glimpse at her lightly toned abdomen, arms, and small teardrop-shaped breasts tipped with dark lavender nipples. All while a thin, leathery-skinned, spaded demon tail swung lazily behind her in a hypnotic fashion.

Then she was on me, slamming my back against the iron-barred wall behind me with her forearm against my throat. I gasped as the force knocked the air from my lungs, her arm refused to let me take it back. Her eyes bore into me with pure rage and seething hatred as she readied a pair of fangs and claw-tipped fingers to tear into me.

"You are going to get me out of this fucking hell hole, understand?" She hissed, pressing tighter to make her threat that much more prevalent.

"Correction," I retorted, my eyes narrowing while my skin took on an ashen hue, my fingers extending into my raven claws. I let my mind sink into that plumbing wrath where the raven resided, giving me more than enough strength to push her off of me and look down at her as my body stretched into my taller form. "We are getting out. All of us."

Her eyes trailed up and down my figure, her scowl twitching with amusement as the corner of her lips lifted into a smirk. I let her appraise me for a moment before she rushed me again, taking a swing of her claws at my midsection. I caught her arm between my triceps and ribs before snarling and whipping my head forward, bashing my skull against hers. The pain was intense, nearly making me falter as I collided with her more densely boned forehead, then I caught her with my free hand and pushed forward. My hand caught her throat and squeezed as I forced her onto the bed in the center of the room on her back and roared down at her.

Our spiteful glares towards each other froze as sounds from a room on the other side of the wall permeated our space. A mix of lustful roars and the cried wail of agonizing desire stole our attention, both of us turning sickened and venomous eyes toward the source of the sounds.

"Weak little- ugh!" the woman beneath me scoffed.

"Yeah, well… not everyone can hold out for a century on that Scheißkerl like I have," I growled, narrowing my eyes at the wall. It made me realize that my left eye was no longer swollen shut. Good.

"You've been putting up with him for that long?" The woman asked, a hint of awe filling her tone. It made me look down at her to see widened eyes of shock staring back at me.

"I escaped once. And I will do it again," I hissed before pulling back and allowing her to sit up.

"And what makes you so sure?" She spat back, giving me a coy look of indignance.

"Because if I don't kill the fucker and escape first, then my mates will do it for me," I grinned, giving her a look of sadistic pleasure at the thought of eviscerating Samael. When the moment passed I looked back down at the woman, feeling my body shrink back to its normal stature and seeing my skin return to its human shade. "Now… let's try this again. My name is Adelaide and I'm going to get us out of here."

I held out my hand, letting it hang in the air while she stared at it. I watched something cross her mind that I couldn't place as she contemplated the gesture. A long moment passed between us before she looked up and gave me a smirk that said she thought I was insane to have any semblance of hope and light left in me. Then I felt her strong grip take my hand in hers, the sound of our palms meeting echoing like a thunderclap inside the room.

"Name's Trish. What's the plan… Princess?"

WHAT IS MY PURPOSE HERE?

That question has been permeating my mind over these last two weeks. A question I cannot seem to find the answer to. I feel as if this is what mortals refer to as '*going through the motions*.' However, I do not understand these motions.

Before this, I knew my role. I had a purpose and a steady routine. Sparse meals, being a proud herald, tracking down children of Nekduamortum, and being used at Samael's leisure for his pleasure. Never my own.

Simple. Menial. Pointless…

The last two weeks with my new master and mistresses have been… frustrating.

I am a puzzle piece with roughened edges and an odd shape that does not fit with those around me. Samael made it so. Despite this, Jason and Haley have tried. Like ones who scan the puzzle, searching for a place where I might fit and gently attempting to align my edges with theirs. They never do.

McKenna, on the other hand, has been one who forces her attempts. She pushes to fit me in, even if the edges are not remotely close. Or I don't fit in at all. It's all been for Jason's sake, I know this, and I've watched her patience wear thin. Then something unknown inside me stirred when she screamed at me.

Last night she slapped me, the first true delivery of pain I had grown accustomed to. Delivered by her, it felt… wrong. I felt something that I hadn't known for so long. Shame. I was ashamed of her disappointment when she claimed that I would never replace Adelaide.

Had I been trying to?

I had simply tried to touch her and offer comfort. Despite being unaware of how to do so. I had offered to cook, in an effort to repay them. A skill I did not possess.

Why am I putting in this effort? And for a master and his mistresses that don't truly want me.

To clear my mind of these thoughts, I sought to continue something that had brought me a sense of acceptance and purpose.

"Very well, let us try again. You managed to not burn entire articles of your clothing off this time," I said, my voice not quite feeling my own.

It was… *odd* to offer encouragement.

"Ugh! I don't fucking get this!" Lex scoffed, her eyes narrowing and her cheek flush with pink. Her latest attempt at trying to beckon her gift of hellfire had just rendered her hoodie to become sleeveless.

"As I said before, this gift of the Nekduamortum resides here within yourself," I replied, placing a palm over the lowest point of my sternum. "Focus on the flame of the underworld residing inside you and call upon it for its assistance."

To demonstrate, I flexed my abdomen, peering down the depths of my mind where that spot resided. It flickered like an ever-present pilot light before I drew that energy from inside me, making it roar to life. I opened my palm where a small hovering ball of flame materialized before I willed it forward. It raced to the end of the alleyway and splashed against a painted target in a shower of cyan flames.

She let out a seething scream, scowling as she mimicked my motions. However, her soul was uneasy. Instead of a small hovering fireball resting in her palm, the fire raced upward along her arm. The flames licked at the side of her hoodie, burning another hole into it before she flung wildly. Once again, instead of a precision throw, the fire swept outward the ground like throwing water from a bucket onto the pavement,

"Fuck!" Lex screamed in anger as her hair roared into a sweeping inferno.

A smooth voice behind us chuckled as he watched Lex's display. I tilted my head curiously at the man. It was an oddity that he enjoyed seeing the underworld nymph struggle. I shrugged off the thought as my eyes fell back onto Lex and furrowed my brow. The pinkish hue of her pale skin due to exertion had deepened to a shade of crimson.

"Gee, Xan," she snarled, folding her arms tightly over her chest as she looked at him with defiance. However, my mind picked up another emotion besides her typical frustration. It was something… more. "Why don't you try it if you're so fucking badass?"

Xander, the werewolf who had taken the duty of being her escort and protection, shoved his cell phone into his pocket and straightened. In another motion, he tugged his cream-colored hoodie over his head to reveal a white tank top underneath. The fabric hugged his figure and contrasted the bluish undertones of his dark umber skin, coiled muscles flexing as he moved.

The werewolf was six feet in height and wore his tightly curled hair in vertical twists, framing his squared features and strong jawline in a picturesque way. His figure was what I'd heard mentioned as that of a wrestler - fitting given his occupation - and carried himself with a quiet pride. In private, Lex had referred to him as being movie-star handsome, a term I was unfamiliar with.

What I found acceptable about Xander was that he didn't parade his strength and body around. Not like other men, lesser men, I'd seen. Ones who had discounted my smaller frame and stature as weakness; that they could overpower easily. Men who were now missing their heads.

Xander's golden brown eyes gave me a look of respect and acknowledgement as he walked past me with his wolf just below the surface. It was an expression that regarded me as a fellow warrior. However, when his eyes fell onto Lex, both auras surrounding him looked at her with carefully restrained hunger. It was the same look I saw every time Jason locked eyes with McKenna and Haley.

A look that… had never fallen in my direction.

I knew the expression of hunger and lust in someone's eyes. I had seen it and felt it on me more times than I could count. The difference was that, back then, it was regarding me as something to be used for their gain. This was… an equal exchange.

Again, a sensation foreign to me stirred and I didn't know what to make of it. All I knew to process was a heat swelling in my core and a twisting of my stomach. I understood the sensation for others but was taught that those things didn't exist for something like me. This had been why I was struggling. I could not deny those sensations, especially when they had been brought on frequently in the presence of Jason, McKenna, and Haley.

Nor could I deny a sudden spot of dampness against the *'panties'*

Haley insisted I should wear beneath my uniform.

"You're saying right here, right?" Xander asked, pressing his fingers against his sternum. I nodded my confirmation. "Makes sense to me 'cause that's about where my other side sits."

"Oooo, your other side," Lex said in a mocking tone, wiggling her fingers to imitate something of a ghost. "Yeah, yeah, so easy for you."

"Please, baby doll," he grinned, happily showing off a pair of fangs when Lex shot him an accusatory glare with a title he'd given her. "Now I can't shoot no damn fireballs or whatever like Grim can but…"

I felt my lips tilting upward with his reference that I'd come to know as my personal title. There was a sensation of pride that he regarded me in the same light as the great being of death itself. However, I knew that he didn't know the distinction between my kind and the great being. The Reaper was the greatest of all celestials associated with death and the children of Nekduamortum - the plane of existence he created from the ether. Dullahans and valravn's, such as Adelaide and myself, were simply messengers and chauffeurs of his will.

As his words trailed off, his eyes closed with reverence and focus before the skin and muscles of his right arm rippled like waves across a water's surface. As a small wave of energy, like a warm static breeze, flowed around him, his umber skin began to sprout a short coat of glossy black fur. His fingers shifted and extended, tipping the newly formed beastly arm with razor-sharp claws.

"Same concept, right?" Xander asked, his eyes opening and moving between his arm and myself.

"Correct," I nodded, my eyes inspecting the arm and taking in its shape for a moment. Then a clear, viscous fluid poured from his fur as the transformation receded. "While you do not contain the ember of Nekduamortum, you do have a source of power that you can call upon in the same manner."

"For me, it's about controlling that beast inside me and what he feels. Not bottling everything I'm feeling inside and letting it pop, more like… telling him what we want to do together. You feel me?" He explained, his eyes settling onto Lex.

"So what, you're telling me just to focus on telling the fire *hey, make a ball so I can throw it at a bitch* or something?" Lex snorted, rolling her eyes incredulously.

Xander and I shared a look before we both nodded at Lex in unison.

"Emotions play a big part. If they're all over the place then you're not gonna get it. But if you're cool and calm as fuck, or a bit of a sociopath like Grim, no offense," Xander explained further, giving me an apologetic look. "It'll be easier."

"Uh-huh, 'cause it's so easy for all of you not to feel a damn thing," Lex huffed indignantly.

"I… I do feel things," I corrected, furrowing my brows. I felt the muscles in my face contort, tightening my lips, cheeks, and throat. I then motioned to my face in confusion. "Like so."

Lex and Xander stared at me for a long moment, unsure of what to say.

"Or things like not knowing where I truly belong and what my purpose is any longer. Truthfully, it is why I offered this service to Young Mistress Lex," I continued, letting out a deep breath while my eyes focused on the pavement at my feet. "Or the sensation of heat I felt when Young Master Xander took off his coat. The tension that occurs when I gaze upon Master Jason, Mistress McKenna, and Mistress Haley. However, I have never allowed myself to address the call for release. Not as Young Mistress Lex has when Young Master Xander departs and she stays the night."

I heard Xander begin to laugh, his warm tone of amusement tickling and dancing across the flesh of my ears and the warmth in my core. Did I enjoy it? No. I knew better than to enjoy it, especially if the frustrated screech from Lex was something to go by.

I deserve punishment for speaking.

"I… was not allowed without Samael's permission. Which he never granted. Nor did he allow me to feel something so… unworthy of me such as pleasure."

The laughter died instantly.

"I feel… fear," I said finally as I looked up at them. "Fear that they would deny me that opportunity. And I fear that I… I am nothing more than a burden, much like I was to him."

Neither of them spoke for a long time, the two of them sharing a wordless conversation filled with a mix of emotions strewn across their faces. Most of which were unreadable to me. The cause was that I had never been allowed it and no longer knew the correct words for deeper emotions or how they might be displayed. Fear and duty were the only ones that truly registered in my mind.

Lex's face was unreadable as she turned away from me and focused her vision on the painted target at the end of the alleyway. She stood there for a long time, breathing deeply with contemplation.

"If Adi returns, are you wanting to replace her?" Lex finally asked softly.

"No," I said, shaking my head. "I do not see myself with a true place in their bed between them."

"Then what *do* you see, Grim? What is it that *you* want?" Xander asked with insistence.

"If they would have me… I would make my home at the foot of their bed," I answered truthfully. "Their obedient and reliant herald

When I turned to look at Lex again, I saw a small, perfectly shaped fireball floating above her hand. It rested there, swaying in an ethereal dance as the flames flickered and swirled softly. I marveled at the perfectly shaped sphere, noting that it may have even been larger than the one I had demonstrated.

She wound up, hurling her arm forward, the ball rocketing forward with immense speed where it crashed against the brick wall with palpable force. A spray of liquid embers erupted in a small, yet impressive explosion, leaving the painted rings glowing with licks of roaring flames. Something warm rose up inside of me like a sense of pride and admiration. When she turned to me, she had fire calmly dancing in her hair and springing from her pupils.

"You. Are *not*. A fucking burden, Sin. Got that?" Lex said, the fire in her eyes roaring with something part of me said was sincerity and conviction.

"Yes, Young Mistress Lex," I replied with a curt nod and found the corners of my vision becoming watery.

"Fucking fuck!"

Jason's angered tone echoed through the alleyway as the garage door opened and a fire in his eyes sparkled violently. His boots stomped harshly across the concrete toward the driver's side door of the Bronco. I could feel wrath and vitriol rolling off of him in heavy waves.

"What happened?" Lex asked, worry dousing the fire in her eyes as she and Xander rushed toward him.

"Bro, you okay?" Xander asked quickly, following on her heels.

"No," Jason growled. "I'm going to fucking kill, Gary."

"Whoa, whoa, whoa, chill dude," Lex said, running to the passenger side where she and Xander climbed in.

I knew Jason would be leaving for McKenna's... Basketball game? It seemed as if it was a very important task for both of them. Moreso as Haley was not able to attend due to her presence required by their Odin, Thomas. However, recalling stories about this Gary person, I knew he did not have anything to do with tonight's task. I realized then that Gary was inconveniencing Jason. Part of me wondered if I should summon Rowan to ride with my master.

Would Master allow me to curse Gary? Or perhaps I could gain favor if I rewarded him with the man's head.

Another part of me wondered if I should ride to McKenna and stand guard at her event. Then I remembered her slapping me and thought that action might make her accusation ring true. I did not wish to incur her disappointment once more.

What should I do?

"Jason," I asked, finding that I had unknowingly placed myself at his door. "Shall I ride beside you? I may be of service in bringing this

Gary to a swifter death.”

“No... I’m not actually going to kill the guy,” Jason said with a deep groan before he turned to me through his open window. I felt his hands encapsulate mine, a pleasurable spark jolting throughout my body, as he placed something into my hand. “But I need someone here I can trust in case Adi comes home and we’re not here.”

“You… trust me?” I asked, my voice sounding like that of a stranger.

It felt odd. Distant and more breathy than usual and heard the accented lilt of my voice. Moreover, I felt my chest tighten as a swell of heat flooded my body and a thrumming beat in my chest.

I... can feel my heart beating.

When I opened my hands, I found my Ananke Ring resting there. Its inlay gave off a faint glow of light blue, no longer the near black it had been my first night with Jason. Instead, it was humming with energy and… life.

“I do,” Jason said as he squeezed my hand firmly. I found myself desperately wanting his touch to remain on me forever. “Protect our home, Sin. And make sure Adi, Mickie, and Haley aren’t alone when they get back.”

“Yes, Master,” I said with finality and a sharp nod as I took the ring and watched him leave.

I felt my lips tug upward as I looked down at the ring, the gesture no longer carrying malice as it had when I'd used it before. In addition, the warmth I felt was not just longing and adoration.

For the first time, I understood what was happening; I was smiling and I was… happy.

As the garage closed, I turned on my heels and made my way back up to the apartment. With the ring in hand, I knew with everything in my being that I had the purpose I was searching for. With that sense of purpose and duty reinvigorated by the thrumming in my chest and Jason's lingering touch, I vowed I would accomplish that task.

Furthermore, with the glow of the ring, I found hope of being more than an idle protector and herald. Jason, my master, had faith in me. He trusted me. And my hopeful duty said that I would never betray that trust; in fact, I would expand upon it.

"I, Sinead O'Hare, do solemnly vow," I said with conviction to the empty apartment. "That I will be more than my master and mistress' abettor and ensign. I am their pale rider. Their protector. Their hunter. And I *will* find the valravn, Adelaide Winters."

Then I made a selfish task and vow for myself; an action that would have seen me punished only a few weeks ago.

"In doing so, I vow - no - wish… to seek Adelaide's forgiveness."

THE DRIVE UP TO SAND HOLLOW HAD ME SEETHING.

I could feel my anger swelling to the point that I could hear an inhuman growl emanating from my throat. Especially once I saw the activity abound in the gravel parking lot of the site. Gary Civka's Ram was easy to pick out among the crowd parked next to a small crew of diesel trucks and heavy machinery. Opposite of them I found the familiar Range Rover belonging to Paul Monroe and Professor Ouray Whitestone's old, beat-up F-150.

I stomped toward the spiritual threshold of the massacre site like a rolling storm where I found Gary getting into Paul and Ouray's faces. The screaming match between all of them was long under way and I knew that it was only about to get worse. This was the case as soon as Gary saw me coming toward him, visibly shaking with rage when his eyes met mine.

"Tell them to get those backhoes back on their trailers, Mr. Civka.

Police will be called if you keep this up," Ouray stated in a calm yet demanding tone.

"Call 'em. I'll be more than happy to see you scum in handcuffs," Gary snarled.

"This is a federal crime, Gary. You will be the one arrested here," Paul groaned, scrubbing his face with his hand.

Passing through the threshold, further activity came into view as the souls of the Sand Hollow Ute Tribe appeared in my vision. The entire tribe went about their routes, repeating their last steps and actions before their camp had been invaded by hostile settlers and destroyed, All *Loopers*, as I called them, aside from the four souls that stood proud behind Paul and Ouray.

Loopers were spirits who repeated their actions. They only had enough spiritual energy to manifest and create laps around the vicinity they were bound to. The kind that appeared and people would try to follow only for the spirit to walk through a wall or disappear completely. *Wakers* on the other hand, like these four, were different. They had enough energy to manifest sentience; they were awake and aware. They knew they were dead, and, if you had the ability to see and interact with them, were the kind that you could carry full conversations with.

They, much like Adi, had more life and compassion in them than some of the living. Despite their traumatic demise. Unless, of course, they had been shitty people or serial killers in their previous life. Those ones were just as dangerous dead as they were alive.

Chipeta was the first to acknowledge me as I came towards the group, her translucent form curtly nodding in my direction. Next to the two-spirit healer of the tribe were her friends and lovers Wakkara and Joseph. The former flashed me a knowing glare as he flicked the bowstring across his bare chest and refused to take his eyes off of Gary.

Did he just ask me if he could shoot him?

Joseph, on the other hand, left no doubts about what he wanted to do as his translucent form rubbed his thumb eagerly across the percussion lever of his rifle. I wasn't sure if he could shoot him, being a ghost and all, however, I didn't want to find out. And neither did Chief Ammon, who nudged the man with his shoulder as he glared forward. The wise old man looked angry, as he should have been, however, I could see something in his eyes that hoped diplomacy and civility would win the day.

"Oh look, the rest of the circus just showed up," Gary scoffed, finally noticing my arrival.

"Aww, comparing me to P.T. Barnum? You flatter me," I retorted, rolling my eyes at him as I stopped at Ouray's side. "But seriously, Gary, this is fucking insane. Even for you. Pack up, take your clowns home, and maybe you won't have the feds coming down on your asses."

"Unless you got the cash, these boys won't be listening to a damn word you have to say, McCrae," Gary laughed, giving me a sneering smile as he planted his fists on his hips.

"Holy fucking shit," Lex whispered, drawing my attention to her. Her eyes were wide, pupils twitching as if she was tracking hundreds of different points. "What is this place?"

Apparently, she could see the dead wandering around behind us.

"Welcome to the site of the Sand Hollow Massacre. Just a lovely place where settlers torched the village of the Sand Hollow Ute tribe and all of its 172 residents," I said, returning my eyes to Gary who scoffed at Lex.

"Seriously? You're trying to disturb sacred land?" Lex growled, her eyes narrowing with anger.

"Sacred is right," Gary chuckled, his eyes looking up at us and beaming with delight. "It's gonna be the jewel of the Silicon Slopes that'll rival those Patterson snobs in Park City."

"Has he never seen Poltergeist?" Xan mumbled, giving the pudgy old man an incredulous look.

"Nope," Ouray and I answered in unison.

Despite the warnings and our persistence, Gary made a motion with his hand and one of the excavators came to life, lurching forward through the spiritual threshold. With a pair of angry growls, Joseph and Wakkara took aim and fired. Both arrow and bullet struck the machinery before Wakkara notched another spectral arrow and Joseph prepped another round in his muzzle-loaded rifle. Within seconds, the excavator halted in its tracks, the gears and engine grinding and choking until they died and left the operator in confusion.

"You are dealing with forces you can't begin to understand, my friend. *Please* tell them to load their machines back onto the trailers and leave," Ouray pressed.

"I'm getting my luxury lots and there ain't nothing you can do," Gary said, narrowing his eyes and growling at the stalled excavator. "I've got a client wanting to buy these lots up and he's got plenty of pull with the state. We're free to do whatever the hell I want."

"Pull with the state or not," Paul sighed, pinching the bridge of his nose. "This still isn't right."

"Gary, money isn't gonna do shit when you have unsuspecting families moving into homes that'll potentially kill them," I yelled, getting into his face and pushing a finger against his chest roughly. "Do you *really* want that on your conscience?"

"What did I say before, McCrae? I'm getting the money from the goddamn lots," Gary snarled back trying to get back in my face and pushing at me. "So why don't you liberal, red-skin-loving pussies bother somebody else."

"Gary," I growled with warning, feeling my teeth grit tight to the point pain thrummed through my entire jaw and my fingers bleached white from how tightly bound I flexed them at my sides.

The Landshark sneered with a smirk, turning away from our group to stomp toward the stalled machine. With a punch to the leg, Gary got the man's attention, who scowled at him in response. Despite the worker's attempts to reason with the old man. Gary yelled something intelligible at him before he attempted to start the excavator up again.

The machine roared to life, rumbling the ground at its start before the operator, at the behest of Gary, began lurching forward once more. As the large metal bucket began to descend, Chipeta rushed forward to put herself in the way of its intended target. Unbeknownst to the operator he was lowering the bucket toward the spirits of children. Spirits who were stuck in a loop of eternal playtime moments before horses had trampled them a century and a half before.

The bucket came to a screeching halt as it came into contact with Chipeata's hands. The excavator stuttered like it was hitting a solid wall of granite, gears whining in protest to the force. As she pushed, I watched as Chipeta's form began to flicker, a sickly black and teal smoke beginning to circle around her feet. An ethereal scream of pain rang out through the field as the smoke began to molt her skin, turning it to a diseased dark purplish green.

"Chipeta!" I screamed in terror as I raced toward her, earning a confused glance from Gary.

When I reached the swirling black mass surrounding Chipeta, I screamed as the smoke touched my skin and sent waves of throbbing pain throughout my body. A wave of sickening nausea hit me, jerking my stomach to the ground, and leaving me lightheaded before the world became weightless around me. The energy sent fire and sickness racing through me as I was hit with a concussive blast of force that hit me like a fist trying to bore its way through my chest.

When my body stopped rolling, scraped and bleeding from hitting the ground like a discarded doll, I found myself twenty feet from where I had been. I grunted as I slowly pulled myself to my feet, finding Gary - or rather two of them - with a look of shock etched across their wretched faces. When my vision cleared enough that I stopped seeing double I watched him begin to slowly back away from the excavator while the operator jumped out and began running.

When my eyes fell back onto Chipeta's form, the sickness of cursed energy had already stained most of her form, inky black tendrils snaking up her arms. The groaning and desperate whines of metal increased as the excavator wobbled and the arm holding the bucket twisted. It then inverted, pointing the bucket at an odd angle toward the sky as Wakkara and Joseph rushed to her side to push the heavy machinery away from her and the children.

Together, the three of them flickered, living shadows whipping around them as the soil and evergreen shrubs around them began to wither and decay. Those same tendrils wrapped around the three of them, sickly veins overtaking them inch by inch. I watched in desperation as I took wavering steps toward them while the three souls slowly began to turn into cursed spirits right in front of me.

I quickly looked around me, seeing everyone's face etched with horror, Lex's hair and eyes beginning to spark with blue fire. She was the only one who saw what I did and I found the same look of hopelessness in her eyes that I felt. Beyond her, however, I saw the peak of Timpanogos looming in the distance. The same mountain range that Adi and I feared being close to because of the overwhelming feeling of a giant being watching us.

"Great Spirit, if you give a shit about them, let this work," I snarled under my breath, turning my eyes from the looming mountain range to the three souls I had began running at full speed toward.

I barreled into the three figures, tackling them out of the circle with every ounce of strength and speed I had left in me. I let out a growl of exertion as I hit them, sending them toppling out of the black swirling mass and I replaced their forms with my own.

I screamed.

The pain of the dark cursed energy roared through every vein, muscle, and bone in my body, my limbs straining as it tried to contort me into its twisted design. I felt the sensation of choking, suffocating on a thick tar-like substance that crawled its way from my gut up my throat and filled my lungs with acrid bile.

The world went weightless once more, however, instead of being thrown, I found myself levitating in the circle as the buzzing in my chest hummed and the tattoos along my arms glowed like fire, bursts of pain radiating in shockwaves from head to toe as they fought against possession and corruption.

The screeching sound of twisting metal and terrified screams forced my eyes open. In front of me, I found the excavator's arm had been wrenched and twisted, now resembling the shape of a thin scorpion's tail as it curled over the cab.

Blinking in astonishment, I felt the rush of air around me as I dropped to the ground at the center of the circle. The ground around me was now glowing green and had the same runes inscribed into my arms burnt into the soil around its circumference.

"You, get another tractor out here. Get to work and bury them all if you have to," Gary screamed from the crowd of workers. He was frantic and caught between wanting to run away from me and having one of the biggest paydays of his life.

My eyes narrowed at him and found that my vision had pressed down into points, my peripherals blacked out as if I was looking through a pinhole of light. The buzzing in my chest and the pain thrumming through my entire body pulsed with a wave of malice as I watched him. The bastard had still been trying to convince the few who would listen to him to get back to work.

This man deserves damnation.

A voice resonating in the back of my mind brought my attention back to my surroundings. The voice had been mine but not at the same time. It was as if my voice had been doubled, one of them shifted an octave lower and then spoken through an old radio. The sound of it sent ice down my spine before my wrists pulsed with a burst of electricity that ran through me like wildfire.

When the heat dissipated, I blinked and realized that I was no longer in pain. Every sickening feeling that had washed through me was gone, replaced by a surge of energy. I felt oddly refreshed and invigorated which drew my eyes down to the glow surrounding my forearms. The tattoos were glowing, outlined in a halo of white light around the black ink. What caught me off guard, however, was small burning embers drifting from my fingers, the same color of glow that had been burnt into the soil around me.

The green embers were… coming from me?

A sudden rumble of a diesel engine roaring to life shook me out of my daze and toward Gary. He was hitting one of the workers who looked distraught and terrified and had forced him into one of the sitting excavators. He was being annoyingly persistent about this job, even for his standards.

"Gary, you need to stop this. Now!" I snarled, my eyes narrowing at the man once more as I began stomping toward him.

"No, this is *my* land, boy! *I* paid for it and I will do whatever the fuck *I* want," Gary raged, balling his fists tightly and shaking them at me.

As I moved forward toward him like a coming storm I found Lex moving in my direction, her eyes solely focused on the heavy machinery instead of me. When her eyes met mine, she gave me a curt nod as we crossed paths, flames beginning to rise and lick from her pupils and hair. By the time she stopped to stand in front of the excavator, her hair was a fiery beacon against the darkening evening sky.

"It's not *your* land, motherfucker," Lex roared, balling her fists which began to glow as cyan-colored flames rose from her hands before she put her palms together in front of her. "It's theirs!"

Fire erupted in pillars across the parking lot as every tractor and excavator was hit with a roaring bonfire that began consuming the machinery. The blue flames burned hot, melting and warping the metal giants into crumpled, disfigured piles of scrap. The only thing louder than the crackling of flames and whining of melting metal in the field was the screams of terrified men. All of them ran and clamored into their work trucks, throwing dirt and rocks as they fled as desperately as they could. They abandoned what they could, soon leaving the field in nothing but the snapping embers of fire and its ethereal blue ominous glow.

And Gary. Alone in front of me.

"I warned you," I said, my voice going cold as I balled my fists at my side. I couldn't help but smirk as Gary watched his dream project, quite literally, go up in flames. "You were told to give this place up, move on, and be a fucking asshole somewhere else. But you didn't listen."

"What… the hell are you?" Gary whimpered pitifully, eyes wide and his voice filled with delicious tendrils of fear.

"Retribution," I answered distantly as I felt every reservation inside me snap.

As I stepped forward, Gary surprised me by taking the first swing at me, his fist whirling lazily in my direction. I ignored it, taking the weak punch in my left cheek before I lunged forward and tackled him to the ground. He took another desperate swing, again ignoring the desire to dodge, and felt a twinge of pain in my cheek.

I had better things to focus on instead of a droplet of blood on my tongue; like how nicely his pathetic mop of hair fit in my fist while I held him down. I bathed in the delight of finally getting to punch Gary after so many years of holding back. He didn't have a contract with my name on it to save him anymore.

My fist pounded against him for a second time, then a third, followed by a fourth. Each commemorated a year that I'd had to put up with his attitude, behavior, and abuse. Fittingly, I heard a pop and felt a surge of pain roar through my hand on that one. Still, I hit him again, calling it vengeance for how he'd treated people. His wife, kids, his employees, the victims of the Sand Hollow Massacre, business associates, sex workers, people in general, everyone he'd ever belittled.

As I came down on him for another blow, I found myself restrained and hoisted backward. Instead of my fist, I kicked outward, slamming my boot into his crotch, and gleamed with pride.

He wheezed, rolling into a fetal position as he clutched himself tightly, his hands not knowing whether he wanted to cradle his ruined face or his shriveled-up dick. Eventually, through his tears and cries of agony, he got onto all fours and crawled away. I grinned and laughed, ignoring the sound of my disembodied voice, wanting to watch this piece of shit man shrivel up and suffer.

"Jason, my friend, you need to stop," Ouray said, his voice cutting through the fog. It helped to drag me out of the darkness that had me hellbent on hurting Gary further.

I was pulled to my feet and then spun around, my vision locking onto Professore Whitestone and Paul Monroe. Both of them usually had gentle demeanors, however, they looked at me with scrutiny. Then their eyes widened and both of them took a step away from me. The brightness in my sight and the glow of my tattoos seemed to fade before I was hit with a dose of reality.

I had just beat the hell out of Gary. And I hadn't cared if I was to go far enough to kill the man either. My mind briefly remembered racing towards the cursed energy before my memory went hazy. I blinked and held up my arms to inspect my wrists which I could feel thrumming with a light burning sensation.

Had I been possessed or was it something else?

The glow of blue flames had died down, leaving spots of fire still burning on the hunks of metal that had once been the heavy machinery. Lex backed into me, her breathing shaky as she stared in wonder at the destruction she'd created with wide astonished eyes.

"I… I did that. Holy shit," she whispered nervously.

"Hey, Jason, lemme see your hand real quick," Xander said, coming to my side and taking my right hand into his. As he held it up to his eyes, pain thrummed like a struck chord when he tentatively touched my index finger. It was swollen and already turned a shade of sickly purple at the knuckle. "Doesn't look broken, but I'mma need to reset it."

Before I could question him, he set the finger, causing me to let out a hissed scream of pain. In that moment of mind-numbing agony I realized that in my haste to beat the shit out of Gary, I had dislocated my finger. I had heard that if you threw a punch wrong you could break your fingers. Until then, I hadn't had the need or desire to actually punch someone.

My first time doing it and I'd nearly fucked up my hand.

"Jason, what was all of this? What in God's name just happened?" Paul pressed, his hands grabbing me by the shoulders to try and shake some sense into me.

"Jason, my brother, I've never seen you act that way before, and your eyes," Ouray trailed off.

"My eyes?" I said, giving the two men a questioning glance and shaking my head in confusion.

"They were black as obsidian," Chipeta said, coming to crowd around beside us. Her arms still had spider web-like veins of inky blackness trailing up them that seemed to be receding over time. "We had resigned ourselves to our fates and instead, you took on the burden of our curse."

"That's impossible… right?" Lex said, shaking her head at Chipeta in disbelief.

The two men in front of me looked from me, then to Lex, and then to a spot where they presumed the medicine woman was standing. They were incorrect. They couldn't see or hear her so they'd only picked up Lex's side of the conversation.

"I… I don't know what happened with my eyes but Chipeta says I somehow absorbed the curse that Gary's crew had started?" I said, more questions in my tone than answers. However, at the mention of a curse, both men took in a sharp breath of air. "Her, Wakkara, and Joseph had stepped in at first, that's why the excavator was bugging out. But… I don't think they were the ones that did that…"

My voice trailed off as my eyes found the machinery that had started it all. I narrowed my eyes at the twisted scorpion tail-looking structure of its bucket and arm. It looked as if it was part of a poorly constructed metal sculpture among the melted heap of scrap beneath it.

"Still, how were you able to absorb the curse?" Chipeta asked as Lex nodded vigorously with her.

"I have no clue honestly how I absorbed the curse," I said with a sigh, making sure Ouray and Paul were still partially involved.

"I have anointing oil in my car. I'm sure the professor and I could give you a priesthood blessing," Paul asked, his eyes carefully watching me as if demon horns were going to pop out of my head.

"No, I'm fine," I chuckled, shaking my head and then looking down at the ground in contemplation.

"What about the blue fire? Was that you, miss?" Ouray asked, his bright brown eyes looking at Lex with interest, his eyes rolling upward to watch the flames dancing in her hair.

"Y-Yeah… that was me," Lex smiled sheepishly, unsure if she should've been proud of admitting her actions or not.

"Does that mean that you were at the Wells Fargo building a couple of weeks ago?" Paul asked, tilting his head with fascination.

"Um… yeah… that was me too," Lex gulped, turning her head away in shame. She then quickly took in a breath and gave Paul a frantic look. "But it was an accident, I swear! A demon tried to hurt Mom and… I didn't exactly know what I was doing with my power."

"Which is why my clan put me in charge of being this lil' firecracker's bodyguard," Xan chuckled, reaching out to ruffle Lex's hair with a jest and snuff it out.

"Your… clan?" Paul asked with hesitation.

Oh boy, this was not the conversation I expected would be happening tonight.

"So… it's all a long story. And, it may or may not affect your beliefs and worldview," I said, giving Paul a small chuckle and an apologetic look.

"Jason, I've known you for a while and I've had to come to terms with ghosts being real. She throws fireballs, which… is definitely something," Paul laughed, giving me and Lex a beaming grin while putting his fists on his hips. "You're acting like you're about to tell me Twilight or Hercules are real or something."

Lex and I shared a careful glance. Paul watched our reaction, his smile falling as his chuckle faded into a choked breath. When neither of us wanted to answer first and chuckle at his self-perceived quip, he gulped.

"Oh…"

Well, this was turning into a long fucking night.

TONIGHT HAD BEEN GOING FROM BAD... TO BLOODY FUCKING WORSE.

It started with contemplating my interaction with Sinead last night, the moment that I had slapped her, which had cycled through my mind on repeat. Part of me wanted to apologize for lashing out. Another wanted to do it again because she was a constant reminder of what I'd lost.

Adi was one of my rocks. One of the three pieces that kept me grounded, and at peace, and made me less likely to fly off the handle. The part of me that saw Sinead as the reason for losing Adelaide said that the headless woman was nothing more than a cheap replacement.

Had Sinead been trying to replace Adi?

No. And I knew it wasn't fair that I slapped her. Nor had it been fair that I said as much to her before I left the house today. The pain and anger I felt had been swirling, building from the moment Adi vanished with that fucking demon bastard, and culminated in my actions. Sinead just seemed to be in the right place at the right time to take out my frustrations. And all she had done was try to touch me when I had been crying.

To top it off, Thomas had called Haley for an emergency meeting with the fangs, taking her away for the night. Then that fucking cunt Gary made it so that I had no one in my corner tonight. Of course, he'd pulled some dumb shit to drag Jason away in an emergency.

The fucking bastard.

So there I was, no one to keep me in check, while I watched my girls struggle against our rivals, Diamond Ridge Junior High. It was halfway through the third quarter, down by 15 and, over the past two weeks we'd gone 1 and 3. Losing tonight would mean my girls, the Canyon Hills Blackhawks, would be knocked out of the junior varsity state playoffs. Beaten by the fucking godsdamned Miners.

Salt in the wound; they were beating us with a girl whose janky ass shot form looked as bad as their dollar store mascot. However, she could pass and drive like a proper star and was killing us on the interior. Which meant she felt entitled to constantly run her mouth on my players. It didn't help that the refs were whistle-happy when it came to calling fouls on us, but not them.

Perfect example, Gentry, our star point-center, was body slammed and thrown against the stanchion as she drove inside off of a pick-and-roll.

She screamed in pain from her shoulder hitting the paper-thin padding of the stanchion. However, instead of drawing the foul that should've sent her to the line for two free throws, Gentry was called for an offensive foul. That meant that not only did our star floor general have to ride the bench, but it gave the Miners possession with six minutes left in the third.

"Watch the switch!" I called out in real-time, as the Miners ran their offense. My eyes darted back and forth over the ten girls on the court, reading for weaknesses we could exploit. "Stay on 15! Hit the pass!"

I grinned wide as the duo of Trista and Mia pounced on the play. The larger of the two girls rolled under an oncoming screen, arms outstretched to block a diving pass into the basket. Instead, it forced the Miners' star player to throw a wayward pass outside. Mia was already on the run, catching the ball mid-pass and rushing down the court as fast as she could.

They had one defender rushing back to cut the smaller Latina girl off but missed the interception of a bounce pass aimed at the taller and stronger umber-skinned girl. Trista caught the bounce pass before skipping it back to Mia, throwing the defender off balance with no chance to bat the high lob pass into Trista's hands. With her arm outstretched, she screamed with exertion as she threw the ball down through the hoop. After dunking the ball, Trista roared with pride as she did a small pull-up on the rim and then dropped to the floor.

"That's my girls! Back down on defense and get another stop," I shouted, happily clapping my hands with one of the first genuine smiles of the night. Pride swelled with the dunk and the knowledge that only three girls in the entire state could do so. And I coached two of them.

Then everything went to shit in a matter of two seconds.

Amidst all of the cheers from our side and boos from their side, I made out several words from the adults in the crowd. I could get frustrated with the comments about telling me to go back to Africa or go back to the zoo. I played them off, grinned-and-beared-it at the highly unoriginal insults and slurs.

Then I heard the one word that made me see red and had a growl filtering through my throat. It didn't take me long to turn around and spot who had thrown the word my way because of how proud they were to say it. Again. It was mildly ironic that it had come from a guy wearing a hat reading Jesus Is Love who hadn't been shy about using the hard R.

Then, before I could confront them, I heard a slew of whistles on the court and turned to see Mia instantly pleading with the ref in front of her. She was getting hit with a technical foul for the audacious act of clapping, however, her eyes had been set on the girl she was guarding. She was being punished for fucking little more than playing the game and being competitive.

"Seriously? A tech for clapping?" I snarled as I ran down and got between the ref and Mia. He rolled his eyes and looked away from me as he made Mia's foul call official.

"If she keeps taunting, she's getting tossed," the ref threatened, pointing at me first and then at Mia.

"*Taunting*?" I scoffed incredulously, staying within inches of the guy as he backed away like a coward. "If you wanna throw someone out so badly, how about some of the bloody parents? They're practically cussing at the top of their lungs in front of the kids."

As if to prove my point, those same parents screamed again, telling the ref to throw me out, only using much more colorful language. Including a certain word, loud enough for everyone to hear. The parents around the couple did nothing but either shoot them dirty looks or laugh. The girls on my team and the opposing team, however, all winced at the word.

I gave the ref an expectant look, my eyes asking him to do something. He, of course, didn't do a damn thing.

Before I could stop myself, I turned on my heel and stomped toward them, rage billowing inside me. I towered over both of them, glaring as I folded my arms tight over my breasts. The wife cowered, however, the husband felt a certain way about himself.

"This isn't some dive bar. Let's not use that kind of language here around kids," I said, as calmly as I possibly could.

"Aww, did we hurt your feelings? Are you gonna cry? Freedom of speech, *bitch*!" The wife said in a whiny voice, mimicking crying motions before outright snarling at me.

I turned and looked at the refs, waiting for a reaction. Still nothing.

"Get the fuck outta here. Job stealing monkey whore," the husband sneered before snorting and spitting a large wad of mucus at my feet.

The refs finally approached me from behind and part of me was really hoping they would handle this situation because I was starting to see red. My beast was feeding off this couple's hate and prejudice like it was wine, making the hair on the back of my neck stand on end, hoping for an easy meal. I had gotten close enough that when I pushed into the husband, his trucker cap flexed so that it nearly fell off his head. All while giving me the biggest shit-eating grins they possibly could.

"Back down to the court or you will be ejected, Coach," the ref threatened.

"Then handle them, or *I* will," I retorted, narrowing my eyes at him.

"Come on Coach, let's just play. They aren't worth the trouble," Gentry said, the tall brunette appearing behind the ref with her eyes full of pleading.

I gave in to that urge and turned to follow the girl back down to the court. I wanted to just win and prove these parents wrong. I wanted to make them stick their foot in their mouth. But I needed the refs to do their damn jobs.

"That's it, listen to the white girl like a good whipped ni-"

The wife lunged at me as she spoke, forcefully pushing against my back as she sneered at me. She, however, never finished her sentence. My fist balled and I turned on her, driving a right hook to her jaw. Her lip was bloody in an instant as she fell to the ground.

Instead of helping his wife up, the husband took a swing at me. It was a sloppy punch that I easily caught in one hand. His eyes went wide when I didn't budge with his force then he fell to the floor as I kicked his feet out from under him.

Hands grabbed me, voices screaming in my ear, as I glared at the two of them slowly picking themselves up off of the bleachers. Before I registered what was happening, I was being dragged toward the locker room by a mix of refs and parents. Then I was officially tossed out of the game.

The last thing I saw was the dejected expressions on every player and coach on both sides. That and Valerie, our mousey computer nerd backup point guard, showing me her phone. She'd recorded the entire incident for posterity and promised she'd send it to me.

Good on her, I might need that soon to plead my case.

I paced the locker room well into the fourth quarter, the muffled sounds of cheers and boos creating a white noise that attempted to drown out my thoughts. The pacing worked and I felt calm until I made one mistake regarding my emotions and memories. The last time we played the Miners, I had nearly been to my breaking point like this.

With that same couple in fact.

However, during halftime, Adi came into the locker room and held me for a few minutes. Her touch and voice distracted me from all of the bullshit to clear my head and think straight.

It had also helped that Haley and Jason threatened legal action since they both knew a pair of really good lawyers who would go to bat for me. Tonight, however, I was alone. My mind latched onto Adi being gone and was tempted by the thought that she would never come back.

I lost it.

An unbearable wave of anger mixed with depressive anguish like a raging river, creating whitecaps around stones of bittersweet memories. They lapped at my control, desperately wanting me to lose what little hope I had left inside me. The barrier that I reinforced with memories of Adi - her touch, the sound of her voice and laugh, her scent, her taste - began to crack.

The sounds of the crowd were drowned out by the crunching of metal, slight stings of pain burning against my fists, and a warm wash of tears streaming down my cheeks. I was sobbing, going off into a fit of rage, and I'd already taken out my frustration on two poor sets of empty lockers before moving to another. I promised I wouldn't take my rage out on anyone living, Sinead withstanding, and instead turned defenseless, lifeless metal into my victims. I'd caved in an entire endcap of lockers when the creak and heavy click of a door filled my ears.

"Coach… Taylor?"

The sound of Mia's voice behind me made me freeze while the sound of her rapid heartbeat filled my ears like drums pounding against my mind. I had a split second of realization when my eyes opened that the skin of my arms was no longer there and had been replaced by the fur of my leopard. The humming breeze of the air conditioning tickled my ears higher than normal and the phantom weight of my tail froze in place behind me. In my fit of rage and anguish, I had gone halfway into my shift and there was no way I looked entirely human. Worst of all, there had now been a witness to it.

Bloody fucking bollocks.

"Is that really you?" Mia asked, her voice laced with fear and anticipation stinging at me from the inside out.

The thought of no longer being able to coach or teach at the school anymore hit me like a wrecking ball. My knees buckled. I was losing everything in the blink of an eye and I fell as a fresh wave of sobbing took over.

"This… you weren't supposed to see me like this," I said, after a long moment, my voice watery and thrumming with anguish. I resigned myself to fate as I turned, sitting with my back against the ruined lockers, showing one of my favorite players and students the monster I truly was. "What are you doing here, Mia?"

"Holy shit, you-"

"Language, young lady," I interjected, narrowing my eyes at her.

Mia stared at me wide-eyed and began laughing, her voice echoing throughout the empty locker room with a hint of joy and amusement. It helped to warm the cold dreariness I was caught up in.

"Yeah, you're definitely still our coach," she snickered. She looked from me, up to the lockers, then to me. Her eyes focused on my cheeks and the hot, wet tracks staining them. "Is everything okay?"

Ah, the big fucking question.

"Truthfully," I began, rolling my head backward to look up at the lockers I'd punched into oblivion. "I'd be lying if I said I was."

"And you'd be breaking your rule number three," Mia nodded with confirmation.

Go figure, she'd throw my own words back in my face. I had them in place as the core values I taught my girls. They were also posted around my classroom. It was something meant for the kids to live by so that they'd be better off in life. I'd never imagined them being thrown back at me.

Rule one; show up. Rule two; work hard. Rule three; don't lie.

"So," Mia started, her eyes scanning the ground at her feet before she made the bold decision of sitting down on the tile with me. "The rumors are true, you and Miss Chavez are brujas?"

I snickered. Then I began laughing at the comment I hadn't expected. Every student and teacher had heard the rumors, sure. Now, however, Mia was one of only two students who had gone and actually asked to see if the rumors were true.

"No," I chuckled and looked at my semi-transformed hands. "I'm not a witch."

"You're something else though," Mia nodded.

I looked at the short Latina girl for a long time before tilting my head and narrowing my eyes at her. Her heartbeat was still racing and an air of nervousness around her that I could taste on the tip of my tongue. But there was something else; an air of excitement and fascination. Then I remembered who I was talking to.

Mia Guttirez - the short and speedy girl with long, dark chocolate brown hair and bronze skin - wasn't just one of my star players. She was also far too bright and analytical for her own good sometimes. Her idea of fun was being nose-deep in a book about some science subjects that were far too intelligent for me to understand myself.

There was a reason she was one of only fifteen students taking AP science and biology classes. Which was why she was the star student of Mr. Ed, our resident science, biology, and chemistry teacher.

The guy paced the teacher's lounge after every visit with her when she'd brought questions after class. Everything from String Theory, parallel universes, a virus that could create real-life zombies, and... cryptozoology.

Fuck.

"How bad is it out there?" I asked, trying to dodge the subject of myself.

"Oh, the parents you kicked the hell out of were thrown out. Get this, they're Brittany Fullbrook's parents!" Mia laughed, shaking her head. Go figure they'd conceived the Miners' star player. It made sense why she would talk so much shit to opposing teams; she'd obviously learned it somewhere. "*But* you missed the other big fight."

"Bloody fucking hell, there was another fight?" I sighed, rolling my head back to hit it against the lockers. Starting a fight had been the last thing I'd wanted for tonight. However, without Adi, Haley, or Jason there, part of me knew that, with my attitude, it had been inevitable.

"Mhmm, the mascots got into it," Mia nodded excitedly, her eyes lit up with amusement.

"Well shit, I would've loved to see that," I sighed, shaking my head and looking up at the ceiling. "Please tell me Bryce won."

Bryce was a tall, lanky, and fairly reserved kid until he put on the costume he wore as Falco, our school's mascot. He was a completely different person under the mask. It was like the cartoonish black peregrine falcon with big aviator goggles and a WWII-style bomber jacket changed him.

Maybe it was the top of the suit that made it so you had to wear the coat open to display a big puffy feathered chest and comically muscled abdomen? Because when the kid was Falco, he was running around, doing backflips, somersaults, and various other stunts to get the crowd hyped up.

He'd also done the mascot thing where they would wordlessly flirt with the players, cheerleaders, and girls in the crowd. It got laughs and blushes alike when he'd come up, sit with them, and put his arm around them while offering giant stuffed animals shaped like a falcon. In fact, it seemed to have worked because the falcon had been kissed on the cheek more times than any of the boys on the junior varsity basketball or football teams combined.

"Bryce totally pummeled Petey the Prospector, stole his mascot head and everything," Mia laughed brightly.

"That's bloody brilliant! Ugh, I wish I could've seen it," I said, sighing with exasperation but wearing a wide smile that most likely showed off my fangs.

"Oh, we're *totally* getting it cause Val filmed the whole thing," Mia confirmed. "Though we probably won't get it until tomorrow morning."

"Oh? Why's that?" I asked, my face twisting to pure curiosity.

"Cause Val is definitely gonna keep him up all night," Mia said, grinning wide. Then she rolled her eyes when she looked at me again and found my face full of confusion. "Don't tell me you didn't know they were dating? That's, like, the *biggest* tea in the locker room."

Realization dawned on me.

"I'll have to have a talk with Valerie, you girls are much too young for that stuff," I said, trying to have a tone of scolding though I knew better.

This was coming from a person who had been sexually active since the age of thirteen and had a relatively high body count. I knew better than anyone that most people started exploring their sexuality at the same time puberty hit us like a ton of bricks. Us adults just choose to ignore it and say that teens were far too innocent to be thinking of anything like that. I, more than anyone, didn't have room to throw stones in a house of glass.

Hello pot, meet my friend kettle.

"Speaking of hot and heavy," Mia beamed with a devious grin. "Where's Hotty McGee and your girlfriends anyway? Do they know about this? Oh, do guys bang when you're like this?"

"Mia!" I said, my eyes wide while I shouted in a scolding tone.

Then my face fell at the immediate thought of Adelaide flooding my mind. "We… Adi…"

"Oh… I'm sorry Coach, I didn't," Mia began, her words trailing off as a sadness of her own took over. She gave me a pitying look like she could understand what I was feeling.

"No, it's okay. We didn't break up but Adi… She's gone missing. Then Jason and Haley both had an emergency with work so," I said trailing off once again. "I'm not sure you're ready for all of this, Mia."

Mia gave me a contemplative look, then moved to stand up, disappearing down one of the isles of lockers. I heard her twisting the combination and a metal clanking sound erupted as the latch to a locker clicked. Then I heard her feet padding back toward me before a couple of small weights landed in my lap. I looked up at her, my head tilted in confusion before I looked down into my lap to see what she'd dropped there.

I looked down at three novels that I knew all too well thanks to both Adelaide and Haley. One of the covers had the image of a black woman in the forefront with a large male figure looming behind her with pitch-black skin and horns. The second book had a white woman with long red hair and large breasts surrounded by four men with animalistic eyes. The third was of a short blonde white woman casually holding a very large male figure behind her with black skin and a white deer skull for a face.

He was holding her as well… by the throat.

I shot a look up at her, readying to scold her for these three books being wildly inappropriate for a girl her age. My eyes were readying to give her a stern glare, however, the clear, cold, and analytical gaze she gave me in return froze me.

"Try me."

I TILTED MY HEAD CURIOUSLY AT THE SIGHT IN FRONT OF ME.

Thomas had called me to the hospital, mostly to have me meet with the fangs, however, this was something I wasn't expecting. We were in Aniah's room, her last night in the hospital and he was here to make sure she got the rest she needed. The way they were holding hands, how disheveled he looked from being by her side, and how they looked at each other confirmed my suspicions. Thomas had fallen for her harder than I'd ever thought possible.

"As my Skoll, what do you think the pack will make of this?" Thomas asked, his eyes roaming over the curvaceous African American woman with a mix of hunger and adoration.

"Honestly, boss, I don't think you should give a damn about what they say," I shrugged, giving Aniah a smirk as she tossed him a flirty wiggle of her brows. "You want her, she wants you, so what does it matter? You're the Odin, you make the rules."

"See, sug, I told she'd be on your side," Aniah teased, giving Thomas a playful jab of her elbow. "Sides, my girl has been getting along mighty fine with that boy you've had her running around with."

"She has?" Thomas asked, furrowing his brow at her and then looking to me for confirmation.

"Oh yeah," I snorted, then gave Aniah a Cheshire smile and narrowed glare. "I mean, they haven't done the deed - *yet* - but gods the girl knows how to scream his name. Kept us up most of the night earlier this week."

Thomas looked horrified while Aniah burst out into laughter, the sound of it filling the room with her melodic cajun charm and tone. Looking at both of them I smiled and sighed, letting my shoulder relax a little. They were great together, they completed each other in the best ways. Just like I had been trying to find forever and found in Jason and Adi. Mickie and I still had our rough patches but we were getting better. A far cry from how we treated each other even six months ago.

We were still mending everything we'd said and done to each other for six years. And, truthfully, I still had patches from my childhood that I was still mending, most of which had been worked through because of the man in front of me.

"If you want my complete honesty, Thomas, I would be an

absolute puta if I didn't give you two my blessing," I said, my eyes training on my alpha entirely. "You allowed Jason in and let me find a place where I feel like I truly belong. And that's by his side. You gave me a home when my parents left for San Antonio and you let me crash at your place most of my childhood. Hell, even when I had my own place, you paid for my apartment from the time I was ten 'til I was 22. You've given me friends, family, a job, and then you allowed Mickie and I to become your Skoll and Hati."

My eyes fell onto the flowers sitting on the bedside table, inspecting the bright yellow lilies that complimented Aniah's dark copper and bronze skin. The same shade as her favorite blouse she'd wear when visiting Thomas at the Volk Haus offices. The same ones that were delivered to Thomas' hospital room three months ago.

"And besides, she sent you flowers and visited you when Moira fucked you up back in August. Aniah was here more than Cam, Eddy, and me," I felt my eyes narrow and the last of my thoughts trailed off beyond words. There was a cold anger inside me that made my wolf stir.

"Like I told you before, Haley, Sam didn't know I'd gotten hurt," Thomas sighed, seeming to read my mind. He knew better than anyone how I viewed his ex-wife.

Puta was chasing dick in Seattle long before Eric vanished, his death just gave her an easy excuse.

Thomas grumbled, letting a low growl trickle through his throat which made Aniah shiver with delight while the heat of his power pricked across my skin like needles. I hated how it seemed like he could read me like an open book. Then again I was, by some accounts, basically his illegitimate daughter with how he looked after me.

"Speaking of which, Aniah has convinced me to finish what Samantha had started years ago before Dean's death," Thomas said, making my ears and brows perk. He gave me a soft smile as I gave him a confused look that widened into astonishment.

"The adoption program?" I asked, my voice going a little breathy.

"Yes," he nodded curtly. "I'm in talks with many of the alphas across the West Coast and Midwest to open up a line to make sure what happened to you will never befall another of our young ones."

"Blame Lex," Aniah chuckled. "I took the girl in not knowin' a thing about the bigger world. I just knew we all end up in the other place in the end and it doesn't matter if we're of the same people. Now there ain't a person alive who could tell me she ain't my daughter."

"So the interconnected pack adoption project is-"

"Nearly complete," Thomas said, finishing my sentence that had trailed off into a distant whisper as I felt my cheeks become wet with hot tracks of tears. "The other alphas and I will be finalizing the arrangements in a meeting during Beltane."

I launched myself forward, wrapping my arms around the big man's neck and squeezing him tight. I hugged him with every ounce of strength inside of me as I buried my face into the crook of his neck, fighting the urge to sob… and call him dad.

This project was because of me. He'd done everything he could to give me a fighting chance at life when my parents hadn't cared. Samantha had laid the loose framework for something I had said in passing when I was a child; about how there should be a way for young ones to find a home with a family from other packs. But it was Thomas who was putting up the foundation and doing all of the heavy lifting.

Because of me.

Before I could hug Thomas any longer - or harder - a vibration against my breast pulled me away from him. He gave me a curious glance as I pulled my phone from the space to the side of my bra. He was a guy so I gave him the benefit of the doubt when it came to not understanding the universal built-in pockets we women had. I narrowed my eyes at the screen to see several notifications.

JASON

Fucking Gary! The dipshit has me heading to Sand Hollow. Mickie is going to need extra love when we get home. See you when I get back. I love you, Little Wolf.

RENEE

Northeast parking garage. Lower level. Meet you in 30 minutes.

"Looks like the fangs are on their way," I said, sighing as I tucked my phone away and ran my fingers through my hair. "Any idea what Sebastian or Reneé want?"

"No," Thomas said with a sighed shrug. "Only that they requested you or McKenna for more information on something."

"I really hate how ominous they have to be," I groaned, rolling my eyes as I moved to collect my jacket off of the chair I had been sitting in. "If you need anything else, just lemme know."

"Thank you, Haley," Thomas said, his attention fluttering back toward Aniah as I made my way to the door.

"My Odin," I said, crossing a fist over my heart and dipping at the waist in a small bow toward the big man.

"Selene be with you, my Skoll," he replied, giving me a curt nod before he turned and moved to hover over the bed with a towering presence that made Aniah giggle like a schoolgirl.

I didn't need to see the two of them get worked up over each other so I promptly left the room and began making my way down the hall. I was nearing the elevators when something caught my eye. I narrowed them as I watched a woman shifting nervously as she ducked into a hidden nook.

It wasn't the woman's actions that caught my eye but the woman herself. Because I knew I had seen the blonde highlighted pixie haircut before.

Ifollowed the familiar-looking charge nurse into the nook where I found the doors to the stairwell. Slipping through the slowly closing door I heard her feet echoing through the hollow chamber as she rushed downward toward the parking garage. I felt my beast rumble with delight as we gave chase, silently chasing the woman to the ground floor and into the dimly lit parking garage until we found our prey.

If it was anyone else, I would have said the nurse was wonderfully attractive with her slim, athletic build, feathered hair, and deep blue eyes. Her narrow oval features gave her a look that was somewhere between conventionally attractive and supermodel gorgeous. If it was anyone else and not the person who had caused so much emotional damage to Jason.

My Jason.

"What are you doing here, Brian?" She said, sneering up at a tall, muscular man leaning back on the hood of a car. Seeing the two confront each other I pressed my back against a corner, leaning enough to watch and listen to the exchange just out of view.

"Baby, c'mon, you ended us over a damn text. I wanna know the reason," Brian said, his voice wavering between angry and pitiful. "Just give me a good reason, Karynn."

"Because *I* don't have time to deal with you anymore," she retorted, folding her arms tight over her breasts and looking up at him with a scowl.

"It's 'cause of that other guy ain't it? *You* said I was better. Fuck, you ditched that idiot for me and now you're gonna go back to him?" Brian whined, his fists balling tight as he got up from his leaning position to get into her face.

My blood began to boil as my wolf batted against the mental cage that held her back. The idea that Karynn wanted to stroll back into Jason's life had my claws pinching against my palms, my knuckles bleaching white from tension.

"Brian, sweety, you're cute when you're stupid like this, you know that?" Karynn snorted, shaking her head with a wide grin.

"I'm *not* stupid," Brian roared, reaching out and grabbing Karynn by the arm with enough force her tanned skin went pale from pressure. She merely looked at the offending hold he had on her then upward to meet his eyes with a scowl.

"Let. Go. Now," Karynn said coldly, her eyes narrowing at him. "I don't even give a shit about the guy. Why do you think it was so easy to dump his limp dick?"

Says the woman who stalks Jason's profile and likes every single one of his posts.

"Limp dick? Honestly, when was the last time we saw our Prime limp?" My wolf scoffed, rolling her big golden eyes just behind my mental barrier.

"Then it's some other guy, right?" Brian snarled, jerking Karynn toward him.

"Ugh! You're so fucking boring," Karynn groaned, doing nothing to pull her arm away from him.

Brian let out a grunt of frustration before his free hand cupped the back of Karynn's head, forcefully pulling her into a kiss. He mouthed her desperately while she had zero reaction to him at all. When he realized she wasn't returning the gesture, he pushed the woman back and stomped his foot like a toddler throwing a temper tantrum.

"Seriously, Brian, what do you want?" Karynn said with a bored tone, giving the exasperated man a look of indifference.

"I want you to get in the car. I wanna hear you say you're not going back to that beta bitch. I wanna hear you say you're mine," he scoffed, his feet beginning to take him in small frantically pacing circles. His hands forcefully gestured his points before he stopped and looked down at her with anger fuming in his eyes. "I want the truth, Karynn."

With anger burning in his eyes, he returned a hand to the top of her head, grabbing her by the hair and jerking her face to face with him. She still showed no reaction to his touch, his anger, or his words. She was baiting him into trying something extremely stupid.

"The truth?" She snorted, an evil smile curling on her lips. "Fine.

Sure you've got a big dick but you have no idea how to use it. Your dumbass hasn't made me finish in years. You don't know how to get the job done."

"That's not what you said last night when I-"

"I was faking you stupid fucking meathead," Karynn whined, interrupting Brian and rolling her eyes. "Hell, I've been faking for four years ever since I threatened to charge that guy with rape when it was your cum leaking out of me."

"You what?!"

Okay, that's enough of this shit show.

As Brian reared back a fist to strike Karynn, I stepped in. Within a second I was between him and the other woman, holding his fist in my palm and easily holding him back with one hand. I glared up at the big man, letting my wolf prowl against the surface of my eyes to give him a hint of the danger he'd just found himself in.

He stared at his fist in disbelief before trailing his eyes down toward me where I stood at half his height and muscle tone. I gave him cold indifference as I threw his fist away, making him stumble back toward the hood of the car that he'd been leaning on.

"Pretty sure she said to get away from her, *Brian*," I said, my tone low and trickling with a primal growl.

"Oh? And what're you gonna do about it?" He scoffed, stumbling back onto his feet and readying himself to come at me.

I shrugged, took a step forward to what I assumed was his car, and reached down. With little more than a snarl, I grabbed the front bumper and lifted it, raising the wheels off of the ground. Then to add a little more to the spectacle I shuffled sideward, turning the car out of its parking stall before dropping it. The car's suspension groaned and rocked to its limit as it bounced off of the ground and righted itself, my eyes never leaving Brian.

For his efforts, Brian's fight or flight kicked in and he stumbled backward, falling on his ass. He whimpered in fear as he scrambled on his hands and knees to rush into the vehicle. Within seconds, the car started and rubber screamed against the pavement as he sped out of the parking garage, nearly taking out several other cars and a cement support structure in his haste to get away.

I was also pretty sure he screamed and I scented the trace of urine.

"Wow, thanks for that, girl," Karynn whistled before chuckling. "I can't thank you enough for getting that monster… away from me…"

I turned to face the taller brunette, the parking garage bathing me in light as she finally saw my face. It didn't take long for her to recognize me and know who I was as I narrowed my eyes on her. With dawning realization etched on her expression, my lips curled into a smirk and I scented the fear and intimidation radiating off of her. My wolf licked her lips at the sensation.

"Not a problem. Gotta be careful around the guys you hang out with, mamacita," I said, my tone coming out in a melodic sing-song tone but held no delight in it whatsoever. "You should also probably be careful of the guys you talk shit about. Never know who you might run into."

"I didn't-"

"No more stalking his socials, got it?" I said, my voice dipping low with threatening malice behind it. "And if I ever hear you be so callous about how you treated Jason or call him limp dicked ever again? I. *Will*. Hunt you."

"I swear I-"

"That guy is only pretending to be a monster, Karynn. Me, on the other hand?" I said, moving to get in her face as a devilish grin curled my lips higher. Fear flashed across her eyes and I knew that, in my rage, my fangs had lengthened and my eyes had probably rolled to that of my wolf's. "Well... Let's just say you insulted a man who happens to satisfy *his* monsters... very well~"

"R-Right! I uh... Thanks?" Karynn stammered as she backed away slowly.

She gave a half-hearted wave before she turned and ran for the stairwell door, hitting it unceremoniously in her rush to get away from me. I sighed as she disappeared behind the heavy metal door, leaving me alone in the parking garage to collect myself and calm down.

"That was a splendid show," said a feminine voice with a thick French accent, gentle, slow clapping sounds echoing through the structure.

Well... mostly alone.

"Is that why you wanted to see me, Reneé?" I asked exasperatedly, turning to find a lithe figure slipping out of the shadows with a liquid movement.

A pleasant smile curled onto her lips, the bright red stain gleaming in the lights of the parking garage. Her lifted brows displayed her amusement as specks of light reflected across her glossy pure black eyes that gave no indication of her emotions. Her playful movements made the wine-red cocktail dress she wore sway open from where it clung tight to her thin hips and supple rear.

The heels of her black knee-high stiletto boots clicked across the concrete toward me as she placed her hands behind her back and tilted forward at the hip. The gesture made her black trench coat open wide and the top of her dress hung down to expose a long valley of pale creamy skin and a pair of small breasts. A brief glance before her long waves of chestnut hair fell, framing her sharp angular features, pouty lips, and small upturned nose.

"No, but it did give me excitement I wasn't aware I was... *hungering* for tonight," she answered, her tone sickly sweet as her fangs gleamed against her lips.

"So what is it then?" I said, rolling my eyes at her forced double-entendre.

This was why I hated dealing with vamps, they always put too much effort into making something into a pun about their bloodlust.

"Straight to business then," she chuckled before standing straight and looking down to idly inspect her fingernails like they were the most interesting thing in the world. "I've come to talk to you about that mate of yours you're so fond of. Red hair, blue eyes, a *delicious* body and mind?"

"What do you want with him?" I asked with a threatening rumble, feeling my body tense, hackles raised as I readied my fangs and claws for an attack. I could feel my lips quivering over my bared fangs like that of a pure-blood wolf. "I swear to Selene if you-"

"No, no, nothing… nefarious I assure you," Reneé cooed, grinning wider as she rolled her head up. The gesture was the same as if she would have had irises and pupils giving me a lidded look. "More of a proposition actually. One where you, McKenna, and I would be mutual liaisons as we bring your man into the fold. It is time after all."

"We're going at his pace, Reneé," I hissed, stepping toward her which only made her grin stretch wider. "He's not ready for everything out there."

"I doubt he'll have time to wade himself into the pool. Especially when we need to know if his skills could help in solving a little problem of Master Sebastian's," the vampire giggled softly, raising a finger to stroke my chin.

"And what would that be?" I shivered, trying to look just to the sides and not meet her gaze directly. I did not need to get mindfucked by a bloodsucker tonight.

"We know his past endeavors have been the demise of a demon, two curses, and many of the more hurtful tantrums of spirits. However, we want to know," Reneé sighed, continuing to stroke my chin before dropping a quiet atomic bomb. "Has he ever dealt with a succubus before?"

McKENNA

I CAME HOME TO A SIGHT I HADN'T EXPECTED.

I expected Jason home in his office or in the kitchen having shots after dealing with Gary. Or possibly him and Haley cuddling on the couch waiting for me. Or, even Lex and Xan cuddling on the couch binging yet another horror movie. Or there was the likely scenario of coming home to an empty apartment and reveling in the pride that my girls managed to claw their way to victory with a buzzer-beater from Mia that would have made Damian Lillard blush.

Or be able to breathe a sigh of relief that Mia herself had taken the news about me so well. So well, in fact, that she was now hoping that maybe - just maybe - the books she wasn't even old enough to be reading might not just be a far-fetched dream after all. I had not expected her, of all people, to be wishing to find her pre-human Prince Adam.

Instead, I found a soft blue glow illuminating the otherwise pitch-black apartment with all of the furniture spread open from the center of the living room. At its center were a slew of papers with a cross-sectioned map of northern Utah printed across their surface. Above it floated a skull wrapped in a swirl of rumbling hellfire, its eyes focused intently and shifting oddly as its bone brows narrowed at the map with scrutiny.

In a wide berth around the map were several objects and candles, strands of blue and white energy stretching between each point to create a pentacle in the center of the room. The star hovered over the map, spreading the glow and bathing the nude form of Sinead sitting at its peak in an ethereal light.

At the lowest two points sat Sinead's ring on one end and Adi's malachite crystal on the other. Seeing the black and pink fissured stone brought back the memory of the day that Jason had stored it in the office. I had felt the world around me crumble seeing him remove it and the hopelessness in his eyes as he did so. The two wings of the star held more of Adi's possessions. One point held a small pile of her favorite smutty books while the teal corset I'd bought her on our first date sat across from it.

I smiled at the memory of her wearing it and the teal thong that matched when we surprised Jason one night. He came home from the store to find Adi, Haley, and me in identical lingerie sets and collars. Jason had nearly dropped a wine bottle in shock.

It was odd to see Sinead's headless body sitting cross-legged, the stump of her neck pouring thick wisps of black smoke from blue smoldering embers. Moreover, the room was flooded with the scent of her, thick with the sweet smell of rain and sage. I then tilted my head in curiosity as the skull dipped down to the map and let out a breathy hissing sound while her body leaned forward and drew a circle around that point of the map.

The flames flickered as if they were running out of fuel, slowly snuffing out before her body caught the skull as it dropped out of the air. In the light of the candles, the flame around the skull flashed out of existence, her human face emerging and her eyes opening lazily as if she'd woken from a long nap.

"Welcome home, Mistress," Sinead said, her voice having a lazy edge of exhaustion to it.

"What… are you doing?" I asked, arching my brow in curiosity as I peered down at the map and then watched her reattach her head out of the corner of my eye. As I looked at the map more intently, I realized what was happening. "You… holy shit, is this the searching ritual you were talking about for Adi?"

I fell to my knees beside her, my eyes wide with excitement as I took in all of the spots she'd circled. I mentally drew an oblong shape around the outermost points including Strawberry, Tooele, Ogden, and

Nephi. In total, she'd mark dozens of points spanning six different counties.

"My apologies… the search was not as conclusive as expected, Mistress," Sinead said, looking down at the map while my beast tasted emotion flooding from her form. She was… ashamed?

"Sin," I encouraged softly, the emotion wafting from Sinead making me lunge at her and wrap her in my arms. I squeezed the petite woman tightly, tears of gratitude streaming down my cheeks onto her shoulder. "This… This is bloody wonderful. H-How did you do it?"

Instead of returning the hug, I felt her flinch instinctively in my arms, her body rigid for a long moment. She slowly began to melt, unsure of what to do with her hands or where to place them as she let me hold her. Albeit uncomfortably.

"With Master Jason, I sensed the signature of his soul always returning here. It was an easy enough pattern to track and is how my kind finds people we mark to return for their heads. A simple method used to outrun us riders is to either stay on the move or cross a large body of water," Sinead explained dryly. "He seems to have chosen the former method which I find curious as if he's not able to leave the boundaries of the state. However, this search still covered an approximate area of 6,000 square kilometers."

I flinched at the large number given and felt shame radiate harder from her form in heavy waves. Now, however, I could taste more emotion from her on the tip of my tongue; one that I knew all too well being next to Jason and Haley.

Wait, is she wallowing in self-loathing?

I pulled back and looked into her eyes, finding a tear trailing down her porcelain cheek. She… was crying. I hadn't even realized it was possible for her. Then I thought about how her demeanor had warmed and become more flexible over the last two weeks. How she felt more… human. I felt emotions battling each other inside me, confused by this development in her. On one hand, I hated the tiny woman because of what she did to Adi. On the other hand, I was overwhelmed and grateful that she'd been able to do something about finding Adi when we had no leads to even start with. Now we did, all because of that same little woman that was crying in my arms.

Sinead took in a deep shuddering breath before raising her head as I slowly pulled away to look at her completely. I then watched her body go rigid, straightening her back and laying the backs of her palms against her bare thighs. I recognized the pose for what it was; absolute and unadulterated submission.

"I… have failed my task, Mistress. I will subject myself to a punishment you deem fit to serve me," Sinead announced, the humanity in her wavering before returning to her usual lifeless tone.

Then she turned her head, presenting her cheek to me as if she thought she deserved to be slapped. I froze at the proposition, my gut wrenching uncomfortably at the gesture. I was used to getting slapped and then launching into a brawl. She, however, had seen it as me punishing her and that, like with Samael, she'd be relegated to nothing but an object.

"I won't slap you again, love," I said firmly, giving the smaller woman an apologetic look. "Please accept my apology and my promise that I won't do it again. I'll work on my anger issues."

"If you needed an alternative form for the release of frustrations, I could have been used," Sinead offered, making me furrow my brow and sigh.

"Sinead, I need you to answer me something," I said, giving her steady eye contact. "Why do this without us prompting again?"

"The ring finally had enough energy to conduct my searching ritual," she answered matter of factly. "Truthfully, I could have performed this a week ago, however, I felt… I felt as if I needed to be more thorough. It… was odd for me."

A wave of shame and regret hit my tastebuds, making me flinch with the increasing hunger, need, and bloodlust. My leopard was getting closer to needing me to hunt.

"Sin, I can taste your emotions. You're ashamed and scared but your eyes and face don't let me know what's going on inside your head," I admitted, reaching out to cup her hands in mine. "I know I've been slower to accept you than the others have and I'm sorry for that. But, love, I want you to express yourself and just be you."

"I… I'm not sure how to," Sinead said, surprising me by intertwining her fingers with mine. "I don't know how to express or put into words the emotions I feel other than fear and pain. It was what he-"

"We're not him, Sin," I said sternly, interrupting her and narrowing my brows. "I'm sorry that I made you feel like we could be compared to that demon cunt."

"I know, not that I am comparing you to him," Sinead assured with a nod. "However, I am unsure you would allow emotions that I… wish to try and express or understand."

"Okay," I said, letting the word drawl. "Like what exactly?"

Sinead's lips pursed tightly with nervousness before she lunged forward faster than I could react and pressed her mouth to mine. It was sloppy, inexperienced, and tentative, however, her lips worked to suckle mine into a long, languid dance. That said, the unexpected kiss delivered more passion than I thought I would ever experience from Sinead, only releasing me to back away and catch her breath.

Her eyes fluttered open, her icy blue pools looking into mine with a pleasant tenderness before she closed them. She quickly turned her head and dipped her chin into her chest, fear radiating off of her in waves. The way she flinched and her body slumped when my lips smacked made it clear she was awaiting an inevitable rejection.

"I… have been desiring to do that for a few days now," Sinead admitted in nearly a whisper, her pale grey skin turning a shade of soft lavender as she blushed. "I know fear and pain like the back of my hand. This, however…"

"You're allowed to try and explain it, love. I promise," I said, smiling softly as the minty taste of her lips lingered on the tip of my tongue. This shy side of her after being so bold was endearing.

"I felt it when Xander took off his shirt. Though, to tell you the truth I feel this far more often," she said motioning toward herself. "When I gaze upon you, Jason, and Haley. This feeling of… tension, heat, and… an urge."

I couldn't help the small giggle I let out as I watched Sinead lean back as she explained herself her motions centering on her lower abdomen as she described the heat and tension. It was cute the way she tried describing being turned on in such a logical and analytical way. I smiled wider as a shiver ran down my spine as Sinead began to speak more freely, her tone becoming less monotone and more melodic with a Gaelic lilt.

She gave me an expectant look then, her brows raised in a mix of worry and anticipation.

"I don't mean to laugh, love, but you know that was bloody

adorable right?" I chuckled softly as I met her eyes.

"I… don't understand. Mortals use terms like that to describe a level of attractiveness," Sinead said, shaking her head as her brows knitted in confusion. She gave me a curious look then as she stood up, carefully putting herself into an on-duty stance. "You… find me… pleasing?"

With her standing above me, it put her entire form on perfect display as my eyes did what her pleading expression begged of me. I roamed over her, taking in her thin form that was fuller and no longer emaciated as she was two weeks ago. She had a pale grey complexion with soft oval features that gave her a dollish appearance and made the icy blue of her eyes captivating. My eyes followed down her small nose, pouty black lips, and long icy-white hair that framed her face.

My eyes travel down across the deepening blush across her chest to her small, perky breasts. Her areola transitioned smoothly, much like Adi's did, in an ombre from her skin to a pair of dainty, erect pale lavender-colored nipples. My mouth watered with the sight of them before I began drooling as my eyes fell down her stomach to between her thighs. There her lithe, ballerina-like frame had narrow hips and a tilted pelvis that wonderfully accentuated a supple peach of an ass. Then my eyes locked onto the figure eight shape of her sex that had a slightly protruded clitoral hood, a pair of tight asymmetrical lips, and exposed inner folds.

"Honestly, love?" I asked, letting my eyes roam up her form to look into her eyes. When she nodded, I stood in front of her and then leaned back as she watched me visually feast on her figure. "Yeah. I bloody fucking do."

"My breasts and buttocks are not too-"

Before she could finish that self-deprecating thought, I dipped myself so I could catch her lips, hungrily kissing her hard and deep. I groaned at her taste, savoring the mint flair of her lips and tongue while I used one hand to brush a thumb of one of her taught peaks while my other snuck around and forcefully gripped her round ass firmly. Squeezing re-affirmingly for good measure.

Sinead took in a sharp inhale as I feasted on her lips, her body shivering as I growled into her mouth and held her tight against me. Our heads rolled in a slow dance together while my tightening hold had her going on her tiptoes to reach me and her hands grasping desperately onto the sleeves of my shirt. Deepening the kiss, she let out a soft yelp of surprise as I caught her puffy bottom lip between my teeth and gave it a tug. We separated with a loud, wet smack of lips that seemed to echo with an ethereal sigh of delight.

"That answer your question, Sin?" I asked, whispering with a dreamy tone against her lips.

"I… I think so," she answered shakily, even more of a Scottish tone filtering through her voice.

"Was that your first kiss?" I asked with a wide grin.

"Y-Yes," she answered hesitantly. "Only his personal concubines were allowed such an honor. My mouth, vagina, and buttocks were deemed as only good for being his cocksleeves."

"Wait," I said, my brows furrowing with confusion. "You've sucked a dick but never been kissed?"

"Unfortunately, yes," she nodded with an uncomfortable look. "And… I know Jason would never deem me as lowly as my former Master did."

"And how are you feeling now overall, love?" I asked, my eyes giving her as much care and attention as I possibly could. "What would you want from me if you could have it?"

"I… I'm sorry," Sinead said, forcing herself out of my grip and away from me completely. She hugged her figure tightly, looking down at the floor with a mix of shame and confusion etched across her porcelain face. "I… have never been permitted these things. I'm not used to having a choice or will of my own and why I… I feel so lost. What is my purpose?"

"That's up to you to decide, love. I know how you feel though, with Adi gone she took a piece of my heart with her. It's why I'm so quick to anger and lash out," I explained, daring to take a step toward her. "Jason and Adi found me and Haley at our lowest points, lifted us up, and found us. Maybe I should have been trying to find you this last little while."

"I do not wish to replace Adelaide in your heart," Sinead said defensively, giving me a cold, determined look.

Gods, she looks so much like Adi right now.

"Then what do you want, Sin?" I pressed, reaching out to cup her cheek and force her to keep her eyes on me.

"To stay!" Sinead declared boldly, stepping into my touch and looking up at me with shimmering eyes. Her accent was completely unhidden now, voice wavering as unbridled emotion drove cracks into her stoicism deeper. "I want to keep my place at the foot of your bed. To serve you, my Master and Mistresses. And to pray that Adelaide finds it somewhere in her heart to forgive me like you have."

Her answer took me off guard.

I watched Sinead for a long moment, tears streaking down her cheeks in an overwhelming wave of emotions crashing around inside her. When she realized she was crying, she moved back, tucking her chin to her chest while her fists balled at her sides. It was like she was desperately trying to reform that protective shell that her time with Samael had built around her.

"I don't expect you to replace Adi, love," I said, earning a look of pain in her eyes before I continued. "I expect you to be your own person, not some glorified guard dog that sleeps at the foot of our bed. You will never be my puppet, you will decide for yourself how you want to live."

Her brows scrunched in confusion and I read the look on her face for what it was. She wanted to do that, wanted to believe she was free, but didn't know how to.

"I'm going to go get in bed, Sin, and what you do is up to you," I said, holding an offer out toward her. "You can either guard the bed like you've been doing or… you can join me."

Before she could answer, I turned on my heels and padded through the dining room toward the bedroom. I made quick work of my clothes, stripping them off and leaving them in a pile by the bathroom door before crawling onto the mattress and readying to slip myself underneath the plush comforter. As I did so, a weight forcefully hit my side, sprawling me backward onto the bed before a weight held me down and I felt the edge of a blade to my throat.

Looking up, I found Sinead, hellfire burning in her eyes with a mix of rage, fear, and anguish swirling inside the flames. Her teeth grit in a sneer as she looked down on me, her hair falling around us like a snowy veil that hid everything except my view of her alone.

"Never cast me aside ever again," Sinead snarled, pressing the edge of her sickle-shaped blade against my skin as she dipped and kissed me with bruising force.

As her nostrils flared with heaving, angry breaths and her teeth nipped at my lips, I felt droplets of hot tears cascading onto my cheeks.

She was on the verge of sobbing as she pulled back and looked down at me. "Please. Never leave me alone. Not again."

With a flash of hellfire appearing from her hand, the blade disappeared and she leaned down, kissing me with as much deep passion and longing as she could offer. She no longer hid her true voice, her accent ringing in my ears like a pleasant, infectious melody that had me leaning upward to meet her movements. Our mouths and tongues danced while my hands reached up, cupping her cheek with one while the other danced my nails across her back. Every touch sent whimpering moans into me, her body shivering with anticipation, and her flesh sprouting a sheen of goosebumps across her form.

Sinead broke the kiss, her chest heaving with shaky breaths as she sat above me, straddling my hips. As her lips left mine, it forced a groan of want from me as I bit my lip and looked up at the smaller woman. Her motion sending thrumming waves of fire through me as her swollen pearl ground against mine. With her eyes on me, she leaned back, planting one hand on my firm stomach for support while the other dipped between her legs. Her fingers traced along the edges of her lips before she spread them apart, revealing her glistening, silken, lavender folds.

"This is what you do to me, McKenna," she whispered, her voice shaking as pleasure coursed through her with her touch. "I… only became like this once during my subjugation and never again. This, however, happens every time I look at you or I hear what Master does to you and Haley."

"Then let's see if I can help with that, love," I said with a purr, licking my lips as I watched her idly trace her wet sex.

I poured my strength into my hips as I bucked, lifting Sinead off the bed before rolling and slamming her back into the mattress. Before she could question what was happening, I rode her, rolling my hips and grinding my throbbing cunt against hers. I savored the droning pleasure made by our lips grinding and massaging each other, leaving small webs of our shared essences clinging from my snatch to Sinead's.

I caught her breath as I kissed her, forcefully taking her mouth into mine and savoring the little whimpers and moans that escaped. Soon, her hips were rolling to meet mine, drawing out the sparks of fire racing through my nerves each time her clit pushed against mine. Her lips submitted to me, letting me open her mouth wider to let my tongue push inside her, finding Sinead's dainty muscle. My larger, rough textured tongue pulled it into a long, slow dance that allowed me to thoroughly savor the flavor of her while memorizing the shape of its new partner.

Sinead's arms wrapped around me, her hand gripping my shoulder and the small of my back with reflexive bursts of strength. For how small she was, it surprised me how easily she pulled me into her with her strength, never wanting the kiss to end. I, however, chose to break the kiss before nudging her head to the side and began trailing gentle kisses and licks down her neck, purring as she mewled under my touch. Then, once my lips passed just under her lace choker, I wrapped my lips over the big pulse in her neck, bit down with a sensual growl, and drank in Sinead's whimpered cry of delight.

I worked that spot for a few long moments, suckling, licking, and biting the tender flesh as Sinead held me tighter. Once satisfied, I pulled back to admire my handiwork, a small spot of lavender bruising already forming around the indentations of my teeth on her skin. She looked up at me with want hanging heavily on her lidded lashes, watching me through a haze of lust.

"That marks you as mine, understood?" I whispered, leaning down to let my voice reverberate through the crown of her ear. With a fang-bearing grin, I let out a long purr, happy to feel Sinead buck and writhe underneath me from the sound of it. "It's our way of showing love and affection to each other just as much as we mark our territory. And Jason and I? We make sure our girls cum as much as they fucking want. Got it?"

"McKenna, I-"

"Shh," I drawled, shushing her before raising myself enough so that her icy blues met my golden greens. I gave her a wide grin, flashing my fangs at her as I shook my head. "You're mine now. No more McKenna, it's Mickie or Mistress from now on."

Sinead gave me a quick bobbing nod before my eyes rolled down to her chest where my large, heavy mounds sat atop hers. With a grinding motion, I drank in more subtle pleasure as her swollen peaks raked across my own, enjoying the view of my umber nipples contrasting the dark pastel color of hers. With a predatory gaze, I dragged myself lower, brushing my lips across her skin and kissing my way down her collarbone and chest before I reached my prize. I rolled my eyes up to watch her as my tongue extended and lapped at the painfully stiff teat like a big cat at a savannah watering hole. The sudden jolt of pleasure made her gasp and let out a high-keening sound that was music to my ears as her hips bucked with anticipation.

I purred as I took her nipple between my lips and applied pressure, lightly suckling it in while my tongue drew lazy circles around it. Sinead let out a choked moan as I suckled and licked her before she thrust forward, burying more of her breast into my waiting maw. Her hands clung to me frantically, fingers snaking into my hair as she held me right where she needed my mouth the most. I pulled back, defying her strength as I came off her nipple with a loud echoing pop before moving sideward and giving the other the exact same treatment.

To draw out more pleasure from her, I upped her hips in one hand and brought up the other, raking my nails across the glistening flesh of her nipple that I'd previously released. She shuddered and spasmed under my touch, her moans coming more freely as I worked her. Then, to up the ante, I dragged my teeth across the nipple in my mouth while completely palming her other breast, kneading the perky mound, and trapping her free nipple between my fingers with a pinch.

"Miss-ckie~" Sinead moaned with pleading desperation, her mind unsure of which name to call me by.

Wanting to hear more of her song, I teased her nipples harder, tweaking and rolling them at my leisure with precise pressure. My teeth, tongue, and fingers worked her until she was gasping and choking on pleasure before I pulled off her nipple with another wet pop. Then, without thinking I squeezed one taught peak between my fingers hard while I bit down on the supple flesh just below the other nipple. As I left another hickie, Sinead thrashed wildly underneath me, her voice letting out an ethereal whine as she stiffened underneath me for a moment and then went limp.

"Sin you okay, love?" I asked with concern at the sudden liquid shape her body took under me, her breath ragged as her chest rose and fell in rapid succession like she was coming down from a panic attack.

"I... I..."

As she struggled to find her words and catch her breath, I lifted myself onto all fours and my eyes scanned over her to make sure she wasn't hurt. I paused as my eyes fell between her legs then, her blush painting the flesh above her mound pink and lavender, her pussy glistening in the light like rain-covered concrete. She was absolutely soaked to the bone.

"Y-You… are concerned," Sinead said, finally relearning how to speak as her breath hitched. "D-Did I fail the task of reaching release as well?"

"No, love," I snorted, shaking my head with a grin as I looked back and forth between her eyes and her drenched, quivering pussy. "I just didn't expect you to cum that hard before I'd even gotten started on you."

"I-I," Sinead stuttered before she went quiet, studying my expression and how my eyes drank her in. After a long moment, she seemed to decide something herself and nodded curtly. "May we continue, Mistress?"

I gave her a nod in response and leaned down to kiss her chest and felt her shudder beneath me. I purred loudly as I began stalking down her body once more, kissing, licking, and grazing my teeth along her stomach and setting her nerves ablaze. Once low enough, I settled between Sinead's legs, dragging my nails down her sides to her thighs which I spread and lifted to give me plentiful access to her.

"Be selfish. Cum and scream for me as much as you want, okay, love?" I said, my eyes drinking in the sight of one of the most delicious-looking pussies I'd ever laid eyes on.

"B-But, what about you, Mistress?" she asked, her breath hitching as I began kissing down her inner thighs toward her center. "How should I serve- oh, Hades!"

I cut Sinead's protests short and turned them into long, screaming moans of pure bliss as my tongue flicked and danced across her protruding pearl. I sent fire through her as I licked and kissed at the thick, swollen bundle of nerves before wrapping my lips around it and suckling liberally. Sinead's strength fought against mine as she bucked and I held her thighs down and apart, pinning her to the bed as I fed on her sensations.

Her breathing became strained and I attacked her clit, teething, suckling, and licking at her with hunger, my pace going from slow and lazy to feverish. Tinges of pleasure-laced pain coursed through me down to my core as Sinead's hands clung to my hair tightly, tugging me down to keep me right where she wanted. That grip tightened as I went lower, tracing my rough tongue between her folds that blossomed open around me. I moaned in delight as I tasted her, Sinead's essence dancing on my tongue with a mix of mint and fresh spring water. A taste that made me feast on her even more feverishly.

I moaned into Sinead's dripping pussy, sending electric vibrations through her core and up her spine, making her bow harshly under my grip. I moved my mouth up and down focusing my attacks on her swollen clit one moment and then plunging my thick tongue into her tight, shuddering entrance the next. I drank her down as I plunged inside of her, tongue fucking Sinead's tight little pussy with greedy vigor. All the while my mind conjured the enticing image of watching Jason fill her.

"Mistress!"

Sinead screamed, her back bowing so hard I had to fight to keep her perky ass planted on the bed. Her hands clung tight, holding my face buried into her snatch as her walls quaked and rippled around my tongue. Her pussy pulsed around me, holding my tongue deep inside of her as a rush of warmth coated it and my chin. I moaned with a pleasure growl into her as waves of her taste flooded my senses and I hungrily drank her down as she came hard again.

Her taste, her scent and the feel of her against me had electricity racing through my body, dancing along my nerves like a wildfire. Added to that were the continual mental images of what could be; watching Jason fuck Adi, then Haley, and then her senseless before turning me into a boneless puddle laying next to them. Her holding me down on her pussy had the same effect as what I felt when Jason held me down and fucked my throat, all of it swirling and coalescing in my core, winding me up with pressure and heat so close to bursting.

I raised my head once the tension in her body began to lift and her muscles eased, purring as my eyes roamed across the petite perfection in front of me. I brought one of my hands from her thighs to trace the shape of her cunt, grazing around the oblong shape of her. She shivered as I grazed around her protruded clit, across her center where she tightened into a neat crease, and then around her entrance where her folds bloomed like a small flower.

"I-Is my shape to your liking, Mistress?" Sinead asked nervously as she panted, twitching with each caress of her. "I have been told its appearance is off-putting."

"Sin, baby, I don't care what he told you. From down here, I've got a gorgeous dame holding me and calling me Mistress," I smirked devilishly up at her as I spoke while my finger parted her folds, tracing her slick silken flesh. She whined in response, her eyes lidding as I teased her. "Between you, Hales, and Adi, I'm bloody spoiled on choices for the prettiest pussies I've ever seen."

"You - mmph - patronize me," Sinead whimpered, unaware she'd just used Adi's catchphrase when we'd teased her.

"No, I'm being *quite* honest," I said, licking my lips as my fingers parted her, exposing the pretty lavender shade of her pussy before I slid my middle finger inside her. She bucked as I sank into her, curling with a come hither gesture that hit that swollen sweet spot inside her. She began riding my finger desperately and I met her movements, soon slipping a second finger inside her to stroke her quivering tunnel slowly. "Impotent bloody cunt had *no* idea what kinda masterpiece he had on his hands."

I stroked Sinead faster, leaving my tips curled so that our combined motions hit that hypersensitive pad inside her relentlessly. Her hands moved from the back of my head to the sheets where she gripped and clung to the comforter for dear life. As I fingered her faster, I used the pad of my thumb to press down on her throbbing pearl, her own movements grinding them together recklessly. All of it together made Sinead sing like a looming storm, her whimpers and cries mixing with loud gasps and yelps of pleasure as my palm began to slap against her mound.

"F-Fuck! Mistress!"

Sinead howled with pleasure, the rougher pace making her body writhe uncontrollably. Intent on wanting to watch her pussy's reaction, I shifted onto my knees and arched my back to lay my chest flat against the bed. Just the sight of Sinead was making my entire body thrum with pleasure as this beautiful woman folded under my touch like putty. My pussy throbbed in time with hers as I stroked her, applying more pressure to her g-spot to bring that fire from her belly outward where I could feast on it more.

She let out another gasping moan of pleasure that filled the room with the ethereal sounds of thousands of whispers calling for me to bring them pleasure. Like a haunting symphony of lust on a cold dark night. And I wanted to make that symphony sing to the gods themselves when she came again.

Then I began to sing with her, eyes wide with surprise as a wave of pleasure hit me like a thunderstorm. I had already been on edge pleasuring Sinead but feeling an unknown mouth and tongue on my aching pussy sent me into orbit. To fight off my climax from hitting too soon before I knew what had caused it, I laid my cheek against Sinead's thigh and bit her with a whining moan.

Sinead screamed with need at my bite except the desire to hold back my climax was put into jeopardy. Her scream and muffled voice came from behind me and I felt her cry out directly into my dripping cunt. Then came the feverish lapping of a dainty tongue that attacked my pulsing pussy with the precision of a marksman, training on every sweet spot I had.

As my eyes rolled back in pleasure, my focus and the pace of my fingering faltered as I found an unexpected sight in front of me.

Sinead's body was writhing, breathing rapidly as I drove into her at a steady pace, her juices soaking my fingers completely. However, her head was now gone and, instead, a small flame of hellfire roiled from her neck. The flames pulsed in unison with her own oncoming orgasm, flickering at the same time her walls convulsed around my fingers.

As I looked over my shoulder, I found the small torchlight of hellfire hovering behind me, blue flames rising from roots of icy white. I blinked in curiosity at Sinead's head floating above the end of the bed, her face buried into my snatch. She didn't let me stare long and I let out a mewling growl of pleasure as her teeth grazed my clit, making my legs quake from pleasure. I was riding a lightning storm of desire as I watched with both fascination and lust as her floating head utterly devoured me.

"F-Fuck," I groaned, my eyes fluttering as her tongue stretched inside me enough to brush against my g-spot. When I resumed my motions, quickly pumping Sinead's pussy, daring to add a third finger to stretch her fuller, she screamed into me and nearly made me buckle. "How… the bloody hell… are you doing that, love?"

Sinead's head retreated and I looked over my shoulder to find her there hovering above my thick, round ass. I bit my lip as Sinead licked her lips, cleaning her mouth of my juices which were smeared across her face and chin entirely. Then she stuck out her tongue and I realized that, although it was thin and dainty, it was long enough to hang below her chin.

"You wanted me to be selfish and I wanted to pleasure you. And since I can manipulate my body separately," Sinead answered matter of factly. Then I shivered with delight as her lips curled into a small mischievous smile. "I believe this is you getting what you asked for, Mistress."

Her floating head disappeared again between my legs, resuming her feast on me as her lips ground against my folds while her long tongue writhed inside me. Then she started to roll her head, making my eyes bug out and my core swelter to a breaking point, as her tongue corkscrewed itself inside me. That put my nerves into overload as fire and electricity began to snap at every inch of my body.

I bit her inner thigh again, making her scream into me and sending another rapid burst of electricity that made my skin burn. As I held off my own scream, whining into Sinead's thigh, I pumped fast enough into her hot, soaking pussy that I was practically vibrating inside her. Her choked, muffled moan began to rise into an ethereal cry that filled the room as I lunged at her dripping cunt. Desperately, I trapped her clitoris between my lips, whimpering and moaning from her eating me from behind while my tongue danced in quick circles over her pearl.

We screamed each other's names into the night, our cries ringing out in an ethereal harmony that echoed across the apartment. Both of our bodies shook as we hit that peak together and our combined climaxes rode us with overwhelming electric pleasure. My legs buckled and my back bowed as my core overfilled and snapped, sending a rush of heat from me and soaking Sinead's face. At the same time, Sinead's body lifted off the bed, her pussy clamping down so tightly she forced my fingers deeper as she climaxed, a small stream of her essence pooling underneath her as she went rigid, quaking violently before falling limp.

As we both came down, I heard a loud thump hit the floor behind me.

Sitting up, I tried to walk on legs that felt like they were made of jelly and found Sinead's head lying on the ground. The hellfire was gone as her head lay in a blanket of her long hair. She was breathing heavily, blinking slowly like her vision was dancing behind her eyes and then we made lazy eye contact as I bent down to cradle her into my hands.

"How do you feel, babe?" I asked, snickering as I contemplated the odd sensation and sight of holding just her head in my hands.

"Incredible," she said with a dreamy tone, it was the only word she could manage.

I brought her back around to the head of the bed, climbing onto it to kneel beside her as I looked back and forth between the two stumps of her neck. I wasn't sure what to do but, ultimately decided to lay her head close to the smoldering stump of her neck. I heard the sound of ethereal whispers again fill the room as smoke reached out like wispy tentacles to grasp her head. They gently pulled her into place and, with another dissonant whisper, she was whole again.

Once she was complete, Sinead began to roll, trying to move off the bed. I caught her shoulder and rolled the dullahan woman back toward me as I laid her beside me. I held her head cradled under my right arm while my left wrapped over her, my hand clamping tightly onto her hip so that I could pull her close. The position cradled her face against the top of my breasts and pressed her hips to mine before I leaned down and nestled my nose into her hair.

"Where do you think you're going?" I asked, nuzzling and basking in the scent of her.

"I was going to return to my post, Mistress," Sinead said, a mix of confusion and concern in her voice.

"What did I say before, Sin?" I asked with a small smirk. "You're not my guard dog or my puppet."

"T-Then I-"

"Your place is here now. And we protect each other in this family," I said, making my voice mix with stern authority and compassion. "Understand?"

Sinead went stiff in my arms then, after a moment, slowly lifted her head so our eyes met. Hers widened with understanding as tears welled in the corners. They began falling slowly, staining her cheeks before I hugged her to me and held her. Soon she was sobbing in my embrace, her hands clutching me as the walls she built to protect herself from her trauma shattered.

"Thank you, Mickie," Sinead said in a quivering voice between sobs as she buried herself tighter into my arms.

I wasn't sure how long we had laid together before her sobbing subsided into silence and her tension evaporated. I hadn't been sure if she even could sleep, because she'd never slept thus far. But gods did she need this. And what better way to get much-needed rest than to curl up with someone you'd just had sex with?

As I held her, my fingers tracing light circles around her back, sleep finally began to wash over me. As I pulled deeper into the darkness of unconsciousness, I briefly heard the front door open followed by a pair of footsteps that paused at the foot of the bed. I still had enough wherewithal to tilt my head up and see the blurred shapes of Jason and Haley standing there.

"Welcome home, my loves," I said in a sleepy tone, not quite all there.

"H-Hey, kitten," Jason said, confusion thick in his voice.

"I have… so many questions," Haley said, a chuckling amusement in her tone.

"Sin might have a lead on Adi. But I don't want to wake her so we'll ask her in the morning," I said with a yawn. "For now just get naked, come cuddle, and kiss me already."

Jason snorted, answering with a sarcastic '*Yes ma'am*' before I heard clothes rustling and falling to the floor. Not to be outdone Haley answered in a similarly sarcastic way, calling me Mami instead. I chuckled at their responses before I felt the bed shift on both sides. I rolled my head to look over my shoulder where Haley's lips met mine in a soft, longing kiss that helped melt away a sense of fear and dread.

Soon, I felt Jason's warmth close by and I leaned over Sinead, our lips meeting in a soft kiss that eased his stress in an instant. His arm tentatively reached over Sinead until his hand cupped my hip. Sinead sighed softly and shifted, her hip moving away from me into Jason. I heard his breath hitch and his heartbeat increase as she snuggled into him instinctively. His throat cleared, obviously trying to ask something and ignore my previous statement to Haley.

"All that needs to be said is that Sinead is ours now."

17

ADELAIDE

ANOTHER DAY IN HELL, ANOTHER PAIR OF DEAD DEMONS.

Of course, Samael had planned for this when he threw Trish and me into a pit with a dozen men. Both of us were panting from exhaustion while groans of pain filled the desolate room as four demons a piece held the two of us down. Our faces were smashed against the stone floor, the front of our bodies being coated in demonic blood, and forced to look up at Samael. The so-called demon lord chuckled as he made his way toward us, his face alight with amusement.

"Good show, bravo," he grinned, sarcastically clapping as he squatted in front of me to meet my eyes. "However, I can always get more of these fuckwits. You really are just wasting your breath by not giving in to me."

"Or you're just too much of a pussy to fight us yourself," Trish sneered in defiance, a fanged grin pointed at him.

His brow twitched at the remark as he looked down at Trish with contemplation for a long moment. He let out a sigh and shrugged his big shoulders before standing and cupping his chin as he walked around the eviscerated bodies of the dead before us. A wicked grin stretched across his lips as he turned on the heels of his cloven hooves, one arm behind his back as he snapped like he had an ah-ha moment.

"You know? The sheep slut might be right," he chuckled darkly before narrowing his eyes at us. "I don't need to fight you two. That would be too easy and, besides, if I did fight you? Neither of you would survive what I can dish out. Instead."

Samael snapped his fingers again, drawing the attention of the banshee woman who had been glued to his side for the past few days. Ever the loyal servant of her new master. He leaned down, whispering into her ear before she floated off toward the entrance of the pit and began talking to one of the guards standing there.

After the two exchanged words, the guard lifted the collar of his suit jacket, speaking into it and then waiting. As we waited for whatever he had in store, Samael squatted again, his eyes watching us with sick amusement.

"See, I don't enjoy resorting to fighting those that I want in my fold," Samael said, his tone raising the hairs on the back of my neck. "Too much drama. And not enough… finesse. You see, I find the mind far more interesting than brute strength. It's about the chase ladies, the long game that I find *far* more fulfilling."

Whimpers filled the cavern as Samael looked over his shoulder and my eyes were drawn to the pair of underworld nymphs that were among his hostages. They looked around nervously, eyes frantic and terrified as they were herded in like cattle across the room. I began struggling against the demon that held me down instantly, my gut sinking from the idea of what he had planned.

Trish screamed in horror as a beast, easily twice the size of Samael, stepped into the pit from the shadows. The massive humanoid man looked similar to Samael's demon form, however, instead of the slight ram-like features he had, the man was more bull than man. The minotaur huffed, steam billowing from its nose as it grinned evilly at the two much smaller women before him before they screamed and tried to run.

Before Trish and I could break free of those restraining us, Samael straddled both of us, pushing a knee against each of our tailbones. With his weight fully holding us down, his big hands grabbed us by the hair, cranking our necks as he forced us to watch.

Over the next two hours, he held us there with amusement. My body screamed in pain from the mix of cragged rocks digging into the front of my naked body while his knee and grip on my hair strained my back and neck. He held us both down, forcing us to watch as we screamed in agony while the minotaur chased the nymphs with glee before he easily caught them in his big hands. Once within his grasp, he brutally forced himself on the women as he used them repeatedly. At one point going so far as bringing them just out of reach of our aid and making us watch the sickening spectacle.

The nymphs were dragged away when he was finished, left battered, bruised, and covered in blood and other fluids. The bull-man bellowed with delight as they were dragged away, holding on by the brink to life while Samael congratulated the bastard on a wonderful performance.

"Ich hasse dich verdammt," I spat hoarsely at Samael as he turned his attention back onto me. My outburst made him laugh like he found me endearing. "I swear to the gods, I'll kill you Samael."

"You may try," he hummed before jerking my head to meet his eyes. "But you never will, little bird."

"Don't call me that," I sneered, glaring bitterly at him. "You don't have that right."

"Oh, but you don't have a choice, now do you Adelaide," he grinned, tossing me aside by the hair.

As he stood again, the banshee floated towards him, a blush and a look of lust strewn across her expression as she looked up at him. Watching her fawn over him made my gut wrench, wanting to hurl at the sight. That was until she presented him with a pair of heavy chains that he gingerly took from her.

"Such a good little whore," he cooed softly before grinning and reaching out with his free hand to grab her by the throat. Forcefully he jerked her form to his and groaned with delight as their lips met in a deep, raunchy kiss. "Be in my chambers when I get back so you can have your reward."

"Yes, Master," she keened blissfully before stepping back, bowing, and then floating away in a hurry.

As she disappeared, Samael's sights set back onto Trish and me, playfully swinging the chains in his grip. Before he got to us, a heavy weight clasped its way around my throat and was tightened uncomfortably as I struggled against my bonds. Once the heavy iron collar was secured, a thick snap echoed across the room as he clasped the chain to my collar and then to Trish's. Then came the shackles that bound our hands behind our backs.

The two of us were forced onto our feet, the sensations in my limbs struggling to keep me standing before he jerked roughly and I nearly fell from being pulled forward. Trish did fall and I was forced to watch as Samael turned, gave her a disappointed expression, and then angrily hoisted her onto her feet by her horns.

She screamed in pain from being grabbed there before he pulled her face to his and scowled. Before letting her go, he leaned in to whisper something into one of her elongated ears, her eyes going wide from his words and tears beginning to freely stream down her cheeks once more.

"N-No, sir. I don't want that," she whimpered and I felt my heart break for her.

She may have refused to share much about herself with me, and could be sassy when interacting with me ever since we became cellmates. However, watching her resolve beginning to crack was taking its toll on me and I could feel it.

Before I could lean over to ask what he'd threatened, Samael pulled the familiar golden coin from his pocket and rubbed it. Arcane energy crackled in front of him as a dimensional door opened before us and my heart broke as my eyes scanned over the landscape. It was all too familiar as he pulled us through the warp and then began parading us around the construction site with glee.

"Almost unrecognizable, isn't it?" Samael chuckled, as our nude forms were dragged behind him and the four demon guards that had stepped through the gate with us. "See, while you two remain stubborn as ever, life moves on *without* you."

The sight was cruel as he dragged us through the newly opened holes in the ground, some of which had foundations already poured. Several weeks ago, this had been nothing more than a leveled field. Now, however, signs of steady development were apparent and tears streamed down my face as I saw a logo I knew well on a banner posted to a nearby chain link fence.

Forrest Homes. A single-family home community with plans starting at $350K. The cleared field was now a subdivision, construction headed by one of Jason and I's long-standing clients, Brandon Forrest. To add even more insult to the already gaping wound in my heart was that this field was the same one we'd come to and I'd lost most of my metaphysical connection to Jason.

This was where I'd lost them.

"You see, while you two hold out being sniveling little bitches that can't seem to get with the program. I, on the other hand, move forward with the future," Samael grinned, holding the chains with one hand, while he motioned to the development with the other. "I've had my hand in everything, Adelaide. You think of only yourself and not the bigger game at stake. One where I, and the followers of Yazmin bring her will to fruition."

"Still going on about that bitch of a goddess?" Trish sneered, her body jerking on her chains angrily. "She won't save you forever, you know that?"

"Oh but she will," Samael growled as he pulled hard on the chains and dragged both of us forward hard enough that Trish and I fell face-first into the cold dirt. "She will deliver a sanctified glory that you cannot even fathom in that tiny little brain of yours. Just like you delivered your sister to me."

"You leave her out of this, you fucking monster," Trish cried while my eyes widened in terror.

Her sister was trapped with Samael? Why had I not seen her before? Unless…

"You're torturing her just to get to me, right?" I growled as I scooped my knees underneath me and then looked up at Samael, rage burning in my eyes. "You really are the biggest Scheißkerl of them all."

"Don't you know it well," he grinned as he turned and stood before me, staring me down with a self-satisfied glare.

"And yet you have no idea how to use it," I smirked back at him, pressing myself higher to get into his face.

As my words bit at his ego, he reared back, my cheek blooming in pain as he punched me across the jaw. My teeth bit hard into my cheek and lips, the taste of blood filling my mouth as I fell to the ground and into Trish's kneeling form. As he turned away in rage I looked up at the half-sheep woman and gave her a curt nod. Her eyes narrowed in understanding as she nodded confirmation before we both got to our feet and stared Samael down.

Sinking into my rage, I reached out for the raven spirit and took hold of its power. My skin turned ashen as my limbs lengthened, my body contorting as I took on the half-raven form of the valravn while gold flames sparked across Trish's fingertips.

Then, before anyone could react, Trish let her flames rage, leaping from her hands across the ground behind us and onto the four lesser demon guards following behind us. As the guard screamed in pain and fell to the dirt, soaked in a napalm-like fire that refused to be doused as they rolled helplessly, we lunged for Samael.

When the big man turned to face us his neck was promptly wrapped up, his gold coin falling and sprouting another gate behind us as the two of us took him down. With the heavy iron chain wrapped around his neck, Trish and I screamed as we pulled, squeezing his throat as hard as the chains and our combined strength would allow.

Samael thrashed across the ground, choking on the remnants of air and saliva as she began to gurgle and suffocate from the pressure. A gleeful smile overtook Trish's expression as his movements began to still, his body growing limp from being choked to death.

When he was completely still, I poured my strength into my arms, the metal cuffs groaning in protest before they snapped. Then, using one of my talons, I swiped at the cuffs locking Trish's arms, severing the bindings apart.

With our hands freed, I turned to face the sheep woman and

growled, a sound filled with a mix of rage and victory. Once I saw that she was okay, I looked around, my eyes taking in the development and seeing the sun beginning to rise over Timpanogos just in the distance.

"When we get to the main road, we'll take it North the entire way. We're only a couple miles away from my mates right now. We'll be safe," I said, my form shrinking back to my human side.

Before anything, I rushed over to the fence, stripping the banner off of it and giving it to Trish to wrap around herself. I, on the other hand, focused on an outfit I could picture myself in, fluttering lights appearing in the space around us as clothing materialized on my body to cover me completely.

"You sure about this?" Trish asked, her brow cocked as she watched me. "Doesn't your boy toy hate demons?"

"Yes, but so do I," I countered, rolling my eyes at her.

"And yet, what am I?" Trish retorted, cocking her hip to one side as she gave me an indignant glare. "Why would someone like me be safe with a demon hunter?"

"Because you're a victim in all of this, just like me," I answered, giving her a pointed glare.

"Uh huh, sure and- Adi!"

Trish's response, which would have been witty or sarcastic, was cut short as she rushed forward, pushing me out of the way of Samael's grip. As I stumbled away from the two of them, my eyes righted in time to find her grabbing at him.

Her hands only found purchase on his suit jacket which he allowed her to strip him out of and use her grip on it against her, trying to bind her in it. I raced forward, my fingers extending into talons, and cut the fabric.

As she fell out of his grip, I ducked under his big arms and tackled him, making him scream as my claws dug their way through his clothes and into his skin and muscles.

I dug through him, tearing into his stomach and sides before I kicked him away and turned to find Trish pulling herself off of the ground. Then I felt the chain around mine and Trish's necks tighten as he grabbed it and pulled us toward him.

In desperation, I swiped at the chain, cutting it in half as Samael lost his grip on Trish. I pulled at the chain, launching myself forward into him to plug my claws through his chest, hoping to cut his black heart into pieces. Instead, he whipped around, flinging me by the chain before I hit something solid and heard a flailing scream follow.

When I hit the ground and got to my hands and knees, my heart sank into oblivion. Several yards away, Trish lay in one of the holes dug for a home with only the foundation risen from the ground. The sheep woman had been thrown into the pit, two of the pillars of rebar lining the concrete walls piercing her through, the corrugated iron bars sticking through her shoulder and chest. She coughed, blood spitting from her lips as she wheezed and her eyes went hazy as her body hung from the rods.

"Trish!" I screamed in a wailing tone, tears flowing down my cheeks as I watched the life drain out of her body.

A hard tug on the back of my neck made the air rush from my lungs as Samael forcefully grabbed me from behind. He bowed my back in a way that it nearly snapped in half, my skin going pale as air was forced out of me. The demon lord dipped low then, laughing with a sinister delight as he forced me to watch Trish die in front of me, helpless to do anything to help.

"Her death is on *your* hands. This is *your* fault, little bird," he growled with delight and then let out a rumbling laugh. "Remember that the next time you think you will ever escape me, you worthless little bitch."

My body went numb as I looked on, even as I felt myself dragged away and the round doorway of arcane energy sputtered around me. The portal began closing as I was hoisted back into hell, the only thing remaining on my mind being Trish. She didn't deserve what happened to her and Samael's words rang true.

She died… because of me. And, for the first time in over a century, my resolve to outlast Samael's will wavered and cracked.

I WAS IN A DARK ROOM WITH ONLY A SINGLE LIGHT ABOVE ME.

Searching the darkness, I found nothing, no visible signs of life other than the faint scent of… something. Sulfur and brimstone. Panic set in, forcing me to choose a direction in the darkness and begin running, the light above me following. As I raced through the abyss, the hairs on the back of my neck stood in fear as the dark throaty tone of Samael's laugh echoed around me.

Running away from the sound in a panic, I bolted faster, trying to get away. I dared to look over my shoulder, finding nothing behind me in the darkness before I hit something solid in front of me and cursed under my breath. When I looked forward, I found myself standing there, my clone giving me the same shocked look I gave him. He was exactly like me in every way except for one thing; his eyes were pitch black.

Laughter rang out again, both of us flinching at the sound before he began to back away.

"Hurry. This way and do not let the bastard touch you," he said in little more than a whisper.

Hesitantly I ran after him, my heart hammering in my chest as we raced forward through the never-ending darkness. The laughter shifted then, no longer the sound of Samael's but others I recognized. Mickie's laugh which normally lit up a room, darkened the depths further. And, as we ran past the source of the sound, I found her standing there with a wide, sadistic grin. As she began to race after us, I found that she no longer had golden green eyes that glowed in the darkness, they were now red.

Next was Haley, giving us an equally sadistic grin and evil, taunting laugh. Her eyes glowed red instead of her golden eyes in the darkness as she too began to chase us. Next came Sinead, Lex, Xander, and others, a chorus of sadistic laughter and a small army of glowing red eyes biting at our heels.

"Jason!" Adi's voice called from the darkness and panic filled me even stronger. I tried to veer off in the direction of the sound, however, my clone stopped me from going to it until I heard her call my name again. "Jason, help me!"

Fuck this!

I broke away from my clone, running into the darkness and

ignoring his protests as I followed the sound of Adi's voice. I followed her voice as my only guiding direction before I saw a spot of light coming up in the abyss. She was standing in the light, looking around frantically and I pushed myself to race to her side until I broke through the darkness.

"Adi, I'm here! You're-"

As I reached out to touch her, sharp pain began to radiate from the center of my gut, my limbs losing feeling as my body began to go cold. When I looked down, I saw a pool of dark liquid staining my shirt and beginning to pour down the front of me where her hand bisected me. As she pulled her clawed hand free, I felt my inside shift with it, blood and thicker things pouring out in a rapid cascade. When I looked up, I found Adi, a wide and sadistic grin stretched across her lips, eyes glowing red, and then she began to laugh.

"You left me to die, Mein Liebe. Now you'll die too," she cooed with a sickly sweet tone before her demeanor became more maniacal. "Pluck and rip and *tear*. Pluck and *rip* and tear. *Pluck* and rip and tear. *Pluck* and *rip* and *tear*. And *feast*!"

Pain shot through me as Mickie, Haley, and everyone I loved threw me to the ground, feeling their teeth sink into me and begin to rip me limb from limb. The last thing my vision saw was the red-eyed figure of Karynn hovering behind Adi, embracing her sweetly as they looked down at me with manic disdain.

"Adi!" I screamed and woke with a start. My eyes were wide, my heart raced far too fast, and a cold sheen of sweat covered my entire body.

Mickie's form appeared in the doorway, her expression filled with a mix of shock, worry, and sadness as her eyes met mine. In an instant, she was kneeling in front of me as I sat up in bed and I was swallowed into her embrace. As she rocked me slowly, my face buried into her chest, I felt Haley wrap me up from behind, the three of us swaying and wrapping me in their familiar warmth. The two of them took turns shushing my oncoming sobs and whispering that everything would be okay into my ears.

Another touch registered as one of my hands that had loosely clung to Mickie was taken into a smaller hand that squeezed mine with reassurance. Daring to look up, I found the dainty fingers intertwined with mine belonged to Sinead as she watched me with frightened eyes.

"Jason, your breathing is elevated and you are sweating. Do you wish for me to draw you a bath or perhaps assist in breathing exercises?" Sinead asked. Her voice was no longer monotone and, instead, held an edge of worry bristling in her Scottish lilt. I realized that most of her stoic, lifeless demeanor was now gone.

Before I could question what happened to change her, I felt a flood of memories enter me as my abilities reawakened. Flashing images of Mickie and Sinead together danced across my mind in rapid succession as I relived the previous night from both of their perspectives. The conversation they had and the realization of how Sinead felt now that she was allowed her freedom.

Secondary to those memories, I saw Haley in the parking garage confronting Karynn and talking to a woman I didn't recognize. I watched her threaten the guy that I'd been cheated on with by lifting his car and scaring the piss out of him. Literally. Then watched as she turned her anger on my ex, barely keeping her control as she fought for my honor. The meeting with the woman after, however, all of her memories went fuzzy as static overtook the visions.

Pulling back from the three women, my thoughts were cut short by the sight around me, making me pause. I realized then that Mickie and Haley were both clad in nothing but cooking aprons, a sea of dark bronze and golden brown skin barely hidden by a thin sheet of white fabric and straps. Sinead on the other hand, stood at the bedside completely nude, the sight of her small perky breasts sitting at eye level.

"Actually, a bath might be a good call," I said finally, turning my eyes up to meet Sinead's. At my answer, she smiled and her icy blue eyes brightened at my response.

With a curt nod, Sinead turned on her heels and began padding toward the bathroom. My eyes followed her curiously and, admittedly, trailed downward to watch her supple, perky ass bounce with her steps.

Then, of course, my mind chose that instant to remind me of climbing into bed last night at Mickie's insistence. And subsequently falling asleep while that same plump rear pressed and ground into me, lulling me into a peaceful sleep.

Until my night terror anyway, which had been occurring more frequently since Adi's disappearance. Mickie and Haley comforting me was becoming more commonplace and, to be honest, sometimes made me feel like a fraud. Especially with how Haley called me her Prime which came with more masculine expectations. I didn't feel worthy of the title.

"I'm sorry," I said, finally taking a deep breath to calm my thoughts. The sound of running water began to echo into the room before I gave Mickie and Haley an apologetic look. "I don't know how to stop them anymore. And… they're just getting worse."

"You're okay, babe. I promise," Mickie said, caressing her fingers through my hair.

"No one's blaming you for night terrors, mi amor," Haley added, gently nuzzling her nose against my temple and kissing my cheeks.

"I know. They just… make me feel more broken than I already am," I admitted with a groan before pulling the two of them tighter against me.

Which, of course, reminded me of my injured finger in an instant. I pressed down too hard on Mickie's bare back and caused a surge of pain to race from my hand and up my arm. With a sharp hiss, I pulled back and pulled up my hand to inspect the finger I had dislocated. My right index finger was a sickly purple from the bruising and swelling and made both of the shifters gawk at me in disbelief.

"Bloody hell, what happened?" Mickie winced as she stared at the finger.

"I uh… may have punched someone last night," I smiled weakly at my reasoning.

"You did what?" Haley snorted, shaking her head as her eyes went back and forth between my finger and my expression. "Who?"

"Gary," I sighed, giving them both an apologetic look. They gave me expectant ones in return, wanting me to explain the whole story. "Okay, fine. Gary may or may not have taken a construction crew to Sand Hollow and was trying to dig right in front of the state historical site monument."

"You're joking," Mickie scoffed, narrowing her eyes at me and shaking her head.

"Nope, I'm being serious," I snorted with a chuckle before my face fell as I remembered last night's events. "Chipeta, Wakkara, and Joseph nearly turned themselves into cursed spirits. I… may have absorbed cursed energy to save them."

"Jason, you bloody idiot," Mickie shouted, flicking me on the forehead for my actions.

"Hey, I'm *your* idiot," I snorted, rubbing where she'd flicked me. "This is what you signed up for after all."

"You sure you're okay, mi amor?" Haley asked as her eyes narrowed and her nostrils flared while she used her senses to inspect me thoroughly.

"I'm okay, I promise. I don't really feel any different and the finger is only because I've never punched anyone before," I sighed with a shrug. I then began to crawl out of bed as I heard the water turn off in the bathroom. "Anyway, I wasn't the only one that had a busy night, right ladies?"

"Tell me about it," Haley sighed, shaking her head. "Job offer from the fangs, threatening your ex, and I'm pretty sure I made her boy toy piss himself."

"Sounds like my night," Mickie chuckled, shaking her head. "Put a couple of racist parents in their place, got ejected, and Mia caught me mid-shift in the locker room. But I doubt the kid is going to run to the school board."

"Wait, she caught you and isn't going to say anything? Shit, Mickie, is Mia blackmailing you or something?" I asked with an accusatory glare. Then I shifted my sights on Haley. "And you ran into Karynn and… threatened her?"

"If I say she won't be stalking your social media anymore will you still be mad?" Haley asked, giving me a sneaky grin.

"You need to spill the details on that when he's in the tub," Mickie chuckled, Haley nodding eagerly in response. "And as for Mia… well to make a long story short; she, Haley, and Adi should have a book club together. Cause finding out about me made her *dreams* a possible reality."

"Wow… okay then," I grinned, giving her an expression of disbelief.

"Jason, your bath is ready," Sinead called from the bathroom.

As I stood, I stared at the entrance for a moment before turning back to Mickie and Haley. I took in a deep breath, letting it out slowly as I collected my thoughts on the visions I'd seen from Mickie and Sinead when they'd originally touched me.

"And you're sure about, Sinead?" I asked carefully, looking back and forth between the two women. "Can we trust her?"

"We can and we will, love," Mickie answered with finality. Her lips curled into a smile as she looked over her shoulder toward the bathroom and then at Haley and me. "You saved Adi, protected her for all this time from what he turned Sinead into. Now, she needs us just like Adi does. If that means we can keep both of them by our sides, I want to take that chance."

"To be fair, la novia, you have had some questionable fuck buddies in the past, however," Haley began, trailing off as she looked toward the bathroom as well. "Personally I think you're right. She needs our help and, if we didn't believe in second chances, I don't think I'd be here now. Would I?"

"No, you're right. I guess it's time I gave her a real chance," I nodded, blowing them both a kiss as I began to stride toward the bathroom. "Love you both."

"Love you too," Mickie and Haley said in unison with a shared giggle before I watched them stand and pad off toward the kitchen.

As I entered the bathroom, I froze in the doorway of the en suite, my eyes locked onto the deep-seated porcelain tub. The basin was filled with pinkish-hued water, steam rising off of its surface while the room filled with the scent of vanilla and cherry. I hadn't expected Sinead to fill the tub and use a bath bomb, nor did I expect her to be patiently kneeling beside the porcelain basin.

She had relegated herself into a nadu pose, thighs spread with her palms resting upward on her knees. She displayed herself as subservient to me as I carefully stepped forward and met her expectant yet submissive gaze.

"You know you don't have to do that, right?" I asked as I drew closer toward her, giving her a relaxed expression as the sweet scents eased my nerves.

"My apologies. It's… habit," Sinead said, her chin dipping as her cheeks flushed with embarrassment.

"Habits are a pain in the ass to break. I get it," I said as I got onto one knee in front of her and gently cupped her shoulder with one hand. As I touched her, her memories flooded my psyche with flashing visions that displayed the routine during her subjugation. The memories and emotions behind them made me shudder and hiss in disgust. "So, I know something happened between you and Mickie last night. And, honestly, I'm happy for you."

"I'm sorry, I should have asked-"

"Sinead," I said softly, my hand moving from her shoulder to catch her chin. She settled against my touch, allowing me to lift her head up so that our eyes met. I wanted - no - needed to help break the cycle of abuse that Sinead and Adi had been put through. And it started with me helping her heal. "I will never require you to do stuff like this. Ever. You know that right?"

"I do," she nodded sadly then tilted her head as our eyes met again. "I remember the basis of your abilities. I am assuming during this physical contact you have seen my memories and felt those emotions. You understand me possibly better than myself."

"I know you see me… as your Dom, which is something I'm still figuring out myself," I said, nodding softly at her. "Adi and Haley are the ones who helped me even realize I had that side of me. And what they've

taught me about being a *true* Dominant is that the Submissives are the

ones who hold *all* of the power. If a sub says no, it damn well means no.

You should be the one getting all of the benefits and everything you need

from that relationship, not the other way around. That make sense?"

The explanation made Sinead pause as she gave me a curious

contemplative look. Her body shuddered as the tension inside her began

to wane and she relented enough to lean into my touch. Her cheek nuzzled

against my palm as she seemed to welcome my touch, seeming almost

humanly affectionate in the exchange.

"Thank you for running the water, by the way. It looks like it'll feel

amazing once I get in," I said, acknowledging her handiwork. "If you want

to stay, you're more than welcome to. But if you want to go out and join

the girls, I won't punish you for doing that if it's what you want. Deal?"

"Deal," she said with a curt nod, her lips tugging upward into a

soft smile as I rose to my feet.

As I did so, I became very aware that I happened to put a certain

part of my body at her eye level. I thought to apologize immediately for

the chance of making her uncomfortable, however, I found her staring in

appreciation at my length, biting her bottom lip while the lavender hue

of her blush spread across her cheeks and chest. Shrugging, I stepped

forward, slowly sinking into the hot water and groaning in satisfaction. As

I lowered myself, I let the heat ease the tension in my body and savored the pleasant burn of relief brought to my muscles that had been strained from stress and anxiety.

She made this perfect. I didn't realize how much I needed it.

"M-may I have permission to speak and… to come closer, Jason?" Sinead asked after several minutes of silence between us. I was so engrossed in the bath she'd drawn for me that I'd nearly forgotten that I wasn't alone in the room.

"If that's what you want, Sinead. That's your call," I said before sinking into the water enough that I could soak my face and my hair. When I came up for air, I found Sinead leaning against the side of the tub, her hand tentatively stroking the surface of the water while tears rolled down her cheeks. "Sin, are you okay?"

"I… apologize, Jason," she said, taking in a deep shuddering breath before she stiffened as I reached out for her without thinking. My thumb dabbed at her cheeks, wiping away the tears before her body seemed to relax and she sank into my embrace."When I first came here I had resigned myself to becoming your tool and to serve my punishment for failing Samael. Now? I find myself drawn to an eagerness to help you, duty-bound to right the wrongs I helped create. I felt ashamed for what I did to you and the Mistresses. And then last night happened… which started with you."

"What do you mean?"

"You said you trusted me."

I did, didn't I?

Truthfully, I wasn't thinking straight when Professor Whitestone called me about Gary. I was being fueled by rage when I left Sinead her ring and left her to protect our home. In doing so I'd made it clear what part of me had been feeling at the time; this was her home too. Had that been the catalyst for everything that happened last night between her and Mickie? Was that the reason for what looked like a ritual set up in the living room that Haley and I'd found?

When I thought back to the memories my abilities had siphoned from her and Mickie last night, one moment seemed to stick out more than anything. It was the moment Sinead had pinned Mickie to the bed, sobbing as she held a blade to Mickie's throat and her pleading words.

Never cast me aside again. Don't ever leave me alone again.

"I know what we have is a massive change for you but I've noticed you beginning to change as well," I said honestly as I watched her eyes carefully while stroking her cheeks with my thumb. "Between helping Lex with her hellfire, trying to make our lives feel more normal, and you not being as cold and indifferent as you once were. Honestly, I'd love to get to know you more. The *real* you."

"In time, you will. I just… I don't remember a time where I've had the freedom to reflect on my life or when I was permitted to be more than in someone's service," Sinead answered cautiously, her mind trying to dig through her psyche to find memories from her life before Samael.

"Adi was like that when I first found her. She was broken and cautious before we learned to trust each other. Now I hardly remember what she was like before and not the flirty, book-loving woman I fell in love with," I said, my eyes going dreamy at the memory of my Adelaide. Sinead furrowed her brow at the mention of me being in love with Adi, a question or thought seeming to cross her mind. "We both helped each other get to a much better place. I… want the same for you."

"Thank you, Jason," Sinead said, a soft smile curling on her lips as she took a deep, shuddering breath. "I'm not sure you realize what that means to me."

"Adi was the one who helped me figure that out for myself. It only seems natural that I keep that cycle going, you know?" I chuckled softly as my hand wandered up to stroke her long silver hair. As my fingertips ran across her scalp, Sinead's eyes fluttered closed and her body shivered under my touch. "The most important thing for you to remember is that you're not a slave here. We,,, *I* want you to think for yourself, do things you want, and be honest. That's all I ask."

"You… say I should be me and as I would wish, yes?" Sinead asked after another moment of me softly playing with her hair. When her eyes met mine, the icy blue sparkled with something akin to happiness. Then her eyes wandered toward the pinkish-hued water, steam still rolling from its surface, as a deep lavender hue spread across her porcelain cheeks. "May I be selfish enough to make a request?"

"Yeah, of course," I chuckled softly, giving her a curious look.

"May I… join you in the bath, Master?"

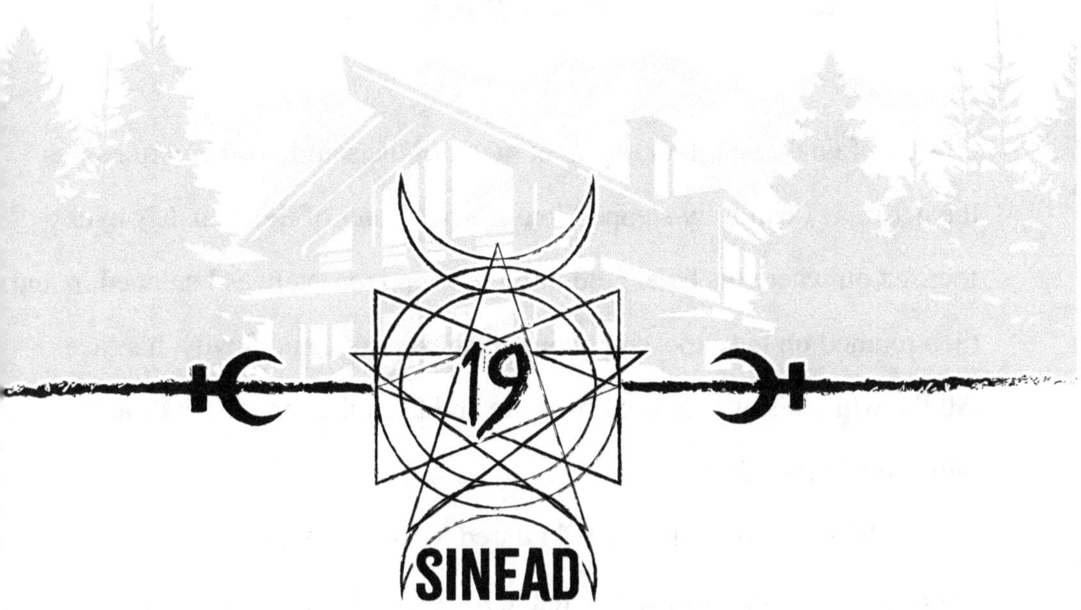

THIS WAS THE FOURTH TIME I'D EVER BEEN SO BOLD.

The first three had come at a severe cost to me and I promised myself I would not make that same mistake again. Now, however, I seemed to have thrown that caution to the wind. The events of last night changed everything, I was no longer a tool to do someone's bidding. I had the honest trust of Jason, Mickie, and Haley pushing me forward down a path I didn't know the destination of.

However, being pushed down this path allowed me to sleep and dream for the first time in decades. A dream that felt more than that. It felt like a memory. One where I rode with Rowan, wind whipping through my hair as we raced along dark emerald rolling hills above a swirling, tumultuous ocean of deep cerulean. A time when I had felt… happy and at peace.

I had felt myself truly smiling in that dream. The same I wore now as I found Jason looking up at me with the same stormy cerulean as the ocean as I carefully stepped into the hot water of the bath. My eyes focused on where his hand held mine to keep me steady as I stepped in and then roamed up his exposed abdomen, chest, arms, and finally, his face. All the while his eyes poured over me and I felt the same hesitation I'd felt with Mickie last night.

"Am I… to your liking?" I dared to ask, an uncomfortable pressure in my belly waiting for the inevitable rejection. Then I remembered the words McKenna and Haley had told me this morning when the three of us woke up. "The Mistresses said that I was to tell you that you have their blessings. I don't know what that means, however."

"It means," he said with a soft chuckle as his hands took mine and applied gentle pressure to guide me downward. "That my dumbass should have told you a long time ago that you're gorgeous, Sinead."

As Jason guided me, I shuddered as the warmth of the water enveloped my body, sensations of comfort, safety, and something else racing across my skin. When I came to rest, I was straddling Jason, the feel of his skin and firm muscles applying gentle pressure to mine. Once I was settled, his hands moved, tracing slow circles along my thighs and hips, his touch sending heat through my entire being that felt more scorching than the steaming water around us. Hot enough that I could feel the burning that darkened my cheeks move downward across my breasts.

"Surely you jest," I said, my breathing becoming quicker as my eyes fell onto the smile curling his lips. The urge to lean forward and kiss him like I had McKenna became nearly overwhelming. "And how… does their blessing involve me?"

"Well… it's how our dynamic works," Jason said, shrugging his wide shoulders as his eyes swayed back and forth. "We're polyamorous. It means we can love and express those feelings with more than one person. We have open communication and we're allowed to bring more people into our hearts and relationships. Technically those new partners can be separate from the others but our dynamic hasn't seemed to function that same way."

"This does make sense to me," I nodded and realized I had moved forward as Jason spoke, my stomach now resting against his. "Should I call for McKenna and Haley to properly discuss my involvement with you?"

"If that's what you would prefer," Jason said, letting me have that choice for myself. A sensation that still felt so foreign. "I know Adi would say yes since she's said I don't really need to ask her permission for more partners. Something about me being touch-starved and needing connections. McKenna and Haley have given me free rein as well as long as they approve of the partner and don't feel like they'd be a threat to us."

I nodded slowly at his response, my elbows resting against his chest as I drew closer to him. I found my thighs tightening as his fingers danced along my skin. Each time they came close to my buttocks I felt my body shiver with delight and anticipation, my thighs squeezing against his hips. Moreover, my position allowed me to feel him as he grew aroused, the length of him stiffening and swelling beneath me.

"I do not wish to be a replacement for Adelaide if that is a concern. I know I would never fill her role in your home. If permitted, I want to seek her forgiveness and take her hand in friendship... if she allows it. Like I should have back then," I admitted, part of me needing to make sure that was never left unsaid. "As for McKenna and Haley they said, and I'm quoting verbatim, *you have my blessing, love. If you want Jason, ask him to be his.* Does this mean you wish to have me in a contractual bond more than the Ananke ring provides?"

I tried mimicking Mickie's accent, which at first had made Jason grin wider. However, as I continued, his eyes widened and his face froze in something of shock or realization. His stiffening body language had another effect as his hands tightened on me, his strong calloused hands tensing against my rear. The reaction my body had to him made my hips roll, sending another deep quiver down my spine and a gasp leaving my lips as my sex ground against his thick length. The sensation made the puckered hole of my ass and the entrance of my vagina tighten with need.

"No contract, just trust and honesty," Jason said, his voice and breath quivering as his nose brushed against mine. "Am *I* really who you want, Sinead?"

"Yes," I said breathlessly, barely more than a whisper as my mind fogged over in a haze.

With my response, fire swept through me as one of his hands trailed up my back and pressed down on my shoulder and his lips met mine. The feel of his lips cradling and taking hold of mine flooded my senses with blissful ecstasy. That sensation melted into a need for more. I sated my hunger for Jason with my lips and tongue, my flesh buzzing with the fresh warm, and salty flavor of him that I couldn't find the words to describe. All while my nostrils flared and took in the deep intoxicating scent of a mountainside forest after a fresh rain that was entirely him.

The groan that escaped his lips reverberated inside me as our mouths parted wider, our heads rolling in a slow dance. However, even though I had initiated, Jason took control, pushing the kiss deeper as he began to feast on my lips and tongue at our combined leisure. The prolonged, deep kiss rewarded him in a low, throaty moan of delight as I savored him, each touch sending more jolts of bliss and hunger coursing through my veins.

He growled softly against my lips as our tongues rolled in an erotic dance before he squeezed a whimpering moan from my throat when his palm that cradled my ass tightened. It had been two decades since I'd wanted a strong, firm grip on my body. I'd forgotten what that sense of desire was but Jason's touch reminded me in an instant. The sensation of need and desire became overwhelming as my bottom lip was trapped between his teeth. His gentle, teasing bite made my entire body thrum with pleasure, my hips grinding my nethers harder against his pulsing shaft and spreading my lips around him.

He broke the kiss, making me whine in protest before the hand that had snaked its way from my shoulder to my cheek tilted me away. Before I could protest, his lips leaving mine he began trailing small kisses and nibbles down the center of my neck to the spot just below my collar. The touch of his lips there made me release another whine of pleasure as my hips rolled harder against him.

"God, I love the sound of your voice, Sin," he whispered hotly, his tone low and trembling from restraint. "I won't be able to hold back much longer, and if that happens, I'm gonna leave a mark here."

His low tone made me shudder again, making me acutely aware of how close we were. My arms no longer held me up from his chest, instead having wrapped themselves around Jason's neck. Instead, his heaving chest pressed against mine, my small breasts melding against his flesh as my nipples, already achingly stiff, ground against him. A wildfire was coursing through me, sprouting from everywhere my body touched his, any resistance to Jason being burned away.

I had come to fear pain in all forms. However, the pleasurable stings McKenna had given me last night reminded me that I shouldn't fear all of them. I now understood what he meant by leaving a mark upon my body and the thought of it sent boiling pressure into my sweltering core. A feeling that Mickie had reawakened last night after so long. I had relished in the undeniable pleasure that pinch of pain her bites had delivered and I wanted the same from him.

I wanted Jason, in his entirety, to be *my* Master.

"Make me- ah~"

My answer was turned from words into a high-keening moan as a low trickling growl filled the air and Jason teethed the flesh of my neck. The sudden shock of pain became molten pleasure that danced across my skin and down my spine. Jason's grip on me tightened as he bit down, drawing my body tight against his and forcing another gasping moan from me as my throbbing clitoris ground against his swollen cock. The firm shape of him melded against me from the base of my lips up to my navel, the thick vein along the underside pulsing against my pearl that made my body sing.

My legs shook with pleasure, tightening around his hips and putting punishing pressure against me. My nails dug into his flesh as my hands squeezed him tighter, my hips bucking feverishly against him as I seized up. The culmination of pleasure and desire that I had been denied for so long became an overflowing inferno inside me that pushed me until I burst. Like a spring that had coiled so tight inside me that it finally snapped under pressure resulting in my pussy throbbing and quivering with heavy, rippling waves as the pressure released.

I.... I climaxed.

There was a ghostly urge that came with that release, a desire that once wanted me to pleasure and seek pleasure from Samael. Now that urge was entirely focused on Jason. Before last night I hadn't remembered what it was, then Mickie brought me to completion three, possibly four times. I remembered waking up this morning, my thighs slick with my desire from the feeling of being cradled into Jason and his length pressing against my ass and back. Between that and how wet I had been when I climbed into the water with Jason, I could no longer deny that I desperately wanted him.

"You okay?" Jason asked, his voice bringing me out of that orgasmic haze fogging my mind. I hadn't realized I sat up in his lap, my chest heaving directly in front of his gaze.

"I am," I answered with a genuine smile as I brought one of my hands from resting against his chest to the bite mark on my neck. I knew it would bruise and I would happily display it beside the one McKenna had given me last night. "I had been denied pleasure for so long I forgot how an orgasm can feel."

"And how do you feel?" Jason asked, reaching up to cup my cheek which I pressed against in response as water dripped down the center of my breasts and abdomen. The sudden mix of warm and cold made me bite my lip with delight.

"Mmm, wonderful," I sighed with a sense of ease. "However…"

From my neck, I traced my hand down my body, watching his stormy eyes following them, delighted that he seemed to pause on my achingly stiff nipples. When I reached my destination, I gently dragged a finger from the swollen head of his cock, down the vein until I reached where our bodies met. I relished that he pulsed and twitched in response to my touch and how much the look in his eyes said he desired me completely.

"Is the mark on my neck the only thing we need to do to make sure I'm yours?" I asked as I slipped my hand around him, shuddering at the discovery that my fingers didn't touch my palm. I stood Jason at attention as I began stroking slowly, earning low moans and growls of pleasure from the man beneath me. "Anything to make me more than your tool?"

"You can be anything you want, Sinead, okay?" Jason said as his hands found their way to my hips, caressing up my flanks as our eyes met once more. "You're not a tool or a plaything. You're a gorgeous woman that I've been stupid lucky to be living with these last few weeks."

My mind fell deep into his eyes, swimming in that storming ocean that drew me deeper into the tides. Inside that storm I found his unspoken promise; that he would always do what was needed to protect what was his. And that included me among the bed of gorgeous women he shared. A promise that made me hold his full length at attention as my hips rose upward to meet him, water splashing around my hips while I shuddered when his head massaged my protruding button.

He throbbed in response, his tip already beading with desire, as I ground against him. I broke eye contact to dip my head and watch him part my lavender folds and press against my pulsing entrance.

"You break this promise of yours to never cast me aside and I will come for your head," I warned with a throaty hiss as the head of his dick pushed inside me. I shuddered, nearly losing my control, as he spread me open further than that bastard of a demon ever had. "It will be displayed on my mantle next to his as a warning to any other potential masters to never cross me."

"Whatever you say, *Princess*," he chuckled softly as one of his hands cupped the back of my head and pulled me forward to hover over him. He kissed me in a soft, yet possessive manner, the emphasis on the title he'd given me making my chest, head, and pussy thrum. "Now-"

Before he could say anything else or tease me further, I drove down on him and swallowed his growling moan with my lips. The sound of him mixed with the shrill scream of pleasure that I let out into our embrace as I impaled myself on him entirely.

My walls milked him with an impossibly tight grip, letting me feel him throbbing inside me like it was my own heartbeat as I was spread open with a fullness I never knew I'd craved. As his thick length stretched me to capacity, pressure was applied to every single spot within my slick, velvet tunnel and sent a lightning storm throughout my veins.

Jason cursed under his shaking breath as our kiss broke and I relished the feel of him as deep as I could possibly take him. To add to that lightning storm surging through me was the feel of his calloused hands holding me. His fingertips sent more jolts of bliss to my core as his grip shifted to cup my hips and ass firmly as we settled into a comfortable position.

I laid my forehead against Jason's, my lips stinging with my wide smile, my eyes fluttering lazily while I began to rock my hips. I found reprieve in the way his eyes lidded and rolled in response to my touch.

The hard, rolling movements made the water lap against me vigorously as I coaxed that storm more, making my breath hitch every time I took him inside me and the water slapped against my flesh. Each pulse and twitch of his swollen dick made me spasm in response as I moved to buck in his lap as if he were a feral stallion.

The droning sting of him hitting my cervix made the fire inside my core swelter to new heights. I bottomed out on him repeatedly and felt an overwhelming pressure against my belly. Looking down, I marveled at the sight of a bulge pressing outward, a testament to how thoroughly Jason filled my aching cunt.

To prolong the sensation of the pressure against my rippling walls, especially that swollen, hypersensitive pad along the roof of my tunnel I sat down completely. Using my hands as anchors against his firm abdomen, I swirled my hips, rolling him wildly inside me and pulling whining cries of bliss from my being. Doubling the sensations dancing across my skin was my throbbing clit grinding hard against his pubic bone, the protruding bulb being massaged in fast, aching circles that had me on edge.

Within moments of my feverish pace, my head rolled back in an ethereal scream of pleasure loud enough every god in existence would hear me. I shook, the water vibrating violently as I hit that crescendo, and went rigid as my body was sent into the heavens once more. I bathed Jason in warmth as my climax hit me, holding me hostage as every nerve ending inside me sang. He throbbed and moaned loudly in response as I squoze and spasmed around him.

Once the heavy waves of pleasure subsided and released me from their stranglehold, I fell forward. I was left a soaked, boneless thing as I fought to catch my breath in his arms.

I sighed in bliss as he held me, stroking small circles across my back and I savored his touch and embrace around me. I smiled, feeling warm, heady, and full as I relaxed in his arms, however, I felt as if something was missing. There was a piece of the puzzle that was our union that still hadn't been placed. It was the piece I had loathed feeling from Samael when he'd reached completion but desired from Jason.

"You… have yet to finish," I said quietly, my body still shaky as I pushed up to look at him.

"But you did, that's what matters," Jason countered with a shrug and a satisfied grin.

"No," I demanded, shaking my head in vehement defiance. I would not allow him to reverse the roles that I'd been freed from. "You will not be used like he did with me. I cannot allow that."

"Babe, you can barely hold yourself up," he replied, my lip quivering as he used the term I'd heard him call the others. I… had joined their ranks. A rank that didn't feel right to hold without his essence leaking from me like I'd seen with McKenna and Haley. "I don't want to push you too hard or hurt you."

"You *stupid, wonderful* man," I growled, smacking his chest weakly, and felt tears beginning to roll down my cheeks. I hit him harder a second and then a third time before words spilled out of me without thinking. "W-Why couldn't you have been my first and only…"

"You really want to keep going?"

"Please, Master," I pleaded, my eyes full of longing and need that had been denied to me for so long. Then I gasped as we shifted forward and my back laid against the edge of the tub.

"If it's too much, tell me to stop. Okay?" He said quietly and I sucked in a breath as he settled me against the tops of his thighs as he got onto his knees.

I nodded eagerly as he pulled back, making me release a sigh of pleasure as his cock receded from my quivering snatch. One hand clasped the edge of the tub, supporting the back of my head as I looked up at him while the other gripped my hips to keep me steady.

His eyes fluttered closed as he let out a growl and drove himself forward, sheathing himself inside my tight, aching cunt and making me gasp with a sudden rush of ecstasy. My legs wrapped around his hips as the position let me hover on the water's edge, the sloshing coating my stomach in a rapid mix of warmth and cold.

Jason found his rhythm within a few strokes, his thick shaft boring into me with a brisk pace that had my body bouncing eagerly between him and the porcelain wall. Each heavy thrust stretched my walls in a delicious way that I quickly found myself craving. Just as much as I loved the way he grit his teeth and grunted with feral need as he took me. The look in his eyes and his quickening pace made my chest ache from how hard my heart was pounding against it.

"M-Master," I gasped as he rocked into me faster, slamming my back against the bathtub wall which had my dripping sex gripping him harder with need.

I could already feel that pressure inside my belly rising, heat sweltering as he sheathed himself inside me again and again. My cries made his cock pulse, stretching my rippling walls further and his next thrust harder. I called for him again and screamed in delight as the result repeated itself, his grip on my hip tightening harder.

He really likes it when I call him that.

Jason's hips rocked in time with the sloshing waves of the tub, his hips slapping into mine with the same force the ocean beat against a rocky cliff. I cried out for him each time he plowed through my tunnel, filling me with that delicious pressure and fullness that made my body temperature rise. Soon the noise of the waves was overtaken by my shrieks of delight and filled the house with the sound of me calling his name like a prayer.

The pressure and heat in my core skyrocketed to its limit as that coil wound up tighter when I felt a warm wetness around one of my achingly stiff nipples. Looking down, I found Jason with his mouth on me, capturing one of my breasts. My body shook as his tongue and teeth toyed with the pebbled flesh voraciously, and sending fire racing across my skin. Then the overstimulation nearly became too much to bear as I heard his breathing going ragged, a testament to how close to the edge he was himself. And that I was doing that to him.

"Oh, Hades," I whimpered, calling out my god's name as his teeth tightened around me and my hands pulled him down against me. I wanted more, I wanted everything Jason had to give and soon my voice was gasping for him to deliver. "Harder~"

His teeth clamped down and his cheeks sank in as he suckled roughly on my nipple, the lavender flesh of my areola disappearing completely into his mouth. I cried out again as he bit down on my taught peak, making sure to leave another welcome bruise that branded me as his.

I let out a shrill cry of pleasure as his fingers dug into the flesh of my ass, leaving marks there while his hips pistoned faster and harder. Jason clung to me like I was a long-lost lover that he finally got the chance to be with and live out his dreams. Like I was the only one who mattered and his entire world had shrunk down to just me.

This was what I craved. To be fucked so eagerly and desperately that felt as if I was needed and that my pleasure mattered just as much, not less.

"Yes, Master," I moaned out with whining breaths and cries of delight as he pounded into my hot, wet sex, my walls squeezing him tighter to try and cling to him as desperately as I could.

My eyes rolled, the sensations of pleasure being delivered pushing me onto a new plane of nirvana. I savored the feel of his teeth and tongue across my nipple, the way his delicious cock pounded against my cervix and g-spot, and the way the harsh waves slapped against my puckered rear.

I wanted him in every way; to feel him driving into my ass, to salivate with him down my throat, and to feel him leaking out of me. Jason was my true Master; who I'd willingly allow to claim all of me and touch every inch of me without fear or hesitation.

"Sinead," he growled, his hands gripping my ass as tightly as he could as he let out a strained husky moan of pleasure.

Then I heard him whisper the word Princess like a prayer right as he slammed forward with everything he had and made both of us collapse into the water with every inch of his cock driving deeper. The force of him being buried inside me, the sound of his moans, and his strained pleading for me sent me over the edge, overflowing for a third time.

I screamed his name, letting it be heard as if I was calling on a deity, as my walls constricted around him, milking his length with everything I had. My warmth coated him in my essence then I felt my walls stretch as he pulsed, each throb of his cock spilling the white-hot heat of his seed into my eager snatch.

I basked in that heat of him as we came together and I felt myself nearly wanting to burst from the blissful concoction swirling inside my pussy. Jason collapsed onto me, his strength giving out entirely as I caught him and we both sank under the lukewarm water in our embrace. Both of us heaving as we tried to catch what little breath we could.

"Thank you, Master," I said after a long few minutes of silence, just basking in the feel of his body against mine in a lazy but loving embrace.

"You're welcome, Princess," he said with a purred whisper that made me bite my lip in desire and give his softening length one last squeeze.

"Gods, you two are bloody fucking adorable together." Mickie purred lustfully.

"Especially the way you call her Princess, mi amor," Haley hummed with lazy delight.

I was startled to find her and Haley leaning against the tub from where they knelt on the bath mat. Mickie circled her finger in the water as her eyes roamed over Jason and me together while Haley watched us with a dreamy glint. I cursed in my native Gaelic tongue which only made Mickie laugh. I flinched when she pulled herself over the side of the tub and then froze when I felt her lips press against my forehead in a gentle kiss.

My eyes went a little wide, not only from the kiss but, as she leaned up, I found that she was completely nude and her large, bountiful breasts were on full display. I found my mouth salivating at the thought of tasting her again and wanting to explore her more thoroughly.

Then Haley stood, my body shivering as my eyes roamed over her luxurious curves and nude form as she strode to where my head rested against the tub wall and leaned down to kiss my forehead as well. Before I could stop myself I felt the top of my head nuzzling my hair against her plump breasts savoring the feel of her warm flesh against me.

I want both of them as badly as I want Jason again.

"C'mon, lovebirds, I'll go warm up breakfast for us," Mickie said with a wink as she rose to her feet and held out a hand toward Jason and Haley extended a hand for me.

"I do feel quite hungry after that," I smiled, finally feeling genuine emotions begin to flood back into my mind after being so distant for so long. I took her hand and, with the help of her and Jason, I managed to step out of the tub on shaky legs. "I shall go get dressed."

"Honestly, I don't mind if you want to show off that cute little ass of yours, Princess," Haley grinned with a teasing sparkle in her eye. "Lex texted and said she and Xander won't be by for a while so we got time to hang out."

The comment made the three of them laugh, Haley making a comment about it being about time the two of them hooked up before I joined in. The first time I'd ever done so. As I stepped out and dried, I bit my lip as my eyes focused on Jason's semi-flaccid length that was still partially coated in a mixture of our union. It felt… right seeing my essence on him and feeling his seed running down my leg.

"By the way," Jason said, giving McKenna a long, passionate kiss before she allowed him to dry off as well. "How long were you two watching?"

"Oh," Mckenna drawled playfully, rolling her eyes that were filled to the brim with mischief. "About the time she threatened to chop your head off."

"I'm surprised you didn't hear the two of us right next to you," Haley chuckled, giving me a playful wink as she licked her fingers which I noticed were glistening with moisture.

Jason laughed and shook his head while McKenna leaned down and cupped her hand around my ear. Her sweet, seductive whispers made me shiver in anticipation as I heard a word of blissful instruction. I narrowed my gaze and strode toward Jason who gave me a confused expression until I gripped his shoulders and lowered him. I hummed in delight as I sank my teeth into the crook of his shoulder and he let out a groan of pain mixed with desire.

"Fuck, Sinead," he muttered softly until I let him go and I marveled at the way his skin bleached from where I locked onto him. "What was that for?"

I gave him a wide, satisfied grin before turning and letting him watch my ass and hips sway with a teasing bounce in my step. Looking over my shoulder, I found his eyes hungrily locked onto my backside and I felt pride swell inside me.

"Now, Master Jason, you're mine. Forever."

IT WAS AN ODD SIGHT, SEEING SINEAD'S HEAD FLOATING BY ITSELF.

After the escapade in the bath, the four of us had gotten some much-needed fuel in the form of reheated eggs, bacon, and some waffles pulled from the freezer. Once reinvigorated with a warm meal, one that was far less awkward now that Sinead actually joined us, we got back to work. Sinead insisted on running another searching ritual, especially since now her Ananke ring was fully charged. If not overflowing.

It was similar to what we discovered with Adi; a healthy romp boosted her spiritual energy reserves to the point that she wasn't spending as much. When I slipped the ring on, the band was humming with power, the inlay glowing a brilliant cyan that matched Sinead's eyes. The ring, however, wasn't the only thing buzzing. As I wore it, the hum in my chest increased, the spot where Tori had told me my magic resided vibrating with crackling static energy.

I felt self-conscious of my nudity as I walked around the apartment so I threw on some sweatpants and a tank top as I studied the wards. There came my second shock. While Sinead sat nude and cross-legged at the head of her pentacle, I wandered toward the corners of the apartment where I'd placed precious stones and candles and had to pause when I investigated the first point. There, even without the candles lit, I could see a faint golden-green glow emanating from the stones and it looked as if runes had been carved into their surfaces.

Haley and Mickie had also gotten dressed not long after I had. Haley was sitting on the couch watching Sinead in the outfit she typically lounged around the apartment in, consisting of a pair of red flannel pants and a loose black tank top. Meanwhile, Mickie strode by my side in her gym clothes; a pair of black leggings and a white zip-up hoodie that she'd cut the sleeves off of. Mickie noticed my reaction to one of the small warding ritual points and leaned down to inspect the humming quartz crystal with me.

"It… smells different than before. That's kind of weird," she said idly, her nostrils flaring as her brow scrunched.

"It's not glowing from your perspective?" I asked, swallowing a lump in my throat. I still wasn't used to the knowledge of having a sort of personal magic so the fact that it was glowing and had runes floating on it was a bit unnerving.

"No," Mickie said, her eyes turning up toward me with a look of shock. "Are they to you?"

"And I'm guessing you don't see the engraved runes either?" I asked in exasperation, drawing out the first word.

"Okay, that's bloody spooky," she chuckled softly before following me back out into the living room.

"Not as spooky as last night," I said, shaking my head with a wry smirk. "Still can't believe I beat the shit out of Gary."

"Mr. Civka, right?" Haley asked, leaning her head over the back of the couch as she watched us enter the room from an inverted view.

"Pudgy bastard, about yay tall, walks like a mutated penguin, and most definitely pulls the whole Scrooge McDuck shtick?" I said sarcastically as I held my hand up to about my chin.

"And has a wife - well ex-wife now - who is a million times out of his league?" Haley snorted and hummed as I leaned down to kiss her.

"Yup, that's the one," I laughed, shaking my head.

"I don't thin I'll ever understand how he pulled a dame like her," Mickie chuckled, holding up her fingers to count her ideas. "She could've had anyone better than that arse."

"Oi ve," Haley groaned, rolling her eyes. "He's lucky you only punched him. If I have to deal with him again? Telling me to *get out of his country, go back to Mexico,* or call me a greasy wetback one more time…

I don't think I could hold back from clawing him to pieces."

As we talked, my eyes watched Sinead every few moments, the flaming skull zipping around over the makeshift map. As she narrowed the search down, the skull would let out a haunting, dissonant whisper that made it sound like some eldritch shadow had come to life. When it did so, her headless body would lean forward to make an X over the point in red marker. As opposed to the circles made of black marker she'd drawn last night.

"Something is still bugging me about his wet dream of the Sand Hollow location," Haley sighed, leaning forward and narrowing her eyes at the map. "Sure, he had some great offers for the lots but that's not his only lucrative property. In fact, his clients have more money going… toward other… developments…"

Haley's voice began to trail off, her brow cocking in confusion as she stared down at the map. Her lips parted as if she wanted to say more but something had caught her deeper attention. She gave me a puzzled look as her eyes went back and forth between the map and me, tilting her head in bewilderment.

"Cariño," Haley began. Her voice filled with affectionate pleading. "Can I borrow your computer real quick?"

"Yeah, sure," I said, my turn to tilt my head in confusion and cock a brow. "Why, what's up?"

Haley stood and marched into the office, where I followed in time to watch her plop down into my seat with a bounce. When I rounded my desk to see what she was doing, I found the Volk Haus logo on the employee end of a login page staring back at me. She quickly went through her profile, opening a tab of clients and scrolling down to Gary Civka whose client profile had a big red warning label on it.

"After Thomas made you and Adi part of the pack, he cut ties with Gary. Pendejo has been livid ever since," Haley idly explained as she leaned in toward the screen, scrolling rapidly. "He said he'll reconsider doing business with Civka Enterprises if Anya takes control of the board of directors, and the company assets, and rebrands it for herself when the divorce proceedings are finalized. And as long as she treats you with respect."

I had no idea Thomas had done that. He'd cut contact with one of his biggest clients for my sake and what he'd put me through. I already owed the big guy for giving me a chance and being able to find my two shifter girlfriends. I owed him for making me and Adi part of the pack as Huggin and Muunin. I was never going to repay my debt to him at this rate.

"Okay, here are all of his projects we had on file, the project investors, and how much they contributed," Haley said as she clicked a button and my printer whirred to life. Once several pages were spit out, she stood to collect them and then looked at me over her shoulder. "Do you have a yellow highlighter by chance?"

I grabbed what she asked for, still confused at her actions but curious as to where she was going with this. Once we were back in the living room, Haley splayed the papers in front of her as she sat at the bottom of the pentacle. Her eyes roamed over the spreadsheets at a rapid pace while the highlighter I'd given her was put to good use.

"What in the bloody hell is going on?" Mickie asked, folding her arms as she curiously watched Sinead and Haley work.

"I have no idea," I chuckled as I came to stand next to her, watching the two with pride and admiration. "I think- Ah, fuck!"

I fell to one knee as the thrumming in my chest turned to pain, striking my nerves like whips from inside me. One of my eyes twitched with pain while a headache put thick pressure against my skull. My open eye drew quickly toward the northeast corner of the apartment when a precious stone sat. It glowed brighter than before, the runes burning hot around its surfaces while the candle behind it came to life with a flickering green flame.

Something is pressing against the wards trying to get in.

"Jason, are you okay?" Mickie said with a mix of shock and fear in her tone. She and Haley both were kneeling beside me, carefully watching my movements.

"I'm okay. I've never felt anything touch the protective barrier before so it caught me off guard," I grunted, hissing as I forced myself to stand.

Both of them instantly raised their heads, noses flaring and eyes rolling to that of their beasts. They gave the ceiling a curious look before looking back down at each other, black and golden green eyes meeting black and amber gold. Both let out rumbling growls as their heads turned toward the door of the apartment and looked ready to pounce on unsuspecting prey.

"Help… me…"

A woman's voice echoed through my head, strained and barely hanging onto what little life was left in her tone. She sounded broken, in immense pain, and on the verge of losing consciousness. Her voice sounded… desperate.

"Haley, keep doing what you were doing. Mickie, will you grab my cross and my rings for me?" I said, growling as I forced the pain into the back of my mind.

"Mi Amor-"

"Pequeño lobo," I said, giving her solid contact through one eye as she tried to growl her disapproval at me. My affectionate nickname for her made her entire body shudder before her eyes bled back to that of her human side. "Please. You were on to something to find Adi, don't let me get in the way of that."

"Jason, we smell sulfur, brimstone, and blood. Lots of it," Mickie hissed, her fists clenched tight at her sides.

"Kitten, I need you to trust me," I said, forcing my twitching eye open to look at her with a plea in my voice and expression.

"Using our pet names is so not fair, cabrón" Haley grumbled before giving Mickie a glance and then slumping as she returned back to her highlighter and pile of papers.

"Bollocks," Mickie growled, sticking her tongue out at me as she turned on her heel to go grab my cross and malachite rings for me. "So totally not fair."

I chuckled as she protested but handed me my jewelry when she met me at the door and I quickly slipped it on. We made our way down the stairs toward the garage where a pair of street bikes were parked next to my Bronco. Interestingly enough, a wooden sawhorse with a saddle on its back sat on the opposite side of the SUV. I made a mental note to ask Sinead about it later as I hit the button for the garage door making it creak as the motor whined to life.

Mickie and I froze as daylight poured in from the alley behind the bookstore and a body lying on the ground came into view. A small pool of blood stretched out from underneath a figure shielded from view by a large vinyl banner and a dark teal-colored velvet peacoat. A scene that looked as if a coroner had dropped off a body wrapped in a makeshift sleeping bag.

Mickie held out a hand to hold me back as she stalked forward, her leggings stretched to capacity as they struggled to accommodate her shifted legs. Her tail swung sharply behind her, twitching in the way cats did when they were on high alert. Ringed spots had appeared against her dark bronze skin as she moved down onto all fours and she stalked forward like the giant predatory cat her beast was.

As she neared the materials draped over the lifeless body, she batted at the banner to test for any response. When she didn't get one, she looked over her shoulder at me, her black and golden green eyes glowing with animalistic power. Her elongated ears twitched as her bestial features looked to me for instruction, wondering what I wanted to do.

"I smell Adi on it," Mickie said, her tone raspy from her partial shift to her beast side. "Think our little bird did this?"

"I'm not sure," I said as I stepped closer, took a deep breath, and narrowed my eyes at a peacoat that looked vaguely familiar to me. The fact that a banner for Brandon Forrest, one of my clients, was draped over the body, did nothing to calm my nerves. "Only one way to find out."

I ripped the coverings off of the body and froze once more as I looked down at the sight in front of me. As I scanned over the figure, Mickie stood with me, a low growl reverberating through her throat as we watched in a mix of confusion, awe, and disappointment.

"Who the bloody fuck is this?"

After a short debate between Mickie and me on what to do with the body, the sounds of a gurgling cough and weak breathing made the decision for me. I remembered hearing someone asking for help, her voice weak and pleading as it pressed against the protective wards. Without a second thought, I crouched down and hooked my arms under the woman's head and thighs. I muttered the phrase for disarming the barrier under my breath as I heaved her upward and headed back to our apartment.

Haley and Mickie snarled at each other as I entered the room with the body of a woman who wasn't Adi, and definitely wasn't human either. Before either of them could jump to fight one another I shot them both stern glares and attempted a dominant growl of my own.

"Mickie, get me some towels to put underneath her. Lots of them. Haley, let's clear a space on the couch so I can lay her down," I growled, my voice far less intimidating than both of them in their beastwoman forms. It did, however, distract them enough to giggle at my attempt to dominate their beast sides.

They worked quickly, Haley clearing off pillows, coats, and Sinead's clothes from the night before while Mickie brought in what seemed like our entire towel collection. Once a few layers were in place, I laid the woman down before the three of us backed away.

"Is she, what I think she is?" Haley muttered with narrowed eyes as she inspected the body on the couch.

I didn't know how to answer Haley, however, what I did know was that the woman definitely wasn't human. The faint scent of sulfur and brimstone radiating from her told me she was a demon of some sort except it wasn't as putrid and acrid as normal demons. It had a sweetness to it that reminded me of a spice like paprika. Adi had used it and Cayenne enough in her cooking that it was confusing my senses.

My eyes roamed over the barely breathing woman, her feathery black hair hiding her eyes was matted from a mix of sweat, blood, and grime. A pair of curled ram-like horns protruded from her temples, obscuring the view of a pair of elongated, slightly floppy ears that reminded me of a sheep. Her facial features were sharper and more elongated, giving her the same animalistic appearance as Mickie and Haley did when they'd taken on their beastwoman forms. Just this side of humans before they became beasts entirely. One distinction was that this woman had a wide padded nose, speckled with fawn spots, that pulled her lips upward, making her black lips more defined.

Her mauve skin tone was marred by bruises, dried blood, and grime that covered her slender bottom-heavy hourglass figure due to her exceptionally wide hips. There, her flared waist gave way to large, powerful thighs covered in thick, soft, black and mauve wool. At the knees, the wool became tightly crimped as her thighs formed a pair of digitigrade calves which ended in cloven hooves.

Looking at her, my first thought was that I was looking at a fae being, possibly a faun, satyr, or some sort of nymph. Her scent however pressed on my senses, telling me I knew better. Especially if her long, thin tail with a spayed tip was anything to remark on.

"I'm not sure exactly," I said carefully before taking a deep breath to clear my nerves. Instead of focusing on what she was or wasn't, I went to the kitchen, grabbed the first aid kit, and returned to patch her wounds. "I think I heard her voice when she touched the wards though. She was asking for help."

Without thinking, I began working on the two gnarly holes in her shoulder and chest that looked as if she had been run through by a pair of jagged blades. My chest hummed with electricity when I touched her and I ignored the sensation the best I could and tried not to notice green embers flickering to life. I cleaned the woman's wounds with as much delicacy and care as possible before laying down wide bandages on the entrance and exit holes. To my relief, her breathing seemed to stabilize as I patched her up.

"Anyway, while you were downstairs, I found something," Haley said, picking up the papers she'd been working with. "Take a look at this and tell me if you see a pattern."

She held out the spreadsheets she'd taken a highlighter to and, at first, I didn't notice anything except a bunch of names, numbers, and highlighted boxes. Then, as I slowed down my search, I began to see what she was pointing out. A series of repeated names who all made identical investments to several of Gary's projects.

"I did it!" Sinead exclaimed excitedly, making us turn to see her standing, head reattached with a wide grin stretched across her lips. "I have narrowed the search down to 150 square kilometers, all of which have high residual resonance of Adelaide's soul signature."

She quickly bent down, picked up several papers from the cross-sectioned map, and handed them to Haley who looked at them with scrutinization. Her head bobbed slowly as she looked over the red X's and then leaned back to look down the highlighted spreadsheet.

"Yeah! I knew a name sounded familiar. See here? Victor Leamas, Leonard Vidali, and Keith Randolph all made identical investments," Haley said, pointing to each red X and then to the corresponding rows and columns highlighted. "Sand Hollow, East Bench, Bonneville Shores, and Shadow Ridge Reservoir. But the largest fiduciary investment from Leonard Vidali was for 13 million here next to-"

"Dry Creek," I snarled, the papers crumpling before the embers buzzing around my hand took hold, turning them into smoldering ash.

"Motherfucker!"

"Jason?" The three women asked in shaky unison as their eyes went back and forth between me and the ash raining to the floor.

"Under our fucking noses, this entire time," I yelled as I began to storm toward our bedroom to get properly dressed.

"You can't... just rush in... half-cocked," a woman's voice said shakily.

I stopped and moved back to the door, glaring into the living room where Sinead, Mickie, and Haley had moved back from the demon woman who was now sitting up. She was clutching the wound across her chest firmly before our eyes met and I was able to see them for the first time. Black sclera surrounded vivid lavender pupils as she watched me intently, her brows furrowing in a mix of pain and curiosity. I realized then that I'd only managed to remove my tank top and was now standing at the bedroom door in nothing but flannel pants.

"Wow… what did I miss?" Lex snorted as she came through the door and paused, looking around the room with a raised brow. "Gone for a day and y'all have a whole ass ritual, ceremony, and shit without me?"

"I found Adelaide, I have been claimed as Master Jason and Mistress Mickie's concubine, and Master found a demon that was one of Samael's prized possessions," Sinead said, not quick to read the emotions in the room. Her excitement, however, did help to calm my nerves at least a little bit. "Oh! Master, may I have a ritual dress? And will Lex be joining your harem of concubines too? The feeling of carrying your semen is quite wonderful I might add."

The apartment was silent for a long moment as all eyes transfixed on Sinead who beamed with pride, her aloofness sucking the tension away little by little. Her smile faltered as she looked around and then cupped her chin in what I assumed was her pondering what she might have said wrong.

"We're not concubines, Sin," Haley chuckled softly, shaking her head as she reached out to ruffle the petite woman's silver hair. "That's just a fancy word for being someone's fuck buddy. We're his girlfriends and mates."

Before anything else could be said, Xander came through the door. The werewolf paused as he looked around the scene before his eyes met mine and an apologetic look washed over his face.

"Hey, Boss," he said hesitantly, reading the room and trying his best to walk on eggshells with his words. "I get this is probably a bad time, but you have a client here, and… they're not taking no for an answer."

Just fucking great. This is all I need right now.

"Mr. McCrae, it's a pleasure to finally meet you in person," said a voice from the stairwell behind Xan, his deep, rich voice humming across the apartment with his Mediterranean accent. My eyes tried to blink away the foaming rage I began feeling again, however, I couldn't seem to shake the blue glow emanating from behind Xander.

"Now's not the time. We were just leaving. Please make an appointment and come back later," I said, trying to hide the disdain and annoyance in my voice.

"Oh, but I believe my appointment is for right now," he retorted as Xander was pushed inside and a man I didn't recognize stepped through the door.

He was a tall, well-built man with an upside-down triangular build of a marathon runner with wide shoulders and thin hips. He had a classical attractiveness to him with his strong, high cheekbones, squared jaw, a wide nose where a pair of thick-rimmed glasses sat atop, and a smooth olive complexion. To add to his air of importance and old-world charm was his navy blue three-piece suit with a pristine white collared button down. It made him look as if he was ready to step into a billion-dollar boardroom meeting or meet with the Queen of England.

What caught me off guard the most, however, was his hair and eyes. At the roots, I saw the beginnings of hair so deep of blue it was nearly black before it swept upward into a rising inferno of hellfire. His glasses then seemed to project the licking flames of his eyes, casting the room around him in an ethereal blue torchlight glow.

Then the feeling in my gut dropped as, once he stepped through the door, Lex, Sinead, and the demon woman dropped to their knees and bowed their heads in reverence. It was as if they saw him as a king or a…

"Dear, I believe you have made your point," an older woman chuckled softly as she stepped in around him.

She was nearly as tall as the man, looking to be in her late 30s, and had a classical beauty to her. Her long red hair fell down her shoulders in curling waves that bounced with her steps underneath a small crown made of roses, lilies, and irises. They emphasized her light brown eyes which seemed to glow like a warm fireplace in winter.

A white strapless dress clung to her voluptuous figure featuring cuts up the sides that rose high on her wide hips to display her long legs and thighs. All while a black silk, sleeveless, hooded cloak draped around her like a flowing cape.

Behind her was another woman who seemed to be the same age as me but far taller, standing nearly to the top of the door frame. She had short, tightly curled, snow white hair which vividly contrasted her dark umber skin that tightened under her well-defined muscles as she took a natural bodyguard stance with her hands behind her back. Her tall, muscular frame was softened by her round, oval features and plump lips that gave her a polished marble-sculpted beauty.

She held herself with an elegant deadliness that had the word *'Amazon'* spring to mind. And she was deadly if the stern, calculating look in her glowing red eyes was anything to go by. Or the image of a pitbull tattooed onto her right bicep that my eyes seemed to be drawn toward.

"We have come to talk to you about a mutual acquaintance. A rogue demon lord that goes by the name Samael Luciano III," the woman said with a more serious tone.

"Who… are you?" I asked breathily, every ounce of tension gone as I looked at the group that had just stepped into our apartment. Then anxiety rolled through me as every candle in the house sprouted to life with blue flames of hellfire.

"I am but one of the three kings of Nekduamortum. We have been sent to acquire your services in retrieving stolen people of ours and vanquishing this rogue demon. Your specialities of course. And you, my boy, have already heard my name before. However, since this is our first official meeting," he grinned, moving effortlessly across the room to shake my hand in a firm grasp. "Please, call me Hades."

21

JASON

HADES, THE LITERAL GREEK GOD OF THE UNDERWORLD, WAS SITTING AT MY TABLE.

When I looked at my circle and what I had dealt with over the years, how was I surprised anymore? Outside of Mark and my Grandma Ruth, no one inside my inner circle was human. I'd been sharing a bed with a wereleopard and werewolf. Adi hadn't just been a ghost, she was a valravn. I'd been cursed by a dullahan before I bound her soul to me and now she too was going to end up sharing my bed as well.

Then there was Lex, who happened to be an underworld nymph. I should have been clued into this eventuality when her species literally had the word underworld in it. Or when she'd casually dropped the knowledge that every single god humans had worshiped in some form or another existed. And that they all resided on multiple planes of existence which they governed.

One of those was Nekduamortum, the amalgamation of what we all believed to be the afterlife, the underworld, hell, and less grandeur versions of heaven. And the plane itself was governed by the tri-council of kings, a holy trinity of sorts, Hades, Lucifer, and Anubis.

Which means if Hades himself is sitting at my dining table, then the woman next to him...

"So if you're Hades... *the* Hades... does that mean you're-"

"Oh, where are my manners," the elegant redhead chuckled, leaning across the table to take my hand and shake it in greeting. "I am Persephone, one of the three queens of Nekduamortum."

Hades laughed, his eyes sparkling with amusement as his voice filled the apartment with an ethereal chorus of distant warm voices. It was similar to what I'd heard from Sinead when her head was detached or when the black smoke leaked from underneath her collar.

"It's not often we visit mortals, but when I heard about you, Mr. McCrae? I knew I had to see you for myself," he said as his hand puffed out a small brilliant blue fireball. Which, surprisingly, left a small teacup in his grasp in its wake. "Despite the wards you had installed when I arrived, I find this home you have built quite charming."

"What does that even mean?" I asked, shaking my head in confusion.

"Like the rest of your home, they may be a little crude in some points, however, they felt built by tender hands that tried to do whatever it took to make your people safe," Hades shrugged, looking around the apartment as he idly sipped his tea. He was right. I had no idea what I was doing when I built most everything myself in the apartment by hand, only that I needed a home for me and Adi away from the scrutiny of my family.

"So you're here to test us and hurt Jason?" Mickie asked, a growl rumbling through her throat while her claws pressed against the table's surface.

"I assure you Miss Taylor, Miss Gonzales, I have no intention of harming your mate here," he said, looking back and forth between the two shifter women. It made me realize that Haley had her claws out on the defensive as well beside me. "In fact, I should be thanking you."

"How so?" I asked, narrowing my eyes at him. Confused by the sincerity his words seemed to hold.

"You've welcomed multiple of my denizens into your home. Treated them with respect and kindness," he said and then turned to look over his shoulder, locking eyes with the demon sheep-like woman sitting in the living room. "Need I point out that you have a lesser demon in your home whose life you saved?"

"All he did was patch me up," she said indignantly, forcing her eyes away from everyone now staring at her. "I was going to leave as soon as they kicked my ass out."

"Oh, he did more than simply bandage your wounds, Valtrishka," Hades said with a smirk.

"Trish! Don't you dare use that name," she sneered, her voice full of vitriol.

"And how exactly do you know all about them? About Adelaide?" I questioned, narrowing my eyes at Hades with suspicion.

"You currently wear the remainder of the Corvi Catena, for one," he said, motioning nonchalantly to Adi's necklace that I finally felt okay to begin wearing again. "Your threshold also still contains quite the pull of a raven's soul, despite her not being here. This is her rightful home. In addition, I feel a strong life force present around Miss O'Hare and your home. However, to make a long explanation short; I know these things because I'm a god."

Ah, yes, such an easy answer.

"Us kings and queens of the realms have a duty to our denizens and we try to know them individually as it were. Especially our ravens, riders, reapers, and others whose purpose is to traverse the bridge between realms and guide souls to where they are destined when they pass from this mortal existence," Hades explained, wafting his hands as he spoke. "Races such as nymphs, hounds, and demonkin, such as tieflings, were not meant to traverse that bridge. They populate the realm Nekduamortum to provide kinship and brotherhood to the souls of mortals."

"Okay, so what about demons? How do they fit in?" I scoffed, giving the god a tight glare while crossing my arms over my chest. Behind him, I noticed Trish shift uncomfortably in her seat as she listened. "And how exactly are demonkin different?"

"Demonkin are those who are of mixed race and heritage. They bridge the gap between all of our people and offer different outlooks, opinions, and perspectives. They tend to be the ones who strive for change the most in how we govern," Persephone offered, looking over her shoulder at Trish.

"Demons by themselves are tortured souls, cursed and meant to be reformed in places like the Nines and Tartarus. Mortal souls who were monsters here in Midgaterra. Dictators, serial killers, those who didn't value humanity, and the like," Hades said with a sigh, uncomfortable about the topic. "Some have tried to walk the path of redemption. Those who have succeeded are allowed to reintroduce themselves and lead normal lives."

"Demons who choose not to mix races, keep their blood pure, are labeled as lesser demons. Unfortunately, there are those among them who then decide to try for grander things; breaking multidimensional law, interspecies trafficking, and theft of souls to gain power. Those who like to be called demon lords," Persephone continued. "The system is not perfect by any means, however. Some simply break containment and escape. It's as common as an inmate escaping custody of your mortal prisons and police enforcement."

"You're fucking gods, why not do better?" I laughed humorlessly, giving them a bewildered look.

"Because demons are snakes and us hounds can't be everywhere at once to stop all of them," the tall, Amazonian woman snarled as she slammed her fist on the table and glared harshly at me. Her voice was rich, smooth as wine, with a deep melodic and sultry tone.

"Easy, Cera. He doesn't know what you've been through," Persephone said in a sweet, motherly tone as she gently patted the larger woman's hand.

"Yes, we are gods. However, we are not the all-knowing, all-powerful, infallible beings mortals think us to be," Hades said, leaning forward with steepled hands. "Truth be told, all power of creation and destruction, the weave of magic, is powered by belief and intention of it. That is what controls the universal fabric of magic which we derive our own abilities from and the more belief and intention is directed toward us, the more we gain."

"So you're saying, what, just because we believe in Jesus, Selene, or Thor; that's what gives them power?" I asked, shaking my head as I tried to make sense of his explanation.

"In a manner of speaking, yes," he nodded. "Imagine… you are being dared to place your hand into a flame."

He produced a large ball of hellfire and bounced it into the center of the table. The orb, about the size of a basketball, sent flames licking several feet into the air above the table. It didn't give off much heat and, instead, felt more ominous than anything, bathing the room in a bright blue glow.

"Do you believe you will be burned if you were to stick your hand into these flames?" Hades asked pointedly.

"Honestly? It's fire so… duh?" I said, cocking an eyebrow and giving him a bewildered tone and expression.

"Well I believe you won't so I dare you to touch it," Hades smiled wide then looked around me. "What do you think, ladies? Mr. Abara?"

Everyone in the room, including Cera and Trish, shook their heads, a small chorus answering a unanimous *no*. Everyone except me believed.

I shrugged, leaned forward, and placed my hand tentatively in front of the ball, testing its heat against my skin. A ringing buzz flooded my chest before I took a deep breath and pushed forward, sinking my hand into the flames. Nothing. It felt warm, sure, however, there was no stinging pain or anything remotely to what I felt should have happened. Playfully, I rolled my hand, waving it back and forth idly before receding and staring at my palm like I was seeing it for the first time.

"How do you feel?" Hades asked, raising an eyebrow with a grin.

"I feel… Wait," I had begun flexing my hand, the heat on it beginning to reside for a moment before it plateaued and I felt something surging within me like an adrenaline rush. I felt like I could go for hours at the gym or do… other things round after round. "What is that?"

"A simple boon in your natural magic," Hades said nonchalantly.

"I'm still having a hard time grasping that," I said, shaking my head with a furrowed brow. "I guess it's there but I have no idea how to use it or what to do with it."

"When you guide the spirits of the dead from this plane to the next, how do you do it? When you released Miss O'Hare from that despicable creature, how did you do it? Your protection wards?" Hades asked, giving me a firm stare that held no room for my own internal debate whatsoever. "When you banish demons to the Nines or to Tarturus, how does one do it?"

"Incantations, rituals, holy water, just basic stuff," I said, shaking my head.

"So do you not believe in the power those tattoos on your wrists provide you?" Hades retorted with a shrug, waving a single finger at my wrists. It made me pause and look down at them with consideration. "Words, runes, symbols, and general practice of rituals - when used with belief and intention - are simply like plugging a cord into an outlet for a small amount of time. You tap into the universal weave for a brief moment. However, if your belief in its power remains, the charge never fades."

"Okay… that makes sense," I nodded. One thing on my mind persisted, why not have this lesson from someone like a witch like Tori? Someone I knew personally. What would bring an actual god to my doorstep, let alone the Hades? "Okay, so what does all of this have to do with you being here? No offense."

"None taken," Hades chuckled, waving a hand casually to bat any offense away. "Firstly, I wanted to check in on my lost denizens personally and offer a way to go home if they wished it. It would mean our dullahan and nymph friends here can return to Nekduamortum-"

"I wish to stay with Master Jason," Sinead blurted out, interjecting herself and possessively wrapping her arms around one of mine. Then, when she realized what she'd done, her chin quickly dipped in reverence. "I'm sorry, my lord."

"I uh… As much as I'd wanna go home to the Styx," Lex chuckled nervously, her cheeks blooming into a deep blush as she looked down and didn't meet anyone's eyes. "Me and Xander we're…"

"Girl, don't be shy, we all know you took Xanny to pound town last night," Mickie snickered teasingly before giving the nymph a playful jab to the shoulder.

"Yeah he did," Lex murmured sheepishly as she looked away even further and tried clearing her throat to regain some composure. She, of course, failed to do so.

"In that case," Hades said, grinning ear to ear as he watched Lex flounder. "The second reason I'm here is to ask for your assistance. The demon lord Samael has evaded me for nearly half a millennium, pillaging cities and tearing families apart every time I got close. Such is the case of Lex, Trish, and Cera."

The comment made both the sheep woman and Amazon turn their heads, looking away with a mix of painful memories flooding their mind. In Trish's case, her expression held a larger air of disgust.

"Well, thanks to Sin, we found him," I smirked, narrowing my gaze at Hades and giving him a sinister grin.

Hades froze, his eyes widening at my revelation before he cleared his throat and fixed his composure quickly. His brows wiggled as he sought to put on something of a level, almost stoic facade but failed as he straightened his tie for the third time.

"Well, it seems we were right to come here. You have already beaten one demon and a cursed soul so I suspected you might be perfect for this task," Hades admitted with a pleasant shrug.

"And what's in it for us?" I asked, steepling my fingers and giving him a firm expression.

"Well, I could offer payment in any currency, or possibly a

trade of services for a favor as well as providing a form of… additional advancements," Hades shrugged.

"What kind of advancements?" I asked, cocking an eyebrow at him.

Hades looked me over for a long moment, giving me a contemplative look that was as if he knew something I didn't. Clearly, because he was a god of course.

"I need to check something first," Hades said, his expression becoming stoic. His eyes fully rested on me, the playful nonchalant demeanor gone in an instant, as he became a picture of who he was in all of the mythology books I read growing up. "Mr. McCrae, would you please stand up and remove your shirt?"

"Excuse me?" I scoffed and gave him a humorless laugh while my eyes traced over him, looking for indication that he was joking. He wasn't.

"Why the hell does he have to do that?" Haley asked, her voice dipping low as anxiety and fear became present in her voice.

"That's bloody fucking creepy, you know that?" Mickie hissed.

"Ladies, please," he said, waving a hand as if to swat their anger, jealousy, and fear away casually. "Persephone and I have a thousand partners waiting for us in our home when we return. I certainly have no intention of adding our boy here to my abode."

"Yeah well it's still-"

"Okay, *fine*, I'll play your game," I groaned, reaching back to take Mickie's hand in mine and squeeze it reassuringly.

I pushed my chair back and stood, gripping at the hem of my shirt and lifting upward, exposing myself to the god sitting across the table. Once it was off I looked around, shrugged, and tossed it onto the table. A long moment passed, confusion and anticipation taking over as I found myself not sure what to do with my hands or body at all.

Instead, Mickie came to stand behind me for support, cupping my shoulders in her hands while Haley and Sinead pressed into my sides. Sinead, returned her tight grip to my arm on one side while the werewolf mirrored her on the other. The weight and presence of them felt comforting, sapping the anxiety from my chest as they held me.

That was until I saw Hades casually toss an orb of hellfire the size of a golf ball which hit me on the left of my chest. The heat of the fire stung on my skin, feeling as if I was in Zi's tattoo shop and they'd begun outlining an intricate chest piece. I hissed with the sudden surge of pain and then blinked when the sensation was gone almost instantly.

"Hmm, that is quite concerning," Hades stated with consideration, his hand moving to cup his chin in thought.

"What? What… is this?" I froze as I looked down across my body and found a patch of faded black ink work covering most of my left pectoral. Instead of heavy black outlines, the ink was faded or nonexistent in some places, making the design incomplete. "What is this?"

"The seal of Saint Alasdair McPherson," Grandma Ruth said, her voice making us all look up to find her quietly entering the apartment. She strode directly toward Persephone and Hades, giving them a soft, welcoming smile. "It's good to see you two again. It's been much too long."

"Ah, Ruth, we were going to come find you once we were finished here," Hades said with a wide grin, bending at the waist to kiss each of her cheeks before Persephone moved in to do the same.

"Oh it's quite fine, my dears," Ruth said, giving them smiles before it faded as she looked back at me. It wasn't disappointment that etched its way across her brow but worry and fear instead. "Oh, sweetie, I should have warned you months ago."

"Warned me?" I asked, shaking my head in disbelief.

That she was friends with gods? Or was this about the tattoo?

Hades strode around the table to stand in front of me, reaching out to cover the tattoo on my chest with his hand. Warmth permeated my skin from where his hand touched as he closed one eye and sighed, his mind searching for… something.

"The seal is an unseen gift handed down through the bloodlines of Silas McCrae, Uilleam Armstrong, Quinn Murdoch, and Lachlan O'Riley," Hades idly explained.

I recognized two of the names instantly.

"And what exactly is it sealing?" I dared to ask, knowing I probably wasn't going to like the answer at all.

"Silas McCrae and Lachlan O'Riley, do you remember what I told you about them?" Ruth asked as Hades' hand covered itself with a sheen of hellfire and I felt heat press into the surface of my skin again.

"They were border clans along with the Armstrongs and were an absolute pain in the ass to the English. The McCraes and Armstrongs were notorious reivers that got their kicks out of stealing the English's horses during the wars," I said with a soft chuckle.

"That explains why Rowan likes you so much," Sinead nodded quietly.

Really, her hellfire stallion approved of me?

"There is more to them than being a pestering force of horse thieves and pirates that helped to keep the English at bay for a time. That war, however, wasn't their first foray into their lifestyle and trade," Hades nodded sagely. "The McCrae, Armstrong, Murdoch, and O'Riley clans didn't originate in Midgaterra."

Hades' words froze me into place as my mind slowly made sense of his statement. With a few simple words he'd gone and added another, deeper layer to what I thought I knew of my family's history. History that I had never learned from Ruth and the epiphany of it all dawned on me like

I was hit by a raging waterfall of truth.

"They weren't… My ancestors aren't from earth?" I asked slowly, nearly fearing the worst of whatever Hades had to say as an offering.

"The ancestors of the four clans, especially the McCraes, have always answered the Call of Death. Watchful guides who have helped souls find their way to Nekduamortum and have been dutiful heralds for the three kings. As such, I have watched over them for protection. But," Hades chuckled and shrugged his shoulders with a wry grin. "That is a story for another time. For right now, we need to be both thankful and cautious of your choices."

"What do you mean?" I asked, my mouth suddenly dry.

"I mean the bond you share with the preternatural beings I find wholly welcomed into your home and life, Jason," Hades said matter of factly. "This seal was placed on your ancestors almost a millennium ago but you are the first to have nearly broken it."

"JJ, have you noticed a change in your abilities?" Ruth asked curiously.

"I mean, I guess?" I said, shaking my head with furrowed brows. "My psychokinesis doesn't take as much of a toll on me anymore like it used to. I can turn the wards on and off a lot easier than when I started. And I can… conjure green fire when I'm angry."

"And when did these changes occur?" Hades asked while giving me a level gaze, coming an inch away from my face like he could see something just behind my eyes.

"I guess the first time I really noticed anything was…"

I froze again.

I had been about to say some time last year but that hadn't been the case. The Sand Hollow site nearly knocked me out cold and had me retching when I crossed the spiritual threshold. When I first met Mickie, every time she touched me it had been a painful spike of memories and emotions. I went from being doubled over in pain and being a very minor empath to an expert one in a matter of, what seemed like, a day. The only thing that had changed was…

I turned my head to look over my shoulders and gave Mickie a worried glance. Her brows raised in solemn realization at nearly the same time I did. Everything changed after I had slept with Adi and Mickie the first time.

"Your close friendship and bond with Adelaide would have eroded this away eventually. But it would have taken decades. This, however," Hades chuckled and let out a relieved sigh. I didn't understand why he seemed relieved though. "Since your first exposure to non-human blood, how careful have you been in proceeding with selecting paramours?"

"Not… very," I admitted sheepishly, my cheeks burning as I refused to meet anyone's eyes.

"Two strains of lycanthropy, two denizens of Nekduamortum, and a hint of energy from cursed souls for some flavor," Hades grinned, giving me a surprised but also proud whistle of accomplishment. Then he gave me another pondering glance that made my blood swirl with fear. "Now what do you suppose would have happened if you had taken Miss Adamos to your bed chambers?"

"Oh dios mio," Haley whispered breathily.

"So um… what would have happened if I had, like, been the one getting freaky with Jason and not Xander?" Lex dared to ask, her voice becoming a little frantic as she spoke.

"Well, my friends, let's just say our Jason McCrae would have become a full-fledged demon," he chuckled, though all of us failed to find the humor in his statement and my stomach began doing dangerous flips inside of me. "And not just the partial one he's always been."

22

JASON

I'M A DEMON.

Well, part demon.

And, of course, Hades didn't bother explaining how much of that blood ran through my veins. Still. Demon? Out of all of the creatures I could have been bits and pieces of; why in the ever living fuck did it have to be a goddamn demon?

"There, that should hold for a long while," Hades said as he pulled his hand from my chest and inspected his work. "And an additional gift for you to use in the future. *If* you learn how to."

With his words, he placed a hand on my neck, hellfire sprouting from his hand and encircling my throat like a collar. I hissed in pain from the sensation of another tattoo being magically etched into my flesh. When he was done, he inspected the design before nodding in approval.

I walked away when he was finished, the thoughts in my head

swirling and driving me to get away from the revelation as far as I could. Instead, I walked into the bathroom, still shirtless to look at the ink on my chest that covered the entirety of my left pectoral. I inspected the design in the mirror. A triple moon spanned across my pectoral while a pentacle and a stretched-out star of David combined over the two circles in the middle. Around it were runes which I didn't know the translation to nor could I decipher if they wore Norse or Celtic in origin.

On my neck, I couldn't help but snort in response to the design that sat there. Because of course, Hades would think it was so fucking hilarious to tattoo a three-headed dog on my neck. Truthfully, part of me wanted to like the design added to my skin, however, at that moment I was not having it.

"So… if he's only part demon, what else is in his blood," Mickie asked as I entered the room once more to grab my shirt off of the table.

"If memory serves, the O'Riley clan were a band of fallen angels. However, his soul had something else there I couldn't decipher," Hades said, his eyes finding me as I joined the group without a word.

I stammered at that tidbit of information.

"So, what, I'm a mutt of everything from Nekduamortum?" I snorted as I looked up at him with disgust.

"Not exactly," Persephone offered, her voice far more comforting than his. "The seraphim people come from Elysivanatum, the plane of the eternals."

"Oh wonderful, a demon and an angel fucked and I got popped out a couple centuries later. That's…. That's just wonderful," I rolled my eyes. I didn't know how to process all of this coming at me at once. It was absurd and I could feel my psyche slipping toward madness. "Anyway, if we're done here, I have things to do."

"Oh, and what would that be?" Cera asked, her brow cocking as she studied me.

"Getting Adi back. And, since I'm living up to my family's expectation of me being a hedonistic monster, I'm going to go and be one," I snarled, then instantly regretted my words as I saw Mickie and Haley flinch at the M-word in my peripherals.

"Sweetie," Ruth said as she came forward and cupped my cheek. "Please don't ever call yourself or the girls that ever again."

"I know. I… I'm sorry," I said, sighing as my head slumped downward. "This is just… a lot to take in right now."

"I understand, but," she said, smiling as she tipped my chin back up to look at her. "I don't need my favorite grandson thinking about himself like that. You've got a good heart, that's what matters."

"Thanks, Grandma," I whispered, giving her a pitiful smile.

"Now, Jason, do you want us to come with you?" Hades asked as he went to Persephone's side, gripped her by the back of the neck, and kissed the top of her head. She let out a soft sigh in response to his touch and affection.

"No," I said, looking toward him and meeting his eyes with a stern glare. "This is our fight, not yours anymore. You hired me to get the job done and that's what I'm going to do."

"I'm coming with you," Trish said abrasively, turning my attention to see her sitting on the edge of the couch giving me a firm, cold glare.

"And why would he trust someone like you, demon," Cera spat, folding her arms tight over her breasts as she stared down her nose at the much smaller woman.

"Besides, you're in no shape to be going anywhere," Haley said, cocking her brow at Trish.

"One, I know the place and I can get you in quietly," she retorted matter of factly, holding up her fingers to count her points. And to emphasize them, strong, billowing flames appeared from the tips of her fingers like roaring torches. "Two, you'll need more firepower than you've got to take him head-on. And three, I owe the Princess for at least trying to stand up to the motherfucker and get us out."

Trish stood then, her hooves clopping against the floor as she made her way to stand in front of Sinead, completely discarding the towels that had been wrapped around her form. My eyes reactively took her in with interest, watching the way her hips swung and her body and feathery hair bounced with her movements. Moreover, it wasn't just that my mind had decidedly deemed her beautiful, it was that I was in the presence of something else. She was a mythical being come to life and stood only a few feet away and the thought was entrancing by itself.

"Besides, if you trust the Warden of all people, I should be a fucking cakewalk," Trish said, tapping her hoof impatiently.

"Warden?" Cera asked curiously.

"Yeah, Sinead here used to be Samael's favorite pet lackey," Trish snarled, shaking with rage as she looked down at the smaller woman. "She was the one who'd come get us from our cages. We'd get beaten, raped, and tortured again and again while she just sat by and watched. Then we got thrown back in our cells to heal up while he went and played with his favorite fuck doll whore!"

Tears were streaming down Trish's face, her voice cracking with anger and pain the longer she went. With a final word, her fists and horns became encased in brilliant gold flames that roared to life as if someone had thrown a match into a pool of gasoline. It seemed like she so desperately wanted to hit Sinead but couldn't bring herself to follow through.

"Does your rage satisfy you?" Sinead asked curiously, looking up into Trish's eyes with contemplation. Trish flinched hearing Sinead speak, something I guessed wasn't common back in the hell hole they'd both come from. "And may I be permitted to seek forgiveness from you as well? Just as I wish to find Adelaide's penance."

"Thirteen years, Sinead," Trish sobbed. "You sat by for thirteen years and now you want to act like nothing happened? I was ten when we first met. I was a fucking child!"

"Master, you remember me telling you how to destroy the Ananke ring, yes?" Sinead asked, turning toward me.

"Um, yeah... You said to break it or throw it in a fire hot enough to melt titanium," I said, repeating her words from two weeks ago with a brow cocked high in confusion.

"But that would-"

"If Trish wishes for me to atone for my sins in such a manner, then I will do so. For hers, Adelaide's, and the other's sake," Sinead said, holding up a hand toward Cera.

"Seriously? You'd destroy your soul just like that?" Trish said, her sobs choking with shock at how easily Sinead had decided something akin to sacrificial suicide would be worth it.

"I am truly sorry for what happened to you and the others. I was weak and locked almost everything of myself away to protect me while I was being, as you said, his fuck doll," Sinead said pointedly, daring to reach out and cup Trish's hands in hers. "Master Jason has given me my freedom back, allowing me to begin to find myself again. And, as it is my choice, I will do this if it helps you. However, only after we take the bastard's head and proudly mount the fucker on the wall."

There was a long moment of silence in the room as everyone looked at Sinead, who had a wide, sinister smile stretched across her lips. She was beaming with pride at her declaration.

"Who… are you? And what… the fuck… did you do with the Warden?" Trish spoke slowly, breaking the silence after several confusing moments.

"I am Sinead O'Hare, herald and guardian of the McCrae Clan. And," Sinead said proudly, standing a little taller and straighter as she spoke. "One of those happily betrothed to Jason Jameson McCrae; one of his mated ones."

Wait, did she say betrothed?

"Okay, hold on," I said, waving my hands in the air to bat away a slew of confusing thoughts that began raining down on me. "First, Sin, you're not giving up your soul. Second, they're right, how do we know you're not going to get us there just to turn us in?"

"I'm with Jason on this one," Mickie said, nodding in confusion before giving a curious glance toward Sinead.

"It took us losing Adi, having Sinead's soul bound to Jason's, and then her actively trying to better herself before we gained any trust," Haley added, trying not to smile and snicker at Sinead's declaration.

Another lull in silence had Trish watching the three women in front of her with contemplation. Her eyes went back and forth between Sinead and Haley for a long time before she turned and fell to one knee facing Hades.

"My lord, my queen, you love bargains, right? Well, I want you to have my soul bound to his. A pact that, if I ever betray the McCrae Clan, I will forfeit myself to the lowest depths of the Nines," Trish spoke with a voice of determination and pride.

"Are you sure about this, sweetheart?" Ruth asked cautiously.

"Well now, I do love a good bargain with high stakes," Hades chuckled softly.

"Now wait a damn-"

"Do it!" Trish commanded, cutting me off with the fire on her fists and horns roaring higher.

"Okay, well then stand, face him with your hands behind your back. Jason, place your hand over her heart," Hades said, answering my bewildered and, frankly, offended glare with one that said there was no time or room for argument. Especially not in the presence of the god of the underworld.

I did as asked hesitantly, gulping hard as Trish stood in front of me and I forced my eyes to stay on hers and not where I placed my hand. Nor did I pay any mind to the way the woman in front of me shivered and let out a small gasp against my touch. Or the way her heart slammed against her chest and her skin heated as my hand splayed over the top of her left breast.

The buzzing in my chest grew stronger as I fought to keep the memories of Trish's abuse at the hands of Samael at bay. I faltered as her memories flashed across my mind in rapid waves, pausing when they fell onto memories of her time with Adelaide. Especially the haunted look on Adi's face when she believed she'd gotten Trish killed.

"Okay, state your name for the pact," Persephone directed as she came to our sides and placed a hand on each of mine and Trish's shoulders. "And then Jason, you'll repeat after me."

"Trisha Geiswyn Chauntae," Trish spoke proudly, her eyes looking at me with pride as she spoke.

"You're real name, my dear," Hades said, giving her a tired glance.

His words made her freeze before her head dipped, lowering her chin to her chest, refusing to meet anyone's eyes. Then she shifted uncomfortably as she rolled her head to look at me through the tops of her eyes with a pained and ashamed expression. She then shot Hades a look of pleading, nervousness radiating off of her in waves before she relented as he gave her a knowing nod.

"Valtrishka... Luciano..."

23

JASON

DID I HAVE A PLAN GOING INTO THIS? ABSO-FUCKING-LUTELY NOT.

Because let's face it, what plan could I have concocted that somehow having Trish riding in the backseat behind me? A plan that involved me riding into battle with the daughter - yes, *daughter* - of the demon I wanted to kill. Learning her true name and heritage had been one thing that would have raised all of the red flags in my mind; except I'd seen what he'd done to her and Adi.

"Are you sure you want to go back there and face him?" Mickie asked, turning in her seat to look at the half-demon sheep woman.

My arm still burned from the ritual Hades had performed with the two of us. With his words, a mix of Latin and Greek, hellfire had covered my right forearm while another inferno spread its way across Trish's abdomen. When the fire had dissipated, the skull of a ram was etched into the skin of my right forearm above my other tattoos. Trish, on the other hand, now had a tattoo stretching across her lower abdomen below her navel. One that featured the same seal etched into my left pectoral with what looked like wings made of Celtic knots stretching toward her hips.

It felt more than a little invasive in my eyes to be branded with the same tattoo as mine. Even more so because, like with Adi when I wore her amulet before, I was picking up brief thoughts, mental images, and emotions that weren't my own. Just like wearing the Ananke ring was giving me hints of joy from Sinead riding the wind with Rowan beside me to keep the edge off.

"After everything he did to me and my clan? Hell yeah," Trish nodded, her eyes narrowed with a churning fire in them. "He thought having an heir with the Embers of Brigit would boost his power, that's why he came after my mother."

I recognize that name from somewhere.

"Samael lured Dame Brigit away, killed most of her core of minotaur crownsguard, and then pillaged our city. He caught her, abused her, and refused to let her get treatment. She died not long after giving birth to me and my sister. I was raised among the horde until I was ten," Trish explained.

"And then the cycle repeated," I nodded, growling angrily as I traveled down a sleepy frontage road until a brilliant array of lights spread the night sky open.

"Anyway, pull over here, Lex and I will sneak into the dungeon and jailbreak everyone we can," Trish said, pointing to the side of the road near a large tree that shielded us from the view of a looming chalet.

"Please tell me your plan isn't to pull up out front, right?" Lex asked worriedly as I got out and tilted my seat for the two of them to get out. She paused only to give Xan a long, deep kiss before she got out, leaving him and Haley alone in the backseat.

"I've got a concept of a plan," I said, giving the two of them a confident smirk. It seemed to satisfy Lex but Trish, on the other hand, lifted a brow in appreciation and smirked,

"See you soon… *Sir*," Trish answered, giving me a mock salute before adding an odd inflection at the end. I could have sworn she winked at me as well.

What… was that about?

Much to everyone's chagrin, my course of action was, of course, to pull straight into the driveway of the enemy like we were going to some fancy party. I surveyed everything as I drove along the paved cobblestone that expanded into a large rotunda with a fountain at its center. The illuminated fountain featured a marble visage of Samael in his demon form standing above the water, chin raised in arrogance.

The rotunda widened at its peak into a massively wide cobblestone courtyard that was flanked on either side by two four-bayed garages. The long garages swept into the face of a gorgeous two-story villa that looked as if it were plucked from a contemporary modern architecture magazine. Along its front was an impressive cobblestone porch with tall white stone square columns that supported black metal roofing illuminated in the moonlight. Lights along the eaves, driveway, and gardens bathed the house in a picturesque glow that made it stand out in the darkness.

I knew the spot where the villa sat because it had once been an expansive horse property with an old early-1900s ranch sitting on it. The property dipped down a hillside toward a creek that I walked along quite a bit as a teenager. Where Adi and I had first met 13 years ago.

Trying to push my anger aside from the idea that Samael had built a prison for Adi and his collection on the same spot I'd saved her, I focused on something else. All of the garage doors were open, moving trucks parked in their tall bays with bits of furniture partially unloaded. Then my eyes focused on the porch.

It hadn't been what I saw, but who.

"The hell are you doing here, Zi?" I asked, narrowing my eyes at the familiar figure to the left of the double-door entryway.

Zi, my long-time tattoo artist and someone I considered a friend, stood guard at the door, now dressed in a set of black harem pants and a matching tank top. Draped over their shoulders was a gold and teal-colored collar that swept down to the middle of their chest like a piece of layered armor. It matched the long gold polearm they held in front of them which was five feet in length and then was tipped with a blade that looked like a straightened sickle.

The woman, standing guard on the right of the door, looked nearly identical but had long dreadlocks pulled backward into a ponytail. She had the same weapon and wore a similar uncomfortable expression to Zi. I couldn't decide if the two of them were stoic, worried, apologetic, or enraged. Their twin expressions finally settled on apologetic as Zi let out a long, weary breath.

"Look, brother, me and my sis don't wanna fight you guys but the Master knew you was gonna pull up," Zi shook their head, scrunching their brow and lip at the mention of Samael. "It don't have to go down the way you think it does."

"If you're siding with that motherfucker, then it does," I snarled and heard my own growl echoing behind me. A chorus like a pack of vengeful animals rose as Mickie, Haley, and Xan let their own snarls of disapproval reverberate through their throats. "How can you work for that bastard?"

"Because he has their souls tied to him the same as I once did," Sinead offered, her eyes narrowed harshly as she stepped forward to be by my side. Her eyes were alight with hellfire while she scanned over each of them as if deciding whose head to take first.

"Lil' momma's right," Zi shrugged, shooting me a look of regret and sadness. "Anyway, we're just the welcoming committee."

"And if we refuse?" Mickie snarled in return, her teeth snapping like she was threatening to tear them apart with her outstretched fangs.

"Atiena," Zi jerked his head toward us and let out another exhausted breath.

The woman, Atiena, stepped forward. As she did so, she became less human as she circled around us with a wide berth. Her stature rose from her mere five-and-a-half-foot-tall stance to seven feet in height, short black fur blossoming across her skin as her oval features lengthened and sharpened into a long, fang-filled snout. Her shapely hourglass figure stretched, keeping her wide hips and shoulders, and large breasts intact while her torso and legs elongated and she sprouted a long, thin tail from the base of her spine above her buttocks.

She had started her journey down the porch as an attractive, human woman with what I'd heard Mickie refer to as *slim thicc*. As she came to guard us in the rear of the group, she'd become a tall anthropomorphic jackal woman, a creature I'd seen only in textbooks about ancient Egyptian mythology.

"You're not-"

"Human? Nah, man," Zi chuckled softly, giving a playful smile as they shook their head. "Me and my sis here are Cynothropes, kinda like your homegirls and your brotha-man, but all descendant from the armies of Anubis. Or what's left of 'em anyway."

"And you never told me? How long have you known about them?" I snapped back, glaring harshly at Zi in front of me as I took two more steps to get within inches of them.

"Like I said, eyes of the gods see all, my friend," they shrugged, tapping a finger against the center of his forehead. "Look, Jason, I never wanted this shit to go down the way it has. But I can only protect my 'lil sis if we do what the Master says. It ain't no bad blood, you feel me?"

There was sincerity in their eyes. However, I wanted to pick it apart until I found the lie. Something we didn't have time for. Instead, I needed to find a way to free them like we'd done with Sinead. But how likely was that going to be? The truth of the matter was that they were given a choice between a friend and their baby sister.

Wouldn't I do the same? I mean I'm doing it now coming for Adi.

I took in a deep breath, let it out slowly, and gestured toward the door behind Zi. I gave them the universal 'lead the way' signal. Everyone around me protested at the idea.

"I'm sorry man, but she's the only blood I got left," Zi sighed and turned toward the door. Once they had a hand on it, Zi paused briefly to look over their shoulder toward me and gave me a remorseful expression. "But believe it, G, if it were her in there instead, I'd be pullin' up just like you are for your raven queen."

Before I could respond, the handle of the door clicked and he swung it inward, revealing a large, spacious foyer and grand room with light wood flooring. Toward the back of the grand hall and well-lit interior, I found the familiar figure of a human Samael. He stood in front of a deluge of grand windows that offered a view of the luxurious backyard complete with a deck and a pool that backed directly to the creek, the center of the yard being the exact spot where I'd found Adelaide's amulet all those years ago.

He was surrounded by four figures with what I counted to be ten more human-looking men and women, all of which stunk of sulfur, taking up posts throughout the main floor. The two figures that flanked his sides had dark skin, one being a tall man already pushing six and a half feet tall with dark umber flesh and equally dark eyes. He had a large, muscular build that held a domineering aura that spoke of being a faithful, strong, silent guardian to perceived royalty. His high sculpted, rectangular features and dark eyes made him a handsome figure but he regarded me as nothing resembling even a small threat to him and his.

The second was a woman with ashen cream-colored skin that stood just shorter than Samael who had attractive oblong features and a cold demeanor on a build that, while shorter, was just as muscular and domineering as the man she stood guard with. Both of them wore the same gold and teal shoulder pieces over a pair of black tactical cargo pants and dark gray tank tops that put their muscular arms and shoulders on full display. They too held the same bladed polearms that Zi and Atiena had, knocking them on the wood floor to announce our presence as we walked inside.

The two other figures in front of Samael turned to watch us with narrowed eyes and harsh gazes. One of them was a man about my height and build wearing tight black leather pants, suspenders, a red long-sleeve shirt, a black leather collar, and a black beret sitting atop short dark red hair. He was handsome with squared, chiseled features, and deep green eyes that soon illuminated with the glow of bluish-green hellfire that licked out of them.

The woman next to him was pale and semi-translucent and looked like she had stepped off the screen of a silent film and transposed into the real world. Her long white hair and short 1920s-style dress billowed in a nonexistent breeze while she floated an inch or so off the ground. Her spectral form had sharp features and hazy white eyes that exuded a sense of eternal sadness, longing, and rage.

"Ah, Mr. McCrae, the man of the hour! So nice of you to finally join us," Samael bellowed with a wide grin and outstretched hands as if he were being humble and welcoming. It was a blatant and obvious trap that I needed to avoid at all costs. "And I see you come bearing gifts for me."

"Where's Adelaide?" I growled, balling my fists tightly as I narrowed my eyes at him while I focused on that spark of rage that seemed to begin boiling at just the sight of him.

"Unfortunately, Ms. Winters wasn't feeling in a particularly celebratory mood. I'm sure you understand how she can be," he chuckled, his smile stretched wide but the mention of Adi's personality made one of his eyes twitch.

"Let's try this again. Where. The fuck. Is Adi?" Mickie snarled, hate and anger permeating off of her like the warm scent of a brewery. It was an odd sensation as her rage danced on the tip of my tongue, daring me to become drunk on the power. As if I could drink it down. "We're taking her home."

"Ah, but she is home, Ms. Taylor. It's why I made this place," he chuckled, waving a hand toward the backyard and the creek just beyond it. Then his eyes dilated as they locked onto Sinead's. "A home you can be a part of as well if only you'd just come to me."

"I refuse… You will return Adelaide to her rightful place immediately," Sinead said, her tone cold with hate and malice as she watched Samael closely.

"Rightful place?" He snorted, his gleeful smile faltering as she spoke. "You, my pet, know where your rightful place is as much as they do. I thought I had taught you better on how to hold your tongue."

"Sinead is not your *pet*," I retorted angrily as my chest hummed and burned with electricity.

I gave into that building pressure of hatred swelling up inside of me and let it take hold. As I did, my vision brightened, the world around me becoming more vivid and saturated with color than before. My senses fired on all cylinders as that electricity spread across my body making me feel as if I were on an endless supply of adrenaline. All the while my skin began turning ashen, a soot-like darkness inching its way up my arms.

"She belongs to *me*!"

"My boy, you do know how to make yourself more interesting don't you?"

SAMAEL SCANNED OVER MY FIGURE LIKE I WAS A BRAND NEW TOY TO DISCOVER.

"I will extend this offer to you; return me my loyal servant, offer up the fledgling nymph, and I will personally take you under my wing," he declared warmly, holding out his arms in a wide gesture. "I will be your guide on this new development of yours and I might perhaps allow you to keep the leopard and wolf as your prizes for your lordship as I ascend to godhood."

"No," I snapped back, punctuating the word with every ounce of wrath inside me.

Samael's face faltered, his smile falling to a thin line of disapproval as his joy and humor leaked away. His arms fell from his welcoming posture, letting his hands sink into his pants pockets, and the four figures let out a combination of their own growls as they regarded us.

"This will not end well for you, Jason," Samael spoke calmly, an edge of anger in his tone. "I will offer once more. Return what is mine by right and you walk out of here alive. If not, I will enjoy breaking you until you are begging me to end your life."

"You know, I was about to say the same damn thing," I snorted with a wide smirk, flexing my fists and feeling a set of claws pinch against my palms.

The demon let out a sigh, then looked back and forth between his subjects with a level gaze that commanded respect and obedience from them.

"So be it," he shrugged, muttering under his breath as he raised his right hand and snapped his finger. "Take them."

A surge of adrenaline began pouring through my veins as I sprung forward, racing to meet Samael who turned his back on us. I wove through the four individuals in front of me with a speed I'd never known. I had every intention of tackling the bigger man, instead, I felt a weight hit my side.

My body bowed uncomfortably before I hit the ground and began rolling toward the far wall. Before I could stand on my own I felt the cold pressure of a metal bar pressed against my neck while a strong warm body pressed into my back. My eyes opened to see the lean, muscular body of a creature resembling Anubis looking down at me.

"Don't do this, J, call 'em all off," Zi's voice filled my ears, their voice slightly more raspy than before as he spoke in their true form. Zi's eyes, though pitch black in front of me, held a look of worry and regret in them.

I snarled, reaching up to grab the polearm against my throat and pushed it forward as hard as I could, making it smack against the end of Zi's snout. They reared back in pain while I dropped toward my knees, slipping out of the hold that had been desiring to choke me into submission.

With a twist of my body, I turned to face Atiena with the weapon still in our shared grasp causing it to turn vertical in her large clawed hands, and used it as leverage to lift my leg and kick outward. The sole of my boot found purchase against her abdomen and I sent her backward against the wall behind her.

The polearm went with her and I turned in time to miss the blade of another that was meant to slash down my form as Zi missed their strike. I reared back and threw a right hook, briefly remembering what Xan had told me about throwing a punch. I connected with the side of their skull, my fist meeting fur and bone, as a tinge of pain spread across my knuckles.

I knocked Zi away, had enough sense to step back, and missed another downward slash in front of me. I swung hard in reaction, connecting my left fist against Atiena's kidney, then hit her a second time with another right fist to her chin.

As Zi and Atiena fell away from me, stunned for those minor seconds, my eyes caught movement and surveyed the scene around me. Samael was now in his half-man, half-ram demonic form, standing taller and stronger than before but was struggling to keep Mickie and Haley off of him. Both women were now transformed, both of their bodies covered in a light pelt of fur, their facial structures taking on a more animalistic appearance featuring fangs, cat and canine-like noses, and elongated ears.

While Mickie had on her black and burnt gold leopard fur covered in dark-ringed spots, Haley was covered in a more lush pelt that was the same color as her dark-tanned flesh but had long patches of black fur. As Haley leaped forward, she sunk claws and teeth into Samael's shoulder and back, making him roar in pain as her bushy wolf tail swished wildly behind her.

Mickie swept underneath him, sinking her fangs into the side of his neck while she held one of his arms in a chicken wing position. One of her hands sank claws into the other side of his neck from where her jaw was latched while the other held his arm in place with claws ripping through his wrist. He was flailing to get the two of them off him, however, each movement caused two sets of clawed hands, fang-filled jaws, and large animalistic clawed foot paws to sink into his flesh and muscles deeper.

Sinead, her head and skull resembling a large bonfire made of blue flames, had drawn the caucasian man and ghostly woman into the massive, glass-walled dining room. The man carried a large scythe while his skull and hair were set ablaze in a large plume of hellfire that matched Sinead's, and swung it wildly at her. She parried it with her dual sickle blades, making it embed itself into the wood of the massive table between them. Sinead then spun on her heels, sending two downward slashes into the spectral woman whose form flickered as they passed through her.

In response, the ghost woman reared back to take in a deep breath and then her jaw opened impossibly wide to let out a high-pitched wailing scream. As the scream began, Sinead jumped down, kicking the end of the table to turn it vertically and give her a wall to hide behind. The movement knocked the male dullahan backward, ripping his scythe from his grip, and knocked one of the demonic goons forward into the banshee's path. The scream ripped through him, tearing red, devilish flesh from the bone before he disintegrated into a cloud of ash and sulfur.

As my vision swept around to the two in front of me, I found Xan in his wolfman form, as he fought off the two remaining Anubis-like creatures in the foyer. His black and dark brown fur resembled that of a timberwolf rippling in the light as he expertly dodged strikes from the two of them.

He grabbed the woman and threw her toward the front door, letting her body crash and splinter the wood before he ducked under a wide right hook from the man, leaped his way up the wall, and then mounted him. Xan rode the much larger creature to the ground before unleashing a flurry of hard left and right hooks that pummeled the jackal man into the floor.

My vision swam then because, as I finally got my eyes back onto Zi and Atiena, the latter hit me with a right hook across my cheek. I stumbled backward, shaking the dizziness and surge of pain out of my head, and managed to duck under her next blow.

I extended my leg and caught the back of her knee, putting her to the ground then threw myself to the side as I rolled out of the way of Zi behind me. They came down on the back of their sister's head with both fists clenched together in an ax handle smash making her grunt in pain and drop to her stomach on the floor.

I tried to do the same thing I'd watched Xan do and jumped forward, planting my feet into Zi's gut while grabbing onto their shoulders. I had intended on riding Zi to the floor but, instead, pain blossomed around my neck as they caught me by the throat and surged forward until my head and back hit against a wall.

I kicked again, hitting them hard enough that they were forced to loosen their grip and drop me. I readied myself for the next round and parried Zi's right hook, trying to swing at them with my left fist, catching them in the side of the face just as they hit me with a left hook of their own.

As I stumbled to the side, I felt something hit the back of my shins and then the world flipped as I lost sense of direction. I hit the ground hard, my ears beginning to ring from hitting the back of my head against the wood flooring. I coughed and gasped for the air forced out of me as I was hit with a hard weight to my sternum. Between the ringing in my ears and the sound of my blood pumping through them, I began hearing a raspy male voice above me in Latin.

My wrists, which I felt pinned behind my head, began to burn like they were being freshly inked, and then the throbbing became tenfold as a sensation of pins and needles crawled up my arms. When the sensation reached the left of my chest, the mark Hades had reinvigorated began to burn with intense heat.

As my vision became clear, the darkness around its edges ebbing away, I saw a demonic form above me. Then I watched the instant shift in his demeanor. His confident recital of Latin stopped as fear flooded into his mind and body. His eyes went wide in terror as his body began to heat up and burn away in a cloud of ash.

Something took over in my mind, pressure thrumming against my forehead, my teeth clenched, and my vision intensified. It was like I was looking at the world through overexposed film. With the demon's weight above me gone, I kicked up my legs and rolled myself in a backward somersault, coming down on the figure that had been pinning my arms. I heard a feminine voice let out a yelp of surprise and then pain as I wrapped my body around hers and pulled as hard as I could. When I landed, I did so coming to my knees behind her and bowing her back in a hard arch while using her own arms to crush her throat.

As I pulled hard enough to cut the oxygen from her, my vision locked onto the back of her exposed neck and then froze in place. Against her crimson-red skin, I watched a mark form, etched like a cattle brand into her flesh.

My mind then caught up to my mouth, not even realizing that I had been speaking at all outside of grunts and growls of exertion. I'd been speaking ancient Latin without my own knowledge. The brand marked into her crimson flesh, which was the shape of a ram skull crossed with scythes, began smoldering with green-colored embers before it desintegrated.

"What the fuck?" I whispered under my breath with a low growl, my voice sounding doubled even to myself. The second tone was a low rumbling growl that was an octave or possibly two underneath my natural voice.

"I… concede," the woman hissed between labored breaths.

I released my hold instantly and backed away, my eyes went wide with shock as I looked down at her form. She collapsed onto her stomach, struggling to breathe and wincing in pain before her eyes fluttered closed into unconsciousness.

Before I could question anything further, I saw a flash of movement in the blurred shape of a black mass before I was forced onto my back once more and felt weight pinning me to the ground. As I forced my eyes back open from clenching them in both pain and surprise, I found two jackal-shaped figures inches from my face. I wanted to spit in Zi's face as they pinned me down but saw Atiena bring a finger to her lips in a silencing motion.

"What just happened?" She asked with a sultry rasp that was a combination of her natural low contralto and the hiss of her beast form. "How did you release her bonds?"

"You tell me. I-"

"Hey," Zi growled, putting pressure on my chest and throat to stop me from saying what I was going to snarl at them. "What I did to you shouldn't have caused this. So what is it?"

"What do you mean what you did?" I snarled back at them, keeping my voice low so only Zi and Atiena could hear it.

"J, I put the blood of Anubis in my inks. That shoulda fought off the demon possession that you got goin' on right now. And ain't no way it shoulda done a demon like that," Zi half-whispered, half-growled back at me.

"The fuck do you mean?" I seethed, pushing up with my body to try and lift their weight off of me only to get slammed back down as Atiena gripped my shoulder and pushed.

"Look, brotha, I knew you was somethin' else. I've been doin' your wrists for a long time," Zi explained in harsh toned whispers meant to make it sound like they were berating me to untrained ears. "I beefed up your protection with a little extra firepower in the clip. But this? To break all bonds completely and turn you into a demon? This ain't me, G."

"We ain't got time for this, Zi," I snarled back.

"Make time," Zi retorted, narrowing their eyes at me.

"I will," I growled back, gritting my teeth and feeling elongated fangs pinch against the inside of my bottom lip. "After I get Adi back."

25

McKENNA

We followed him like two shadows hot on his trail. By the time we made it to the demon ahead of us, my beast side had already climbed into the driver's seat. Part of me wanted to veer off to take care of the Anubis figures that had charged Jason in an instant, however, I stayed the course. Doing so, when Haley and I hit Samael, we hit him in unison with sextuple the strength it would have had if we had been human.

He hadn't had a chance to move or counter us for the first few moments of our assault. Samael became victim to a wild storm of punches, kicks, claws, and savage bites that rained down on him like a torrential force. Our claws dug into him again and again, ripping the fabric of the once pristine, expensive suit he'd had on into pieces. Once his flesh was exposed, it became marred in gashes and lacerations that carved into his flesh and muscle. Together, we'd turned his body into what resembled a cornfield if the person driving the oversized tiller had been three sheets to the wind.

Taking on his demon form hadn't saved him either. The added mass of his body as well as the appearance of his large curled ram horns gave us an advantage. Haley and I took turns grabbing onto one of his horns and jerking his head to the side to spin him off balance.

When Haley would forcefully twist his head and body to her side, it opened him up and gave me room to dig my fangs and claws into his flesh. Then, as he was twisted around, I kept him spinning so that Haley had open flesh to tear into on her turn.

By the time we had him spinning in circles, he was nearly naked and the three of us were drenched in his thick, blackened blood. We'd turned his wood floor into a scene that looked as if someone was splattering oil across its surface.

He began trying to bat at us but I moved quickly and wrapped him up, putting him into a chicken wing submission hold while Haley tore into him deeper. As I pulled on his arm, I got low enough that his neck was exposed to me again and the smell of his blood hit my nose like a fresh buffet. I let out a rippling snarl as I bit down, forcing my teeth through his flesh and muscle, snapping at him with vicious intent.

His blood was hot on my tongue, carrying an added spice to the familiar flavor of copper and vanilla candy that I normally enjoyed.

Instead of swallowing, I let it pour from my mouth trying to avoid the sour aftertaste Samael's blood held. We bathed in his blood, drenching mine and Haley's body in the acridly sour, viscous fluid.

He roared as we both bit into him, tearing chunks of flesh from his neck and shoulders on both sides. Samael spun wildly, gravity shifting our bodies just enough that, when his arms came up to grab us, he found purchase. As gravity righted itself, I felt air swooshing around me then hit the ground and began rolling violently. I skidded across the grand hall into the massive dining room, narrowly missing Sinead's feet.

I hit the far wall with force, the plaster and sheetrock imploding from where I struck and found myself halfway into another room behind it. Pain radiated throughout my body from where I'd hit the floor with my legs, torso, and head throbbing with every pulse of my heartbeat.

I groaned and rolled myself from the hole my body had created and felt my vision rectify itself in time to see someone coming down on me. I had enough time to duck the swing of a giant reaper's scythe followed by an ethereal scream. It reminded me of what I'd heard Sinead do, only this voice was male.

I rose upward and spun, planting a foot hard into the guy's chest. Before I could launch myself forward to rip him to pieces I watched another scythe split through him, the curved blade tearing through his chest cavity. A dark stain that turned his red shirt black began to blossom outward like an unfurling rose as the viscous liquid spread across his chest and torso.

Then the man was forced to bow backward at an unnatural angle as the blade tilted with a malicious force and he went to his knees. Behind him, Sinead appeared, her flaming skull roaring with an ethereal scream as she stepped down on her scythe. With the male dullahan incapacitated for a brief moment, she grabbed his flaming head from his shoulders. Behind her, the spectral woman was taking in a deep breath, readying to unleash a hellish scream.

When her jaw stretched unnaturally wide, Sinead forced the dullahan's head into her mouth, her ungodly scream muffled by the foreign object blocking her. Another ethereal cry of agony from the man rang out as his body began to twitch and convulse violently, inky black smoke erupting from his neck in explosive billows.

When the scream faded, the spectral woman fell backward, her eyes rolling into the back of her head as she passed out but remained visible. The man, on the other hand, fell limp. All that remained of his head was a skull, which fell to the floor and shattered with its impact.

"The hell just happened, love?" I said, catching my breath as I stood and looked down at the unmoving body beneath me.

"I… killed… the bastard," Sinead grunted as she forcefully ripped her scythe from the dead dullahan and turned a wary eye on the spectral woman. With a curt nod, she heaved the scythe properly into her grip and trained vicious eyes on Samael. "Come, mo ghràdh, let's take this mother fucker's head."

"Sounds like a perfect date to me, sweet thing," I grinned, letting out a sadistic laugh.

The two of us ran forward just as Samael was lifting Haley by her throat and she kicked at his forearm frantically. Before he could choke the life out of the werewolf, Sinead and I were on him, striking together in unison. Sinead's scythe tore through the arm holding Haley like a hot knife through butter, severing the massively muscled limb from his body.

His bellowing scream of pain was his only reaction before I pounced onto his back, grabbing hold of his horns and hitting his back with all of my weight and momentum like a missile. I rode him down, delighting in the sickly crunching sound made as I forced his face into the floor and dug my toe claws into the muscle of his back.

The force of him hitting the ground threw me forward and I rolled end over end before my feet caught the wood flooring. I skidded to a stop in a pouncing position, my feet and hands creating jagged trails through the wood grain. My tail waved wildly as I held myself with my torso low and my ass high in the air.

I cackled like a madwoman, a grin stretched ear to ear, as Samael slowly tried to pick himself up with one arm. Blood was flowing in thick, black rivers from his nose and mouth, making him lose traction repeatedly.

We'd learned our lesson the first time; we hadn't let up on him or gotten too cocky from the get-go. He'd also clearly underestimated our tenacity this time around, nor did he expect Sinead to side with us.

"One of the rings on his hand disappeared," Haley coughed, rubbing her throat with one hand as she looked forward. Only one of her glowing amber eyes was able to open. "Any idea why?"

"I killed one of his honor guards," Sinead said proudly, a smile stretched across her lips as she watched Samael's pain with amusement. "He has another Ananke ring on that hand so I would believe the dullahan was tied to the other."

"That mean the rest of the bling is the same?" Haley asked, shaking the pain out of her system as she rose into the same pouncing position as me.

"Only one way to find out," I chuckled, digging my claws into the floor and feeling my muscles coil, readying to launch myself toward the demon lord.

Haley and I screamed, a mix of a primal leopard yowl and wolven howl filling the villa as we raced forward, hitting Samael with everything we had. Our combined weight and momentum hit him across the face where I stopped in place and latched on.

Haley, however, continued forward, leaping up toward the ceiling after sideswiping him, digging claws into the sheetrock and plaster. Her

muscles coiled tightly before bolting downward like a meteor, ripping

a chunk out of the roof with her. She plowed into the top of his skull,

making him fall to one knee in disorientation before she wrapped her arms

around his throat and pulled.

As Haley's muscles rippled, strangling the life from Samael, I

grabbed at two golden bangles around his wrist and began tugging. When

he realized what I was doing, he had the wherewithal to pull, fighting me

to keep them on. I snarled at the big man as Haley and I pulled him in two

different directions.

Lifting a foot to dig my feet claws into his forearm, I tugged with

everything I had, hoping I'd take his entire wrist with me. He jerked and I

kept my grip on him until he swung hard enough that the back of my head

hit one of the panes of glass overlooking the backyard. The force shattered

the entire sheet and my vision began swimming. He threw me the opposite

way and I heard two loud snaps as I hurtled across the room.

After landing unceremoniously, I sat up slowly and I realized I held

half of the two bangles in my grip. Then I watched them with curiosity as

they began to disintegrate. I heard wretched screams and turned in time to

see the Anubis creatures, which Xander had been fighting, begin to shake.

With terrified looks in their eyes, both of them seized up, backs

bowing as they convulsed and clutched at their chests. Unnatural screams of pain and agony tore through the foyer, making the remaining glass shiver with the force. Then they went silent as the two of them fell to the ground in crumpled heaps, life leaving their vacant eyes.

Then I heard Haley scream.

Refocusing and blinking away my shock, I raced forward toward Samael, hellbent on hitting him again as hard as I could. Instead, I found myself getting hit by Haley who was thrown across the room toward me. I was forced to catch her limp body as I slid backward and hit the wall near where I had landed moments before. She growled as she began to move, coming back to consciousness as my arms wrapped around her midsection and I leaned in to press my cheek against the side of her neck.

"Caught you, love," I said, letting a playful purr slip out while my eyes narrowed hatefully at Samael a few yards in front of us.

"Gracias, la novia," she sighed into my arms, reaching up to give my shoulders a reassuring squeeze.

As Samael moved to stand, I found where he'd thrown Sinead as I watched the two other Anubis creatures, Zi and their sister, help her onto her feet. The three of them glared at Samael as Sinead gave them the bangles she'd removed from the demon's severed arm.

She'd handed them their own freedom.

We'd found Samael but not Adelaide. And she, more than anyone right now, deserved that freedom for herself. As I helped Haley stand and become stable, I closed my eyes, lifted my nose to the air, and took in a deep breath as my nostrils flared.

My senses flooded with familiar scents. I poured through all of the sensations, trying to find just one in particular that I knew so well. I mentally crossed out and filtered through which I recognized and which I didn't, however, I found myself hitting a wall. I could scent Adelaide but she'd been dragged through the entire mansion, every room having that faint scent of her that hit my senses like walking into a fresh bakery.

I savored the faint sweet smell of her at every opportunity my beast could find. One simple fact remained; Adelaide was here in the house. Somewhere. She was possibly feet away from us freeing her or she could be on the other side of the compound. I didn't have a solid direction to follow.

Samael's scream broke me out of my thoughts, my eyes settling back onto him with a rage-filled growl. He lifted the arm Sinead had severed back to himself and muttered something under his breath. From our viewpoint, I spotted the Ananke ring still on his finger and watched the glow signifying the lifeforce of the soul bound to it dim.

Meaty tendrils sprang from the two sections of his body, reaching for each other before they caught and pulled in a sick, macabre display. While his arm reattached itself, some of the deeper gashes across his form Haley and I inflicted healed themselves in rapid time.

The air was rich with the smell of sulfur as the wounds closed, smoking and hissing as the flesh soldered itself back together. He bellowed with laughter, looked around the room, and scowled at all of us. His honor guard was gone, the banshee being the only one still clinging to life while the rest of us stood strong against him.

"This is your last chance, you fucking peasants," he roared with anger as he looked around the room and saw how much of his backing force had been dwindled. "Return what is mine and when I ascend to godhood under Yazmin's rule, you will know sweet suffering and a quick death."

He then pulled something from his pants pocket, or what remained of them, and flipped a large golden coin. When he caught it and rubbed across its surface with his large thumb, an inky, black void began to swirl to the side of him, creating a doorway that seemed to open up in the fabric of reality.

A dozen more lesser demons began stepping through the opening and into our plane of existence. Each of them scowled, giving the air viscous snaps of their fangs while marking the rest of us as enemies with their cold pitch black eyes.

Then the room filled with an overwhelming scent of earthen pine, rain, and the smell of ozone after a fresh lightning strike. From the side of the room to my right I saw a familiar figure that I nearly didn't recognize step forward and my heart began to thrum in my chest. I hadn't realized I had held my breath and I let it out slowly as my eyes trailed over Jason's form.

Gone was his pale white skin, becoming replaced with darkened flesh that looked like he'd been through a thick cloud of ash and coal that turned his forearms, chest, and eyes completely black. His eyes were now pitch black, pinholes of bright blue light shining where his pupils would have been. All the while his deep auburn hair looked as if he'd dyed it a red so deep it was almost black. The most surprising feature on him, however, were the two lyre horns emerging from the top of his skull, forcing his hair to part for them as they rose upward.

"Over my dead body," Jason snarled, his voice layered with a thick, raspy tone that was far lower than his usual timber. It sounded as if he'd carried a beast inside of him and now he and the monster deep within were speaking as one. "Lord Hades sends his regards."

My heart skipped a beat and heat flooded my core. I did a double take to make sure I was seeing Jason correctly and scented the air again. Sure enough, despite the change in appearance, nothing could beat the evergreen forest and rainy fall smell he had to him.

Was this him letting his demon side out?

"Where is she, you bloody cunt?" I growled, speaking before I could even think to stop myself. "You can still let her go and live, or does my man have to wipe the floor with your arse?"

Mickie, what the fuck was that?

I scolded myself for letting my ovaries speak before my brain. Embarrassment ran through me before a sense of fear overtook it when I saw Samael snort and kick his hooves in response. While words earned a hateful snarl from Samael, Jason, my apparent semi-demon mate, gave me a seductive smile.

"You won't make it far enough to find her, you fools," Samael grunted as his eyes scanned the room for who to hit first.

"Sin, Haley, search upstairs," Jason growled, moving his head side to side as if to ease the muscles in his neck as he began walking toward Samael without an ounce of fear in him. "Xan, search the basement."

Samael roared again, marching toward Jason only for him to disappear and then suddenly reappear behind the big man in a flash. I rushed forward as I saw Samael swing one of his massive arms toward Jason, screaming for him to get out of the way. My eyes went wide in astonishment as I stopped short when Samael was forced to stop mid-swing. Because his large fist was halted midair by Jason's much smaller hand. Jason grinned, showing off a pair of long, sharp fangs as he caught Samael's fist and began chuckling in amusement.

"My turn."

When he walked through the crowd in that new form of his, my heart began slamming against my chest as hard as it could. I was in awe of him. He had been handsome before and I had thoroughly enjoyed seeing him with his shirt off or even less before today. But this?

Dios tenga piedad de mi alma

The coal-dipped skin, pure black eyes, and horns were checking all of the boxes in my head that appeared during my reading time. Especially from the books Adi and I read together.

Between him catching Samael's fist with one hand and his commanding tone with Sin and me, a fiery heat was racing from my core across my body. I was so starstruck I hadn't noticed Sinead at my side, jerking hard on my shirt and forcing my attention to her. Our eyes met, mine full of awe and lust met her bewildered expression.

"Master told us to go," Sinead said.

"I know, I just… Jason-"

My words were cut off as we found his form being thrown at us, forcing Sinead and I to catch Jason, skidding backward as we clutched him. My wolf rumbled as his scent hit us stronger than ever before. Both of us wanted to deny his original command and stay to help fight.

"Thought I told you to go find Adi," he rumbled, his chest vibrating as his doubled voice spoke. My heart thrummed faster when his eyes shifted to the side to look at me.

"We can help, mi amor," I pleaded, clutching his arm tightly. Possessively.

"Find our Adi," he snarled as his eyes shifted back to watch Mickie bolt between the demon's legs, rise smoothly, and latch her teeth just above his kidneys. "Fucker has her here somewhere."

"Jason-"

"Sé un buen lobito y encuentra a nuestro pajarito," he prodded hotly, his attention fully on me as he spoke. The doubled voice and the presence of a low-timbered growl gave me a heady feeling.

"Si, Papi," I hummed with a light moan.

Putos ovarios traidores, ahora no es el momento

What had once started as a joke to get him riled up was backfiring.

It had gone from a joke to an unlocked kink and then to something more in the span of the last three months. Now, there was nothing in my mind that would ever betray my prime, or a command given, no matter how much my beast and I wanted to stay and help.

Instead, I let out a snarled growl and grabbed him by the hair to tug him toward me. Our lips crashed in a quick, yet ferocious kiss that left me breathy and him rumbling with delight. The pinch of his fangs on my lips did nothing to douse the heat rising in my body before I pushed him back and narrowed my eyes at this demonic form of my mate.

"Sé un buen chico y ayuda a Mami a joderlo," I purred in his ear before finally yielding to Sinead's efforts to pull me away from him.

I shivered at his wide, fanged grin as he nodded and we went our separate ways. Once I was back in the here and now, Sin and I hit the stairs next to the foyer and ran for the upper level. When I scented sulfur directly ahead of us, making the round on the landing in the middle of our ascent, we both bolted.

Sinead raced forward, her reaper's scythe appearing in a plume of blue hellfire as she bound toward the wall, somersaulted off of it, and came down on a guard at the top of the stairs. I went the opposite way, hopping onto the banister railing, running up it like a gymnastics table, and using it to jump high over a second lesser demon in front of us. I landed behind him, wrapped him tight into my arms, and then came down on his exposed neck as he struggled to free himself. An entire section of his throat and neck was ripped away with my teeth and I fought the urge to gag on the taste of demon blood filling my mouth and throat.

My wolf *hated* the taste of demons.

As he fell to the floor in a pile of ash, smoke, and sulfur, I ran down the short hallway and slammed myself into another guard. She was violently speared over my shoulder before I slammed her against a wall, breaking the sheetrock and wooden stud beneath it under our combined weight. I grabbed the front of her face, digging my claws into her flesh despite her screams of protest, and then hammered her against the wall and floor. She too disappeared in a plume of sulfur and smoke.

I saw a fourth guard coming out of my peripherals and turned to face the man only to watch him get hit. Hard. His sharply bowed back came upright and I noticed the two small sickle blades sticking out of him. Sinead had snuck to my side and threw her blades, landing one between his beady black eyes and another right into his chest cavity. My wolf growled with approval of her talent for the hunt.

With the fourth guard down, the spare bedroom now empty of lesser demon goons for us to dismantle, Sin led me back to the top of the stairs. The first two guards we'd taken out had been guarding a large set of black, wooden double doors which Sinead and I proceeded to kick down. We were ready to fight after our big entrance, however, the room was silent as we walked through them into a giant master suite.

The main bedroom itself took up more than half of the entire upper floor with expensive-looking wood floors, massive dark stained wood built-in bookshelves, and a personal wet bar. In the center of the room pushed against the far wall was a gargantuan four-poster bed that made a king size seem small in comparison. I made a mental note to find one of its size for us and Jason.

However, as beautiful as the big wooden bed was, my gut and heart sank as I looked up at the figure tied to it. Adelaide was chained to the front posts of the bed, suspended by thick iron chains that cuffed her wrists and held her a few feet off the ground. Her head hung forward limply, her long strawberry-blonde hair falling over her face like a curtain. It was made more red than usual by the dried blood that stained it in various places. She'd been pseudo-crucified, chained up like a broken and bloody angel at the foot of the bed for everyone to see.

"Adi," I choked out, running forward to inspect her for more injuries as I took in her entire beaten and bloodied nude form. I quickly shot a glance over my shoulder at Sin who used the two small sickle blades to cut through the chains and drop Adelaide into my arms. "I'm here, la novia. I got you, baby girl"

"H-Haley?"

Her voice was dry, filled with an exhausted rasp. Her eyes

remained closed as she teetered on the brink of consciousness. She felt heavy in my arms as I hugged her to me tightly, cradling her limp form against mine while I settled down onto my knees.

"Sin, get her some water," I said, turning to look at the dullahan over my shoulder.

I heard Sinead move toward the wet bar while I rubbed slow circles across Adi's back, whispering into her ear. They were a mix of words of encouragement, pleading for her to wake up and hang on, and reminding her that I was there for her. I heard the tinkling of glasses, running water, and then footsteps that approached me quickly from behind.

After some gentle repositioning, I cradled her into my arms, laying her back while Sinead tentatively held a glass mug she'd found to Adi's lips. She began pouring slowly, letting Adi hydrate after some prompting, and we watched with bated breath.

She came back to full consciousness and looked around the room slowly before her eyes finally fell back onto me. I gave her the best smile I could muster before Sinead offered her more water. Her eyes were on me completely as she finished the mug and took a few deep breaths.

"Hey beautiful, welcome back," I said, grinning dumbly at her but was more than happy to get a small smile and a chuckle out of her in response.

"Where is-"

Adelaide's expression fell to a scowl and she kicked herself into a backward somersault out of my arms and onto the floor. She crouched down onto her hands and knees and an unnatural hiss overtook her as the raven skull materialized and sank down to cover her face like a warrior's mask. Her fingernails extended into razor-sharp talons that dug into the wood flooring and, in her new position, she resembled a cat with its hackles raised. Despite her weakened state, she was ready for a fight.

"Adi, wait it's-"

"I'm okay with this outcome," Sinead answered solemnly and then settled on her knees in a submissive position. She extended her arms, sliding the two sickle blades across the floor toward Adi, and gave a sage nod. "Please do as you would with me, Mistress Adelaide."

"Pendejo, we don't have time for this right now," I growled, leveling my gaze at Sinead and scowling at her before turning my attention to Adelaide, watching her carefully.

"We will *make* the time," Sinead retorted, her voice filled with a mix of annoyance and purpose. "Because despite how you, McKenna, and Jason may feel about this, the only one whose opinion matters to me right now is hers."

Adelaide and I were taken aback by the comment as Sinead moved forward on her knees and lifted her head higher to bare her throat to Adi. Her eyes were closed, waiting with anticipation, and making it clear the only one who could truly decide the dullahan's fate was Adelaide.

I hated how calm she was about offering herself up like that. But I could understand it. Part of me had wanted the same with Mickie if my death would have brought her happiness.

It was a moment of selfishness on our part, offering ourselves up to appear weak to those we saw as better people. I had dolled myself up for Mickie when I had confessed my feelings for her, hoping that she'd see me and not the threat we'd been to each other for years. It had been a selfish act to hope that would open her heart to me, to find that spark Mickie and I had once had together.

I had been lucky enough that Mickie had seen through my facade and realized that the spark we'd once shared hadn't died out completely. It had still been there waiting to reignite. Now Sinead was offering the same thing.

Sin had mentioned that Adelaide had once tried to extend a hand of friendship at one time. Seeing them together, I realized that Sinead had completely let go of that notion. The part of her thought that there were no second chances for Sinead in Adelaide's eyes winning the fight.

"Oh," Sinead said, furrowing her brow and tilting her head back down to look at Adelaide. "I did bring you some essentials. These are necessary for you, after which I will offer my life to you once more."

"Would you stop talking like that," Adelaide growled, her teeth clenched in rage before both of our faces were covered in a quick flash of hellfire. When the light dimmed again, I watched as Adelaide's face softened before her mouth opened to say something. "And what essentials…"

When my eyes followed Adi's it was to a spot directly in front of me on the floor. There, in front of us was a neatly folded and laundered pile of clothing, putting the dual blades between Adelaide and the pile. The small stack contained the outfit that Adelaide had once said was her favorite; a pair of light blue capri jeans, a white long-sleeve blouse that she wore in a way that nearly hung off of her shoulders, a teal thin-strapped tank top, black lace underwear, and her favorite tan heeled boots with a rhinestone strap.

"Who… are you?" Adelaide asked, her brow cocked in confusion but the look in her eyes said she was in a state of mixed emotions that had not only confusion but remorse and appreciation mixed in.

"I am simply Sinead O'Hare," she replied, a small smile stretching across her lips.

"La novia, what happened to the new title you used in front of Hades?" I chuckled, shaking my head at the petite woman in front of me and shooting her an incredulous look.

"I still need time to completely… *workshop* the new ones," Sinead answered, tilting her head in confusion as I watched thoughts rolling endlessly inside her head.

"New titles?" Adelaide scoffed, giving Sinead an incredulous look as the dullahan mentally tried coming up with an overly long title.

"Yes," Sinead answered slowly as she watched the floor then turned a bewildered glance up at Adelaide and me. "Using the McCrae clan seems fitting. Especially after Lord Hades revealed to us that Jason's clans served the Call of Death, right? But do I add the title of *Princess* that Jason gave to me? Is it too pretentious to declare that I am a girlfriend to Mickie, Jason, Haley, and, if it is permitted, you, Adelaide?"

She shook her head then and quickly brought up her hands, pointing at her neck where she prominently displayed a matching pair of hickies.

"Do these signify this? Or should I go about another method of being claimed?" Sinead continued before coming to a slow stop. "What… is so funny?"

Adelaide began snorting which melted into boisterous laughter that filled the room like the tinkling of bells. Her hands covered her face, muffling the sound, however, the blush that spread across her skin conveyed the overwhelming joy she felt. Then, in her uncontrollable fit of levity, Adelaide let out a second snort that mildly resembled the sound of a pig. I couldn't hold back after that and joined her in our shared delirious bliss.

"Fuck, I needed that," Adelaide sighed after a long few minutes, while Sinead looked on a mix of horror and bewilderment etched across her face. Then a sadness crossed Adelaide's eyes and her gaze became distant. "How much did I miss?"

"Oi ve, where to even begin on that one," I groaned, rolling my eyes because even just the last 24 hours was a lot to take in. "Well, for starters, Jason is downstairs fighting Samael and he might be winning? I'm not sure. Um also… he's part demon or something? And we met Hades so that… that was something."

"Hades? *The* Hades?" Adelaide looked up, eyes wide as she stared back and forth between Sinead and me. Then her gaze focused on the dullahan with intensity. "Wait, you said something about the Call of Death?"

"Yeah," I shrugged and looked up to remember what exactly the literal god of the underworld had said. I was seriously still trying to wrap my head around that one by itself. "The four clans or whatever, Jason's descended from two of them? And they were, like, demons or fallen angels or something like that so they always answered the call. What am I missing?"

"I guess the skull hasn't shared everything I should know," Adi groaned, her eyes rolling before she looked back down. Her gaze shifted between the blades and the clothes Sinead had set out for her. Then she furrowed her brow and looked up at me, her eyes narrowing. "And wait… girlfriend?"

I froze and my eyes went wide as I became stuck in the moment, giving Adelaide my best deer in the headlight impression. A slow, nervous smile crossed my lips as my brows upturned to give her an apologetic glance. I felt terrible that Adi hadn't been there to give Sinead her blessing with Jason.

"She helped find you, Adi," I said nervously, my eyes floating back and forth between the two of them. "Sinead… isn't the same person you knew her as before. She doesn't want to be Samael's tool anymore."

"So you, Jason, and Mickie?" Adelaide asked slowly.

"I… haven't," I let the word hang in the wind before looking down and felt my cheeks begin to burn from the memories of this morning that began to flood my mind. "We didn't know where to look to bring you back and… I'm sorry I let you down."

"You didn't," Adelaide whispered as I felt her hand slip into mine and squeeze tightly. Then she turned her gaze up to Sinead and gave her a contemplative look. "Sinead, are you sure you're not going back to Samael? Are you going to turn on us as soon as he calls for you?"

Sinead took in a deep breath and scowled hard as her eyes met Adelaide's, small hellish flames rising from her pupils. The anger in them then transferred to her hair as a small plume of blue flame began rising from the top of her head and her long white hair began to billow in a nonexistent wind before it too began to spark with fire.

"No," she growled out finally, her Scottish lilt coming front in center as rage took over her voice. "I wish to take his head and mount it on the wall inside Master Jason's office. Right next to that cunt named Gary that has vexed our Master. But *only* after we complete our task of saving you, Mistress Adelaide."

"Gods that's hot," Adelaide chuckled softly and let a wide grin cross her lips with delight.

Before either of us could register her movements, Adelaide launched herself forward, wrapping her arms around Sinead in a tight hug. Adi all but straddled the dullahan's waist as she squeezed tightly until Sinead finally relented. Her stiffened body melted into Adi's embrace before Sinead cautiously let her hands gently cup Adi's hips, the fire in her wide eyes died immediately as they were replaced by flowing tears.

"I... I'm sorry, Adelaide For everything before," Sinead finally said quietly, still staring off into the distance. Then the dam broke and Sinead collapsed into Adi's arms, sobbing woefully into her shoulder. "I never... want to be that weak again."

"You're not weak. I know what he's like, the same as you. What matters is that you're here now," Adi answered softly, digging her fingers into Sinead's hair and scrunching the back of her shirt.

The hug lasted for a few more moments before Adi reached behind her to grab the clothing Sinead had brought her and stood. We both watched as Adelaide dressed, a look of confidence and fire radiating from her before she adjusted the raven skull on top of her head with a nod. Then she let a wicked grin cross her lips at the same time a loud roar rang from downstairs followed by a booming sound that shook the entire villa.

"Now… Let's let Sinead make good on that promise and get us a demon's head."

I HAD JUST ESCAPED THIS HELL AND NOW I WAS BACK.

Gods, I must be fucking insane.

This time, however, something felt different. Maybe it was Jason's rage or the way he was so determined to get the Princess back but something inside me pulled at me to do this. Maybe it was the slave crest etched across my lower stomach. Which I had zero desire to talk about to anyone or address in the slightest.

Though, would Jason have been so willing to let me help if I didn't offer myself up on a silver platter? Part of me said he would have trusted me - eventually - but the girl didn't have time for those semantics. We'd address the fact that I traded one life of servitude for another some other time. When we were alone, of course, I didn't have a nymph hot on my heels.

We raced up the hill from the creek to the back of the chalet, a view I'd seen plenty of time from the asshole's domain. Funny how I'd always thought of it as the perfect escape route and now, here I was, doing things in reverse. Any guards around the perimeter were pulled toward the inside, leaving the path in front of me clear.

Which means Jason drove straight up to the front door.

"Great, my new master is an idiot," I scoffed in a mix of disgust and dismay.

"Yeah, definitely some white knight syndrome with that one," Lex chuckled softly.

"Ugh, those ones are always the worst. Always getting themselves killed and hit," I said, shaking my head as we rounded the outside of one of the garages and I quietly opened the door.

"Eh, he's not so bad once you get to know him," Lex retorted, a shrug in her voice.

My eyes narrowed as I looked around the interior, skimming over the moving vans and finding two doors. One led inside from the garage, the other looked like a pair of metal double doors surrounding a large metal column in the back corner of the garage. The entrance to the garage wasn't guarded, however, the scent of sulfur in the air led my gaze toward a man in a black suit creeping toward the open bay door of the garage.

When he crouched and raised a rifle to take aim at Jason and the others, who looked to be having a conversation with the front entry guards, I moved. With his attention on the rifle in his hands, he never noticed the faint sounds of my hooves against the concrete running toward him. When he did, I ducked to slide underneath him as he swung the rifle while I went between his legs.

In a matter of seconds, his vision went from peering down a scope to hitting the concrete with his full weight.

Before he could let out a scream of pain to accompany the sickly cracking sounds of his nose and jaw being broken, I came down on him. My knee drove into the back of his neck, crushing his throat as his breath came out in gurgles and choking sounds.

Then, before I thought to grab him by the head and snap his neck, my eyes spotted a scabbard strapped around his waist. With a grin, I grabbed the hilt of the blade and drew it, reveling in the sound of the melody it made as the forged steel came free.

"Lucifer be damned, you brought me a present? Baby, you shouldn't have," I said, my voice a sing-song teasing tone as I whirled the pommel in my hand and was met by the satisfying song of metal being driven through skin, bone, and viscera.

The demon's body twitched several times before it disintegrated in a plume of sulfur and ash, the weight below me vanishing into nothingness. I regarded the pile of ash with disgust as I stood and tested the new blade, letting it spin and whirl through the air with ease.

I inspected the rapier, watching the metal glint off of the illumination the lights outside offered. I smirked as I swung it once more, letting the blood on its tip spray across the concrete before bending down to pick up the belted scabbard.

"Really, you *shouldn't* have," I mocked, scowling at the ash beneath me as I used the loose black blouse McKenna had given me to clean off the rest of the blood. I hilted the blade with a satisfying '*shlinck*' sound before securing the belt around my hips.

"Damn girl, that was fuckin' cold as hell," Lex said, walking toward me with awe etched across her face.

I shrugged as we walked toward the metal column and opened the doors to a chrome-lined freight elevator. Hitting the button, the doors accordioned open, allowing us to step inside the illuminated box where I pressed the only feasible option on the two button pad. Down.

"Yeah, well, when you grow up in the pits and you're forced to fight other demonkin, wayward souls, and tieflings that don't know any better," I said, forcing the memories of my early childhood from my mind. "You get *very* good at being cold."

"And… he's… your daddy dearest?" Lex asked, making me flinch as memories of the last ten years hit the back of my mind and made my head sting.

"Un-fucking-fortunately," I growled, reaching down to find

comfort in gripping the pommel of my newly claimed sword.

"Right, bad topic," Lex nodded softly out of the corner of my eyes as we watched the door.

"Let's just-"

As the elevator pinged, and the doors spread apart, two more demons turned to look at us with disbelief in their eyes. They reached for their weapons, however, before they could swing a pair of rifles up at us, I was there.

I drew the sword again in a vertical quickdraw that drew the edge of the steel upward along one of the demon's forms, splitting his body in half. As his bisected form fell apart in a cascade of black blood, viscera, and sulfuric ash, the one next to him became engulfed in a quickly raging cyan inferno.

I gave Lex a contemplative look as her hair, eyes, and fists rolled with hellfire licking off of her as the demon screamed in agony. My eyes watched her just in time to see her do a double leap off the walls of the elevator, catching the burning body of the demon in front of her by the neck and driving her to the ground.

It looked similar to something I'd seen in the pits from other fighters who were obsessed with something on Midgaterra referred to as professional wrestling. I didn't get the extra showmanship of a simple move but could appreciate the athleticism behind it. Especially as she got up and brushed remnants of sulfur, ash, and smoke off of her form before giving me a look of indifference.

"So, if my master is such a great guy, why didn't you take him for a ride instead of wolfboy?" I asked, trying to steer the conversation away from me as much as I could. I smirked as her pale cheeks bloomed with a bright shade of red as I brought up the wolf; Xan or whatever his name was. "You reek of his scent and don't get me started on how mushy the two of you were on the way here."

"We weren't that mushy-"

"You mean aside from the brief makeout session and thinking he was the only one who heard… What was it again?" I said with a smirk, lifting my head and pressing my finger to my chin in mock contemplation before I attempted to mimic her voice. "*Oh Hades, Xanny, you gotta do that thing with your fingers again. Next time you should take me from behind and-*"

"Hun, shut the fuck up," Lex scowled with indignance, unable to hold back from smiling and giggling at the teasing. Or was it because I'd made her think about him again? "Okay, and to answer your question. Jason is cool and all, but me and Xan just have a ton more in common."

"A nymph and a werewolf have commonalities?" I asked with incredulousness as we walked out into the basement and began looking around the massive expanse that was hidden away underneath the main structure.

"When you spend the better half of your life living here in Midgaterra, you forget a lot about your life in Nekduamortum," she said with a haunted tone in her voice, drawing my attention to her as she looked around.

The expanse was lined with dozens of cages that filled it from end to end with multiple rows of pens made of steel bars and glass panels. Cages the Princess and I knew well because the glass was reinforced with arcane wards that made it impossible to use your abilities to escape and left you at the mercy of the wardens. It displayed the interiors perfectly and put the occupants' sadness and melancholic expressions front and center, causing Lex to stifle a sob.

I could tell that she and I both recognized the various creatures in the cages. Another dullahan, two more banshees, and another cage holding a lesser grim reaper. Another demi-anubis woman placed her hands on the cage, a pleading look filling her eyes as she regarded us. The cage next to her held a Giltine - a woman with long white hair, pale skin, and sunken features with an owl perched on her shoulder - who licked the glass, displaying her impossibly long, yellowish tongue. All while a small pack of hellhounds in the cage across from them lifted their heads with interest.

My eyes followed Lex as she walked forward, tears flowing down her cheeks as she stopped at another cage and put her hands on the glass.

Inside, a large shepherd breed dog with emerald green fur that gave off an ethereal glow looked at her with mournful eyes. I waited with bated breath, hoping the creature didn't let out three baneful howls as it was accustomed to doing.

"I-It's a cu-sith… I… always wanted one as a kid," Lex said, her voice choked with a mix of disbelief and depression. I nodded at the faerie dog that was tasked with guiding souls across the bridge between worlds, the same as the dullahans, banshees, valravns, and reapers did. "They… they're all from Nekduamortum or have something to do with death."

"Samael believes if he greedily collects them and makes them adhere to his will *he'll* become a new god of death," I scoffed, shaking my head as I regarded my so-called father's endeavor. "They're nothing but a hobby to him."

"Help… us…" said a dreary voice that turned our shared attention to another cage.

"Lex… is that you?" said another voice, this from a woman who shared the cell with the first.

The nymph ran toward the cage, dropping to her knees in front of the two emaciated figures inside. One had dark umber skin with long bright blue hair and eyes while the other was pale with hair grown out to her knees which shared the same cyan hair and eyes as the other two.

"E-Erato? And… Clio? What are you two doing here? How long-"

"Since he came to the village," Erato, the dark-skinned woman, answered weakly. "We… never escaped like you and some of the others did."

"Where is everyone else?" Lex asked, her eyes widening as flames rose from her eyes to give off a hollow glow of hope.

"They… didn't make it," Clio, the pale woman, answered, confirming Lex's fears and dashing her hopes.

I wouldn't tell Lex that I'd seen the two of them before. Not more than a day ago, these were the same underworld nymphs that Samael had forced Adelaide and me to watch as a corrupted minotaur chased them and then assaulted them in front of us.

"So our mothers… they…"

"Lasted as long as they could," Clio answered, finishing Lex's thought for her.

"When he'd break them of their will to survive or fight they began withering," I said, watching a mix of anger and despair wash over Lex as she looked up at me. The two women clutched themselves tightly at my words, nodding curtly in confirmation to say that I told the truth. "If his collection became too far gone to serve their purpose to him or refused to serve him as he wanted? He gave them to the horde as trophies and prizes for them to claim."

"Only two pieces of his collection were never given off to the horde," Erato said, her eyes narrowing at me. I could see the disdain in her eyes, clearly making it known publicly that Adelaide and I had been the only exceptions to his rule.

"What are you doing here, Lex?" Clio asked, ignoring her cellmate's pointed look at me and focusing solely on her old friend. At Erato and I's shared answers, the hellfire on Lex roared to life in a blazing inferno that cast the vast space in an ethereal blue glow.

"My friends and I are here to kill Samael and to release you," Lex answered with conviction, hints of rage and pain making her voice crack. Her eyes scanned over the entire room before she raised her voice so it could fill the dungeon. "To release everyone!"

I heard footsteps racing toward us, the sounds echoing across the cages. Two more lesser demons emerged from the darkness at the opposite end of the room, their eyes solely focused on us. My hand went for the blade at my side and then I froze and tilted my head at Lex as her hellfire became an uncontrolled bonfire next to me, bathing me in warmth.

"Burn, motherfuckers," Lex screamed as fire raced forward like flames in a trail of oil that exploded once it reached the two demons. The two froze in place as they were engulfed, their screams drowned out by a scream filled with rage and pent-up emotions that Lex had carried with her. "Burn!"

A second explosion rocked the cavernous space, filling it with the sounds of raging flames and heat that warmed me to the bone and bathed me in its embrace. The darkness was swallowed by the blinding light of Lex's flames until she fell to one knee in exhaustion and her fire came to a screeching halt. When the flames sucked back into Lex's body, a good portion of her clothing was burnt away, flaking off of her in ash and leaving the room entirely in silence.

Then small, gentle popping noises filled that silence one after the other. Before the room could be filled with silence once more, Lex's sobs echoed through the chamber. I was left in stunned astonishment as, while Lex stared at the floor, sobbing as all of her emotions poured out of her in that instant, a frail figure moved slowly to her side. The heat and explosion of magic had been so intense that it had broken the wards locking all of the cages and its occupants cautiously stepped forward.

Standing behind Lex were her two nymph sisters, squeezing her with reassuring grips that made her look up with shock at their presence. Then her eyes looked from me to the room as the occupants of the cages began to crowd in front of her and me as if we were a pair of generals and they were our armies waiting for us to give them a command.

"You said you're here with your friends?" Clio asked carefully.

"And her boyfriend," I smirked, delighting in the scowl then gentle smile Lex offered me. "I don't suppose the Princess is down here is she?"

"Who?" Erato asked with a cocked brow of confusion.

"A valravn named Adelaide. Have you seen her?" Lex asked with hope before it faded as Clio and Erato gave each other a distant expression.

"He hurts her the most," Erato nodded, her eyes shifting to look at me out of her peripherals. I didn't enjoy the look one bit.

"If she's not down here then that can only mean she's up in the submission den," I answered, my fists clenching with rage.

Lex stood then, her hellfire springing back to life weakly, her hair swirling with flames as her glowing eyes locked onto mine. There was a confidence in her that I had just seen recently. Before it had been with Adelaide, her righteous conviction drew me into the belief that we could escape together. Then it had been with Jason whose same conviction and drive had caused me to do something I'd never thought I would; give my life over to him. Now it was Lex, her conviction filled with strength and will to finally put an end to the monster just above us.

Or had it all come from Jason and that's what he inspired in the two of them?

The crowd parted as Lex turned on her heels and began marching toward the opposite end of the room. Toward the sounds of battle that I could faintly hear coming through the ceiling. Watching her, I felt my own gold-colored celestial fire spark to life, warmth flowing across my eyes and horns as I began to follow after her in stride.

With renewed confidence and drive, I smirked wide as the creatures we released began filling the chamber with the echoes of their footfalls behind us. I'd always wanted a hellish army at my back when I faced my father and because I'd bonded with Jason, my dream was coming true.

I snickered with delight as I drew the rapier at my side and watched as golden flames raced across its blade, lighting our way up the stairs. I ignored the bewildered expression Erato gave me as she followed behind Lex.

"In that case, hun," I said with a wicked grin, twirling the blade to produce a ring of fire at my side. "Let's go hurt *him* more."

MY SURROUNDINGS WERE BLURRED AT THE EDGES, MY FOCUS BEING ON ONE SINGULAR POINT. SAMAEL.

The rage I felt for the big goat man had my chest buzzing with lifeforce and magic that I still wasn't entirely sure how to tap into. I just knew it was there. The same way I knew, without a shadow of a doubt, that my voice was no longer my own. The same voice which had commanded Haley and Sinead to continue their search for Adelaide.

She was here. Somewhere. I just needed to buy enough time for them to find her. Part of me thought that, once she was back in our possession, we should run and get away from this fight. She was the only reason that mattered to be here, to save her and get her out of this hell hole. Another part said that wasn't good enough and she would never be truly free until this fucker was in the ground.

The latter was the louder of the two voices and subsequently won over my inner turmoil. Even with Samael opening a portal of some kind, using that damned gold coin of his, I shot forward once more. I speared myself through two lesser demons that stepped in between me and him. One was sent end over end with an arm extended in a clothesline while I wrapped the other into my grip.

The one I brought with me had his yelp of surprise cut short as I drove him into Samael. One of his curled ram horns pierced the demon and turning it into a cascade of blackened blood, sulfur, and ash.

The force of me driving the demon into Samael made the big man stumble a step backward before I stole one of his own moves. I headbutted Samael but, instead of my forehead cracking against his, I speared the newly appeared horns on the top of my skull into his. They didn't go as deep as I'd preferred. I growled in rage that I hadn't been able to take him out with that one rush. However, his pained scream and the sight of blood running down his face from where I'd pierced him satisfied a savage part inside of me I never knew was there.

"You could have escaped all of this if you would have just left her alone, Sam," I snarled as I stared down at him with rage. "Now I'm going to make you pay for even thinking of touching my Adi in the first place."

"She was never yours to have, boy," Samael snarled before I felt his big hands grip me in a crushing, vice-like embrace as he tugged me off of him.

I fucking hated being called *boy*.

He held me up so easily like I weighed nothing to him and it made that rage inside me spike. I'd told the girls I refused to be weak, that they wouldn't have to save me every single time. And I fucking meant it.

The rage made my chest thrum with electricity slamming against my ribs as green and - interestingly enough - golden embers began to float around my form. Then Samael's eyes went wide as I seethed and extended one of my hands to an inch within his face.

"Trish sends her regards," I taunted before I willed that thrumming buzz of energy down my arm to my palm before it exploded in a mix of ethereal green and golden fire.

Samael let out a bellowing scream of agony as fire engulfed his face, forcing him to drop me and begin to frantically slap at the flames that were burning away his fur pelt. It left an acrid smell in the room as the scent of burning flesh and hair permeated the air.

Then, just as he was snuffing the flames out, Samael was hit by a black and golden-furred rocket that sent him rolling wildly from the living room into the kitchen where his banshee servant still lay, unconsciously floating in the air.

"Didn't realize you could shoot fire, love," Mickie rumbled with a snarled grin, extending a big, clawed hand to help me.

"Neither did I," I snorted, licking my lips and cringing from the taste of blood along the insides of my lips and cheeks.

"Just one more thing to add to our conversation after all this," Zi said, smirking as they and Atiena stepped up behind me. I gave the Anubis shifter a coy look over my shoulder, my mind still surging with questions as to when and why they had infused Anubian blood into the ink of my tattoos.

Then my eyes settled on the sharpened blade of the polearm they and their sister carried.

"Mickie, get behind him and drop him to his knees," I said in a cold tone that didn't match the grin stretching across my lips. Then I reached out to snatch the weapon from Zi's hands, "I'mma need to borrow this for a minute."

Before the jackal shifter could protest, Mickie launched forward with a wide berth, bounding off the glass walls and upturned furniture to reach her destination. Just as Samael came to stand again, he was hit with a sickening force in the back of his knees. Blood sprayed from the taught ligaments as Mickie dove through his legs, claws extended and slashed at the tendons that kept his kneecaps in place.

As his knees hit the floor again I raced forward with the pole in hand before feeling the urge to leap and twist my body end over end to bring the blade down one Samael. With a whirling arc of force, I slashed at him, bringing the blade down the center line of his chest and abdomen, more blood blooming down the front of him. A snarl of rage ripped from my throat as I realized the big man had acted at the last second to move himself backward enough that the blade didn't cut deeper.

As the metal clanged and embedded itself into the edge of the once pristine wood flooring, Samael surged forward. His fist caught me across the face, sending me hurdling backward in a chaotic flight before I landed harshly against three bodies. Mickie, Zi, and Atiena had to stop the attack they were collectively gearing up for to catch me instead. The force of my collision not only leveled the three of us but sent us skidding backward across the floor once more.

"I'm going to enjoy breaking you. *All* of you," Samael roared as he stomped forward toward me.

Despite the blue pinhole of light around the edge of my vision, I began seeing red with rage. My entire body was on fire. The buzzing sensation in my chest curled out through my whole body and made every nerve dance on the edge of a lightning storm.

"Not… if I… break you… *first!*" I growled, my voice starting low before it grew with husk and volume.

My voice crescendoed into a scream of defiance as I slammed one fist against the ground and raised the other to catch his. Instead of the intention to stop his punch, however, a bright green light billowed from my hand, blinding everyone in the room with the sound of a loud, roaring explosion.

When my vision cleared, the pure white edges ebbing away to reveal the scene around me again I had expected to find Samael's fist in my hand. Or at the very least feel pain splash across me from his strike. Against my palm, instead of feeling the short, bristled goat fur of Samael's knuckles, I was touching warm, smooth flesh taught with the feel of finely tuned muscle.

I blinked rapidly, clearing my vision to get a better look at what I was seeing, and froze at a sight that had me calming that rage and turning it into something more akin to bewilderment. Standing tall and solid above me, holding Samael's fist back with one hand was Cera; the woman who'd accompanied Hades and Persephone in my home just an hour or so earlier.

She stood her ground, brows knitted in confusion that marred the stoic look on her face that I'd come to recognize during our brief interaction. Confusion turned to curiosity as she stared down at me, something of a look of recognition and realization etching across her soft, rounded features before she turned a cold gaze toward Samael.

A rumbling growl reverberated in her throat before the muscles in her right arm wound tight like metal cords, bunched, and then sprang forward. With a hard shove, she sent Samael rolling backward, tumbling to where Mickie had dropped him just moments ago.

She regarded him with coldness before her gaze flitted back to me and extended her free hand toward me. I took it, feeling a radiating heat from her palm and strong grip as she hoisted me to my feet. My neck still craned to look up and meet the bright ruby color of her eyes before I watched her full, pouty lips tug carefully into a faintly amused smirk.

There was something about the way she looked at me, something just beneath the surface of her gaze that I felt like I recognized but couldn't place at the exact moment. She broke the gaze and turned to offer a hand to both Mickie and Zi before helping Atiena up to her feet last. As she did so, I became acutely aware of the burning sensation across my neck.

Where Hades had left a tattoo on me.

"Do you always drag your mates into your war against demons?" Cera asked cooly, her deep wine-like voice raking nails across my nerves.

"Not always," Mickie chuckled softly, her tongue extending to lick the blood off of her lips with a sadistic grin. "Sometimes it's a war against bloody cursed bitches."

Cera chuckled softly at Mickie's remark and turned to face Samael. A sadistic grin stretched across her lips as she pounded a fist into her open palm. She looked as if the thought of killing a demon brought her joy. If not a bit of sadistic pleasure.

However, I snuffed out that glint of desire in her eyes as I stepped forward, gently brushing my fingers down the rippling muscle of one of her arms.

Instead, I was the one to give Samael a sadistic, joyous grin.

"Cera, cull the herd, starting with the weakest of them," I purred, mocking Samael's words from the first time we'd faced him. Then, before anyone could say anything to stop me I began striding forward, fists balled tightly at my sides as I went toward Samael like an oncoming storm.

"This war is mine."

29

ADELAIDE

DARKNESS HAD BEEN HOLDING ONTO ME FOR SO LONG THAT I WAS SLOW TO WAKE.

Being stirred, I expected another beating, another assault, more torture, or being used by the horde once more. I had expected to never find salvation again. To be trapped here forever. But I had gotten Trish killed so I deserved it. However, instead of opening my eyes to see Samael again, I found a golden-skinned angel staring down at me.

Then I saw Sinead standing over her shoulder and my anxiety took over, sending me deep into my fight or flight reaction. Part of me wanted to take on my raven form, devour her soul, and bathe in her blood. When she offered up her blades, however, that part of me was taken aback.

When she offered me clothing and her head in the same breath, her voice hit me and I realized that, for the first time, I was no longer looking at the dreaded warden. I realized once again that she had been a victim just as much as I had been.

It was a glimpse into the woman she was before Samael sunk his claws into her. The one I could have known for two decades now if I had been able to sway her away from his influence.

The laughter we shared was something I'd never expected, however, it was everything I had needed in that moment. What had given me the energy to regain a part of myself just for that moment. Then when I heard about Jason? It sent a surge of adrenaline coursing through my veins and I knew I had to see him as quickly as possible.

After dressing and having Haley and Sinead flanking me on my sides as we raced down the stairs, I froze at the landing. I wasn't sure what I had been expecting from the accounts of the two women, however, what I did see was beyond words.

Jason, my best friend, my savior, the love of my life, was trading blows with my abuser. The boogeyman that had haunted me for so long. I hadn't expected to see his skin turned ashen as if he'd nearly bathed in a tub of coal.

He looked so much like me when I let the raven take over. His deep auburn hair had turned black with two horns sticking through the now disheveled waves that had become messy from the exertion of the fight. Then there were his eyes; black as mine in my raven form with bright blue pinhole lights for pupils that streaked with his quick movements.

He looked ethereal, menacing, and gorgeous all at the same time. Enough to make me freeze and watch him in awe and wonder.

"It's kind of freaky but sexy at the same time, right?" Haley chuckled, letting me know that she had stopped with me. I looked over to find her grinning ear to ear, a blush spread wide across her cheeks.

"Master is… extremely attractive in this state," Sinead confirmed and I couldn't help but chuckle and look to my left to see her standing there with us. I found the odd color of her blush fascinating because what I had always thought was just pale, almost snow-white skin was actually a soft shade of bluish-gray. She gave me a tentative glance and then looked away quickly. "Sorry, have I misspoken?"

"No, Sinead," I sighed with a dreamy smile. "No, you have not."

Jason was thrown across the room only to be replaced by Mickie launching at Samael. She dug her claws into his chest before Jason grabbed Samael by the ram horns and slammed his knees into the demon's nose. The spray of blood that poured from my tormenter made me grin maliciously as a fire rushed across my skin and swelled in my core.

"Girls, did our boyfriend just get hotter?"

"Yup," Haley and Sinead answered in unison.

Samael bellowed then, a wave of dark energy surrounding him like a case of armor that grabbed at Jason, Mickie, and several other figures that I didn't recognize. With a thunderous burst, the energy threw them outward. His chest was heaving as he looked around and let out another roar that made the entire house shake from the wave of demonic power that poured off of him like a raging fire.

With a deep breath, he raised his fist to show off a faintly glowing ring, the same one he'd had when we fought him the first time that bound Sinead's soul to him. The deep lacerations that were strewn across his body began healing, stitching themselves back together as a woman's scream of pain scratched at my ears.

Following the deafening sound I found his banshee bride flickering in and out of view. Her soul was being forcefully sucked out of her and draining what little left of her life force was left to heal himself.

"No, no more," I growled under my breath and felt my body begin to shift.

"If it is war that you want, Mr. McCrae, then war you will have!"

My wings beat around me as I leaped into the air, rushing forward with the wind swirling around me before I made it to Samael in less than a second. My lengthened talons grabbed him and I screamed as I hit him, the force throwing him with all of the strength I had.

The big man went flying, hitting the pane of glass behind him and shattering it upon impact, forcing him to tumble onto the back deck. He roared in pain as large shards of glass dug into his flesh, cutting him open in various places as they stuck out of him and became stained with blackened blood.

Once outside, I soared into the frigid night sky and then curled back around in a wide curve as I grabbed him once more and drove my shoulder into his chest. As I came to a stop on the ground Samael went flying, his body sent crashing through a massive brick and steel pillar that supported the upstairs deck. The same one he'd gone out onto to enjoy a glass of wine after using me each morning and night over the last two weeks.

"Did your plan for war account for me?" I growled, a long grin screeching across the avian shape of my beak to show off long rows of sharp fangs. A shimmer of joy glinted in my eyes as the deck fell into pieces around him.

"Or me?" Sinead snarled as she appeared behind Samael just as he began to stand.

A flash of hellfire from her hand sprouted a handle made of bone before the fire jumped to it and became a long flaming stream of a whip. The bright blue strand of flames jumped as she spun and the air cracked as the end wrapped tight around his neck. As his legs went out from under him, the flaming whip picked Samael up and Sinead spun around quickly.

When the line went taught, he was sent through part of the villa's rear-facing wall, all of which were large panes of glass. He went from one end of the house toward the other before the centrifugal force sent him directly toward me.

I grinned wide as my wings beat again and took me airborne, catching him with my feet talons by the horns while I soared. Once we were nearly three hundred feet into the air, I dropped him and then circled back, putting my body into a freefall before I caught up to Samael's form, adding my momentum to his. I used him like a demonic wrecking ball to punch a large hole through his roof into his bedroom, caving it in completely with the combined force of our descent.

His crash nearly took him through to the main floor; which I was partially sad didn't happen. However, knowing that the four-poster bed that had caused me so much pain and torment had been utterly destroyed gave me elation. Then, before he could get to his feet, I grabbed one of the massive wood beams from the corner of the bed frame, reared back, and swung as hard as I could.

The force of the blow took him off his feet, through the outside wall of his bedroom, and then down to the ground floor below. I couldn't help the maniacal laughter that came over me as I walked through the hole his form had made. It was all that he would be able to hear as I briskly jumped from the upper floor with little effort and stalked forward toward him.

Moreover, I couldn't hide my glee as I turned to look back into the villa and saw creatures, his trophies of death mythology, pouring from the basement. All of which swarmed the demon horde he'd brought as his backup. Seeing who led the charge made me freeze and a cold sting of tears fell down my cheeks.

Trish! She's alive!

I watched Trish and Lex tear through demon after demon, several being split into pieces with a sword while others were immolated with fire that couldn't be snuffed out. Better yet, I saw her exact revenge on three demons that had assaulted the two of us only a few nights ago.

Moreover, I watched a gorgeous umber-skinned woman with short, crimped white hair and bright ruby eyes roar with rage before her human form rippled and the body of a massive three-headed pitbull took its place. It was a mix of relief and pride that made a fire of confidence swell hotter inside of me as I turned back and looked down at Samael.

"It's laughable now. Isn't it?" I scoffed with a humorless chuckle. "I was scared of you for… *so* long. I felt so fucking weak because of you. So how does it feel, Sam?"

Samael began laughing, turning his head up to look at me through those pitch-black eyes, his lips curled into a wide grin. His look of glee made me scowl, the rage inside me beginning to burn and send a fire across my entire body. To the point that I felt prickling sensations dancing across my ashen flesh.

"It feels like you have still learned nothing, little bird," Samael gloated. Then his smile stretched wider. "Persedeo."

A jolt of ice-cold electricity shot through my body at that one singular word and I stopped mid-step toward him. My mind fought like hell, trying to will away the sudden urge his voice had on me. However, a jolt of pain that pierced through my chest and head had me falling.

The seething pain forced my eyes shut and I sucked in a breath through my teeth as my head swam. It felt as if I had one of the worst hangovers I'd ever experienced. When my eyes opened I found myself on my knees, arms behind my back, and my chin raised to the sky looking up toward the stars.

It was the position I always found myself in right before a particularly brutal beating.

"You are bound to *me*, remember?" Samael said, his voice holding a vicious rasp that had my very soul bracing for the first slap I knew would be on its way. Then Samael stepped into the frame of my vision, his towering form blotting out the stars and first drops of snowfall above me.

Samael reared back, readying to slam a massive palm across my cheek and I let out a hiss to force myself to stand. I found myself still frozen in place, unable to move like the force of gravity was so strong it refused to let me move. Before I could take the hit, I heard a meaty smack and opened my eyes again to look up and see a familiar figure standing in my vision.

Even through the ashen skin, I could see a fresh tattoo that I had seen only twice since its inception. Within the black ink, I made out three distinctive skulls stacked on top of each other above a vertical triple moon; a leopard, a raven, and a wolf.

Jason's body shook as he held back Samael's hand with his arm while his free hand sent hard right hooks into Samael's ribs one after the other. As Samael raised his other arm to strike down on Jason a blur of black and amber fur pounced on him, twisting the demon away from Jason with a palpable amount of force which took him off balance from the dual attack.

The momentum didn't last, however, as Samael regained his bearings quickly, his wrist moving so that his big hand grabbed Mickie by the tail and swung her like a whip into Jason. The two of them went careening sideways. As they toppled over each other across the ground, Sinead charged forward on her hell stallion and came down on Samael with her scythe. The demon narrowly ducked out of the way and grabbed her, plucking her off the back of the steed's back, and threw her.

She crashed through the side of the villa, putting a large hole into the wall before her form disappeared completely underneath the rubble. Haley appeared in the air, pouncing onto Samael's back and grabbing him by the horns as her wolven jaws sank into his neck. As fresh blood sprayed into the night sky, Samael roared in pain and began flailing.

During his movements he reached back, managing to grab her by the waist and rip her off of him like she was nothing more than a tick. I watched with horror as her body slammed onto the ground beside me. However, his spell forced me to helplessly stay in my position as I heard her cough up blood.

Samael grunted, holding his neck where Haley had torn a large chunk of flesh and muscle from him, as he scowled down at her. He roared again as he lifted his leg, intending to come down on her with his massive cloven hoof and stomp her into a pulp.

Instead, a blazing inferno of golden flames erupted across his body, filling the air with the scent of burning fur and skin. A second inferno of bluish-green fire mixed with it as Samael was ignited by two different sources covering him in a whirling wall of fire.

I saw two figures step into my field of vision, Jason on one side, the teal-colored fire pouring from his open palms as he heaved and snarled at Samael. The second source was Trish, holding the pommel of a blazing sword against the open palm of her left hand that roared with golden flames. Both of them stood guard over me as they torched the large figure beyond.

Samael screamed and roared through the flames that ate at him before they began to dissipate, being snuffed out from the inside of the whirling firestorm. As the flames were choked out, Samael stood taller. His hulking frame was even more massive than it had been before as he shrugged off the last of the flames and grinned.

"My turn," he snorted with glee before turning his open palms towards Jason and Trish, firing back with two massive blasts of teal-colored fire.

Both of them screamed and I heard the sound of bodies crashing back through the rubble behind me. From Jason's side, I heard what I assumed was the final large pane of glass being shattered as he was sent through it. On the other, I heard the sickening sound of Trish's body crashing through brick, steel, and sheetrock with a loud shriek of pain.

"I must say, little bird," Samael said in an amused sing-song voice before stepping over me completely. "This little group you've assembled around you could be quite formidable. If you all were under my control that is."

I shrieked in pain as one of his big hands came down on me, jerking my body to the side as he wracked me across my face. The force was enough that I was left slumped to one side, made to watch Haley struggle to roll to her side and lift herself up. She spit blood and then rolled her wolven eyes up to look at me, a pleading wish inside them begging me to stand up and fight.

"How precious, how fond you are of each other," Samael snickered to himself as he grabbed me by the hair, gravity not wanting me to leave the ground. I was stretched against my will, my body crying out in pain as my limbs were forced upward despite the tug of the earth that sought to keep me grounded to my knees. "Maybe I'll finally break you if you watch her die. Just like your whore for a mother."

Time *froze*.

My face went slack as my eyes widened at the mention of my mother, an expression he noticed, and began laughing maniacally. There was so much sick humor and boastful light in his eyes as my body felt a rush of cold numbness fill every nerve inside me. He watched me and then looked down at Haley, shaking his head with a delighted grin.

"You didn't know?" He asked with an incredulous laugh. He reared his head back, bellowing his astonishment and amusement into the night sky and falling snow. "You imbecile, all of this was never truly about you. I never wanted a mutt when I could have had the pure blood of a valravn. But that bitch had to go and make things difficult."

"Scheißkerl! What are you talking about?" I asked, my voice filled with a sense of haunting sorrow and rage.

"You, my worthless little slut, were nothing more than a silver medal when I was this close to getting gold," he sneered, holding up his free hand and pinching his fingers together. There was a vicious sparkle of pride in his eyes. "All I had to do was get rid of her shitty little family."

"You… you attacked our village?" I asked, horror making my blood run even colder until I felt like I was made of ice. "It was-"

"You mortals make it so fucking easy. You always have," he laughed again, his voice becoming teasingly melodic. "A whisper here, a rumor there, and then just wait for the dissension to happen on its own."

With a grin, he raised his free palm as he began letting out a humming war cry, lewdly patting his mouth in a mock gesture that I'd come to understand as being a cruel racial slur.

More than that, it was hauntingly familiar, a quieter mocking tone of the war cries that had inhabited my nightmares for nearly two hundred years. My fear of the native people had been misplaced from the beginning, all of the trauma, the nightmares, PTSD, and panic attacks were all aimed at the wrong target from the time of my death.

All of it had been Samael. It had always been *him*.

"But the bitch was a tricky one, I'll admit that," he shrugged with his big shoulders and then looked back down. "She didn't break and bend to my will, even after I had one of my horde inhabit your father's dead body and shoot you in front of her."

The same numbing rage I felt when fighting Moira began to take over and the world began to go silent around him, Samael's voice beginning to fade into a mumbling tone.

"But the last trick she played on me was binding your dying soul to that stupid amulet that she had you run off with," Samael continued, his voice growing quieter as I sunk deeper inside myself. "Your soul for hers in a last-ditch attempt to make you a pure-"

His voice disappeared from my senses.

Every single ounce of hate and wrath I had inside was flowing like a torrent now, washing away all other emotions. Every sense inside me was numb other than one thing, a small chant of a mantra that flowed through my ears. The raven's wrath consumed me whole.

Rip. And. Tear. And. Feast.

Rip. And. Tear. And...

"Hey, Sam!"

I heard Jason's voice through the darkness, calling to me like it was a lifeline out in the ocean. The sound of his voice pulled me toward it, a distant speech about how I had a new family or something. I wasn't entirely sure.

As I reached through that eternal abyss and finally caught hold of something in my hand. It was a beaded texture like an iron chain with a black crystal that felt as if it were as tall as me with a blotch of pink that crawled up its edges like webs of lightning.

I heard Samael's roar of protest through the darkness as my mind began drawing closer to the sound of Jason's voice and I could feel his warmth spreading throughout me. It was the same warmth of his I felt when we were cradled in each other's arms in our bed with the heat of Mickie and Haley pressed to my back. The numbing rage was fading away, replacing that distant calmness with the warmth and heat that I'd found in my second chance of life.

I realized then that Jason was speaking words in Latin.

Ligare dimittis!

The sound of a raven's cry erupted into the night sky that was so loud and deafening that I felt Samael stumble backward and my limbs moved weightlessly. Lights were pouring out of him, the small orbs mixing with the falling snow and blinding me in the process as they shot into the night sky.

The backyard accompanied the raven's cry with the ethereal screams of thousands of people. It was then I realized that the cry was my own and the demon's eyes twitched in pain as the shrill sound filled his ears and rang through them like a blaring bullhorn. Then his grip loosened around me.

I felt my fingers flex and twitch as they curled into fists and I rolled my neck, easing the pressure that had built up there in the peak of my spine. All of which should have been impossible with his will over my soul intact and Samael in control. No, he was no longer in control of me at all.

My legs moved, pushing my knees up to my chest as Samael

continued to try and regain his bearings, all the while my hands and talons wrapped around his forearm that gripped me by the neck.

With a hard thrust, I slammed my feet against his chest, drop-kicking him as hard as I possibly could. The force should have brought me with him but my wings beat, forcing me to stay in place and I heard a wet snapping sound followed by liquid splashing against the ground.

That splashing sound was then overpowered by a larger one and when I looked down I found Samael struggling to pull himself from his backyard pool, the lights illuminating the water beginning to cloud over as an inky black substance filled it, staining the waters with his blood.

He wavered in his stance, beads of water twinkling like small stars over his body as the light of the moon caught them. I looked curiously at where the water was becoming stained, noting he was missing something until I looked down and found that his right arm, from his elbow downward, was now lying on the ground at my feet.

I grinned wide as I saw a faintly glowing ring on one of his fingers before plucking it and turning to look over my shoulder at where Jason was kneeling on the ground. As I walked towards the demonic form of my boyfriend, I looked over my shoulder at Samael who grunted and whined in pain. With shock and horror strewn across his face, he took notice of his missing limb.

"This is the last piece in your collection, right?" I laughed sadistically as I turned to watch the chaos inside the villa.

The released creatures inside, including the two Anubises from before, a tiefling, Trish, Lex, Xander, and the Cerberus shifter woman, were decimating both the home and the remainder of the horde he'd called for backup.

I frowned as I got to Jason and noticed that one entire side of his chest and torso was a complete mask of crimson but I couldn't see where it was coming from. I gave him a worried look as he clutched that side with one hand. Instead, he ignored the injury and shook his head with a smile before taking the ring from me.

He muttered something in Latin once more and the banshee that had been fighting by Samael's side appeared. She gave the two of us a grateful look as she took the ring from Jason and then flickered out of existence.

"Now it's just you against us, no more tricks up your sleeve. No more games to play, Samael," I growled under my breath and turned to face my past - my boogeyman - one last time.

Sloshing water caught my attention and I watched the ram demon, now looking deflated from what he had been. Gone was the wide muscle mass and tall, looming figure that had been so imposing it tormented my dreamscape for over a century. Instead, he was barely taller than Jason who now had more muscle mass and definition than he did. Samael had been reduced to nothing more than a sad, skinny demon who was running for his life.

He's afraid... Good. Now he knows how it feels.

As he climbed the side of the pool and pulled himself onto its edges as far away from me as he could, he was hit with a bolt of fur and claws that sent him reeling to one side. Mickie appeared, having hit him like a bullet before grabbing him and throwing him to the other side of the rear end of the backyard where he met a hard clothesline maneuver offered up by Haley.

As he stumbled to get back onto his feet, a hard right hook from Sinead connected, busting his nose once more as he wobbled and fell onto his back. She stomped one of her boots onto his chest to keep him down before one of her sickle-shaped blades appeared in her hands and she slashed him, crossing his chest in the shape of an X.

"You took everything from me, Lord Samael. Now we return the favor," she said to him coldly and then looked over her shoulder toward me.

"You tortured me, broke so many others, and drained them of their lives, and for what? Where is the all-powerful demon lord that I could never seem to escape," I snorted incredulously as I came to stand over him.

He looked like a pathetic mess and part of me hated myself for being afraid of him in the first place. That same part of me began blaming myself and others for being weak and stupid for believing that this poor, sad thing in front of me had been a monster to us all. He was nothing, and he somehow made us feel lesser than him.

"If the pits taught me anything, it's that the weakest of all are the oppressors who need their greed to keep them afloat. Well… look at you now… *dad*," Trish scowled as she put a cloven hoof on his chest and held her blade to his throat.

It wasn't lost on me at how she spat her last word with so much hate and anger, the flames curling around her horns, eyes, and sword burning even hotter than before.

His face twisted as he began to laugh, low and pathetic at first before it filled the space with a booming, deep tone. He was succumbing to the madness and his eyes lit up with bright glee as he looked up at both Sinead and me. Samael was on the brink of death at the hands of two of his most prized possessions, because that's all we'd ever been to the greedy bastard, and yet he laughed.

"You will not survive what is coming, little bird. Nor will you, my pets," he sneered, a grin stretching from ear to ear. "You could kill me but that won't stop the ascension of the queen of the gods."

"What the hell is that supposed to mean?" I snarled and began reaching down for him.

Samael roared as a wave of demonic energy knocked us away. Sinead, Trish, Mickie, Haley, and I fell backward onto our backs and knees. The concussive burst of energy had us reeling, forced to pick ourselves up off of the ground and I had to shake my head free of the ensuing feeling of nausea and lightheadedness.

My ears were ringing from the blast and the blinding white edges of my vision slowly faded back into technicolor. I heard another loud crash and my head snapped up to see that Jason had tackled Samael when he'd begun to run, hoping to flee across the creek lining his backyard and into the woods.

I got to my feet and started to give chase, hoping to be by Jason's side in a mere second when I stopped as I got to the edge of the property. A wave of memories and nostalgia hit, forcing me to stop in my tracks as I looked around and I felt tears begin to cloud my eyes,

"This… Is it really?" I whispered quietly to myself as I took in the surroundings.

It wasn't as thick of a forest as it once had been, but I soon recognized a tall warped oak tree on the other side of the bank. I'd once tried to hide there in hopes the things in the forest wouldn't find me. In hopes he wouldn't find me. I slowly stepped into the cold, fresh water that flowed around me and felt the tears cascading down my cheeks.

A Russian olive tree caught my attention, remembering the time I hoped its thorns would protect me. Next to it was another smaller oak tree that had the initials of two lovers carved into it. I had run my fingers over the indentations so many times, wishing I would do the same someday.

I remembered discovering the freshly carved grooves as I returned to this plane outside of my mother's necklace. I remembered seeing two people giddily laughing as they snuck away down the creekside holding each other tightly. They had been so in love and the tree had bore witness to it while I'd just missed the proclamation by mere seconds.

Then my eyes trained on my feet and fought the urge to fall to my knees because that same tree had bore witness to the beginnings of my new life. Just more than a decade ago it had watched a broken young man, wanting to escape the world with the pistol in his hand.

He'd traveled the creek bed to find the perfect grave and found my mother's necklace instead. After falling to his knees, clutching his head in pain, he dug just beneath the creek's surface and found the chain before pulling the amulet free and me along with it.

I looked back over my shoulder at the villa collapsing in on itself from the destruction inside and then back to my feet once more. Of course, he'd built his castle here. His would-be fortress was at the foot of where I'd always return to after I'd been healed enough for him to come and haunt me once again.

This was the crux of all of my issues, trauma, and salvation rolled into the spot where I stood.

This, where I was standing, was where Jason had found me and rescued me from Samael. And here we were, almost reliving the past as he'd done it once again.

A pained scream from Jason rang out through the creek bed and my head snapped to find him, falling backward and clutching his injured side. His back hit the shallow island in the middle of the creek he and Samael had been on and now I could see it clearly. There was a deep gaping wound running up his side from hip to chest while his blood dripped from Samael's horns.

Samael, barely functioning, pulled out his gold coin once more and gave it a flick. An electric charge filled the air as the space not far behind him tore open, light cutting through reality itself to open a slit wide enough for him. It was like looking through a narrow doorway, a warm secluded beach being superimposed against the cold, snowy night sky, the creek bed, and the sparse woods around us.

As Samael turned to run, Jason let out a snarl and hurled himself forward, wrapping one arm around the demon's waist to hoist himself up and wrap his other arm around Samael's throat from behind. The demon grunted as Jason pulled, both of them dragging each other back and forth on the edge of the small berm. They both struggled while their feet filled the air with the sounds of scuffling rocks and water.

"You're not getting away that easy, you son of a bitch," Jason growled and then threw himself to the side and released Samael, the demon falling and crumpling into the shallow water.

My feet moved toward them, splashing through the rocks and water to get to Jason who stumbled and put his arms up in a boxer's stance. As Samael rose, he was hit with a right hook, pushing him back a few steps before he centered himself and launched a left hook in return. I watched them trade blows for a few seconds as I stomped closer to Samael, the demon not seeing me coming until the last second.

With a last-ditch effort, Samael lowered his head and charged, jamming one of his curled horns into Jason's chest who let out an agonizing scream. The scream turned into a snarl as spittle dripped from Jason's lips in exertion, blood flowing from the wound in a river.

Still, he persisted.

He cocked his fists together and began bashing at the back of Samael's skull until he managed to dislodge himself from the horn and hit the demon hard enough that his eyes glazed over. The two of them grinned at each other, however, for far different reasons.

"You will die, Jason McCrae, and I will find refuge with my queen Yazmin," Samael laughed, letting out wheezing breaths of exhaustion. "You cannot stop what is coming."

"I might not stop you," Jason spat, his grin growing wide with a mix of pride and mania as he looked up at where I stood. Which was right

behind Samael. "But she will."

"Fick deine Konigin," I snarled with a throaty rasp as my jaw

lengthened, and my extended talons grabbed Samael's shoulders from

behind, my form now towering over him.

Samael let out a wailing scream of terror as my raven-shaped beak

opened wide enough to take him in. My jaws snapped around the demon

- my abuser - as his screams became muffled inside my jaws. The razor-

sharp teeth pierced him like serrated rows of blades that tore through his

flesh. Hot liquid poured into me as blood filled my mouth with the taste of

copper, vanilla, and fiery spice. The heat was almost too much to bear as I

drank it down regardless, bypassing my instinctual urge to gag.

His thrashing movements calmed as I closed my mouth tighter,

his free arm falling into the creek limply, severed from his torso. My arms

moved from his shoulders to his waist where I began to push forcefully.

My ears filled with a mix of muffled screams of terror and the

sound of wet cracking which resembled a water-soaked log slowly being

snapped in half. His thrashing turned to convulsions as his body went into

shock from the sheer amount of pain and suffering he was in.

I delighted myself in that suffering.

Turnabout for all of the times he'd severed a limb from me for not

pleasuring him, the times he cut and mutilated me for not giving him my servitude. I was giving him all of the pain he'd done to me over a hundred years in one fell swoop and he was finding himself weak and powerless for the first time in his useless existence. It was exactly how he'd made Trish and I feel, how he'd broken Sinead and so many others. And how I imagine he wanted to treat my mother.

This wasn't retribution or some disillusioned form of cleansing the wicked. This was revenge of the sweetest kind, plain and simple.

I yanked my head to the side and heard the sound of his unmoving lower half fall to the ground before I spit the other onto the ground a few feet away. I scowled harshly at the demon with every ounce of hatred I had toward him and then tried to let the satisfaction of the kill wash over me. But it didn't fill me with a sense of happiness in the least.

I... did it.

I had finally fucking killed my Freddy or Michael, the one who haunted, stalked, and made my life after my first death an absolute hellish nightmare. The man who had caused me so much pain and torment, the source of my trauma, was now on the ground bleeding out. But all I felt was a cold numbness wash over me. He was gone but none of it actually mattered.

It meant nothing. Just like how his body began to shrink in on itself, his flesh and form crumbling into ash that wreaked of putrid sulfur. As the ash began to flicker away into the night sky and mix with small snowflakes, a small ball of dim light began to drift upward.

Its glow was a sickening yellowish green in color but hummed with pure power and energy like rain against a powerline. I grabbed the ethereal balloon, the size of it filling most of my hand as I looked at those around me who watched in a mix of terror and awe.

"Your queen forgot something," I mused with a smirk as my eyes reflected the halo of the glowing orb inside them. "Dinner time, mein Haustier."

I tossed the ball into my awaiting mouth, cringing at the extremely sour taste of it before I forced myself to swallow. I felt the burn of it flow down into my belly as my form shrunk, becoming entirely human again as my veins and senses came to life with the feeling of thousands of insects crawling underneath my skin.

Moreover, I felt all of the exhaustion and pain from going days without food, sleep, or rest wash away. The residual pain of the beating I'd taken from Samael earlier in the day slipped into nothingness as well. Instead, the energy filled me to the point I was feeling like I was on a caffeine high and an adrenaline rush mixed together.

"That was so fucking spooky, love," Mickie said, making me turn to the side to see her, Sinead, Haley, and Trish walking toward me.

"But you're back, that's what matters," Jason said weakly, limping toward me as he clutched the largest of the wounds on his torso tightly.

When my eyes went wide, he waved off my concern. "I'll be fine. How do you feel?"

"I… I feel," I tried to hold back my concern for him, knowing his priority was me. I decided I'd quickly answer him so that we could focus on patching up his wounds and getting him home.

Aside from the rush of energy flowing through me, how did I feel? I felt…

Thump-Thump. Thump-Thump.

My vision went hazy as the sound of a massive heartbeat pounded against my consciousness like the sound of war drums directly next to my ears. The rush of energy and enthusiasm was quickly replaced with pain as my skin began to feel tight like it was constricting against my muscles and bones. Dizziness and nausea began to swim through my mind like a thick fog that made me have to brace my leg to catch myself from falling over.

Thump-Thump. Thump-Thump.

I heard the sound of Jason cautiously calling my name, a distant song of an angel in my mind as I felt myself drifting into an abyss. I was being pulled into the depths of my mind like a flowing current that only seemed to get stronger as I began to fight to stay awake and alert.

The massive drums of that pounding heartbeat began to quicken, their volume crescendoing until the ringing in my ears became a steady high-pitched tone that grated along my insides.

The building volume of noise, pain, and power mixed into a violent storm that coalesced inside my chest and pushed at my ribs. The pain was so great, I was gnashing my teeth, gritting them until my jaw went stiff and I tasted my own blood from the inside of my cheeks trickling into my mouth. The sudden taste of it made my eyes shoot open with realization.

And then I screamed.

Floods of power flowed from me in rippling shockwaves that blew back the branches of trees and water around me. The gravel around my feet hovered in the air weightlessly as if gravity itself had been turned off. The pressure around my body billowed and wound up until everything exploded with an audible *boom*, sending wind and shockwaves out around me until I was a crumpled mess in the basin of the creek bed. The world came back into view as the white edges around my vision faded and I was able to look up and see what had happened.

What happened? I felt a surge of energy, then pain, and then nothing. I feel fine now. I feel alive! I feel free… Completely free.

"Is everyone okay?" I asked, my voice sounding hoarse from screaming as I looked around and watched the others slowly climb to their feet. "Sinead? Haley? Mickie? Jason? Trish?"

"Jesucristo," Haley groaned, shaking her head and blinking rapidly. Her smile made my heart flutter and my body swell with warmth. My golden angel. "I'm okay, la novia."

"I appear to be unharmed as well," Sinead answered next, though I saw her adjusting her head to be set correctly.

"I'm fine. My ass is just fucking freezing," Trish snorted, turning my attention to where she slowly picked herself up off her haunches in the frigid water.

"I'm okay, little bird," Mickie answered next, getting to her feet and idly brushing her pant legs free of dust and debris. She chuckled then, giving me a bright wide grin that had my heart pounding and butterflies churning in my stomach. Gods I'd missed that smile. "What in the bloody hell was that?"

"I'm not exactly sure," I sighed, sitting up to look down at my hands and inspect them like I was looking at them for the first time. "Jason, what do you think?"

I had begun to smile as I watched my hands but then paused when I didn't get a response. His name was on my tongue as I looked to where I'd seen him before and found his body shaking as he tried to stand. His demon side of him I'd never known before was gone and his pale skin returned to its normal shade. No, it wasn't his normal shade, he looked far paler other than one entire side of his body completely stained red from blood.

"Jason?" I said, my voice already beginning to crack from the tears that were racing to the surface.

"Adi," he whispered, his voice barely audible like it was taking so much effort just to say that one single word.

With one last breath of exertion, he stood completely, his body swaying limply before he stumbled backward. I screamed his name and my legs kicked at the ground beneath me as I raced toward him. Jason was standing in front of the doorway that Samael had opened to make his escape and it was closing. However, Jason was far too close to it.

He gave me a warm smile and then his eyes, those beautiful cerulean seas, dimmed to a gray as consciousness left him and he fell backward. His form disappeared into the open portal to somewhere I didn't know or recognize before it closed around him. I raced to where he had been only a second ago and pawed violently at the air, touching only the cool night sky of the creek bed.

"Jason! No, no, no, no," I frantically fell to my knees and began digging at the water and rocks below, desperation taking over as tears poured down my cheeks to quench my horror and agony.

And all I could do was scream into the night sky.

Jason… was gone.

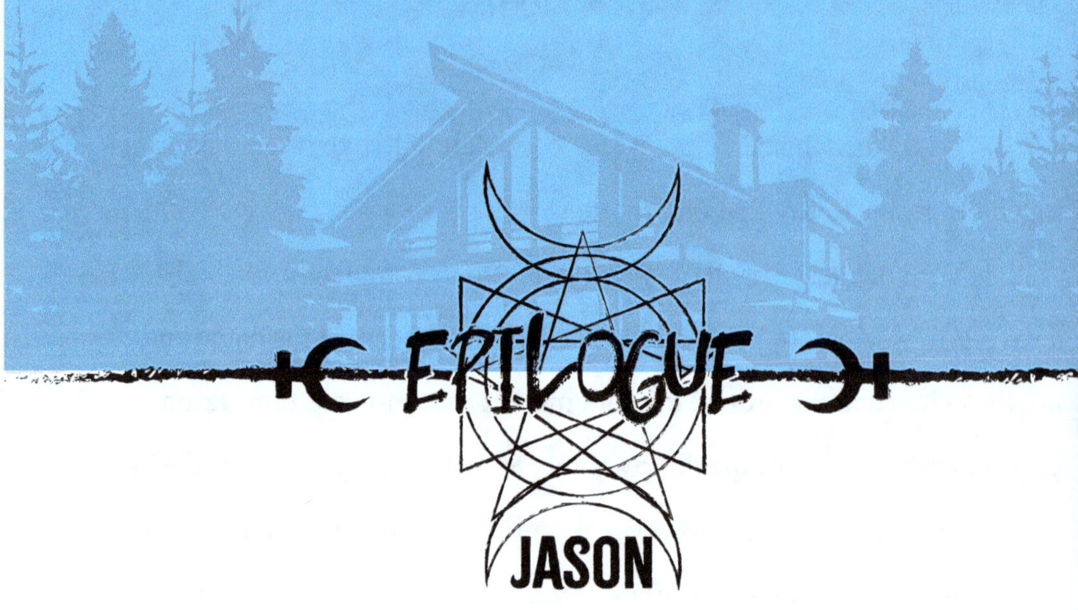

I MADE ADI CRY AGAIN.

The last thing I remembered before falling into darkness was the look on her face. The pain and anguish etched across her gorgeous features. All I wanted to do was run to her, hold her, and tell her everything was okay because she was free. We could have gone home together for the first time in nearly a month.

But, of course, I had begun to fall unconscious as my body grew colder by the second.

The fight with Samael had taken everything out of me physically, mentally, and emotionally. The only thing that I could think to do was lie down and sleep. It's what my body, heart, and soul had desperately needed.

There in the darkness, I felt like I had woken up from a long night's rest, no longer bleeding out and no traces of the immense pain

I'd felt. I knew that was probably a lie, made into a pseudo-reality by whatever this dark void was. I was surrounded completely by the everlasting darkness; however, I felt like I was on solid ground with no discernible temperature.

It wasn't warm, nor was it cold, it just… was.

With a grunt of exertion, I sat myself up before getting to my feet to stand and looked for any direction. With none in sight, I shrugged and began walking despite part of me telling me I should stay put. After some time had passed I saw a pinhole of light and began making my way toward it, taking what felt like nearly an hour. I marveled at the realization that my feet didn't hurt and I didn't physically feel like I'd been walking that kind of distance.

Had I seriously just walked, what, two - maybe three - miles and I don't feel a thing?

The pinhole of light eventually became the size of an empty room, the light having no true source for its glow or origin. But what startled me more than the ghostly light was that, when I entered it so did someone else on the opposite side.

The man walking toward me… was me.

I was in the same dreamscape as I'd been in before but this time his transformation was more complete than it had been. I had a part of me that recognized that this was what I'd become after I'd released Zi, Atiena, and that tiefling woman from Samael.

The realization of what I'd become made me pause and take him in entirely, looking over my own visage whose hair had become black, had a pair of lyre horns rising from his forehead, and eyes darker than I'd ever seen save for the bright blue pupils. His skin could have been considered more pale than mine, however, in reality, he was ashen gray; other than his arms up to his biceps, a mask across his eyes, and part of his chest and hips which were completely black.

"So do I call you Jason, or do I call you something else?" I asked, genuinely curious about how to address him properly.

"Honestly, yes? I think anyway since we're the same person and all that," he answered with a shrug and a voice that seemed to be a little deeper and raspier than mine.

The two of us began circling the space and each other, my eyes drifting back and forth between him and the outlying darkness surrounding us. I nodded curiously at his answer, still unsure what all of this was or what this meant in the long run.

"Okay, so… Jason," I began, feeling odd talking to myself and referring to him as myself. "I guess my first question is what is this or where are we?"

"Technically," he answered with a sigh, taking his turn to now look around the darkness as well. "I guess the easiest way to explain it is that we're sort of in our mind or soul, whichever you prefer to think of it."

"And you've just… been here the whole time?" I asked, furrowing my brow as I contemplated his answer.

"Yeah, pretty much," he nodded with a chuckle. "I guess you could say we've been connected ever since you used your ESPer abilities. That's when we would have connected the first time."

"So my psychic abilities, that's you?" I pondered, tilting my head as I paused as I watched him do the same.

"Truthfully, it's just us," he shrugged and turned to look around.

He was shirtless and I noticed for the first time that a pair of black wings rose from his back. At the center was the tattoo Zi had inked nearly three weeks ago, except it was different. It was the stacked skulls; a leopard for Mickie, a raven for Adi, and a wolf for Haley. Except it had three more totems added to the pile. Two of which were easy to decipher with a pair of crossed scythes at the top for Sinead, and a ram skull resting beneath Haley's which I guessed indicated Trish. However, the last skull at the very bottom of the stack seemed to be blurry or smudged.

"I guess the best way to think about it is," he said, turning back to me with his chin cupped in his hand. "When we first connected… Imagine us walking through a crowded mall and we brushed up against each other. Most times you'd ignore the person who touched you and chalk it up to being accidental on account of it being so crowded. But you looked back to see who brushed your hand and found me."

"So, what, if I would've just ignored you in that crowded mall situation… The abilities would've just gone away or something?" I asked, cupping my chin in thought then.

"Possibly. Would have saved us all that fucking trauma, maybe could have been normal. Hell, we might have been popular and had more than just Mark and Adi by our sides," he replied with amusement as he pondered what could have been as well. What was odd was that, as he mentioned Mark and Adi's names, they appeared out of the darkness, laughing and smiling as they held a conversation neither of us could hear. "A lot of people have the same gifts we do, they just choose to ignore them and eventually lose touch with how to use them."

"Use it or lose it, that makes sense," I chuckled, tilting my head curiously as I watched the silent Mark and Adi with interest. It reminded me of the first time they'd officially met at Piper's after beating Moira. As I thought about that night, Mickie, Haley, Jen, and the Council appeared beside them, all having silent conversations. "So, is this where all of the memories go after we touch somebody?"

"I guess it could be, I never thought about it that way," he said, smiling as he watched the memory of all of our friends conversing and laughing together replaying on a loop.

"Okay so if this place and you are the source of… whatever we can do what else should I be expecting? You know other than being faster and stronger than normal, 'cause I know that happened. And what about that green fire or whatever it is?" I began asking, my words becoming more rambling as I went. My eyes seemed to latch onto his wings.

Was I... going to learn how to fly? Was that even remotely possible?

"Eh, you'll find out in time," he laughed and waved me off nonchalantly. Then his head turned to look up toward the source of light above us and I began hearing the distant sounds of waves and seagulls. "Besides, we don't really have the time anyway cause you're about to wake up."

I am?

I heard my own, unfiltered voice repeat the question consciously as the void faded away and the light expanded. The light became blinding as noises began to fill my ear with a warm, pleasant song of tranquility. It was a song that pushed my consciousness to the surface and soon it became the deafening sounds of gentle waves and seagulls, no longer hearing that darkened version of myself.

The scent of freshly baked bread, rose, and lavender began to fill my nose, lulling me awake as my eyes slowly opened to bright warming light filling the room I was in. I was lying on a bed that wasn't the most uncomfortable one I'd ever slept in. However, the nervousness of not being in my own bed caused me to panic, wanting to get up and run as fast as I could.

I realized then, as I blinked sleep away and began taking everything in that I could hear a soft, decisively calming voice humming a tune I didn't recognize somewhere in the distance. I pushed myself to sit up and hissed as my side screamed in protest of the movement. The pain rocked me and nearly forced me back into a lying position. Instead, I gritted my teeth and slowly opened my eyes once more to adjust to the bright lighting and the subtle smell of the ocean.

Which, I knew couldn't be correct because the Pacific Ocean was nearly a thousand miles away from where I lived. And I hadn't been back since I turned 21 when Mark took me to San Diego for a late birthday present as a boys trip together. And we definitely hadn't stayed in an oceanside villa like the one I was in now. Despite the fact, he definitely would have had the money to do so. I had just been stubborn and refused to make him spend more than necessary on someone like me.

"Shut up, Jason, you know better than to think like that."

Was that... Adi and Trish's voices?

The room itself looked as if it was made of white clay and brick pillars creating the corners and essential framing such as windows and doorways. All of them were smoothed to perfection and showed off marvelous craftsmanship, the walls being made of smooth, polished beechwood that was artfully bleached by salt, time, and algae.

The brick and wood were wrapped in garlands of fresh herbs and foliage while white silk drapes covered the windows. Together they created a light and warm visual that made me feel relaxed and at home, begging me to just lounge and enjoy the sounds of the ocean and a calm spring day at the beach.

The sound of light tapping against the stone flooring drew my attention to the foot of the hand-made bed where I cocked my eyebrow in confusion. I locked eyes with a large white bird that I nearly instantly recognized as a swan. Then it turned and quickly padded out of the room, its feet flopping against the floor rhythmically.

The fluttering of wings drew my attention elsewhere as I heard a soft hooting sound just before a pair of smaller white birds took flight out of the window. Had those been pigeons or possibly doves? As they flew off I saw the endless expanse of a bright blue ocean lapping gently along the shoreline set against a sunny blue sky that had sparse clouds with a slight pinkish tint to them.

"Ah, you're awake, me lad."

A woman's voice which had a heavy Gaelic dialect turned my attention to the doorway and I locked eyes with its source. It belonged to a voluptuous feminine figure that was tall with a lightly toned frame of pale white skin. Her flesh was covered in large patches of dark freckles across her bare shoulders, cheeks, and the bridge of her nose. Her long, flowing hair was a bright shade of red curls that caught the light outside. It gave her the impression of having a mane of luminous fire cascading down her back and shoulders. The light caught it the same way with her eyes.

I found myself staring into a pair of the brightest emerald green pools that sparkled as bright as the ocean below us. Then my eyes were drawn upward to the small, intricately woven crown nestled along her forehead, the binding reminding me of an iron woven Celtic knot around an emerald centerpiece.

Seeing me awake brought a wide smile that captivated me, making me watch her every move with intensity. I felt more nervous than I ever had as the arguably most beautiful red-headed woman I'd ever seen in my life bounced toward me eagerly. Her tone and smile felt welcoming but the ethereal, almost celestial-like beauty had me guarded and finding it hard to swallow, let alone speak a word.

"Let's get your bandages exchanged and see how your wounds are looking," she said with a voice that reminded me of tinkling bells.

Her sage green silk dress flowed as she moved across the room to pick up a large woven tray full of small mason jars, vials, herbs and plants, and bandages on it. It felt like I'd been plopped into the past with all of the holistic and herbal remedies readily available at her fingertips. As she walked, the gown tightened against her figure to display wide curvy hips, a soft abdomen, and large breasts that threatened to bounce free. She filled out the dress in every way that seemed to barely be able to contain all of her.

And just to make my mouth feel even more dry was the fact that she didn't seem shy about her looks or the sway of her body whatsoever. Even as she leaned over me and tenderly ran her fingers along my side and chest while bending over at the waist. All of which had her immense cleavage directly in my line of sight.

My attention shifted to the wood-ribbed roof as I let out a hiss of discomfort while her fingers nimbly pulled at something attached to my skin. Once the initial discomfort had subsided, I found her pulling off homemade gauze; something that resembled snakeskin.

For how badly I had been injured by Samael, I had expected the bandages to be more soaked through. I was only showing traces, which meant I had to have been out for a long while.

"Where am I exactly?" I asked cautiously as I furrowed my brow, watching her prepare another couple of strips of snakeskin and gauze bandages.

During the preparation, she picked up leaves that I couldn't identify, crushed them in her free hand, and then sprinkled the remains onto my skin. Next, she opened several of the vials which looked like they contained oil of some kind. When she poured them onto the wounds, I flinched from a sudden spike in pain.

"Sorry, lad, I should have warned you that it might still sting a little," she smiled with a shrug.

Then she laid the skin and bandages against me and then gently smoothed them out with her hands to ensure they'd adhere. I flinched in terror then because I saw movement on the bed next to me before a long white snake with black scales that looked like hundreds of diamonds overlapping each other began to slither its way up her arm and onto her shoulder.

"Should have warned you that my friend here has been keeping you company as well," she mused before bringing a finger up to gently pet the snake's nose. It answered her touch with what I visualized to be happy tongue flicks against her finger.

At least it was friendly, right?

"You'll find quite a few adders roaming around the premises but as long as you are kind to them they'll tend to leave ye be. As for where ye are… Do you not remember, lad?"

"I… don't," I said, shaking my head and closing my eyes in confusion as I tried to pour through my memories. "The last thing I remember is a fight. I was trying to save my girlfriend but I… lost too much blood. I remember falling backward into this… I guess a portal is the only thing I can call it. Then I woke up just now."

"Aye, well I don't suppose it's been as quick as ye recall then. You've been asleep for quite a while since we found ye," she said, cocking an eyebrow as she looked upward out the window as she pondered everything. Then she grinned wide and let out an excited giggle. "Ah, and what a find! It's not every day ye find a mortal in Aardeotheous."

"I… wait, are you saying I'm in the... what was it - celestial realm?" I asked, quickly sitting upright and locking eyes with her, giving her every intense emotion of realization I had to offer.

"Ah, see I knew ye were a wise lad," she laughed brightly as she playfully punched me in the shoulder. "Quite an interesting one as well with ye traces of demon and such flowing through ye veins and all that."

"Yeah, I'm still not sure how to process that one," I snorted, giving her an apologetic look.

"Aye, not a harm at all," she retorted, waving off my concern nonchalantly. "Ah, I've gone and forgot my manners though. You, me lad, can call me Brigit."

She held out her hand, offering it to me to shake and I moved to take it but froze at the last second. Two things hit my consciousness like a speeding truck, forcing me to freeze. Firstly, I was in the realm of celestials. A plane of existence that housed a large portion of every god and goddess civilization had ever worshiped and prayed to since the dawn of man.

Moreover, Grandma Ruth was dedicated to our family's genealogy and learning about our roots. Secondly, she'd talked at length about who our clans prayed to long before Christianity came to the isles of Scotland and Ireland. I recognized the name instantly.

"You're... *the* Brigit?"

"Aye, I am," she laughed. "Good to know some mortals still who I am after all this time."

"Okay," I sighed and let out a deep, long breath as I tried to calm myself down and speak more in my normal tone and volume. "So I fell through a doorway into Aardeotheous. The Celtic deity my ancestors prayed to happened to be the one to find me. And now I'm in her... bed..."

"No, lad," she laughed heartily again, patting me on the head like I was some lost puppy or something. "This isn't my home ye're in. I was just asked to make sure ye get ye wounds healed and have ye feeling in top form."

"Okay, then... who's home am I in? What god or goddess would care to get me patched up by the mother of healing, music, and ironwork herself?" I asked incredulously, furrowing my brow.

"That, my dear, would be my doing," said the harmonious voice of a woman. My jaw promptly began to go slack as my eyes fell onto the goddess in the doorway.

Standing there, with a halo of golden light behind her, was by far the most beautiful woman I'd ever seen in my entire life. My girlfriends withstanding. Her aura alone elevated her over everyone else in comparison and I drank in her form. She had wide hips, a shapely hourglass figure, and long toned legs that made her stand at six and a half feet in height.

A sheer white silk dress hung loose from her hips to show off everything from her upper thighs downward. From her hips, the dress clung tightly like a second skin displaying every subtle curve and roll of her flesh before barely covering her exceptionally large, bountiful breasts that gave Mickie's endowment a run for her money.

Her soft blue eyes brightened as she watched me look at her, lighting up with amusement and shining like crystalline waters. Her long golden hair fell down in lapping waves around her like an endless sun-soaked beach. It made her olive skin, long oval features, pouty red lips, and high cheekbones more striking as if she'd been a marble statue brought to life.

"My uncle speaks of you in high regard after you were able to dash Samael Luciano," the woman said. Her voice was sultry, seductive, and regal all rolling into one that filled my mind like a sweet red wine. "It made me wonder if you would be up to the task of proceeding with a trial I might have given to someone else before now. I'd like to discuss the details of employing your… unique services, Jason."

"You want… to hire me?" I said, my voice shaking with nervousness, still taken aback by this woman's presence. "But you're…"

"I am," she grinned wide as she stepped forward around Brigit and took one of my hands in both of hers. She finished the gesture by bringing my knuckles to her lips and kissing them, sending an electric jolt of energy throughout my entire body.

Could she blame me for being too stunned to move?

She gave me a knowing look of delight as she traced her fingers across the back of my palm. Then she rested her fingers lightly against one of my thighs while I struggled to swallow a thick lump in my throat.

I watched her eyes trace over me before they settled in my lap for a moment before looking up to watch heat flush my cheeks, chest, and more with a pleased smirk tugging at her lips. Then I watched her eyes trace a slow, wandering pattern as she took me in, humming with delight before our eyes met once more.

I became aware that, other than the bedsheet, I was completely nude in front of a pair of honest to gods…

Well… goddesses…

I also became acutely aware that both of them gave me the same look I'd seen quite frequently that Adi, Mickie, and Haley had given me. A look that made me wish I had something to drink to get rid of the dry feeling forming in my mouth and throat.

"No need to be so formal or shy, my dear. You flatter me, I assure you. However, it would be rude to not properly introduce myself to a guest in my home," she giggled softly before laying one hand gently against her chest while the other pressed against my hip next to the bulged sheets. "I... am Aphrodite."

THE SAGA CONTINUES IN:
LILITH'S LOUNGE

ACKNOWLEDGMENTS

If you've made it this far, thank you for reading.

Still here? Then seriously, from the bottom of my heart, I cannot thank you enough for reading and taking a chance with this story of mine. If you enjoyed it please do not hesitate to leave a review on Amazon, GoodReads, or wherever you found me.

First and foremost, I need to thank Matthew Lillard and the team behind Thir13en Ghosts because without them I would have never found inspiration for the Jason McCrae series.

In all seriousness, thank you **Aly**, my wife, my muse, my baby bird, for always supporting and believing in me even when I'm at my lowest. Without you and your unconditional love, I would have given up on everything more times than I care to admit. I owe everything to you, especially my renewed love of literature. Without you I would have never fallen in love with the novels that inspired me to write and showed me the ways of the 'why choose' romance genre. And most importantly, thank you for giving me two wonderful little girls that help bring my life purpose, fulfillment, and love. Even if they are as bratty as their mother.

Ryane, my birthday twin, and second wifey. You and Aly have given me inspiration for helping develop the strong, beautiful, and wonderful women that I've loved to write. Thank you for loving me and being there for me, even when I've been my most fucked up. And thank you for the best friend Aly and I could ever ask for. I love the two of you more than you will ever know.

Seth, **Todd**, and **Skylar**, for being my best friends and brothers when I've needed you the most. Thank you for always being supportive, pushing me, and having my back.

Dad and **Mom** for raising me to go after my passions, even if you don't understand or necessarily like them. Yes, mom I write monster smut, it's fun so I'm going to keep doing it. Dad you are the true MVP through the process of making this novel. You're an unbelievable badass for being a huge supporter and fan of this series stepping up to being a beta reader when I needed one.

Tam Delakor, my author bestie and mentor. Thank you for guiding me through the process of being an independent author and taking me under your wing from day one. Thank you for being a friend, brother in arms, and massive supporter of my writing career. Take care of yourself and your heart, my guy.

In loving memory of Colleen Ruth Cannon.

Thank you for the light you were in my life. It was because of you I picked up my first Michael Crichton and Laurell K. Hamilton novels and sent me down the urban fantasy pipeline. Without you, I would have never had the dream to turn my writing into nothing more than an idle way to get my dreams out of my head and onto paper. And I will always regret not having the chance to properly say goodbye.

I love you Grandma.

ABOUT THE AUTHOR

Matty Baggins is a hermit living somewhere behind the Zion Curtain with his wife, two daughters, and fur babies. His writing journey started at a young age because he wanted to document his lucid dreams (the ones that weren't Final Destination movies). When not taking care of his family he can be found with a frappuccino in hand, daydreaming about gorgeous - bratty - shifter/monster women, while perusing Barnes & Noble or gaming stores. If conversation with Matty is desired, approach him cautiously with shiny click-clacks, D&D minis, harem mangas, horror movies, or screamy music. His hobbies include Sunday D&D sessions, video games, horror movies, anime, and making angry music while hiding behind his drum set.